C.C. HUMPHREYS

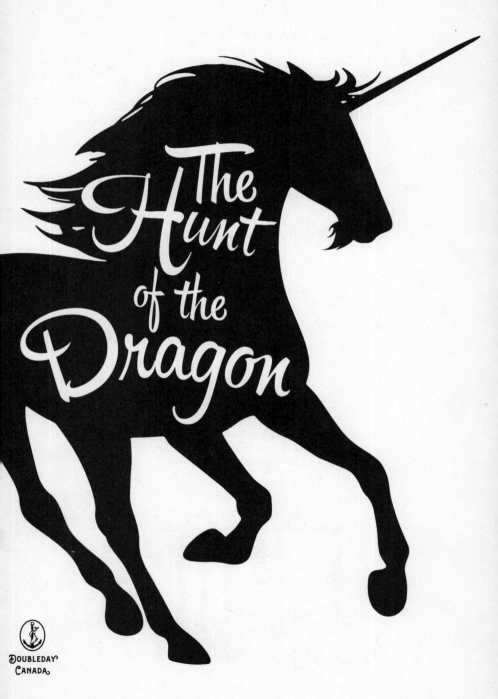

The Hunt
of the
Dragon

DOUBLEDAY
CANADA

Doubleday Canada and colophon are registered trademarks of Penguin Random House of Canada Limited

Library and Archives Canada Cataloguing in Publication

Humphreys, C.C. (Chris C.), author
The hunt of the dragon / C.C. Humphreys.

Issued in print and electronic formats.
ISBN 978-0-385-67712-7 (hardback).—ISBN 978-0-385-67713-4 (epub)

I. Title.

PS8565.U5576H85 2016   jC813'.6   C2016-902462-8
                                                 C2016-902463-6

Jacket images: (city) © Natalia Bratslavsky | Dreamstime.com; (unicorn) © Svetlana Alyuk | Dreamstime.com
Jacket design: Jennifer Lum

Printed and bound in the USA

Published in Canada by Doubleday Canada, a division of Penguin Random House Canada Limited

www.penguinrandomhouse.ca

10 9 8 7 6 5 4 3 2 1

Penguin
Random House
DOUBLEDAY CANADA

TO AMY BLACK

—*So we did it!*

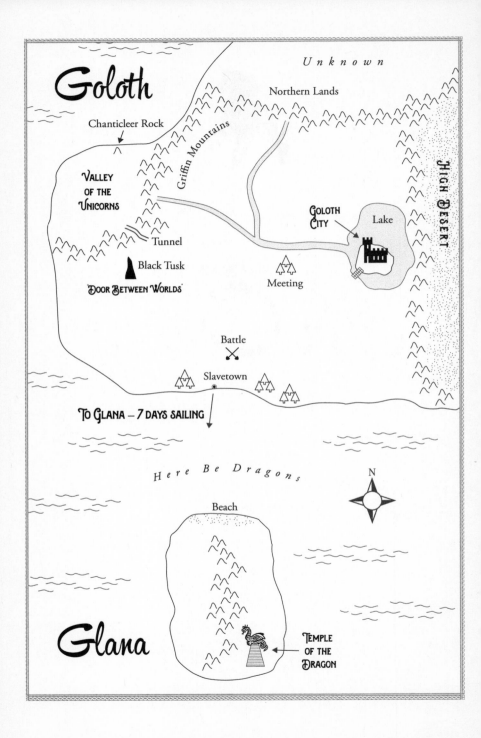

Stir Crazy

I

Manhattan Traffic

Bike lanes? What was the point of them? When no one in New York could care less?

Like this jerk!

Elayne swerved around the delivery truck, perfectly parked between the broken white lines of the bike lane. Swerved wider when the delivery man's assistant stepped from the cab. As her left grip missed him by a hair, she saw a flash of startled eyes, heard the Spanish curse as she whipped by, felt the single finger jerked up to accompany it. Simultaneously, tires screeched, a horn blasted. Her manoeuvre had forced another driver to brake hard and she heard him scream, "Stupid kid!"

She looked back. Two fingers were raised now. A small price to pay. Because she was in the clear, the lane empty, and nothing but tail lights accelerating away ahead. Sixth Avenue was free for a block and a half, just one taxi across the junction and way over to the right. But she also saw the lights on West 22nd go from green to amber.

No way! Miss this light and she'd hit every one between here and school. She'd be late for class. Again.

"Not going to happen," she muttered, rose on her pedals, and kicked it.

Her bike was a Shinmayo hybrid and she was fast. Even so, the light had been red for two seconds before she took it anyway. This required her to dart between a lady with a stroller and a businessman pulling a carry-on suitcase. The lady screamed; the suit swore; three crosstown horns sounded a blaring discord. It was easier on the north crosswalk, just two people freezing as she swept by. She glanced back without dropping her speed. Five fingers now stood at attention—though one of them might have been the baby's rattle. Made seven fingers by 23rd Street.

Close to my record, Elayne thought, turning forward—just in time to see the yellow taxi, which had been all the way over on the other side of Sixth Ave, now right in front of her. Not in time to do anything about it.

Kerang! Her front tire plowed into the cab's rear fender.

Schling! She shot forward, launched like a missile from some medieval siege weapon—trebuchet, she thought, history class. Her knee banged the rear windshield but that didn't slow her much, though she managed to twist around the cab's rooftop hoarding, which her foot caught. That held her, that and her hands plunging onto the car's hood. She braced herself and, hanging upside down, stared into the startled wide, brown eyes of the African taxi driver.

"Hi!" she said.

The wide eyes narrowed. A furious blast of his native tongue burst forth—disparaging her eyesight, her riding skills, and finally casting slurs upon her parentage.

He paused to draw breath, no doubt to continue. And Elayne thought, Uh-uh. I'm the one on a bike. You're in a cab in the bike lane.

It was time to unleash her superpower.

"I doubt you have a licence, dude. But if you do, why don't you shove it where the sun don't shine?"

His face, poised for further insult, froze. Not surprising, she thought. Couldn't be every day in Manhattan that he was insulted in perfectly accented Swahili.

While he gaped, word-lost, she slid off the roof. Her knee hurt from where she'd struck it, so she limped to the rear of the cab. "Great!" she huffed when she saw her front tire bent near in half. Third one in three months. "I hope you got insurance, buddy," she said in English to the driver now rising from his seat.

The driver had obviously decided not to believe he'd just heard Swahili because he replied in English, "You! Crazy girl! You break my taxi!"

"What, a dent in your fender? You shouldn't have stopped here, man."

"You break!" He pointed up and Elayne saw that the rear windshield had a nice starburst crack. No wonder her knee hurt!

"You pay!" He grabbed her arm. "You pay!"

There had been a kind of whining in her ear from the moment she flew over the cab. This now went up a pitch—and then ceased altogether. The murmur of the small crowd that had gathered, the many honking horns, the beep-beep-beeping of the crosswalk guide, each faded until she was in an almost undisturbed stillness. All alone with her fury.

"Well," she said, disengaging her arm, "in for a penny, in for a pound"

Then she lifted her bike and hurled it through the windshield.

They sat in the waiting room, her father and her, silent. Except it was the sort of silence that shrieked. She could feel the words roiling around inside him, how he was fighting to keep them in. Once he began he wouldn't be able to stop. The last time she'd had "a biking incident," which had involved a jogger and a Shih Tzu, he'd let rip, vowing all sorts of penalties. He'd waved his arms about, spittle had flown. His French ancestry, he'd said, apologizing later. But he hadn't truly apologized because he'd remained really, really angry.

In a way, she preferred fury to the silent treatment; the "disappointment" that was one of his main tactics. She could provoke him. She'd become good at that in the last couple of years. At home she might have done, but here? The waiting room of the medical practice, one of the swanky Midtown establishments, was eerily quiet. The walls were an indeterminate shade of cooling blue, the plants a restrained emerald. The faint music was only a tad up from elevator: classical, not famous, reassuringly bland. The receptionist sat behind a desk, her hair a spray-sculpted helmet, her dress a gentle lilac. She had a broach on the left shoulder, copper, a heraldic design. Peering closer, Elayne saw that it was a griffin. She had an urge to go up to her and say, "Do you know how they hunt the griffin in Goloth? With nets and one-eyed men for bait!" But she suspected the woman heard similar things most days, this being a psychiatric practice and all. Her smile would not shift though her finger might creep toward the panic button.

Nah. To get up meant moving her leg. And that was still painful.

She shifted the ice pack on it, and her father spoke, his voice forcedly calm. "How's the knee?"

"Better," she lied. "How's my bike?"

She'd had to call him, of course, once the police showed up and it was clear they weren't going to just let her go. "Protocols, ma'am," the cop had said. "Ma'am," though he couldn't have been much older than her. So she'd waited, and Alan had come and been all "diplomatic"— which essentially meant bribing the taxi driver.

It was as if he read her thoughts, part of them. "They don't own the cabs, you know. Just lease them. So all damages would be down to him. He'd been in the US six months, saving to bring his family over from Kenya."

"Yeah, yeah," she said, affecting boredom but feeling bad. "Let's hope he doesn't meet them in his cab. He's a terrible driver."

"Elayne—"

There, he was about to begin. Get it out. She could see the flame in his eye. But then the receptionist had to spoil it all by leaning forward and saying, "Dr. Leibowitz will see you now."

Her father rose. "I'll come get you in an hour," he said, curtly.

"Wait! Isn't it your final pitch to the client?"

"It is. But I'll put him off."

"Dad, you don't have to do that."

He'd been talking about this deal for weeks. A complete remodelling of a brownstone in the East Village. He'd become the hot architect in town. Sought-after before; deluged with offers ever since . . . well, ever since he'd risen from his bed in the hospice where he was dying of leukemia, completely cured. They called him "the Miracle Man." Which he was—even if the miracle was because a unicorn had laid its horn on his chest and taken the cancer away.

My unicorn, she thought, seeing him for a moment, his magnificent creamy whiteness. My Moonspill.

She reached up, took her father's arm. And maybe the contact passed a current between them, and with it her thoughts, that name. They had a way of often thinking exactly what the other did. The anger in his eyes passed, and he sat again, placed his hand over hers. "Elayne," he said, his voice softer. "I don't mean to be . . ." He sighed. "I'm just worried about you. You keep promising to . . . to calm down. And then—"

He gestured to the ice pack on her knee.

"I know. I know! I will. I swear."

A little smile came. He held up a finger. "Pinkie swear?"

"Better than that. I swear . . . I swear on Moonspill's horn. At least—" She shrugged. "I will when I get home. And I'll get home by myself. Really."

He considered her a moment. "All right, if you're sure. But straight home after your session, young lady. I'm still figuring out how long to ground you for."

"You can't ground me! I'm eighteen. I'm an adult."

"You're seventeen until tomorrow. Which means I've got—" He glanced at his watch. "Eight hours to devise some fiendish punishment."

The receptionist cleared her throat loudly. "Ms. Alexander?"

"You see. 'Ms.' She knows I'm an adult. Go!"

He shook his head, rose, and went. "Second door on the right," the receptionist said.

Elayne took a breath. Her father had booked this new therapist after her last "incident" with the Shih Tzu. Nice coincidence that it came on the day of her next one. He'd seemed quite excited about this doctor, said that this might be "the one." But he'd said that about the other three. Because there's always this teensy-weensy problem, she thought, as she stood there, willing herself to move. Recovering from trauma was based on talking about it, getting the facts out there for the therapist to evaluate. Re-living it in order to deal with it and move on. But revealing the truth of *her* trauma was the straight road to the psych ward.

She stood, swayed as pain hit her stiff knee. Besides, she thought, who says I'm traumatized anyhow? Why can't I just be excited? Proud. She looked at the receptionist. "I mean, if you'd tamed a unicorn, cured cancer, and started a revolution, you'd be proud, right?"

The woman stared back a moment, a gleam in her eyes, then said, her voice all sing-songy, "Second door on the right."

Oops, thought Elayne, as she limped through the archway, did I just say that out loud?

The corridor beyond had a thick carpet and highly polished oak doors. Hers had the name "Dr. G.R. Leibowitz, M.D., Ph.D." engraved in copper plate on . . . a copper plate! Fancy, she thought, and knocked. A moment's pause then a firm, "Enter!"

Enter? Really? What is this, a play? Sighing, she pushed open the door.

She knew, at first glance, that she wasn't going to like Dr. Leibowitz. It wasn't the long, straight blond hair that made her look like a folk singer, nor the paleness of the observing eyes. It was more that she was a woman. Elayne knew she was better with men, able to figure them out faster and deal with them accordingly. She'd spent years dealing solo with her dad after all—but her experience with women was largely confined to teachers. She could get men to focus on what she wanted to focus on—her mother, dead since she was an infant. She'd gotten over it, she knew—how could you miss what you'd never really known, right? But male analysts would nod in sympathy, hand her the Kleenex— and so be steered away from any discussions of what truly might be bugging her. The land of the fabulous beast, and all that. Only one shrink had ever gotten anything out of her. A woman.

The doctor did not rise and, ignoring Elayne's offer of a hand, spoke in softly accented English. "Elayne. Dr. Leibowitz. But you may call me . . . Dr. Leibowitz." She gestured to a chair.

Oh God, Elayne thought, an Austrian who tries to be funny. She'd placed the accent straight away. It was part of her superpower, of course. She decided she wouldn't start speaking fluent German. It would open up all sorts of questions she'd rather not answer. So she sat, said, "You can call me maybe."

"Excuse me?"

Ah! Not that funny then. And though she looked to be only in her thirties, the doctor wasn't going to play the "we're both young women together" card. Good. "Never mind. How are you, Doctor?"

"No, Elayne. How are you?" She leaned forward over her desk, looked down. "Your knee? It is swollen, yes?"

"Some."

"Would you prefer to lie down?"

She indicated and Elayne turned. She'd missed the couch, a long, dark leather affair. Really? She sighed. She'd done one semester of psych at Columbia. The accent, the couch? Come in, Dr. Freud. She glanced up at the framed diplomas on the wall. Yup, the Ph.D. was from the University of Vienna. Oh, this was going to be fun!

She turned back. "I'm good."

"Excellent."

The doctor reached, slipped on large, horn-rimmed spectacles—honestly, this could be a movie, Elayne thought—and peered down at the open file folder before her. There was a lot of paper in it. Dr. Leibowitz's three predecessors had made a lot of notes. They'd had to justify her father's $400 per hour after all. She'd tried to persuade him that he was wasting his money, that she was fine. But the bike accidents—none of them her fault!—together with what had been officially described as "night terrors," though she considered them just heightened bad dreams, had convinced him otherwise.

Leibowitz read for near a minute then looked up—over the lenses, keeping in character. "Poor Elayne. You appear to have had several 'accidents' in the last two years. Why do you think that is?"

Elayne shrugged. "Why do *you* think that is?"

A smile came—though it did not enter the blue eyes above glass. "I think you will find this works better if I ask the questions and you answer them, yes?"

"Why would that work better?"

The smile left even the mouth. "Elayne," the doctor said, "I have read these notes quite extensively. All my predecessors on your . . . case write that even after several weeks of trying you are most, uh, unforthcoming. How can I help you if you won't let me in?" Elayne was about to reply—with a question, of course, like, "Why would I want you in here?" when Leibowitz continued, "All my colleagues say this except for," she glanced down, "Dr. O'Reilly."

Damn! There she was, the one queen in the deck. Sinead O'Reilly. Irish with that wild red hair and the big laugh. She had actually made Elayne talk. Tricked her into it, in a way, with her own tales of Ireland, leprechauns and the like. After a few weeks of lulling, Elayne had thought, what the hell, had offered the "U" word and a couple of stories to back it up. O'Reilly had offered nods and an increased dosage of medication.

"You appear to have talked with her quite extensively. Once even, she writes, in what appears to be Gaelic, though she did not tape the conversation and does not speak it herself." She looked up again. "Did you?"

"Which? Talk extensively or in Gaelic?"

A slight colouring flushed the doctor's pale skin. "Both."

It was time to lead this hound astray. "Well, obviously I don't speak Gaelic," Elayne replied. "And as for telling her stuff—well, I wanted to please her. You know, because I never had a mom."

She sniffed, bent her head to conceal her smile. Take that, Dr. Freud, she thought.

She looked up again—to Leibowitz's unsmiling face. "So all that is written here," she gestured down, "all you told her, were simply tales?"

"Uh-huh."

She took off her glasses, laid them down, leaned forward. "And so you do not believe in the reality . . . of unicorns?"

There it was. Out in the open. She kept her face straight and Moonspill from her mind. "Of course not, doctor." She gave a little laugh. "What? You think I'm here because I'm crazy?"

Leibowitz did not laugh. Did not move, apart from a slight shake of the head. "Crazy is not a term we use, Elayne. No one thinks you are crazy. But we all believe that you are suppressing some trauma." She gave the word a serious Germanic smack—"trowma"—then continued, "And that you are challenged. We—your other therapists, your father— want to help you meet those challenges. To help you succeed at university where, I understand, and despite all your promise, you are not doing so well. To help you avoid . . . accidents." She nodded at the ice-packed knee. "So do you understand why you are here?"

"So we can talk and then you can give me a new pill to make me better?"

She used her "little girl voice." Leibowitz ignored it. "I could prescribe more medication. Increase the dose. Though you seem quite resistant to pills—if you take them always, which some of my colleagues have doubted." She shook her head. "Do you know why you are here, with me?"

"No."

"Because I specialize in FAD."

Elayne smiled brightly. "Oh goody. I always like to be in on the latest fad."

"F-A-D. It stands for Fantasy Affective Disorder. Have you heard of it?"

"Nope."

"It is when young people—mainly, but not exclusively, girls—get morbidly stuck in a fictional, specifically a fantasy, world."

"Get out! That's not a thing!"

"Oh, trust me, it is a thing. It is my thing." She frowned. "You would be surprised to learn how common it is. It is connected to GOS—Gaming Obsessive Syndrome—though that is mainly a problem with adolescent boys." She leaned forward, peering over the frames. "It is healthy, of course, to identify with, to imagine yourself fully in a world that cannot be real. It is unhealthy to be stuck there, to be unable to distinguish between what is and what is not." She tapped the papers before her. "Dr. O'Reilly made the diagnosis but it is not her field of expertise." Her eyes glinted. "It is mine. In fact I wrote my thesis on the disorder." She waved her hand at her diploma. "Though that was more concerned with alien abduction fantasies, the principles are the same."

Elayne wanted to scream—I wasn't abducted by aliens, I was summoned by a unicorn! But she knew that would only confirm the doctor's hypothesis. And she wasn't here to make it easy for her. Nor for her dad. He'd betrayed her by bringing her to this woman. Because he knew the unicorn wasn't a fantasy. Hell, the Miracle Man knew it better than anyone.

Apart from her. "Look, doc—"

"May we try something?"

"Like what?"

"There's another reason I've had such success in the field." Leibowitz smiled. "I use a special technique. Journey to the very root of the fantasy where I am able to . . . dig it up, yes?"

Her English was near perfect. But it was a German phrase she'd roughly translated here. *Ausgraben.* Elayne wanted to offer it to her. But then she'd have to get into why she spoke all known languages—and several animal ones as well. Which would only complicate matters, sanity-wise. So she just asked, "What technique?"

"Hypnosis."

She sighed. "One of your colleagues, Dr. Tanner, he tried hypnosis. Didn't work on me. I am . . . *unempfänglich*—" She said it in German, couldn't help herself, wanted to see those pale blue eyes widen again.

They did. But Leibowitz didn't comment, just said, "Oh, I think I have an ability that perhaps my American colleagues do not. Shall we try? Shall we take this journey, you and I?"

What the hell, Elayne thought. With Tanner she'd pretended to go under, then strung him along with some apparent "revelations," mostly of a teengirl kind. Got him quite excited, the old dude, until he figured out she was playing him. Exit Tanner, enter O'Reilly. Now here was another opponent to be played. To be beaten too. Fun! After all, she'd never taken a Freudian. "Sure. Let's try it," she replied.

"Excellent." The doctor reached to the edge of her desk, to a small wooden case. She pulled a lid away and set a metal arm moving. "A metronome," she said. Unnecessarily, as Elayne had taken five years of cello. Tick . . . tick, it went, the rhythm slow but not too slow. She then pressed a button on her desk and soft music filled the room from hidden speakers. Tanner had been an Indiaphile and it was gentle sitar he'd tried to lull her with. This was chanting. Greek monks?

So far, so obvious. Any second now the doc would tell her to—

"Relax, Elayne. Close your eyes, take a deep breath in, hold it for a moment, then let it slowly out. Repeat. In . . . and out. In . . . and out."

Elayne breathed, which she was planning on doing anyway. She also considered how long she should give it before she "went under"—not too long, she thought—and more importantly, what fantasy she should concoct. Since unicorns were already out there, she'd have to stick with them. But she wasn't going to go anywhere near the truth, since no one believed it anyway. What was that book she'd read when she was eight? The seven pink unicorns? That would do. FAD diagnosis here we come!

"Are you feeling relaxed, Elayne?"

She delayed her reply, made her voice sluggish. "Yes."

"I want you to imagine you are slowly descending a long staircase. Just focus on the stairs. Count them down with me. Twenty, nineteen—"

"Eighteen." Nine, she thought. I'll make nine and then I'll stop and—

"Elayne!"

The doctor's voice was so sharp Elayne opened her eyes. Leibowitz was staring at her, her own eyes narrowed. "Elayne," she said again. "Please do not waste my time nor your father's money."

"I'm not, I'm—"

"I do not think you are susceptible to the common techniques. Resistant anyway. Come." She stood and gestured. "Let us go to the couch. Maybe it is too soon for this. Maybe we shall just talk for this session."

Oh, that was too easy, Elayne thought, rising and hobbling over. I didn't even get to describe Pink Wind. The unicorn who farts glitter.

"Just stand for a moment, at the end."

Elayne, about to lower herself, halted. The doctor stood about two feet in front of her. She was quite small, and Elayne was taller than most. "I apologize," said the doctor. "I was a little short with you there." Elayne bit back the obvious reply: you're a little short with me here too! Especially as Leibowitz seemed genuinely upset. "Please, may we start over?" She offered a small, beautifully manicured right hand. "Welcome to my office."

Elayne shrugged, reached.

As soon as their hands met, the doctor grabbed hard and jerked her forward. "Sleep!" she commanded, her voice hard and low.

Shockingly, Elayne did.

2

Going Under

There was still a part of her that knew what was happening. That she was lying on a couch in a shrink's office. That questions were being asked. What she'd lost was the ability to resist or deflect those questions, which annoyed her. How had she fallen—literally, she supposed; she had no memory of descending to the couch—for a different hypnosis technique? She, who could see every analyst's trick?

And yet? Elayne felt relief surge through her. Because wasn't this a chance to talk about what had happened to her? She never could, except to her father. If she even hinted at it, people thought she was deranged. Like Dr. O'Reilly had, writing all those notes that Leibowitz was now scanning. But under hypnosis wasn't she expected to reveal her subconscious? And if Dr. Leibowitz took it as teenage fantasies, as metaphors to be deconstructed, so be it. She would know what she was saying were truths. It might just help. Her dad could be right: if she didn't bottle it all up, maybe she'd have fewer bike incidents!

"Tell me, Elayne. How did you meet the unicorn?"

"He summoned me to Goloth."

A rustle of papers. "This 'Goloth' is a parallel world, yes?"

"Kinda."

"A world where 'all our myths live'? Is this correct?"

"Many myths. Fabulous beasts live there anyway."

"Fabulous beasts. Do you mean monsters?"

"Not in the horror movie sense. Monsters are creatures made up of different animal parts. A griffin has the body of a lion, the head of an eagle, the—"

"Elayne, I know what monsters are. I have studied my Jung." Dr. Leibowitz took a deep breath. "Does anything else live there?"

"Ordinary animals too. Along with some humans."

Elayne could hear a finger tracing down a page. "Medieval humans?"

"A medieval world to us, yes. Peasants. Knights. A king."

As soon as she said it she had a flash of him—Leo, the arrogant prince, handsome as hell but a total tyrant. He had tried to kill Moonspill. He'd wanted to marry her.

"A king? I see." A pause, another rustle. "How did you travel to this world?"

"Through the tapestries."

"These are the Unicorn Tapestries that are kept at the Cloisters Museum here in New York? The famous medieval ones, yes?"

"Yes. There's a door you can open if . . . if you have the right key."

"A key? And where did you find this key?"

"I didn't find it. I . . ." She swallowed. "An ancestor was given it. She was the daughter of the man who wove the tapestries. He wove the door between worlds too."

"But this key is . . ." another shift of papers, "a part of a unicorn's horn, yes?"

"The tip of one. The unicorn broke it off so my ancestor could always come back if she wanted to."

"But she did not. You did. And you knew this family, uh, story, from childhood, yes? About this unicorn and his . . . his relationship with your ancestor. Also a teenage girl, yes?"

"Yes."

"Interesting." Elayne heard a nib scratching on paper. And then the doctor continued, "I want you to go deeper now, Elayne. To imagine . . . no . . . to see! To see this unicorn before you. What would you say to him now? This . . ." Another finger slide. "Moonspill?"

Moonspill! It was the first time his name had been mentioned. And it set something off inside her. Not a memory. A feeling—that extraordinary feeling of being joined to him, linked to the unicorn's mind. "Ahh!" she breathed out on a huge, shuddery sigh.

She heard the creak of a chair, the doctor leaning forward. "Where are you now, Elayne? Yes. Go there. Go . . . deeper!"

Deeper? Why not? She'd go anywhere if she could be with him. She'd go . . .

Maid.

    Moonspill!

    You are hurt, Alice-Elayne.

    My knee? It's nothing.

    Let me.

He comes toward her slowly, so slowly, giving her time to take him all in. Her Moonspill. Her monster. No pink cuddly toy. A fabulous beast. A horse's head and body, marbled whiteness like a monumental statue, half as big again as the biggest stallion. But with the beard and the splayed hooves of an enormous goat.

She reaches a hand to him, runs her fingertips down the velvet of his muzzle. He bends to the hand, allowing the caress, as he would for no other person. Now she sees what she has longed for most: one of his eyes. Sees it, falls into it, into that dark blue immensity, that galaxy of stars.

Maid, he says again, but not out loud. Why would he? There is no need for speech, not when their minds can be linked like this, the two of them utterly joined, as she has been to no other being, ever, not even to her father to whom she is as close as only an only child can be.

But words are the smallest part of it. Greater is touch, his mind wrapping around hers like a silken scarf, cool to ease her, then warm to hold her, enfold her. Two years since last he'd held her so. Two years of being alone.

Her sigh came long, shuddering again from her depths. A voice followed, from far away now.

"Tell me, Elayne. What are you feeling?"

You want me to tell you? Of what floods every part of me? This certainty, these truths: that I was never whole before. That, without this, I will never be whole again.

"Yes, good. Good. Let the tears come."

It is your pain that brings the tears, Alice-Elayne. Let me touch it. Let me take it away.

You are! Just by this, you are.

Even so . . .

He lowers his head. The horn passes before her eyes, that glorious spiral of ivory five feet long. He lays it against her swollen knee. Instantly a coolness comes that spreads over the hurt as his mind did over hers, bringing the same ease. More, bringing pleasure, a tickling delight.

"Yes!" She laughs out loud.

"No!" That voice comes again. "The pain. Focus on the pain."

But how can she, when all the pain is going? Moonspill is here and he is taking it all away. For that is what the unicorn does, this healer of beasts and man. He takes away pain and with it all heartache. Especially that. For did he not return with her from Goloth to New York and cure her father? Did he not lay his horn on Alan's ravaged body and draw all the cancer out, though the drawing nearly killed them both?

"My father. He healed my father."

"Yes, Elayne. Your father. His recovery was a miracle. So you have created a bringer of miracles, haven't you? But how can you ever repay that gift?"

Moonspill raises his head, his task done, all her pain gone at his touch. His eyes narrow and that rumble comes, that one, oh-so-rare, when he is amused. *Repay? How can she not know? That I summoned you to my aid, Alice-Elayne. That you were the one who saved me, me and Heartsease, my mate. When all was lost, you found us. Reunited us. Repay?* That rumble again. *It is I who owe you.*

No, Moonspill. We . . .

"Now, Elayne, you see him, yes? He is clear before you, yes?"

"He is. Oh, he is."

"So now . . . dissolve him! You may let him go. Let the bringer of miracles go, Elayne. He has done what you need. In the real world—"

As suddenly as they were joined before, his mind leaves hers. As slowly as he came, the unicorn begins to back away.

She stretches for him. *No! This world is the only one I want. Nothing else comes close to being joined to him, to Moonspill. Nothing ever will. Don't try to take him away!*

"Elayne! Calm. You are safe. Lie back again, please."

No. No, no! Don't leave! Moonspill, I beg you. Stay. Or . . . or let me come with you. Let me come back to Goloth.

She tries to move. To lift herself. But it feels as if she is bound to the spot where he left her, where he last touched her. At a distance now, against a huge setting sun, blending into its light, just as she last saw him, he reaches her again.

You will not find me there, maid. For Goloth as you knew it does not exist. I have gone. All the unicorns have gone.

The shock of it runs through her. *Gone? You can't have. Gone where?*

But he does not answer. Instead, there is only a flash as he merges with the light.

"No!"

That voice from outside, its harshness such a contrast to the one that's just vanished. "Elayne, that is enough for now. I want you to wake up."

She stretches her fingers to the light. Some of him must still be there within the flame of the sunset. Some trace that she can bring into her heart to keep her warm.

"Elayne, listen to me. On 'three' you shall—"

There is something there. Something stirring still. He's coming back, she thinks, flushing with joy. *Moonspill! she cries.*

Maid?

She gasps. It is not his voice. Not a caress but a jab. No warming silk but a bucket of burning coals. She cries out, in agony, hears from far away, a woman's voice calling her name. Stuck where she is, powerless to respond. Only listen.

So you are the maid. The Summoned. The words come flat and hard on sibilant esses. *The one who started a revolution.*

Revolution. No! I didn't. I only helped Moonspill. I . . .

Chaos followed your helping. You are responsible. For every action has a consequence. Yours left civil war. Slaughter of innocents. Goloth in flames. A chuckle came. *And flames are where I live.*

"Elayne? Elayne! Stop thrashing." A hand on her again. "All right, this is enough. You need to wake up. One—"

You are right to fear. For I will hurt you. You and everyone you love.

"Two!"

But you will come to me anyway. You will have no choice.

It isn't just a voice now. Within the setting sun, inside eyelids she cannot force open, something glows brighter. A small light, growing rapidly larger.

"No!"

"Three!" A silence. "Wake up, Elayne. Open your eyes."

Not yet. Not until you hear. Not until you see . . . Me.

"Elayne? Elayne!"

Someone's tugging her arm. Trying to pull her upright. But she cannot rise, cannot look away. She can only watch the light within the light grow larger. Till it focuses . . . on an eye! Vast, shimmering, an iridescent green, at its centre the slit of an iris, a gash of red that widens into an orb—and then into a lake of blood.

"Elayne! I'm going to call—"

The voice again. It is both a hiss—and a caress. And it speaks now of desire.

Admit it, Alice-Elayne. You long to return to Goloth. There are other adventures to be had here, after all. You may have ridden a unicorn. But surely what you really want to do is fly a dragon.

The eye flashes fire. Her scream is long and loud.

3

Chicken Marengo

It had taken quite a lot of persuasion for the doctor to let her go. First Leibowitz wanted to call her father. When Elayne refused—he'd be in his big pitch session right then—a cab was suggested. "I think I've had enough of cabs today, thanks," she'd replied, rubbing her knee. Finally, after ever more flippant answers, the doctor had accepted that her patient was fit to go. She'd even re-acquired her Germanic cool, after being briefly thrown by Elayne's shrieking and thrashing and general impersonation of the possessed.

"We made good progress today, I think," she'd said, reaching out her hand.

"Fist bump?" Elayne replied, offering her knuckles. She wasn't going to be tricked into her subconscious again. Leibowitz declined contact, accompanied her to the front desk, and fixed her next appointment, returning to her office with a smile on her face. Well played, Elayne thought. She had to admit, if this were an international soccer match, Austria had just scored the first goal.

"Anyone home?" she called as pushed open the front door.

Silence. Dad was still at his meeting, probably wouldn't be home for a couple of hours yet—which suited her fine. She could use the time. To prepare dinner—it was her turn. And just to think for a while. Process.

What the hell had happened at the doctor's office?

"Food first," she said aloud. There was something meditative about cooking and since there was just the two of them, her dad had trained her from an early age. When he'd gotten sick, she'd really stepped up her game, to try to keep weight on him. His grandmother had been French, and he loved that cuisine, so she'd immersed herself in daubes and moules and aioli.

Her dad had taken up origami while he was ill. He was always folding paper into unusual shapes on which he'd write notes. One stood on the kitchen counter now—a Viking longship, complete with mast. It seemed a shame to dismantle it, but he always said they were meant to be transitory things, here and gone. So she unfolded it and read two words: Chicken Marengo.

"Yes, boss." She put olive oil and butter in a wide pan, chopped and then started to sweat some onion. The dish was one of his faves because he was also a military history nut—forget galleries; they'd walked battle-fields on their holidays in Europe. This dish would allow him to discourse again on how it had been created for Napoleon himself from the ingredients readily available after his great victory over the Austrians at Marengo. "Onions, garlic, tomato, thyme, mushrooms, bread, chicken," she recited under her breath. "And wine, of course," she added, reaching into the fridge. A medium dry white was required—and his favourite was in the fridge, Veuve de Vouvray. "What the hell," she said, and poured herself a glass. She'd be eighteen tomorrow. Legal. Well, maybe not in New York, but in lots of other states, for wine at least. Though legality had never mattered too much to a household governed by French rules. Her dad had given her watered wine to drink from age ten.

Delicious scents began to fill the kitchen. She hummed as she sipped and cooked. Trying not to think of what had happened earlier. Trying not to think of what she knew she would do when the dish was in the oven.

And then it was. Topping up her wine, she crossed to the living room. Their loft in the Meatpacking District was open plan so the pleasant smells still reached her. She flopped into the deep, old leather sofa, took a gulp of wine, then reached for the book. Didn't open it. Just ran her fingers over the frayed emerald cover, over the faded embossed words.

The Maid and the Unicorn.

Different maid, though they shared a name. Alice-Elayne. Same unicorn. Moonspill.

It always sat on the table. Her dad would often glance through it, but she rarely did. She found it too painful. Because this book was where it all began. Reading it, on this same sofa two years ago—two years, how could two years have passed?—had set her on the road to Goloth and all her adventures.

She took a breath. Opened the book. There it was, on the first page: "The Incredible yet Nonetheless True Tale of Alice-Elayne Robochon: Her Adventures in Goloth, Land of the Fabulous Beast, and What Happened Next."

She looked up to the window. The light was fading on an early spring night. Out there horns blared, a distant siren wailed, someone was shouting about bad driving. Out there was the everyday world of New York. While in here . . .

She looked down. The "incredible tale" of the ancestor was just that. "Incredible," in the literal sense: not to be believed. For how could anyone believe a tale that began in medieval France with a brilliant weaver who was saved from death by a unicorn using his special power: to heal, to remove poisons from a body? Believe that the unicorn then persuaded the weaver to weave him a doorway to another world— Goloth, the land he came from, and to which he, Moonspill, was so desperate to return. Believe that the weaver was forced to go through to that world by another man, a supreme hunter who'd stalked the unicorn and would not be denied his prize. How those men, trapped there by the closing of the door—which could only be opened by a touch of the unicorn's horn—then set about remaking that world, in their different ways. How the Hunter became a tyrant king, killed the weaver when he opposed him—then chose unicorns to be his enemy, and his descendants' enemy, a vendetta to last through all time . . .

Until a second Alice-Elayne—herself—ended it. Because the first had made a pact with Moonspill when he helped her escape. That either she or, if too much time had passed, one of her descendants—each new girl-child being named for the weaver's daughter—would come if he needed her. Needed a maiden.

Who could believe all that? She never would have. Until she'd been the maiden Moonspill summoned.

Lost in memory, she didn't hear the key in the lock, the door opening. Only his voice.

"Hey!"

"Hey."

Alan inhaled deeply. "Mmm, that smells good. Chicken Marengo?"

"As commanded, mon Empeurer."

"Actually, Napoleon was only First Consul at that battle. The emperorship came later." He let go of the door, came over, and put his bag onto the table.

"How was the meeting? You get the deal?"

"Oh yeah. They loved me. Hence . . ." He reached for his bag, pulled out a bottle of champagne. "Ta-dah! Double celebration. Eve of birthday and—" He came over, flopped down. "How was the shrink?"

"She was German. Austrian, actually."

"Ach ja? Ist zat zo?"

"I know! Total cliché Freudian too. 'You vill lie on zee zofa! Ve are going to explore your *trowma*.' I thought she was going to smoke a cigar!"

"In Manhattan? They'd burn her effigy in Times Square." They both laughed. He quieted first. "But did she have any, uh, insights? Early days, I know, but—" He shrugged. "I am worried about you, kid."

"I know, Dad. I'm sorry." She squeezed his arm. "Well, she did hypnotize me."

"Really?" He'd half risen. Now he flopped back down. "Did it work?"

"I don't know. I . . ." She'd decided she wasn't going to tell him about the dragon probe. She couldn't explain it to him. Hell, she couldn't explain it to herself. In fact, sitting on the subway coming home, she'd concluded it wasn't real, just a stress-based hallucination. There were no dragons in Goloth. "I saw Moonspill though."

"Yeah. And how was that?"

His voice was calm, but his gaze intense. "Oh great. I mean I've dreamed of him, of course, but this felt like I was really, really connected to him again. He even laid his horn on my sore knee and I swear it feels way better. See?" She stretched out her leg to show him. "But there was a lot of weirdness too."

"While hallucinating a unicorn? Can't think why." He smiled. "Tell me more."

"Moonspill said he was no longer in Goloth. That Goloth itself was in flames." She paused, hearing again the sibilant, ecstatic voice that had actually told her that. "It terrified me. I mean, you've only got to look around the world to see what usually happens after a revolution. The tyrant is overthrown, everyone dances for, like, a day. And then they all start killing each other. Civil war. Chaos."

"And since you believe you started that revolution, of course you're terrified."

"I didn't, I just—"

She broke off as he picked up the book, flicked to its endpapers. There, carefully attached to the back covers, were the pages she'd added. Her dad had gotten her to write down all her tales while they were still fresh. Thought it would help her to get it all out.

He opened the last page, cleared his throat. "'I was caught up in the moment. Moonspill had just escaped with Heartsease. He had defeated the tyrant. But what about tyranny? And since everybody was looking at me, I gave them the word they wanted to hear. The name by which their rebels had always been known. I screamed, "Weavers!" It was another first—I started a riot. Though it looked more like a revolution. Perhaps they begin the same way.'" He put down the book, continued, "I always thought it was cool that their rebels called themselves after our ancestor's profession."

"Yeah, but Dad, all that doesn't mean—"

He interrupted. "You are bound to feel worried. And guilty. So no wonder that under hypnosis you conjured up the one being you most wanted to see—and that Moonspill brought you the news you most feared to hear."

Elayne still didn't want to think about it. "You should be charging the four hundred bucks an hour, Doc."

He wasn't deflected. "It's pretty obvious. You don't have to be a Freud."

"But I am a-freud. In fact, I'm terri-freud."

They both laughed—then he took her hand. "Shall I tell you what frightens me most?"

"Of course, Dad."

"That all the night terrors, the accidents, your problems at school—they are all because you want to go back."

"Where?"

"Goloth. To see what's happened to your friends. To that two-headed snake you talked about—"

"Amphisbaena."

"Yes. But mostly to Moonspill."

Go back! It was what she most feared. It was also and equally what she most craved. But she couldn't let that show on her face.

Yet he must have read it there anyway because he continued, "Which is why I have commandeered the only vehicle that could take you." As he said it, he reached beneath his turtleneck sweater and pulled out, attached to a silver chain . . .

The horn! The tip of Moonspill's horn! The only way to get between the two worlds.

"Hey," she cried, suddenly furious, "that's mine!"

She lunged for it. He leaned hard back, then stood up, tucking it away.

"Ours, Daughter. It belongs to our family."

She stood too, faced him, her face bright with anger. "No! You gave it to me."

"Because I thought I was dying and you needed to know the stor—"

"You *were* dying. And I used it to go to Goloth and bring you back the one thing that could cure you. In case you've forgotten!"

She took a step, her hand reaching to the shape beneath the wool. His hand closed over it as he stood his ground. "A unicorn in my living room is something I am unlikely ever to forget. Nor the curing." He shook his head. "But now I am well—and I am also your father. I am meant to look out for you. So until you've convinced me that you have no intention of trying to go back to Goloth, this," he patted his chest, "never leaves me. Even when I sleep."

As suddenly as her anger had come, it left. "But, Dad. I'm worried. That . . . vision. The unicorns are the protectors of that world, and all the creatures in it. Man and beast, fabulous and otherwise. If they've left—"

She broke off. He took her hand, still stretched toward him. "I know, lovely. I am as worried as you are. I may not have gone but I know how much I owe Moonspill. Owe Goloth. I owe them everything." He gestured to the book on the table. "That's my history too. My ancestors. And my daughter who risked her life to add to that history, and to save me, while I did . . . nothing." He took a deep breath. "I bet if Leibowitz got her hands on me, she wouldn't need hypnosis to diagnose me with a big dose of survivor's guilt."

She squeezed his hand. "That's crazy talk."

"No, this is crazy talk." He crossed his eyes, and ululated, "Uggle sprangle wazzokey." He smiled. "Runs in the family." His smile faded. "But I would do anything now—anything!—to save you from further danger. Including being the guardian of the gate."

"OK, Dad." She knew he could be tough when he needed to be. It was what she'd missed so much when he was sick, her strong father. "I consider myself saved."

"Good." He squeezed and released her hand. "And I consider myself hungry. Where's my dinner, child?"

"Coming." She took a few steps toward the kitchen, stopped, and turned back. "Can you take my birthday off tomorrow?"

"Haven't you got school?"

She did. She wasn't going to tell him that though. What was one more missed class. "Nah."

"OK. You sleep in and I'll wake you with French toast in bed. Deal?"

"Deal." She smiled. "Is that what Napoleon had for breakfast the morning after Marengo?"

"I suspect he had cold chicken. Which mine will be if you don't hasten to the stove, child."

"Hastening, First Consul."

She turned but his voice halted her. "You know how much I love you, Elayne, don't you?"

His voice had changed, gone soft. She turned back. He was standing where she'd left him, one hand still at his chest, wrapped around the unicorn's horn inside his sweater. "Uh, sure, Dad," she replied, puzzled. "Me too. I love you too."

4

NIGHT TERRORS

"I love you."

She says it. Out loud. She is no longer asleep. She is not awake.

She does not say it to her father. She says it to the unicorn.

She is in her room, in her bed. In the Meatpacking District of New York City.

She is in the dungeon of the Castle of Skulls, in the City of Goloth. For there is Moonspill, as she found him there that day. After all their adventures, separate and together, it has come to this.

Maid.

Him in her head. Not the usual caress. A groan of a voice.

What have they done to you?

They have drugged me. I will still fight in the arena. But I will not fight well enough to defeat the tyrant. He will kill me before his people. He will prove his right to rule.

She laughs. She swaggers. *Not on my watch.*

Is that what she said? Time changes everything. Stories change with each telling. This she knows. She is not certain, in her bed, two years later.

But she is certain in the dungeon.

So she says to him, *You brought me here to tame you. You thought that if I did, you could think, not run mad. Think and free your love, your mate Heartsease, from the tyrant's prison.*

Instead I have only joined her here to die.

No. For what if you do not need to be tamed? If you need something different? If you only need to meld with me?

Meld?

She laughs again. There in her bedroom. There in that cell. And then she leans her head against his flank and closes her eyes.

She closes her eyes. Opens them to bright sunlight in the middle of the night.

The arena in Goloth City. A coliseum where animals are slaughtered, for the delight of man. She is in the stands, a prisoner, a helpless witness to the climax of the ritual—the sacrifice of Moonspill by Leo the king-elect. The hunt and death of the unicorn.

She is not helpless. And Moonspill is no longer drugged though he feigns that he still is. A touch of his mate's horn has cleared that poison as Moonspill's had cleared her dad's cancer.

It is true, her father says, suddenly there, in the bedroom, in the arena.

Dad, she cries, delighted. You came to Goloth.

Did I not say I would? he replies.

She takes his hand. She squeezes it. Watch this, she says. You're gonna love this.

Moonspill is jabbed with blades, chased and savaged by hounds. Unicorns run mad in a fight. It is their strength. It is their weakness. For if he runs mad, how will he do what he needs to do?

But he is not alone. She is in his mind now. When he wavers, she steadies him with a thought. When the red rage is about to sweep over him, she calms him with a word.

Remember.

And when he falls as if finished before the king, when Leo descends with his cruel spear to give him the killing thrust, Moonspill knocks it aside with his horn. And the next blow and the next. Then he strikes himself, again and again, and it is Leo parrying, Leo stumbling up the hill, Leo on his knees, Leo looking up at his death in a thrust of sharpest ivory.

In an arena, in a bedroom, she holds her breath. A heartbeat. One more. And then Moonspill rises on his hind legs and roars. Roars his triumph. Roars for his mate, Heartsease, who runs to join him. Together they kick down the stadium gate and run off into the night.

And everyone's looking at me, she thinks. Even the defeated king on his knees. Looking up at the maid who tamed the unicorn. Even if she didn't.

There's a silence, waiting to be filled.

She fills it with a word—the name for the rebels who had been waiting through centuries of oppression for this moment, for this silence.

Weavers! she cries.

Her father has her hand now. He looks concerned. "Elayne," he says, "you're OK. You're OK. Wake up now. Wake up!"

"But look what I've done!" She screams it. "Look!"

She points. At people starting to kill each other. At children running. At a city in flames.

"Look what I've done," she sobs.

"Elayne," her father shouts. "Wake up!"

Elayne woke up, even if she wasn't asleep. Night terrors were like that. Caught between two worlds. Unable to get out of either.

"Elayne! It's OK. It's OK."

He pulled her close, murmuring calming words, held her while she kept sobbing. When the first storm had passed, he reached to her night table and grabbed her water. She gulped it, spilling some. "Breathe, sweetheart," he said. "Deep breaths."

While he rubbed her back, she took several. Eventually they became less shuddery. She reached past him, grabbed a Kleenex, blew.

"Better?"

"A little."

He moved farther down the bed, so he could see her. "Bad one, huh?"

"Could say that."

"Want to tell me?"

"Same old stuff."

"The arena?"

"Yeah. The dungeon first. Moonspill and I joined our minds. It was as amazing as . . . it was the first time. Then I helped him defeat Leo—"

"As you did."

"As I did." She sniffed. "But then I cried out the rebels' name: Weavers—"

"Which is where I came in."

"Yes, but you were there too this time. In the arena. Seeing it all . . ."

"I was?"

". . . seeing the chaos that followed. People killing, dying. And after Moonspill came to me during hypnosis, said the same thing—"

She broke off. He took her hand. "Darling, you can't *know* that's what happened next? Come on, where's my smart daughter? You have to know that this is your fears speaking. Not your truths. It's the great unknown. Isn't it is just as likely that the tyrant was overthrown and that your shout ushered in a new age of freedom and democratic rule?"

"I guess." She swallowed. "But why doesn't it feel like that?"

"Because you're dwelling on the worst outcome, not the best. It's how you roll. Disaster will fall. Didn't you always believe I'd die of my cancer?"

"And would've done, if I hadn't brought a unicorn to cure you."

"Exactly!" He grinned. "See how it all worked out? As it may well have in Goloth."

"How will I know? For certain?" A tear ran down her cheek. She wiped it away. "How will I ever know?"

"You won't. But what you'll do is learn to live with the uncertainty." He squeezed her hand, then stood. "I was making some cocoa. I'll bring you a cup."

"I didn't wake you?"

"No. I was up."

"Doing what?"

"Thinking about you." He smiled. "Marshmallows?"

She wiped her nose and smiled too. "Is there any other kind?"

He went. She bent down, pulled the duvet up around her, lay back and looked at the ceiling. The night terror had been so real, as they always were. And as always, it had left her shattered. Though she did feel as if it had eased her somehow. Seeing it again. And her dad was right. Maybe it had all gone brilliantly. Maybe they were raising statues to her in Goloth City. A great big one in the main square. Her on Moonspill. The maid and the unicorn.

She yawned, felt herself slipping away, straight into the sleep she craved. And a few minutes later, though she felt a hand on her shoulder, heard her dad say, "Sleep, darling girl. Daddy's going to take care of everything," she found she didn't want to wake up. Even for cocoa.

5

THE RETURN OF THE SNAKE

She woke with a start, sat up, looked at her clock. Nine forty-seven. Wow, she thought, long sleep. Needed it. Dad must have let me sleep in. Then she remembered why.

"Because it's my birthday," she said aloud, and lay back.

He was probably in the kitchen now, making her French toast. She felt a little guilty, telling him that fib about no school. He knew she'd cut classes. That her grades weren't what she was capable of. But he didn't quite get how dull she found the whole thing. In fact she was thinking of dropping out for a while. Going travelling. Maybe she would talk to him about that today, on their outing. Now where would they go?

She took her lower lip into her mouth and chewed. But it didn't take much thought. "The Cloisters," she said. If she couldn't see the real Moonspill, except in dreams, at least she could visit his woven double.

There were no noises coming from the kitchen. Dad was probably waiting to see "the whites of her eyes," as he liked to say. She'd flash those, have a shower while he cooked, eat, tell him where she'd like to go.

She got up carefully, pulled on her track pants, tested her knee. Not too bad if still a little bruised from the cab contact. Better though. Ibuprofen or hallucinated unicorn's horn? She'd take both.

"Dad?" she called as she opened her door. "I'm up." Silence. She walked down the corridor, into the main room. No one there. She yawned. He'd probably gone out to get some fancy vanilla for the French toast. It was like his cocoa. He paid fortunes for the chocolate, never used a brand powder. Life's too short for cheap cocoa, he'd say.

She looked at the kitchen. On the counter, where he'd leave her his origami notes, stood a unicorn.

She smiled. Picked it up, stood it on the palm of her hand. It was about two inches tall, including the half-inch horn. A beauty. There was probably a note inside. But she didn't want to pull it apart just yet. She'd wait for him, so he could do it carefully and then put it back together. Her first birthday present.

Setting it down, she went off for her shower.

"Dad?"

She came out of her room, towelling hard. Her dark hair was so thick it always took an age to dry.

No reply. Strange. She'd taken at least half an hour. The scent of eggy bread, vanilla and Quebec maple syrup—like his cocoa, only the best—should have been filling the place.

She stopped and looked at the unicorn. Her heart started to thump hard. She crossed, fumbled it open, careless of the delicate folds. She ripped it a little, but not enough to confuse the words. The terrible words she'd suddenly, certainly, known would be there.

Elayne, my darling daughter. I have gone to Goloth.

She gasped, staggered, sat on a kitchen stool. When she could breathe again, she read the rest.

I have worried, ever since you returned, that you would want to go back. Life here must seem very dull after your adventures. And you've never settled. I can understand why. I only met Moonspill once and I long to see him again. How much more must you?

I also understand your worry for the land and its people. That is why I am doing this. I am going to see what's happened there. I plan to be gone no more than two weeks. Enough time to learn what you need to know so as to give you some peace. I hope to find a new world that you helped begin, a struggling world perhaps but one on the road to some sort of balance. Not the world of your night terrors. But if I do not find that, I promise I will return swiftly and help you live with what is, knowing you can make no difference. You only have to look at the world today to know that an individual rarely can.

"But I did," she cried out, then wiped away the tears that were now making the words hard to see. Read on.

I do not do this only for you, my child. I always felt that I owed Moonspill, all Goloth, a huge debt. Perhaps I can repay a little of that now. Remember, I am Weaver's blood too.

I love you deeply. And will be back before you know I'm gone.

Ton pere,

Alan

PS I know you're cutting school. Go! I want to see your first A when I get back.

PPS French toast is prepped in fridge. Use the good maple syrup. Happy Birthday!

"No!" She slammed the paper down, staggered back, stumbled to the sofa, fell onto it, couldn't stay there, got up, ranged about the loft, seeking, finding nothing.

What was she going to do? What the hell was she going to do?

There was only one way to get to Goloth. One door—the tapestry. One key—the horn. And her father had that. He was there now, she was sure. About to embark on all the adventures—terrifying, exhilarating—that she had. She couldn't decide if she was jealous or furious.

No. What she was, was scared. Really scared. There were so many ways to die in Goloth. "Dad," she sobbed. "Come back!"

It took ten minutes, but she cried herself straight. There was absolutely nothing she could do. Except do something else. If she sat around here worrying for two weeks she really would go crazy. Wouldn't Dr. Leibowitz love that!

Her father had left her two things: French toast and an order. She set about making the one, and started planning the other. A different route to Columbia U. "Eighth Avenue. No bike lanes. Just traffic."

Her anger lasted her till Midtown. There was nothing to fuel it. Everyone was driving like wusses, being courteous. In New York! Every light obligingly changed when she approached it.

Fury had kept her fear away. When it went, terror returned, doubled. Dismounting, she pulled over to the curb, bent over her handlebars. She thought she was going to be sick. When she'd dry heaved a couple of times, she realized she had nothing to puke. She'd managed one bite of the French toast before throwing the rest out. There was a power juice joint over on Park and 44th. She'd drink a protein smoothie and try to get her strength back. Only problem—the direct route led through Times Square.

She hated it for two reasons. One, it was the worst of New York to her, the place that most people in the world associated with the city she otherwise loved. The giant screens flashing ads, the outlandish costumed people posing for photos for money, the vendors selling crap, the hordes of gaping tourists. Welcome to America. Buy! Buy! Buy!

Yet there was a second reason why she hated it, avoided it. A very personal one. And when she reached the square, one swift glance told her it was still there. Indeed, if anything, it had grown.

Right opposite her stood a unicorn. Not a hallucination. A unicorn. Or rather, a man in a unicorn costume. He was all pink and glittery, with cascades of foil for a mane. His horn was stubby and kinked near the top, where he must have run into something. He looked like a joke—but that didn't stop people crowding around him, taking his flyers. And it wouldn't stop many of them boarding the tour bus behind him, the one that proclaimed, "Unicorn Tours."

She wanted to cross, move away, keep her head down and go. But she found herself staring like any dumb tourist. Because the tour bus was one of the new ones, a screen running the length of its side. On it, a movie was showing, a mixed montage. Some of it was a slick promotional video. A horse, done up like a unicorn with a spiralling horn and a beard—though with horses' hooves, not cloven, like real unicorns had, duh!—galloped across a grassy meadow. First alone, then with a girl on his back. Classic maiden look: long dress, long blonde hair, impractical riding heels. But what made Elayne stare, longingly, was the footage the slick video was interspersed with. Rough, grainy, blown-up from cellphones, so blurry it was hard to tell sometimes what was there. Not surprising really, she thought, as she watched herself and Moonspill gallop across Columbus Circle and vanish into Central Park. It had been midnight, after all.

She shook herself, crossed against the red, ignoring the bike bell blares. Thank God it had been a freezing, snowy night when she'd ridden Moonspill through the tapestries from Goloth to escape the hunters; the weather not quite as bad when she'd ridden him back two days later to escape. Still, if there had been any decent footage, they'd have shown it, then she might have been recognized, and how could she have explained that?

People were divided: most thought it a hoax, a student prank, a horse decked out like in the bus's promotional movie. Some maintained it was a conspiracy, that the CIA or terrorists had slipped drugs into the city's water supply and mass hallucinations had ensued. A large minority believed fervently in the reality of the unicorn—many now boarding the bus that would take them on a tour around the "route" the unicorn and girl had ridden, all the way to the Cloisters Museum.

She shook her head, took another step. Then something else caught her eye. Moving words.

". . . be another New York monster mystery?"

She froze. One of the square's giant screens was broadcasting the daily news. An anchor was talking. There was a blurred photo behind her, with her speech appearing in text below. "Details are still a little hazy. But it appears that at 7:45 yesterday morning, municipal workers made an amazing discovery," Elayne read. "It slithered out of a storm drain near Union Square. Not one of New York's legendary albino alligators. Something even more extraordinary."

Then the picture in the background took over the whole screen. And even though she recognized the subject instantly, with the kind of shock that takes all breath away, she still found herself reading the words that appeared.

"A two-headed snake. But this is not like a Siamese twin with two heads on a joined body. This snake has a distinct head . . . at each end."

A man bumped into her from behind. "Pardon me," he said, in Czech. She understood. She could have answered him in his own language. If all her words, in all languages, had not been taken away by the words on the screen above her. Which was ironic, she thought, when she finally could think again, considering that the two-headed snake in the photo had given her the gift of tongues in the first place.

Her nausea vanished. Her body filled with energy. She even smiled. Because if Amphisbaena—the two-personality, two-headed snake— had come through the tapestries, they had to have unicorn's horn. So they were able to go back.

They were able to go back with her.

6

THE DARK WEB

There was only one problem. Where the hell *was* the amphisbaena?

If her phone hadn't been crushed in the encounter with the cab, she'd have sat down on the curb and started googling. Instead she mounted and kicked it uptown—through Central Park, and all the way to Columbia, where she headed straight to the library and to a computer.

First, she watched the news reports, read the print. There wasn't much more than what she'd seen on the screen in Times Square. Amphis and Baena—she knew them as two separate beasts though they were joined—had slithered out of a drain in Union Square and been grabbed. They'd been taken . . . ? No, there was no mention of where. "To be studied by a team of scientists" was the only reference. There was already a lot of speculation. There was footage of several snakes that had two heads, but of the Siamese twin variety, never with a head at both ends. Many comments called it a hoax. Some linked it to the "great unicorn con." Frustrated by the lack of any clues, Elayne found herself clicking and following, watching the grainy footage of her and Moonspill again, absorbed.

"Never took you for a conspiracy nerd."

The voice startled her out of her screen trance. "Huh?" she said, looking up, squinting, since the figure above her was silhouetted against the spring sun streaming through the Columbia library window.

He moved into shade, resolving into . . . "Oh, hello, Huy."

"Hello, Elayne."

Huy—pronounced "We"—Phan, her fellow first year student, dropped into the vacant chair beside her. He was one of the few people she talked to from class. Maybe because he was a bit of a loner, like her. Maybe because he distinguished himself from the hipster crowd by dressing relentlessly old fashioned, as she did. She'd first noticed him even before he transferred from pre-med because, although he wore the identical white coat and earnest expression to the rest, he also wore gold pince-nez glasses, complete with beaded cord. Free from the medical life, his clothes had caught up with his eyewear. Today he was wearing a tweed three-piece suit, with a fob watch. Since she was in an ankle-length brown-velvet skirt—hell on the bike, but she tucked it into her belt and didn't care that she looked like a cycling chocolate macaroon—the two of them would have fitted right into a Henry James novel.

"Whatcha doing?" he asked, gesturing to the screen.

She nearly clicked off the pages she had open. But he was the one guy at school she could trust, maybe a little. "Oh, you know. Research."

"Not updating Instagram like everyone else?"

He gestured around at the students, gawking at screens. "I'm not on Instagram. Or anything actually," she replied.

"Me neither." He peered again at her screen. "But I don't spend much time on these sort of sites either. Research, eh?"

One eyebrow rose, making a thin brown line above his gold spectacles. He'd be quite cute if he wasn't so . . . formal, she thought. But when she thought about what he might be like informally, she blushed and ran her hand through her hair, shrugging it off her shoulders. She thought of making a joke of it, changing the subject—but then he spoke again.

"So," he said, "do you believe in unicorns?"

She kept a straight face. "Of course. Doesn't everyone?"

"Every nutbar."

"So how do you explain these?" She gestured at the photos—they were the cell ones of her and Moonspill on the ride through Manhattan.

He snorted. "Please. Five minutes in Photoshop and I could have you riding that unicorn up the Champs Élysées, stark naked. Oh—" He actually blushed then too, and his eyes went wide. "Uh, not that I would, of course. I mean I don't—"

It was rare to see him break his cool. She quite liked it. "Don't worry, Huy," she interrupted. "You're just making a point."

"Well, yes." He swallowed. His fingertip was close to a photo of the special snake. The two heads were clear, with a human hand beneath each one, squeezed around the neck. "What's that?"

She brought up the wiki page. "It's called an amphisbaena." She swallowed. "Mythological beast. Spawned from Medusa's blood, so it says. You know—the Gorgon?"

"Uh-huh." He scanned the words. "Does it also turn people to stone?"

"Don't think so."

"What, no magical powers?"

"Um, I think I read somewhere that it's, like, the teacher of languages." She swallowed. "It knows all languages, living and dead, and can, if it chooses, teach someone all of them in about a minute. If it chooses," she repeated, licking her lips. She didn't think it would be a good idea to tell him that was exactly what Amphis and Baena had done to, for, her. Given her her superpower. Moonspill had wanted her to have it, knowing it would help her in the treacherous world of Goloth. And he'd been right. Knowing what people were planning for her when they thought she couldn't understand them had saved her life more than once.

"That'd be useful. Then I wouldn't have to spend all that time in the language lab." Like her, Huy was studying linguistics. They also had to learn to speak at least three languages fluently to achieve their joint ambition: join the UN translator program. She knew he spoke Vietnamese. He didn't know that she spoke . . . everything.

He shook his head. "I'm surprised though. I'd expect this from the *New York Post*. But it's unusual for the *Times* website to run a fake," he said, pointing.

"Why does it have to be a fake?"

"Come on! I may have dropped out of medical school but . . . a head at each end? How would it . . ." He paused a millisecond. "Excrete?"

Strangely, the question had never occurred to her. I'll be sure to ask them when I speak to them next, she thought. "I suppose they'll find out when they examine it."

"You mean when they dissect it."

She froze. "Dissect?" Another thing she hadn't considered. "You don't think they—"

Huy shrugged. "Eventually, sure."

She hesitated. "Uh, where . . . where would they do something like that?"

"Why, you want to drop in? I don't think it'll be open to the public."

"Just . . ." She shrugged. "Curious, I guess."

"Uh-huh." He gave her a skeptical look, then grinned. "Would you like me to find out?"

She tried to be casual. "Um, sure. Whatever. If you, like, have the time."

"It won't take any time." He smiled. "Move over. And just make sure no librarian is passing."

"This isn't legal?"

He chuckled. "Nope."

He swung his chair in beside her, put fingers on the keyboard. They flew. Despite his clothes and style, Huy was obviously a computer maestro. A blur of sites appeared, passwords were entered, boxes clicked on. After less than a minute, he leaned back. "Bronx Zoo," he said.

"What? How did you—?"

He tapped his nose. "If I tell you, I'll have to *keel* you," he said in a bad Mexican accent, then sniffed. "Dark Web. It's kinda like the brain—80 percent of the Web is hidden, seemingly unused. It's where the cool stuff lives. Just need to find it—before they find you."

"'They'?"

"The Powers. There'll be a trace on this computer already. I may not believe in unicorns but I sure believe in 'they.' So speaking of—" He leaned forward, fingers poised.

"Wait!" She shot her hand out, held his for a moment. They both looked at their joined hands, before she withdrew hers. "Before you click off, can you download me a map of the Bronx Zoo?"

"I can do that on the normal Web."

"A security map?"

"Oh." That quizzical eyebrow lifted again. "I probably could but, uh, why?"

"Um, maybe I could put on a white coat. Sneak in for the, you know, examination?"

He stared at her a moment, then placed his fingers on the keys. "Uh-huh," he said for the third time, tapping away. Within a minute he raised a finger, held it for a moment, then plunked it down. "There. I've sent it to an untraceable address."

"You've done this before, haven't you?"

"Once or twice." He grinned, got his phone out, brought up a screen. A couple of taps, and the printer beside the computer began to spit out pages. "I've also learned to cover my tracks." He turned back to the computer, fingers flying. "You know, there's an old expression of my mom's. Translates literally as, 'You want to catch a snake, you better wear thick gloves.'"

She was mesmerized by the shifting screens, his dancing fingers. "'Khi con muôn bắt con rắn,'" she murmured, "'con phái mang dôi gǎng tay loai dây.'"

His fingers shot off the keys as if he'd been burned. "Whoa! You speak Vietnamese?"

"Oh no, no. Just that phrase. I, uh, heard it once."

"Once? Your accent is better than mine!"

"Well . . ." She shrugged. "If you learn something new, you may as well learn it properly."

He stared a moment, then returned his eyes to the screen, his fingers to their work. "I knew I was right about you," he said, typing fast.

"How so?"

"You are amazing."

"Oh." She was glad he was so focused forward, so he couldn't see her blush. Again. She had a tendency to blush blotchily, she'd discovered.

"And . . . sign out!" With a last flourish, he turned the screen off. The printer had finished and he bent to the papers, collected them, held them out. But when she reached, he pulled them back. "I don't know what you are up to, Elayne. You don't have to tell me anything but . . . I'm intrigued. Your impeccable Vietnamese has only confirmed that. So I've decided something."

"You have?"

"Yes."

"What?"

"I'm coming with you."

"Where? When?"

"When you break into the Bronx Zoo. Cuz I think you may need my help."

7

BREAK-IN

Getting into the zoo was not a problem. They met at the south gates at the last admission time and bought a ticket like anyone else. Staying in after the zoo closed was trickier.

"Really? A tree?" Huy raised that one quizzical eyebrow again.

It was obviously a talent—and one that was beginning to annoy Elayne. But she knew she was easily annoyed just then. Wedged ten feet up in the branches of an oak, with people continually walking along the path beside it, there was a constant fear of discovery. Then there was the concern of what she might hear from Amphis and Baena—*if* she reached them—not to mention what she would do with the news. And, yes, the tree, which continued to drive remorselessly into her butt. Still. "You'd be more comfortable if you'd dressed for the occasion," she said, pointing at Huy's attire. "What part of 'breaking in' didn't you understand?"

He huffed. "I think this is quite suitable."

"Sure—if you're the Count of Monte Cristo."

To be fair, Huy *had* changed. He'd shed the tweed three-piece—and returned in a black velvet frock coat and matching trousers. He snorted. "This is at least half a century after the Count," he said, flicking leaf mould from his knee. "It's warm. And anyway, he was breaking 'out' of the Château d'If, not in."

Despite her discomfort, her worry, Elayne couldn't help her grin. Huy was probably the only person she knew with whom she could bandy the works of Alexandre Dumas, pere. Apart from with her own "pere," of course.

Her grin vanished. How could she even forget him for a moment? Where the hell was her dad now? There were so many ways to die in Goloth. She had to get to him fast. And the only possibility of that happening waited in the building ahead. She hoped.

Huy hissed softly and put a finger to his lips. Elayne listened, and also heard the footsteps. Someone passed below them, whistling—in the seven o'clock gloom of an early April day, she thought she could make out a zookeeper's peaked cap.

The whistle, the steps faded. "You sure it's here?" whispered Huy.

Elayne peered through the tangled, leafless branches. The building was about fifty yards away, and night lamps lit it dimly. "That's what the man said," she replied.

"And you believe him?"

She thought back. They'd arrived at the zoo and headed for the first logical place—the Reptile House. Of course, the amphisbaena wasn't on display—it would have been mobbed. There were locked doors marked "Staff Only" that led to the back of the tanks and cages. They'd loitered before one, peered in when it opened—but the guard who'd emerged shooed them away. Then she'd gotten lucky. They'd split up to look for other ways in and Elayne had been outside when a back gate opened and a guy came out, pushing a wheelbarrow. He was singing a song—in Bahasa, the language of Indonesia. Which of course she spoke, like all other languages, fluently. She broke it up a bit when she talked to him, so he didn't get suspicious. And she had been to Java, where the man was from, with her dad when she was twelve. Eventually, she'd swung the conversation around to the two-headed snake. He was surprised she knew of it, but being a snake keeper he'd actually helped settle the new arrival.

"In the Wildlife Health Center," she said now, nodding to the building. Apparently, Amphisbaena was not entirely well—further cause for worry. "Do you think we should go now?" she asked.

"And leave this comfortable tree?" He shook his head. "They've only just shut the zoo. Let's wait a little while." He adjusted his position, still looking pained. "So, Elayne, you'll have noticed I've held off on the questions of why the hell we are sitting in a tree waiting to break into an animal infirmary to see a two-headed snake . . ."

"For which I'm grateful."

"But can I ask you this?" He shifted. "Why'd you let me come and not . . ." An eyebrow lifted. "Your boyfriend?"

She'd wondered if that question would arise. Was that why he was there? And trying to figure out how she felt about that was an extra problem she didn't need right then. "No boyfriend."

"Really? Pretty girl like you? I'd have bet there was some dashing Lancelot in your life."

Pretty? She was glad the dusk hid her blush. She'd dated, of course. But boys her own age . . . after what she'd been through, normal conversation and activities kinda bored her. And inevitably during the date she'd say something weird that would freak them out.

But "Lancelot"? Her mind went straight to Leo, the king-elect of Goloth. He looked every inch the Arthurian hero—tall, long blond hair, muscular. Wore armour well. And soon after her arrival in Goloth he *had* saved her life when a griffin had snatched her, nearly dying himself to do it. But he'd also tried to use her in his "quest": to kill a unicorn in the arena before his people and so prove his right to rule. Even offered his hand in marriage. Kissed her.

She shuddered. She could be queen of Goloth now, if she had played along. But then Moonspill would be dead. "Nah," she said. "No Lancelots."

She said it the French way, as if it rhymed with "Romeos."

He smiled. "Fair enough," he said, and settled back against the trunk.

They waited, as the dark drew on. There were a number of comings and goings into and out of the building and for about twenty minutes they watched in silence, apart from little moans as stiff limbs were uncoiled, stretched. Eventually, the last person who'd gone in left. She gave it five minutes. "Let's go," she said.

She dropped the backpack she'd kept beside her, followed it, then ran across to the building, Huy a pace behind. There was a loading bay, a large shuttered steel door at the back of it. Straw lay about and in that—"Oh, gross," Elayne exclaimed, lifting her sneakered foot, then hopping over to a step edge. She was glad there wasn't enough light to study it. It smelled bad enough.

"Oh, tough!" Huy chuckled. "But, hey, elephants get sick too. There's super-sized crap everywhere."

She looked up. He was standing by a smaller, human-sized door beside the shuttered one. "Thanks for the warning," she said, scraping. "How did you manage to miss 'em?"

He smiled. "I'm wearing calf-leather Ferragamos, sister," he replied. "Even turds live in fear."

"You are so weird."

"It has been said."

He pulled his laptop from a satchel. A couple of presses and a screen came up. "And here's something I prepared earlier," he murmured.

She peered. The screen was a series of numbers. "What are they?"

"Security codes for every building in the Bronx Zoo." He looked up at her. "I am the Dark Knight of the Dark Web."

"You're certainly the Dark Dork," she replied. "So which is this one?"

She pointed at the buttons on the door lock. He sucked in his lower lip, scanning, then grunted and stabbed a finger forward, pressed a four number combo. A click came, and he pushed the handle down. The door opened. "We have fifteen seconds."

"Before what?"

"Before the alarm goes off." Snapping the computer screen shut, he stepped inside, Elayne tight on his calf-leather heels.

There was dull internal lighting. A faint beeping came from beside the door. Huy stepped up to another box, tapped some numbers. The beeping ceased. He gestured for her to precede him up a corridor lined with doors.

She turned to him. There was a speech *she'd* prepared earlier. "I think you should wait here."

"What? Why?"

She hesitated. "Uh, there are things . . . I really need to do this next bit alone."

He considered, then shook his head. "There may be more door codes. You need me." He pointed ahead again. "Lead on, Macduff."

"That's 'lay on, Mc . . .' oh, never mind!" She stared at him. He didn't look like he'd listen to reason. "OK," she said, setting out, "any clue where they might keep snakes?"

He shook his head. "Couldn't find any maps of the interior layout. We'll have to follow our nose." He sniffed, winced. "Which won't be pleasant."

The first doors opened onto offices, laboratories, nothing in them but equipment and chemicals. Marching farther down a corridor that receded into the dark, Elayne inhaled deeply again, wished she hadn't. There were a number of funky odours; whatever was on her shoe was just one. There was musk of beast, the acrid tang of urine—*urines*? Plural anyway. Food in various stages of decomposition. Overlaying it all, the whiff of strong disinfectant.

All nothing compared to what hit them when they opened the door at the corridor's end—a blast of stink that sent them both reeling back, gagging. Mastering her stomach, breathing only through her mouth, Elayne stepped back and peered into a vast hall. The dim lighting showed a caged-in gantry ahead, which ran almost the length of the building, its far end lost in gloom. Spaces loomed each side.

"Shall we?" she said, her hand before mouth and nose.

"Ladies first." His reply came even more muffled. He had a large Hermès scarf pressed against his face. In one corner she saw the initials HPD worked in purple thread. Shaking her head—she'd have to revise his nickname to Dandy Dark Dork—she stepped onto the gantry.

There were pens either side of her—cells with slick walls, at least fourteen feet deep. Her eyes adjusting to the light, she saw a dog-like creature in the far corner of the right-side cell. It rose up, tottered forward on shaky legs, sniffed at her. Hyena, she thought. On her left side, in the center of a heap of straw was a coypu, who didn't rise but lifted a pig-like snout in her direction. The next on the left contained some kind of deer with two babies who broke off suckling to glance at her for a moment before resuming while their mother stared.

They advanced slowly. It was the same all the way down, like some mini Noah's Ark, a selection of animals though not usually in twos. A bison was in a cage beside a camel. The incontinent elephant—Indian, she could tell by the small ears—was about halfway down. Beyond her, the pens were filled with yet smaller cages within them, and steps down—to birds. Cockatoos, parrots, toucans—the exotics on one side. A hawk and an owl side by side on the other. Each beast looked up as they passed.

"How come they're all so . . . quiet?" Huy whispered. "Is that normal?"

"What do I know," she replied, also in a whisper. "It's a little creepy, right? As if they are . . . waiting."

"What for?"

It was like the cue for an orchestra. For suddenly and simultaneously all the hitherto silent patients of the Bronx Zoo infirmary started calling! Trumpeting, squawking, howling, barking, all came, a great cacophony of animal sounds that had them both clutching ears not noses. "What the hell?" shouted Huy. "We better get outta here! Keepers are going to come."

He turned, took three paces. "Wait!" she called, hand raised. Then she put fingers to both temples, closed her eyes.

When the amphisbaena had given her the gift of tongues—literally, because it had stuck both its tongues into her ears—she'd asked if the gift included the ability to speak to animals. Apparently she could, though most non-fabulous beasts weren't really interested in much more than their own desires—feeding, mating, chasing, sleeping. Plus they didn't have mouths with tongues, or lips to shape words. But she'd been told that if she thought something hard enough, they might hear and might respond.

So she thought now, hard. Please, she begged. Be quiet!

As suddenly as the uproar came, it stopped. Not one chirrup more came from any of the cages or pens. Only a gasp from Huy, staring at her wide-eyed. "You—" He pointed, his mouth moving, no more sounds coming, until, "You . . . whimpered—"

"I did not wh—"

"You did. And then they all shut up!" He dropped one hand, raised the other to his forehead to wipe it with the silk scarf. "OK, you are officially beginning to freak me out."

"Well, you ain't seen nothing yet." She meant it as a joke but the concern on his face only grew. "Listen, I can explain." She stopped. How could she? It would take weeks. And she couldn't begin now, anyway. Because she was there for a reason. She had to find—

"Alice-Elayne."

The hissed call came from farther along the gantry, where they had not yet reached—and she recognized the voice instantly. Turning from Huy, she ran to the next pen, looked down. And right in the middle, in a glass tank, lay a twelve-foot-long, two-headed snake.

"Amphis and Baena," she cried.

8

${B}$AD ${N}$EWS FROM ${F}$OREIGN ${L}$ANDS

The head at the left end raised. The mouth opened. But the next words came from beside her. "Holy shit!" gasped Huy, the last of his cool abandoned to total astonishment. "It's true—a snake with a head at both ends! Unbelievable!"

She knew the snake was about to speak—which might give Huy a heart attack. She shushed with a raised finger then turned to the young man. "Look. Can you wait outside? Keep guard?"

"And leave this? No way."

"I need a moment alone with the snake."

"Oh-kay. Weird, even by your standards."

"Listen . . ." She paused. What could she say? "It's going to get a lot weirder, trust me. You may not be able to handle it."

He snorted. "You should hear the stories of how my parents escaped through the jungles of Vietnam. This snake is tiny!"

"No! You don't understand. Oh! Please just go." She stamped, and a waft of elephant poo rose up. She really didn't have time to explain this. Keepers could return at any minute.

Huy shook his head, smiled. "You mentioned Dumas earlier,

right? Well, aren't we the Three Musketeers? 'All for one, one for all.'"

"There's only two of us!"

Huy gestured down. "Three."

"Four."

This number was supplied from below and came on a deep, upper-class English voice. Huy didn't look, just stared at Elayne's mouth. "I didn't know," he said slowly, "that you were a ventriloquist."

She took a step. People fainted, she'd heard. She never had but she could try and catch him if he did. Save him from spoiling his velvet frock coat. "I'm not," she said, putting a hand on his arm.

"Yea, but I am. 'Tis the advantage of not having lips to betray, but all engines of speech within the throat."

Huy did look now, and swayed, grabbed the railing before him, didn't fall. Impressive, really, thought Elayne, since a snake's head had risen to the top of its tank and was eyeballing him. While speaking mellifluous, old-fashioned English.

Speech was, however, beyond Huy. "Erk," was all he managed.

Sure that her companion was firmly standing, she turned. "Hello, Amphis."

"Maid." The snake bobbed its head in a sort of bow. "We hoped that you would find us."

"Ack," contributed Huy.

"So you are here for me?"

"Marry, we are. On a matter of urgency. Goloth is in peril."

Elayne looked at the creature's other head. Amphis was always the polite, well-spoken one, trapped forever in a quasi-Shakespearian way of speaking. While the other . . . "What's up with Baena?" she asked, pointing.

The craning head turned. "We suffered some injury in our apprehension. Mainly down Baena's end. The attendants at this castle gave him some sort of infusion in a needle. It makes him sleep. It's preferable, for when he wakes—"

"What the—"

Elayne was surprised that Huy hadn't totally freaked and run. "Are you OK?" she asked, squeezing the arm she still held.

"Oh sure." He giggled. "It's a talking snake."

Amphis got in before she could reply. "We are not truly a snake, youth, though it appeareth so. We are the amphisbaena, 'the one that goes both ways.' And we are both the keeper and the giver of language." He rose higher. "Where art thou from? Thou dost not look the same as the maid. Prithee, speak! I would learn thy native tongue."

"My parents are—"

"Stop!" From her previous experiences, Elayne knew how the amphisbaena, so in love with language, would be lost in words. And this was not the time. She snapped her fingers. "Later, Amphis. We haven't got time. Focus. Peril? Goloth?"

The snake's head opened its mouth—but it was a different voice that came. Higher pitched—and not English. Not, anyway, in the strictest sense. "Yo, homie. Be fly, dog. I got this."

Elayne's gaze whipped across. The second head had risen. Baena's eyes were just half open and he had what could only be called a wide grin parting his scaly mouth. "Baena?" she gasped.

"Hey! AE! What's happenin', sista? Give me some scale."

He jerked upward, but Amphis tugged the other way, pulling him back. "Forfend, knave," he cried. "You are not in your right mind." His eyes flicked back. "The substance he had of the apothecary has deranged him."

"And not you?" Since they were, essentially, one body, she couldn't understand how one was drugged and not the other. Was this the time to clarify Huy's question about excretion? Probably not.

Yet before either she or Amphis could speak, Baena did. "I'm not buzzed out, bro. I'm inspired!" Suddenly he looked Huy up and down. "Man, that coat is cold."

Huy had at last rediscovered words. A few, anyway. "Wait," he said, his voice breathy, "are you speaking . . . in rap?"

"Not just speak, yo. I flow."

"Nay, nay, Baena. 'Tis not the hour for—" He looked at Elayne. "A warder here, while he cleans, plays music such as I never heard before. It comes into a box from the air." He shuddered. "It is execrable."

"Phat is what it is. And it's not just music, man." Baena's grin widened. "It's a way of telling a story. So leave me to tell my girlfriend here all she needs to know, with style. You down with that, brother?"

Instead of objecting, Amphis sighed. "It may be for the best, maid. He would only interrupt our discourse and confuse all with his 'style.'"

"Got that right, dog."

"Wait." Elayne lifted a hand. "You are going to tell me why you're here—in rap?"

"Yezza!" He tipped back his head and cried, "Come on!"

"Forgive me. 'Tis probably best to humour him," sighed Amphis. Then he began to make a series of strange sounds—clicks, little explosions, percussions. All in rhythm. At the other end, Baena was nodding in time, swaying back and forth.

"Uh, Amphis? What are you doing?"

The snake broke off from his sounds. "I believe the term is 'beatboxing.'" He shivered. "It was only when I agreed to accompany him thus that Baena would let me listen in silence to the night warder's sounds. NPR, I believe they are called. Most educational. Though your world has become exceedingly strange—and your youth in severe danger from Grand Theft Auto. Hep!" He started swaying in time to his other end. "Spuff. Kwak. Eh eh eh. Huh."

"Wait! Night warder?" she exclaimed, looking around.

At the other end, Baena rose up. "All right. OK. OK. Uh-huh. Uh-huh. OK. All right. Uh-huh. Let's bust a rhyme." And while Amphis beatboxed on, he took a deep breath, then began.

"So once upon a time came Alice-Elayne,
Brought through the tapestry, called to her destiny,
Summoned by a unicorn, cryin' through his spiral horn.
They made the walls tumble down, Leo lose his crown,
Rebels known as Weavers made the mighty monarch frown.
    Get down.
Those Weavers in his palace, man, tearing up his arras, man,
Till his hunter brothers cried, enough of the chaos, man,
Obey us, or pay us, for you will not dismay us."

Amphis stopped beatboxing; Baena stopped rapping—but started singing a harmony as his brother began, in a rather beautiful tenor, to sing the chorus.

"Freedom has a price, it's always mixed with blood.
It washes the streets, floods every field,
Seals in heartbreak, in uncivil war,
Where the ones who suffer most are the ones who have the least."

As he finished, as both inhaled—Elayne shot up a hand. "Civil war? So the nobles fight the Weavers?"

"Weavers?" interjected Huy.

"Uh, their name for rebels."

"Indeed they do. It has been a terrible time—"

Baena, who'd been threshing his end more violently, suddenly shouted, "Yo! Listen up now." Reluctantly Amphis did, while his brother launched into the next verse.

"So the times are bad enough, yo, everybody suffers.

The strong get stronger, the weak get rougher.

Can it get worse? Another curse? Dig it:

The People of the Dragon is the subject of this verse.

Pirates from a foreign shore, stealing gold and more

Evil to the core. Wanting flesh to feed their gods.

These gods are real, getting them to steal,

Dragons craving flesh and blood for every single meal."

Elayne jumped in. "Oh. My. God. I knew it. Dragons. I . . . I felt one." She shook her head. This wasn't the time for that. "But since when are there dragons in Goloth?"

"All thought they'd vanished from the world. But they slept on the island in the middle of the ocean, Glana. And woke again, when the turmoil came. The people of the island worship the dragon as a god. And will do anything for it."

"But where's Moonspill in all this?"

Amphis turned. "Can you take over, young man."

"Sure."

Elayne jumped. Stunned by what was happening, she'd actually forgotten for a moment that Huy was there. "You . . . you're very cool with this."

The young man smiled calmly—though there was a wild glaze to his eyes. "Hey, as soon as the two-headed snake started rapping, I figured it out. Remember Sherlock Holmes? Dispose of the impossible and what remains, however improbable, is the answer." He licked his lips. "So a two-headed snake is impossible. A snake that can speak, doubly so. Let alone rap." He shrugged. "Ergo, the only explanation is that this warehouse is filled with airborne hallucinogens. So my choice was either freak out or go with it." He grinned. "So I'm gone! Yow!"

And with that, he started beatboxing along with Baena, who seemed content with the idea.

Amphis spoke again, "After you left, and the revolution began, Moonspill and his mate Heartsease decided they would never be safe in Goloth again. So they went over the mountains to the Valley of the Unicorn, where the rest of their kind had gone hundreds of years before."

"Over the mountains?" Elayne gripped the rail before her hard. "It explains why I . . . I kinda felt I'd lost him. I mean, we never talked but there was this . . . this connection. But then it dropped. Like a line gone dead. He was just too far away." She reached up, pushed her hair off her forehead. "But he and Heartsease were always the guardians of Goloth. Of all the other fabulous beasts. I can't believe they just, uh, abandoned them."

Amphis wriggled his head. "They tried to persuade all the fabulous beasts to go with them. Some did, yet many did not—and those that remained are hunted now, as man is hunted, to be sacrificed—"

Beatbox licks had built to an explosion. "Enough," Baena shouted, "I got this now, dog."

Amphis sighed. "I do wish he would not call me that. Besides, wretch, 'tis the chorus again first."

"Murk the chorus! Ow-ooh!" He began.

"No unicorn can call her now, so the snake has come to warn
    her now,
Amphisbaena, no stranger to the danger, but driven by
D-E-S-peration to try and save the nation.
His world is rent asunder, not just mankind going under.
Mother, father, sire, dam, manticore to lamb,
Taken to the dragon feast, food for the fiery beast.
So maid, you must come back, or see Goloth burn,
For only you can cross the mountains, persuade Moonspill to
    return."

Baena had driven himself into a frenzy. Swirling up and down the length of the coil, he now began chanting, "Na na na-na, na-na-na na," as if he was appealing to a very large crowd.

Amphis, who was being whipped violently the other end, managed to lunge and seize his brother around the neck. Through a mouthful of scale he mumbled, "Cease, Baena, thy song is sung."

His brother writhed a moment more. Then his eyelids fluttered. "Yo. I'm straight," he replied, and closed his eyes. "You take the real talk, bro. Ni-night!" On that his brother released him, and Baena sank slowly to the floor of the tank.

"Mayhap he'll sleep now," Amphis said. "Whatever medicament they gave him makes him crazed, then soporific."

"OK." Elayne pinched her nose between her eyes. "Some things I need to know."

"Ask."

"So you've come to take me back?"

"To beseech you to accompany us thither, aye."

"But why? What is it you think I can do?"

Amphis rose a little higher in the tank, eyes widening. "Cross the mountains of the griffin to the vale of the unicorn and persuade Moonspill to return."

"Oh? Only that?" she gasped. "But what will happen then?"

"Then?" Amphis took a deep breath. "You are the maid who tamed a unicorn and ended the tyrant's reign. But the chaos that followed was too heavy a price to pay for freedom. The civil war was terrible. Yet when the Glanasa came—" The wide eyes narrowed with memories. "Their cruelty surpassed all horrors hitherto. The factions of Goloth must unite to resist—but they will not, so caught up in their own enmity. Some even help the invader, to gain favour. They are deluded. For all will end up as food at the dragons' feast. Taken to be sacrificed, in hideous ceremony, on the island of Glana."

"And you need Moonspill to stop that?"

"Moonspill—and you." Amphis glanced at his brother's head, then continued. "There was a gathering of some who resist the Glanasa. At it, Baena suggested we come here and for once the fool was right. The maid and the unicorn once brought hope to the land. Reunited, you would bring it again."

She went to speak, to protest. But it was Baena who spoke now. He didn't even raise his head, or open his eyes. "You the only one got game, sista."

"'Got game'?"

It was Huy that answered. "He says you are the sole person with the skills to achieve the desired outcome."

She looked at him. He was still grinning. Huy was a whole other set of questions that needed answering. How was he so damn cool about all this? But that was for later. For now—what the hell was she to do? Three pairs of eyes were staring at her, for even Baena's had opened a tad.

She felt it, an equal and opposite tug, like someone had her guts in their hand and was twisting them. The daily terror she'd felt in Goloth, matched to the daily thrill. She'd never been more frightened. She'd never been more alive. Doing battle with yellow cabs was nothing to taking on a tyrant. Besides, in the end, what choice did she have? There had only ever been one—from the moment that morning when she'd unfolded a paper unicorn and knew her father was gone. "Look," she said, "I don't know how much game I got." She raised an eyebrow at Huy. "Is that the correct usage?" She swallowed. "But I'll come."

Everyone breathed out at once—double snake and fellow student. "Then I suggest we make all haste," said Amphis. "Though we do have a problem."

"Just the one?"

"The first of several, mayhap." His head turned to his brother's, from which little snorey whistles were coming. "Baena cannot stay awake long. And when he does we cannot roll as we are wont because of his injury." His tongue flickered out, ran around his mouth. "How will we speed to the Cloisters Museum?"

"So you did come here the same way?"

"Aye. The unicorn tapestry is the only door between the worlds."

"But how did you get through it? You need a horn."

"Before he left Goloth for good, Moonspill shed a piece of his horn for us. In case of great danger, he said. Here 'tis." Immediately he retched and ejected a piece of yellowing, slime-covered horn.

"Ewgh!" Elayne and Huy made the sound simultaneously.

"Ah, apologies." He bent, sucked up the horn and goo again, to further bleats. "So we have the means to go, once we get there. And you still have yours, of course."

"Actually, I don't." It seemed like the right time to tell them. "My father took it. He went through this morning."

"What?" Amphis's eyes went wide. "There is great danger there."

"I know! I'm worried sick. I—"

The sound of a shuttered door rising came muffled yet distinct through the building. "The night warder," Amphis said, as they all jumped. "We must make haste."

"Yeah, but how? We can't just tuck you under my friend's frock coat."

"No you can't—you'll ruin the lines." Huy jerked his head back. "Outside the door, there's a wheelbarrow. I think they use it to bring in food."

"Marry, they do. Mayhap it will serve."

"But then what?"

"One thing at a time . . . sista!" Huy darted back down the gantry. When he opened the door, Elayne could hear distant whistling. Beethoven. It had to be the NPR-listening night warder.

Huy returned pushing a wheelbarrow with one huge rubber tire at the front. He stopped before the pen. "How will we—?" he said, looking down its steep steps.

"We can travel thus far," said Amphis. "Rouse, rogue."

A shiver travelled the length of the scaly back. Baena lifted his head. "Can't you let a brother sleep?" he mumbled, but lifted himself. Amphis led, sliding over the tank's edge, then up the steps, through the small gate Elayne opened, then up into the wheelbarrow, their thick coils filling the whole thing. "Time to get ghost," Baena said, laying his head down and immediately recommencing his snoring.

Elayne looked at Huy. "He wants us to go, fast," he said.

"How? The only other door this end must be the animal entrance. And it has about eighteen padlocks on it."

"There's one other door. A big one—in the elephant's cell."

With Huy following with the wheelbarrow, Elayne ran back up the gantry. He was right. There was a big shuttered door—the elephant was the only animal too big to bring in along the gantry and down the ramps. She looked. The elephant filled most of the space but beyond . . . "It's padlocked too," she said, "and listen." They did. The whistling was getting closer, Beethoven's *Heroica* nearing a climax. Out of tune, the way people are when they are whistling with headphones on. "We'll never get it open in time."

"We do not need to open it. We only need to go through it." Amphis rose up as he spoke, thrust his head over the railing. And started calling. In Urdu. The elephant obeyed immediately, rising to her feet as Amphis broke off to say, in English, "The doctors who examined us were Indian. They reminded me what a beautiful language it is, isn't it?" His head wiggled side to side in that characteristic Indian way. Then he reverted to Urdu again, yelling instructions down.

"Uh, Elayne—what?"

Huy was pointing down into the pen where the elephant appeared to be listening intently. "Ah. I told you—the amphisbaena is the teacher of languages. It knows, literally, every tongue on the planet. And—" she tipped her head to listen, "apparently Kamila used to work in the lumber industry before she came to America. She can lift, pull and," she nodded down, "push."

They both looked. Kamila had lowered her head, pressed it into the steel and, to Amphis's continual shouts of Urdu encouragement, now proceeded to shove. The shuttered door was designed for various purposes but apparently not to resist a working elephant at full push. The door bent, buckled, and then, with a huge crash, fell out.

"Hey!"

They jerked round. The night warder stood in the doorway, reaching up to jerk out his ear buds, disbelief rapidly displaced by fury on his face. "Who the hell? What the hell are you—"

"Run!" yelled Elayne, whipping open the pen's small gate. And run they did. She followed Huy as he bounced the barrow down the steep ramp. The guard ran too, giving chase. And the elephant ran, freedom before her, trunk raised, trumpeting loudly into the clear night. It charged south, where Elayne remembered from the zoo map the "African Plains" lay. Perhaps she could sniff her mate.

They ran east. Over her shoulder, Elayne saw the warder hesitate, looking after the respective fugitives. Then he took off after the elephant, shouting into his walkie-talkie. Shouts and trumpeting filled the night.

They had luck. By the time they reached the Bronx River Gate, both it and the car park entry beyond it had been flung wide, no doubt to admit whatever was making all those siren sounds; ambulance, police and fire trucks were heading their way. They finally paused by the bike rack where her bicycle was chained, to heave in air.

"And now?" Huy wheezed.

"We need to get . . . across town . . . to the Cloisters Museum," Elayne managed. "Subway."

"Subway!" The echo came on a croon from the barrow. "That's fly."

9

BACK

They had a lot of time on the subway. A few clicks on Huy's computer showed that the quickest routes would require them to change lines four times, from the 2 to the 4 to the D to the A, including at Grand Concourse—the Bronx's busiest station. A third route took longer, but it meant only two lines and a bit of a longer walk to the Cloisters. One station in the Bronx wasn't wheelchair accessible, so they'd had to bounce the barrow up and down stairs and escalators, drawing some strange looks. Huy, at the first station, had sacrificed his frock coat to cover up Amphisbaena. Surprisingly he didn't complain about the cold, nor the fashion outrage. He was too busy being curious—and Elayne had a lot of explaining to do.

He accepted the whole tale—of Goloth, her time there, kings and beasts and unicorns—with relatively few gasps. Well, she thought, a rapping two-headed snake will cure anyone's skepticism.

"So, after this unicorn took away your dad's cancer," he said, as casually as he might have commented on a sporting triumph, "you rode him back to Goloth again via the museum?" It was the first time he'd interrupted with more than a whistle. "And that's where all these photos

were from? Phew! You started an industry, girl—and a million conspiracy theories."

"I know. And no doubt Amphisbaena's sudden appearance and dis-
appearance will start a million more." She raised the coat. One snake
head lay atop the other. Both were snoring. She was worried about them.
They weren't completely well. "That is, if we *can* make them disappear,"
she added, chewing her lip.

"And your dad? You certain he's gone through?"

"Oh yeah." She thought back to his words and the look in his eye
the night before. She swallowed and stared out at the tunnel walls
speeding past. Where are you now, Dad? she thought, as if sending him
a message, then leaned over Huy's computer, open on his lap. "Are you
sure you've got all the codes?"

"Yup. The Cloisters' firewall is about as medieval as their exhibits.
We can get in." Huy tapped his computer. "But I can't do much about
the human guards. Except give them some Muay Thai moves."

"Seriously? You do that? Thai kick boxing, right?"

He nodded. "You?"

"Black belt in macramé."

They both laughed, tension making the joke better than it was.
When they fell silent, he said, "So was it all beasts and adventures? Was
there no time for . . ." He paused, then spelled it out. "L-o-v-e?"

"No, no. Nothing."

There must have been something in her voice, because Huy did his
single raised eyebrow thing. "Uh-huh?"

"Um—" It was insane. The moment the word *love* had been spelled
out, an image of Leo, the tyrant king-elect, popped into her head. Which
was ridiculous because she didn't love him. Quite the opposite. He was
"the man who would slay Moonspill," after all, to prove his right to rule.

He was handsome of course, in a total TV star way. Buff, blond. And he had kissed her—twice, in fact, when he was trying to use her to defeat Moonspill. Once she'd slapped him, once she'd gone along with it to lull him. That one had lasted a little longer. She shivered. Still, villain though he was, he had more things going for him than the few trust-fund brats she'd dated since. At least when he kissed her, he didn't try to take a selfie at the same time!

She looked at Huy. He was still staring at her, eyebrow high. Was it appraisal? Interest? She felt a blush coming on, spoke fast, aggressively. "Why the interest, man?"

Beneath his coffee cream skin, he gave a blush that must have matched hers. "Oh, did you think . . . ?" he said. "Oh, no. Sorry."

"No, no. No, that's cool. I mean, I'm not . . . you are not . . . uh—"
Awkward!

"No, Elayne, you misunderstand."

His formality, one of the things she liked about him, was back. But he also looked away, and it was the first time—aside from when he was watching a two-headed snake rapping—that he looked slightly less than totally in command.

They'd come to a station. The doors opened, someone came in and sat not far away. "Look," he said, leaning in, speaking softer. "There are a couple of things you need to know about me."

"Only a couple?"

He was not put off. "First . . ." He paused, took a deep breath. "I'm Canadian."

It was not anything she'd expected him to say. "Oh no!" she cried, putting the back of her hand to her forehead. "Tell me it's not true."

"I know. Shocking. But that's where I'm from, *eh.*" He emphasized the last syllable, then blurted, "And I'm gay."

"Oh."

She didn't give her reply any weight. But he carried on as if she had. "It's not that you're not . . . if I wasn't, I'm sure you'd—not that you'd necessarily be interested in—"

"Oh. Oh, sure! Yeah. Whatever." Jeez, Elayne, she thought, why do you always become thirteen when this sort of stuff comes up?

"So I just thought I'd say . . ." He swallowed, looked straight at her. "That I've got your back. Because I like you. You're amazing. As a friend. Not—" He broke off, then smiled. "And Baena's right—this is fly."

"Indeed. I was only now thinking how very fly it was."

They laughed. Fell silent again. Then Huy looked up. "Three stops," he said. "I'll, uh, just re-check those numbers."

The three stops passed fast. Just as well, Elayne thought. I'm going to have plenty to deal with in Goloth without leaving a potential boyfriend behind. How much more "long distance relationship" could you get? Different countries? How about different worlds?

To their relief, there was an elevator at the 190th Street station, so they didn't have to bounce the barrow up the stairs, nor go back down for her bike. She'd thought it was a little crazy bringing it, but she wasn't going to leave it chained up in the Bronx—a Shinmayo hybrid would be stolen fast. And she couldn't take it home. Not with a snake in a barrow.

She shivered. And not when I'm not sure if I can do this, she thought. Gotta keep going. Just gotta keep . . .

They walked the long paths of Fort Tryon Park in silence. Soon she could see the dark outline of the Cloisters Museum. It had crenellations, turrets—large parts of it were constructed from genuine monasteries and castles from Europe. She'd always loved it because it was well done, not Disney "ye olde Middle Ages" in the least. If only she was there to enjoy the view!

She'd always entered and left—twice on a unicorn!—by the front entrance, where all the tourists came in. Huy had a better idea. As they crouched in some bushes at the back, he flipped up his computer screen. "See this plan? It's the café. It's set up around the monks' garden, yeah?"

"So?"

"Café. Needs its own entrance to bring supplies in." He tapped. "That's the door on the map," he raised a finger, pointed, "and that's the door before us."

Elayne looked up. There was a wooden door about twenty paces from where they were. She looked at the screen again. "But the tapestry gallery is up there. We'd have to go upstairs, through most of the museum to get to it."

"So?"

"So we'd have to pass a gazillion guards to get to it."

He looked at her over his pince-nez. "Do you even know what a gazillion is?"

"Doesn't matter. We'd still be caught."

"Two. There are two on security at night."

"Still. Two guys. With guns."

"True. But they'll be busy."

"They will?"

"They will. They will be busy . . ." He placed his hands on the keyboard. "Over here."

His fingers flew. "Uh, what are you doing?" she asked.

He smiled. "This," he replied. Then he jabbed a finger down.

There was one more moment of silence—and then chaos. On the far side of the buildings, alarms sounded—more than one, wailing in different frequencies—while lights began to flash in three distinct areas.

Elayne gasped. "What have you done?"

Huy snapped the computer shut. "Got us in. Let's go."

"You—"

She had no choice. This was their chance.

He ran, pushing the barrow. She wheeled her bike. She still didn't want to leave it and besides it had occurred to her: wasn't it time that Goloth had two-wheeled transport? It was a long walk to anywhere on the other side of the tapestry. Why not ride?

There was a problem at the door. Huy kept tapping numbers and the lock kept on not opening. From the mid-distance they could hear shouts. From farther away they could hear sirens: the first responders were on their way. "Come on!" she yelped.

"I'm trying, I—oh my God!" He looked up. "It needs a key too."

She squinted, saw the keyhole. "What?" She looked up. The walls were too high. Police sirens were getting nearer. One by one the alarms within were getting switched off. "Crap! We'll have to go. Come back in opening hours. Try—"

The interruption came on a hiss. "Pray ye both. Stand aside."

"Yo, give a blood some space!"

Two heads had risen from the barrow. They slipped out of it, shot forward, using their big body to shove the humans aside. They bent to the door, stuck out two thick tongues with forked ends—and shoved them into the keyhole.

"What? So you do breaking and entering now?"

They couldn't answer Elayne, for obvious reasons. But after just a moment both their tongues stiffened, and then came a distinct click. Huy shoved the door—and they were through.

"'Tis useful to be able to open doors if you wish to spy on man," Amphis said.

"No, dog," said Baena, as Huy brought the barrow forward again. "Time we rolled on our own. Let's jet!"

The snake pushed into the museum. Elayne followed, wheeling her bike, and Huy, snatching up his coat from the barrow, brought up the rear.

There was no time to creep, the sirens and shouts told them that. Elayne took the lead as she'd been there before. There was a back stair beside the café, and she ran her bike up it to the main floor. The dark confused her for a moment—then she saw the entrance hall to her left and it oriented her. "This way," she yelled, began to run—until she realized she could go quicker on rubber and leapt on her bike. Amphisbaena formed into the hoop that was their fast mode of travel, though she could hear Baena groan in pain. Huy just ran.

They burst into the tapestry room. There they were, the medieval masterpieces her ancestor had created. But there was no time to admire them, not with the shouts from down the hall, the sounds of cars skidding to a halt outside, their sirens loud now, so loud. She heard someone yelling for backup. So they had a moment. And a moment was all they needed.

She dismounted, crossed fast to the panel titled *The Unicorn Leaps Out of the Stream*. It was within the tree in that tapestry's centre that her genius ancestor had woven in a door. Now she was there, that gut war came again. Excited. Terrified. But there could be no pause to think. Besides, her father had gone through only that morning. What if he was just a push through the weave away?

She turned to Huy. It felt a little sad to be leaving her friend. But shouts getting closer meant there was no time for a big farewell. "Thanks for everything, Huy. Later."

"Whoa! What do you mean, later?"

There was no time. "Come on, Amphisbaena. The key. Take us through."

Footsteps coming fast. A man shouting down the corridor. "You in there! Put your weapons down! Lie on the floor! Do it!"

"Maid, I should tell you, the door on the other side has been moved to—"

"Later!" called Baena, mumbling because the horn was in his mouth. He hurled himself forward.

"Erk!" was all Amphis managed as he started slipping into the tapestry.

Grabbing scale in one hand, bike in the other, Elayne dove.

It was the same darkness she'd gone through before. The bike led, and now she was holding tight to its handlebars, her legs trailing behind, falling slowly, as if on a parachute. She knew it wouldn't take long.

Then she felt it—a heavy weight on her left leg that she couldn't shake off and couldn't see because of the dark. She opened her mouth to yell. Which was a mistake seeing that it filled instantly and completely with water.

The Return of the Maid

10

BACK TO GOLOTH

Drowning. Not what she had expected on her return to Goloth.

She was thrashing in the water, her mouth full of it, her head pulsing with noise as if a thousand sirens sounded within it. One thought cut through it. It was true what they said: when you drowned your life did flash before you. Manticores morphed into monkeys in a zoo, unicorns pulled carriages in Central Park, she was kissing Huy—

Stop! The thought came clearly. *This is not my life. I never did tha—*

The front of her sweater suddenly jerked into her throat. Something had hold of the back of it, something—someone?—that was now pulling her up. She rose, broke surface—

"Gack!" She spat out water, took a huge breath, coughed violently. Now she was being pulled across the surface. But the sweater was doing nearly as good a job as the water had in choking her. She reached a hand back, expecting to feel a scaly mouth clamped there, Amphisbaena saving her. Instead, she touched a hand.

A hand? Whose?

She nearly fainted from lack of air before she could answer the question. But then her bottom ground on rock, the grip loosened, she took another whooping breath—and someone yelled, "Push!"

She scrabbled her heels against the stream bed, hit some sort of earth lip, got her hands back, heaved herself up onto the bank, flopped there. She couldn't lie flat because her backpack was still on. She took in air and relief at the same time. She hadn't drowned! And neither had the person gasping next to her, who'd rescued her. The person—

Dad, she thought and whipped her head around. "Huy!" she cried. "What the hell are you doing here?"

He squinted up at her. It took her a moment to realize what was different about his look—he wasn't eyeing her over his pince-nez.

"Came for the ride," he wheezed.

"You came for . . . how the—?"

"Held onto your leg."

"Wha—? Why?"

"Why?" He sat up, spat into the stream. "All those cops about to rush in? If they hadn't shot me, I'd have had to explain . . . everything!" He shrugged. "I think I was looking at five years, minimum. Or more likely indefinite detention in an asylum. This seemed a better idea." He sniffed, looked around. "So this is Goloth? Huh. Looks like Vermont."

Elayne looked too. They were on the bank of a small river, in a forest. It was daytime here, and felt warmer than New York—seasons and times didn't correspond between the worlds. She had no idea where in Goloth they were. Amphis had only had time to yell that Moonspill had moved the door before they were through it. And where was he? They? No sign of snake anywhere.

She shook her head. One thing at a time. "Look," she said, sitting up and taking off the dripping pack, "you have to go back."

"Why?"

"It's dangerous here."

"Exactly."

"What do you mean, 'exactly'?"

"It's dangerous. You need me. You'd have drowned without me."

"I would not." Now that she was looking at it, the river looked more of a stream. They must have just landed in a pool.

"Besides," Huy continued, "where's the door?"

"I—" Elayne scanned the surface. It would be kind of hard to find. "Well, the amphisbaena will show you." She stood. "Amphis? Baena?"

The only reply was a burst of chattering, a squirrel somewhere close by, angry at intruders. When it stopped, the only sounds were the gently gurgling stream and bird calls. "Looks like the snakes," said Huy, "have jetted. So we're on our own."

Elayne grunted. Part of her was glad she wasn't alone, especially if she'd lost the snake. Part was very worried. It was hard enough keeping herself alive, she knew from experience. But looking after someone else—

"Hey!" she cried. Something had broken surface in the stream. Not a snaky head. "My bike!"

She slipped off her backpack, jumped in. The stream was indeed shallow in most parts, though she slipped up to her waist once. She grabbed the handlebars, dragged it back and onto the shore. It dripped but it seemed intact apart from a bent front fork, which she straightened between her knees. "Uh, why did you bring that again?" Huy asked.

"Because it beats walking. Which I suppose I'll now have to do since you're here," she grumbled. She still couldn't make up her mind whether she was pleased about that or not.

"And you're not worried about introducing bike technology to a medieval world?"

"This is not the past—our past. Nor is it full of tribes hidden in the Amazon rainforest who have avoided contact. A bike can't do them much harm. Besides, it sounds like they have plenty of other stuff to worry about. Uh, what are you doing?"

Huy had stepped back into the stream. He bent over, seeking in the water. "My computer. I was holding it when I came through. Damn!" He shrugged, straightened. "Would have been useful."

"How? I doubt even the Dark Dork could get a signal in Goloth."

She'd had to raise her voice a little, as that squirrel had come nearer and was objecting ever more vocally to the intrusion. She wondered if she should try thinking him calm but decided on words. "Chill, fella," she said, "we're just going to—"

She got no further. The angry chitter did stop—or maybe it was just drowned out by the sudden blast of a horn, and the yells of the many men rushing through the trees.

They were swiftly surrounded by a dozen, all armed. Some pointed bows with arrows notched, others held spears, axes. One, the largest man there, huge and red-bearded, hefted a rusty-bladed sword. "Do not move!" he shouted. "We'll slit your throats as soon as look at ya."

They'd had no time to do anything but put their hands up in the air. Though as she did, even within the sudden shock, she realized that the man had not shouted the command in English, which was the "official" language of the world, spoken by all but especially by kings and nobles. The man had used Dramach, the ancient, peasants' tongue, spoken since before her ancestor the weaver unwillingly accompanied "the Hunter" to Goloth. Since that first Leo had only spoken English and he had rapidly become ruler there, he had insisted that everyone learn his language, rather than the other way around.

She knew Dramach, of course. The gift of tongues had seen to that.

But she wasn't going to let their captor know that. So it wasn't just terror that made her use English and blurt out, "Don't hurt us, please."

The man started, peered closer at them, then shouted in the same language, "Sit!"

They sat, back to back, both keeping their hands behind their heads. He then reverted to Dramach, ordering his men to lower their weapons, all save two who were commanded to bring their spears uncomfortably close to the prisoners' faces. Then he squatted before them, sword thrust into the dirt, and hung from its guards. "Who are you? What are you doing in Scragar's forest?"

She hadn't heard of such a place in her previous times in Goloth. And he thumped his chest when he said it. So she thought she'd try, "Lord Scragar, we—"

The guffaw from all the men silenced her. "Lord? I am no poxy nobleman!" he bellowed, thrusting his face close. His face was largely hair—a tawny beard that ran from the cheekbones down, a thatched halo of rough brown above. His eyes were red and gummy, and such teeth as he had stuck out at all angles, yellow and filmed. They suited breath that had her gagging.

"Uh, Weaver?"

"Nor no poxy rebel neither! Pox on 'em all! We serve no master, we!" He turned aside, not very far, spat. "Scragar looks after Scragar's gang." His men gave a shout, which he acknowledged with a tip of his head. "No one else. I feeds them, I clothes them, I—" He looked past them and his eyes shot wide. "By the three heads of Cerberus, what is that?"

Elayne turned. It was her bike. She'd left it on its kickstand. Judging by the reactions, she realized Huy had been right: Goloth wasn't ready for the bicycle. Scragar leapt up, all his men backed away, several making the sign she'd grown used to on her previous visit because it was always being made at her: a sort of "Avaunt, Witch" gesture, formed by thumbs and forefingers joined at the tips, thrust out. Another man stepped forward and jabbed his spear at it, fortunately missing the tire but hitting the spokes. The bike fell onto its right side—and right onto the rubber bulb of its horn. "Bepp!" it blared—but it had never had such an effect on pedestrians in New York as it did on Scragar's gang. They scattered, one fell into the stream, all did a lot of avaunting. The rear tire circled, making a faint clicking sound. Only the leader himself did not quail, but stepped forward, sword raised above his head, about to bring it crashing down upon the monster.

"No!" yelled Elayne. "It's not dangerous. It's . . . it's not alive. It's . . . it's . . ."

"A vehicle," said Huy. They all turned to him. "Like, you know, a cart."

"A cart?" Scragar bellowed. "It is like not a cart. It is—" Suddenly his attention was on Huy. He stepped toward him. "You! You are darker, like people from the sea. But your eyes are . . ." He groped for a word, settled on, "Narrow. And your apron," he continued, jabbing a finger into Huy's black velvet lapel, "is soft!" He spat the word disgustedly, then looked at Elayne, who'd dressed for the snake heist in ski jacket, black turtleneck, wool pants, boots. All soaked. He reached, shoved a finger into down. "Soft!" he shouted again as if insulted by softness. His fingers uncurled and curled on his sword hilt.

"Scragar?"

It was a small man who spoke, the only one there without a weapon, though a large ox horn hung from his shoulder. He was a little older and slightly better dressed, in that he wasn't wearing a mishmash of smocks and trousers tied up with rope but a doublet and what once could have been hose if the stockings weren't so smeared and ripped. "What is it, Glot?" grunted Scragar.

The man came forward, stood on tiptoes, and whispered something in his leader's shaggy ear. Scragar nodded, grunted—and then his bloodshot eyes went wide. He pulled the smaller man aside from the others, who were clustered around the bike. "The maiden?" he hissed. "She who rode the unicorn?"

"'Tis her."

It was hard not to react to the words, to yell out that yes, I am Unicorn Girl and you'd better take me fast to someone in authority. But he'd breathed the words in Dramach, and she wasn't prepared to reveal that she knew it. Besides, she thought, this was where her father had come through, only twelve hours before. Perhaps this gang had grabbed him too. Stick with them and they might reunite dad and daughter.

"This can't be her, Glot," Scragar continued, not very softly. "The maid is said to be beautiful. She has flame for hair and always dresses in pure white." He glanced back and sniffed. "And she is taller. As tall as me."

"I was in the arena when the revolution began. She passed a hand's breadth from me." Glot closed his eyes for a moment, breathed deeply. "I will never forget her."

"If you are right . . ." Scragar scratched at his chin. "She is worth gold. Much gold."

"But who will pay more? The man who was king? Or Big Weaver?"

"Hmm." Scragar drew in his lower lip with yellow teeth, then blew it out again. "Let us take them to our camp. Keep them there and send to Weaver and King. See who will pay most."

Glot turned. "And the dark youth?"

Scragar's eyes narrowed. "Maybe he is Glanasa. Maybe just a freak. Either way, we'll take him to the slave market on the ocean. They'll pay too. If he is one of them, they may pay ransom to have him back. If not . . ." Yellow teeth were bared again in a grin. "I hear the dragon likes different-flavoured meat each meal."

Dragon! Elayne nearly yelled the word out. So everyone here knew of them!

Someone shouted from the riverbank, someone else argued back. All looked—and Elayne saw what was causing the dispute—her backpack. Two men were tugging it between them. But with a roar, Scragar was up and over to them, snatching it from both their hands. There was a certain amount of snarling, like pack dogs over a bone. Then the two men backed down and Scragar lifted the bag, shook it hard. Things rattled inside but nothing fell out. He shook it harder in frustration.

"Let me try." Glot came forward, holding out his hand. And it seemed that in matters that required intelligence, the big man deferred to the small. He said he'd been in the city, Elayne thought. He probably knows a few things.

But not how to undo a zipper. He tried various techniques—threw the bag up, caught it, swung it. Only when nothing worked did he pause, look closer, seize a tab, pull. The zipper gave a little and with a cry he continued pulling. As it was the main one, and he was holding it upside down, something fell out almost immediately.

Everyone leaped back from the yellow foil object. It glinted in the sun and Scragar kicked it toward the prisoners. "Energy bar? Really?" whispered Huy. "You couldn't have brought a gun?"

"I don't have a gun. And I thought, in case I needed to come straight to Goloth, I'd pack—"

"Silence!" bellowed Scragar, in Dramach, glaring at them. Then he snatched the bag from Glot, shook it harder, until something else dropped to the ground—a metal canister about six inches long. As Glot bent, picked it up, Scragar said, "What is this?" in English.

"Be ready," Elayne whispered to Huy under her breath. Then aloud said, "Scent."

"Sent?" The hairy face wrinkled. "Who sent it?"

"No, uh . . ." She thought then continued, "it's perfume."

"Perfume." It wasn't a question. He'd heard of it. "Perfume for women."

"No. No, no. This perfume is for men."

"For men? Ha! Impossible."

Glot was shaking the can. "Nay, 'tis true, Scragar. Some men at the court, they used it. Usually it comes in flasks but—" He examined the can's plastic lid, the yellow safety tab at the top. "Perfume comes out here, from the hole. 'Tis for the body, yes?"

"Oh, no," said Elayne, coming onto her knees, Huy rising beside her, "this one's for the face, the beard. It's a mist. Lovely smell! You pull the yellow tab off, press down," she mimed pressing the button, wafting it over her face, her eyes wide open, showing her pleasure. "Shall I show you?"

"No," said Glot, drawing himself up to his full five feet. "I know. I lived in the city." He pulled the tab off, lifted the can and pointed it at his face.

"Nay!" shouted Scragar. "I am leader. I want perfume." He bent down to Glot. "Mist me."

The small man nodded, lifted the can and pressed the nozzle.

The screams were very high-pitched for a big man. Understandable, really. She'd always supposed that bear spray would hurt. A lot. "Run!"

yelled Elayne, and Huy was off, following a faint deer trail down the riverbank path. She didn't run, though. The gang had fallen back in shock and her path was clear. Sprinting to the bike, she lifted it, sent it rolling, kicked the kickstand up, and was astride and pedaling like a maniac before anyone could do more than shout.

MAN AND WOLF

Plenty more cries came from behind her as she followed the path through trees. She caught up with Huy after half a minute. "Bear spray?" he said.

"Uh-huh. In case I met another manticore. This was better. Damn it, though," she said, swerving around a log, "they've got my backpack."

The shouts and horn blasts were fading as they entered a thicker stand of trees. The path got narrower. She looked at him. He was running fast, easily. "How long can you keep that up?"

He smiled. "All-Ontario under-eighteen cross-country champion. Two years. Those Neanderthals have no chance." He glanced at her front wheel. "Can you ride that?"

"I didn't win any prizes," she answered. "But I did five days on the Appalachian Trail on this last year." To emphasize the point, she took some big air over a tree root. "Gnarly!"

He looked pained. "Elayne, one of the reasons I like you is that you don't engage in 'teen speak.' Proper usage, please."

"Oh," she replied, "you are just going to love it in Goloth . . . dude."

He glanced sideways, stuck out his tongue—so didn't see the tree branch. He ran into it full force, forehead to bark, his legs swept from under him, dropping him hard onto his back.

"Huy!" she yelled, skidding to a stop, lowering her bike, running back. He wasn't even groaning. He was out. Immediately the shouts came clear and a lot closer. The horn sounded.

"Oh no. No!"

She looked around. The brush surrounding the faint trail was thick salal. Bending she grabbed him under his arms and dragged him off the path. It was hard going. He was heavier than he looked, and the little bushes were so thick they slowed her. She gave up ten feet in, dropped him, ran back to her bike, threw it into another dense patch. She could feel the vibration of running feet, shouts getting closer. Yet what chilled her the most as she hurled herself after the bike was a new sound—a terrible howl.

Hound, she thought, as she buried her face in the earth. I didn't see any hounds.

She was only just in time. Men ran up. Go on! she thought. But they didn't. They stopped about three paces from where she lay.

"What is that—dog? Wolf?" a familiar voice barked, speaking Dramach. Very carefully she raised her head, peered through the shrub. She could only see a small part of Scragar's face—a very red, very swollen part.

"Dog," Glot replied. "Could it be—"

"No. Not here. Not this far west. Demons and curs!" Scragar jabbed his fingers into his eyes, whimpered in pain. "I want that girl. When I find her—"

"Shh!" said Glot.

"You dare to—"

"Listen!"

The intensity of Glot's hiss made even Scragar go as silent as the other men who'd run up one by one. But Elayne realized quite quickly what he'd heard. Not a bark. The clicking of a wheel going round and round.

"There!" screamed Scragar.

She was right by it. She had no choice. She leapt up, turned to run—and a huge hand fastened around her neck. "Got you!" cried Scragar, jerking her out of the bush, slamming her down onto the path, knocking her breath from her. She didn't pass out, though, could see as if through a mist as first her bicycle was dragged out, thrown down beside her—and then Huy was pulled out by his heels. He was groaning slightly, but not back with them yet. "Huy?" she whispered. No reply.

"Silence!" roared Scragar. "You witch!" He raised his rusty sword high above his head.

Then Glot spoke. "The ransom?"

The sword stayed high, Scragar kept breathing hard, the tears cascading down his reddened face from eyes narrowing to slits. She thought he was still going to strike—until he lowered his sword to rest the blade on his shoulder.

"Ransom, yes." He bent, glared at her. "But you run again and they will not be ransoming all of you. Understand?" He looked to her left. Huy's groans were on words now, and his eyes were fluttering open. "But this one? He runs too fast. Kill him!"

"No!" screamed Elayne, coming onto her knees her arms raised over Huy. "Please!"

Yet it wasn't her prayer that stopped them—but Glot again. "If we kill him, the slavers will pay us nothing, master. For ransom or . . . it is said the dragon will only eat live meat. Keep him alive too, for a few days. Till we reach the coast."

"He runs fast," repeated Scragar, glowering, rubbing his face, "fast as the girl on her like cart."

"Then, Master," said Glot, drawing out a long bladed, serrated dagger. "I'll make sure he can't run at all, eh? We'll throw him over a donkey."

Scragar ran a hand over his streaming eyes. "Do it."

Four men came and seized Huy. Awake now, he began to writhe, to shout, especially when they flung him onto his front. Two more held Elayne as she lunged forward, crying now. "No. Please! No!"

Glot bent and slashed one of Huy's velvet trouser legs all the way up to just past the knee. He laid the dagger there, but flat on its side, right against Huy's bulging tendons. He didn't cut, yet. Instead he looked at Elayne, still straining against those who held her. "Perfume? Funny maid," he said, and raised the knife.

There was light in Glot's eyes, light on his blade—and then light on the other piece of metal that appeared suddenly. And it was only because Elayne was staring so very hard at the raised hand that she saw the arrow head that burst through Glot's wrist. Screaming, he fell forward, the only one moving for a moment, everyone else frozen, silent. She felt the grip loosen on her arms, just a little, maybe just enough. But even as she bent to punch whoever held her, she saw that Huy had beaten her to it.

Jerking his right arm free, he snapped his elbow fast into the face of the man who'd held it. Flipped onto his back, kicked his right leg clear, bent both legs to his chest, then drove his heels hard up into another brigand's face.

It was all she saw. She twisted her arm in, so that the man on her right had to let go or have his wrist snapped. But she didn't have to do anything to the man on her left because another arrow took him in the shoulder, spinning him away.

She was up, and Huy was too, dropped into his Muay Thai stance, but swaying slightly. She could see the welt discolouring his forehead. Scragar was before them, sword lifted again. But he didn't have time to bring it down because there was a snarl, and then a blur passed them in a flash of grey fur and large canines. These dug into Scragar's sword arm, and then he was falling, yelling.

It was enough for the rest. To a man they took off, scattering through the brush in all directions. Only Glot and Scragar remained, the first staring in disbelief at the arrow lodged in his wrist, the second rolling back and forth on the ground, screaming, trying to stop the vast hound— or wolf, Elayne wasn't sure which—from ripping his throat out.

A piercing whistle came, three notes. With a last good shake, the hound released the man, who curled up into a ball. Then the beast ran back a little ways into the trees—just as far as the man standing there. The man who, while not releasing the tension on the string, was slowly lowering his bow.

"Set," he called, and the dog went, disappearing into the forest in the direction the rest of the brigands had fled. A bark came, followed by a human yelp. Then the man came forward, swiftly moving out of the shadows that had partly obscured him. He was dressed from ankle to neck entirely in a green so dark it was nearly black, which, as he neared, Elayne saw was all some kind of leather, both shirt and leggings. He had a black cape trailing behind him from his neck, a black, wide-brimmed hat pulled low, and a red scarf that concealed his entire face except his eyes.

His voice came muffled from within it. "Are you well, you and your companion?"

He still had his attention and the bow held on the writhing man, but Elayne realized he was speaking to her. Her heart was still thumping and she managed to blurt out, "What? Oh. Yes. Well. Quite well. Thanks for asking."

He grunted, leaned, toed Scragar with the tip of a worn boot. "You know me?" he said softly.

"Yes," Scragar gasped from between clenched hands.

"Yes?"

"Yes . . . lord!" the brigand whimpered.

"Then remember that a judgment is coming to this land. And you will be held responsible."

"I . . . I will remember."

"Now go."

"I will, lord!" He dragged himself to his feet. His eyes, near closed now, streamed, and he clutched a savaged, bleeding hand. It had been a bad day for Scragar. Elayne almost felt sorry for him—until she remembered what a shit he was.

"Stop!" she called, as he started to move away, and when he didn't, she strode across, grabbed his shoulder, spun him around. He cringed, bending so low he was looking up at her. "Did you meet someone else in the forest today? A man, about fifty?"

Though Scragar's eyes were almost shut, they contrived to widen a little. "You speak Dramach! You *are* the maid! Forgive me. Oh, forgive me!"

He reached for her hand; she snatched it back. "Forget about that. Tell me."

"No one, lady, no one. I swear!"

"Pah!" Annoyed, she waved him away. Sniffling with pain, he disappeared into the brush in the same direction that his men had gone, Glot whimpering beside him, both yelping as the dog ran past them back to its master.

"Let us away," the man said, stooping for the bandit's sword, then rising to slide it through straps across his back.

There was something about his voice, now he wasn't growling orders to beast or brigand. Something familiar. "Uh, why would we go with you?" she said, as she tried to remember. "Who are you anyway?"

A low chuckle came. "I had forgotten how you always answer a command with a question." He paused, then added, "Alice-Elayne."

He turned, and for the first time she could see his eyes above the mask. They were steel blue.

"Leo?"

12

CATCHING UP WITH OLD ENEMIES

The king-elect of Goloth had changed.

Not only his clothes. The last time she'd seen him was at the arena in the city two years before, dressed in flowing, pleated crimson. It was the day he was supposed to slay a unicorn before all his people and prove his right to rule. But when Moonspill, guided by her, had defeated him, it had been the spark of the revolution that had consumed the land.

He'd pulled down his mask when she said his name, regarded her with the slightest of smiles at her astonishment. His face had changed too. He'd been maybe twenty before. He'd had long, styled fair hair. This was now shaggy, gathered with a piece of leather, and looked like it could use a wash. He'd been clean-shaven too, with a touch of youthful chubbiness about the jaw. She couldn't see that, as it was now covered in a thick and untrimmed blond beard. The leather he wore covered a hard, wiry body; before he'd had the bulked muscle created by a meat-heavy diet and constant training in armour.

However, it was within the so-blue eyes that the change showed most. They'd always contained guile, manipulation, arrogance. Now she saw a hint of uncertainty within the blue, a wariness.

All these impressions went through her mind as she stared. Which meant that she must have been staring a while. Which prompted the distinct, "Uh hum," throat clearing from beside her.

"Oh, sorry." She turned to her friend, standing there, hands on hips, looking at the two of them. "Huy, this is, uh . . . the king! Um, elect? Or—"

"Leo," he said, stepping forward. "I am king no more. You are the maid's . . . companion?"

"No. I mean, yes," Huy replied. "I am her friend."

Leo studied him a moment, then nodded. "And her bodyguard, is that correct?"

Huy barely paused before replying, "Why, yes. Yes, I am. Huy Phan."

He'd raised a hand to shake, but Leo bypassed it, grasped the other's forearm, forcing Huy to do the same. This held for a moment until Leo spoke. "You fought well, and without weapons. You must show me the way of it sometime."

"I'd be delighted."

They both stared, gauging the other, then dropped their arms. Leo turned back to her. "So, maid, I ask, I do not command. Will you accompany me now?"

"Whither?" Elayne smiled to herself. One hour back in Goloth and she was already speaking all medieval-ly.

"Away, first. It is possible that Scragar may muster enough courage and troops to attack again."

"And where are your troops?"

He smiled. "You are looking at them." He bent to run his hand over the large, soft ears of his hound, who inclined his head slightly to the touch, though his large brown eyes never left the two strangers. "This is Wolf," Leo continued, his touch shifting to the beast's neck and the thick grey-black fur there that went on to cover the large, muscled body. "I did not have time for a more inventive naming when I rescued him from a hunter's snare, since he was trying very hard to kill me. Fortunately for me, he was but a pup then. And either his mother or father was one, I am sure." He laid fingers on the dog's head. "These are friends, Wolf. Friends."

At last the beast turned his stare away to the forest. Immediately, he gave a small growl. Leo looked up at them. "Can I tell you whither we are bound when we are bound thither? My hound senses some danger here still. It may be Scragar. It may be a manticore. I have seen the spoor of one these last three days while I waited. Last night I heard his hunting song."

He'd stepped away through the trees and Elayne's question did not halt him. "Waited for what?"

"For you, maid," he replied, as he kept going.

"Uh, what's a manticore again?" Huy asked.

"A monster. Looks a little like a tall guy, if the guy had a triple row of really big, sharp teeth. But it has a lion's mane and body—except for the tail, which has a ball end that flicks poisonous darts. What else?" She tipped her head back. "Oh, yeah, they're man-eaters."

"Great!" He gave a nervous laugh. "Well, I vote for going with the handsome dude with the big bow and the wolf dog. You?"

"Sure."

She ran back, retrieved her bike. They soon caught up with Leo on the faint deer trail he'd taken. He glanced back, did a double take. "What manner of mischief is this? More witchcraft from your land?"

She'd told him a little about New York in her previous visit here. "It's . . . my ride. Like a, uh, a cart without a horse?"

It sounded lame but he nodded. "You ride this. Good. I did not reckon on two of you coming and I only have the one steed. Swiftsure."

He waved. A large stallion was there, its reins looped around a tree. The animal backed away, threw his head up and down as far as he was able, but soft words and a stroke calmed him as Leo unhitched him.

Elayne heard gurgling, then spotted the glint of sunlight on water. "I think we're quite close to where they caught us. Can I just check? I have some things."

"Be swift."

The three went to the river, followed it back. They came quite swiftly to the clearing where the brigands had ambushed them. To her delight, the backpack was still on the ground, its contents scattered about. "They must have just taken off after us," she said, kneeling to stuff things in.

Huy helped, retrieving various items. "You really planned, eh?" he said, handing her a coil of rope, some matches, a pocket knife, chocolate bars and—"Soap? Really?"

She smiled. "You have no idea how smelly one can get in Goloth. Medieval, right?" He held up a bright orange plastic pack. "It's a medical kit," she said, reaching.

"That's not a medical kit," he said, letting her take it. "This," he said, peeling up his shirt, "is a medical kit."

Next to his skin was a cloth belt. In black ink was stamped across it "Médecins Sans Frontières."

"Why have you got that? You didn't know you'd be coming to Goloth."

"No. But the news said the snake was hurt, and in case we did get to it . . ." he shrugged. "My elder brother, pride of my parents, was a doctor with this group for a while. He knows just what to pack for a disaster." He lowered the shirt, glanced around. "Which this has all the makings of."

"Hey! We're alive, aren't we?"

She shoved her kit into the pack, checked it again. She had one change of clothes. But it was actually warm, unlike New York, and all the running and fighting had largely dried her out. Besides—

Wolf chose that moment to growl. "Something, someone comes." Almost on Leo's words, there came a burst of . . . singing. A high-pitched but very tuneful run of notes. Not very far away.

"Manticore!" she squeaked. "Forgot to tell you. They sing." Putting the yellow safety tab back on the bear spray, she dropped it into her pack, zipped it up.

"Maid! Can your bodyguard take your horseless cart? You may mount before me. I needs must talk with you."

"Uh—"

"I'll gladly mount before him if you won't," said Huy, under his breath.

Elayne turned. "Do not flirt with the king! Or whatever he is." As another run of notes came—closer—she shoved the bike at him. "Remember this is a Shinmayo. The gear system is—"

"Oh, please!"

Wolf started barking louder, facing into the forest. Elayne ran to the mounted Leo, who reached down, lifted her easily, and placed her before him. "Wolf! Set!" he called, and the dog ran into the forest in the direction he'd barked.

"The manticore will kill him," Elayne cried.

"He will not get close enough. They are not fast and Wolf will keep his distance and delay him a little only." With that, he tapped his heels into Swiftsure's flank. "Yah!"

They set off at a gallop, slowing to a measured canter when Leo looked back and saw that Huy was fast, but not as fast as a horse. They went through a stand of trees. These ended and opened onto grassland. Within a few hundred yards, Wolf joined them; while behind, from the edge of the forest, came the rising, melancholy notes of the manticore's song.

She'd met a manticore when she'd first come through the tapestry before. She had nearly become its breakfast. But Moonspill had saved her.

One memory triggered another—and she felt a lurch in her stomach, sudden breathlessness. "Hey!" she turned her head toward Leo. "Did anyone else come through while you were watching?"

"Anyone else? This man you asked Scragar about?"

"Yes."

"You say he preceded you through the doorway between worlds?"

"Yes."

"Why?"

"He's my . . . another of my companions." She'd been about to say "father." But Leo had been her enemy. He'd tried to use her on her previous visit to capture and kill Moonspill. The leather bandito-chic thing was interesting, and she could see he had changed. But he said he'd been waiting by the stream for her. So he obviously had a plan to use her again. There were lots of reasons why she still shouldn't trust him. "It's, uh, complicated," she continued. "He wanted to go ahead to, you know, reconnoitre?"

He regarded her a moment. She sounded pretty lame, she knew. But then rather than question, he shrugged. "I was near the stream where Amphisbaena left me for most of the time. But the manticore tracked me, and my choice was to move for a time or kill it. So I moved. It is possible that someone came through then." He paused to steer Swiftsure around some rocks. "Though now you say it, I did notice some strange tracks. I had no time to examine them as the manticore had wind of me."

"Strange how?"

"At a glimpse I would say . . ." He took a deep breath. "They were not of this land." He nodded ahead. "And they pointed east, the way we now take."

Elayne peered forward. Could her father be just ahead? Dad, she thought, sending it out into the world like a shout, where are you? Then a sudden fear took her. "Could the manticore have—"

"No. It followed us, the opposite way to the tracks. Until I was able to double back and lose it for a time."

"Another one?"

"It is the only one of its kind nearby."

But there were other beasts. Not to mention Scragar and his crew. She glanced back—and saw, thrusting from the forest, the towering basalt spire known as Black Tusk. Somewhere near its base was a glade where the old portal between worlds had been, in the folds of a big oak. "So the new door is close to the old one," she said.

"Aye," came the reply. "But no one, save the unicorn who moved it and the snake that is its guardian, knows exactly where it is." He leaned around her so he could see her face. "What became of the amphisbaena?"

"I don't know. He—they—came back with us but then were gone."

"Hmm." Leo grunted. "The beast is strange. It could have felt it accomplished its task when it delivered you to me."

"Delivered?" This did not compute. "You sent the snake through?"

"In a way. Though it desired to go also. It saw the doom that would befall this world if . . ." He hesitated. "If a miracle did not happen."

"But—" There were so many questions that she could ask; she had to settle on one. "But the fabulous beasts hate you. You hunt them, kill them in your arena."

"No more." He looked ahead grimly. "Now it may be that only the fabulous beasts can save Goloth. They, you—" He sighed. "And perhaps, with the Gods' good favour, me." She went to speak but he forestalled her. "Maid, there is so much to tell. I can tell it but mayhap it would be easier if I do so without your questioning."

"Mayhap. No guarantees." She was suddenly ravenous and delved into the backpack she'd swung before her when she mounted. "Power bar?" she offered, pulling one out, ripping off the foil.

He squinted. "What is't?"

"It's, uh, cake. A kind of cake." She held it up to his mouth.

He bit off the end and his eyes went wide. "Delicious," he mumbled, chewing.

She looked back. Huy was keeping up easily. Too easily. The grass on the plain was cropped, even and gently sloping down the valley—so he was riding with no hands. "Power bar?" she called.

"Sure." He caught the one she threw, ripped off the foil, bit, and called up, "How did you know Pink Cherry was my fave?"

"Wild guess."

She looked ahead again. When she'd come to Goloth the first time, she'd had a terrible fear of riding. But galloping across the plains on a unicorn, learning to trust him entirely, even as he learned to trust her, had cured her of that. Plus all the horseback-riding lessons she'd taken back in New York. Leo rode easily, totally in command. "OK, ready. What's the story here?"

"A sad one." With a sigh, Leo began.

13

The Late King's Lament

"Woe to the ruined land!"

Leo sighed as he stared ahead. "How much did the amphisbaena tell you?"

"Some. Not sure how much I understood since quite a lot of it was in rap."

"R-ap?"

"Uh, too difficult to explain." She tapped the back of her head into his chest. "Tell it your way. I know that there was a revolution—"

"You know because you were there. Because you were the spark that lit those flames. Nay." He shook his head as she began to speak. "I am not blaming you. The tinder for it had been laid for years. My ancestors laid it, all the Leos that preceded me, including my own father, with their tyrannies, lesser and great. From denying people any freedom. Placating them with certainties. A land where it was safe to grow crops. A festival every year where beasts could be slaughtered for their delight."

"Bread and circuses," Elayne murmured. "Never mind. Go on."

"In the beginning, I could not see it any differently. For had I not been raised from birth to be the next tyrant? The Weavers held great rallies and my spies told me of their plans. A parliament of equals. Laws that made sure no man was above another. Disaster, as I and my kind saw it." He shook his head again. "So my nobles rallied to me and we set out to crush the Weaver-rebels. And if we were not as numerous as they, we were nearly all soldiers, trained for the hunt, for battle." He shuddered. "Have you ever seen civil war?"

"No." She thought of the news reports on television, nightmares from around the globe. "Not first-hand."

"Trust me, maid. You do not want to. It is not just the fighting, the ambushes, the killing. They are bad enough. The first time one kills another man—" He paused. "It is not what I'd been told. But even that is not the worst. The worst is that the innocent suffer the most. Farmers, who just want to provide for their children, see their livestock—and their sons—taken for war. Their crops burned, their villages . . ." He swallowed. "Most die away from the battlefield, those who take no part, who want no part. They die of starvation, of the pestilence that comes. During ceaseless raids and counter raids."

He broke off, staring ahead again into some bad memory. She recalled a line from the rap—actually the chorus that Amphis had sung, as beautifully as any manticore: "Where the ones who suffer most are the ones who have the least."

"Go on," she urged softly.

"I continued to fight, as my followers wished. Until the day we raided a village." He inhaled deeply. "We'd been told that the villagers were Weaver supporters, hiding them, feeding them, storing their arms. I arrived late—and saw what my so-called nobles had done in our cause. Children's bodies were—" He shuddered. "I did not speak. I could not. I could only turn my horse and ride away."

He sniffed. Was he crying? Elayne couldn't quite swivel her head to see. Besides, this was Leo, the man who'd used every trick to try to get his way. Why should she believe everything he said? "And then?" she asked.

"And then I went to the forests to the south of here. Lived amongst the great trees. I found Wolf early—" He glanced back at the loping dog. "Which was fortunate for me or I doubt I'd have survived without his warnings. I hunted—not fabulous beasts, only meat for my pot. Traded meat with villagers for other things. I . . . lived. And I even found some peace in the silence under the canopy. At least when I was awake."

At that, she did force herself around to look back at him. He stared back. This *seemed* a very different Leo from the youth she'd met two years ago. Still. "Go on," she said again.

He began as if he had not paused. "Yet I learned something else 'neath the branches—that you cannot have peace if the world does not. You cannot cut yourself off from humanity if humanity is suffering. No, not just humanity—if everything in creation is suffering. Civil war caused much of that. And then the Glanasa came." He took a deep breath. "And it got much, much worse."

She remembered from her first time in Goloth how she'd been mistaken for someone from Glana because she was dark-haired when most in the world were fair. "Tell me about them," she said.

"Glana is a huge island in the great ocean to the south, where the lands are hotter. We thought they were the only other humans in our world, but now we know this is not true. Sometimes they came to trade—we had metals that they coveted. They had foodstuffs, spices, and . . . what was in that cake you gave me?"

"Uh, chocolate?"

"So. They have something similar, darker, more bitter, that we called cacao." He nodded. "Sometimes they came to our shores to raid, though had not for many years. My father had fought them twice. Beaten them. They did not have our armour, our bigger bows. It was useful to have an enemy outside our land. It made the people happy to be . . . protected." He sighed. "But when civil strife rent our land, they came in ever greater numbers. They seized some of our weapons. They stayed, built forts on our shores. Then they began to push inland. And because we fought each other we could not unite to fight them."

"You say 'we.' But weren't you in the woods?"

"I was. And I was happy enough in them. Until a snake came and recounted to me the woe of our land." He smiled. "A talking, two-headed snake. 'Twas . . . a marvel." The smile vanished. "The amphisbaena told of the Glanasa pushing ever deeper into Goloth. Of how they did not slaughter if they could avoid it. Because what they wanted were living humans—aye, and fabulous beasts like him too. Bodies to be sacrificed and fed to their god."

"A dragon."

His gaze whipped to her. "The snake told you?"

She paused. That feeling she'd had in the doctor's office came back to her like an echo. If an echo can make breath catch and skin flush cold. It was not something she could share. Not when she didn't understand it herself. "They told some. That the dragon had slept for years, had woken up, wanting . . ." She gulped. "Feeding."

"Aye." Leo nodded. "There is little more that we know for sure. For though many have been taken to Glana, none have returned. Yet some of our people have learned a little of their tongue and helped them in their conquests." His voice got harder. "These traitors have reported what they've discovered. Of great ceremonies of chanting, drums and song where the men, women, children, yeah, the beasts of Goloth too are chained alive to rocks for the dragon to feast upon."

"That's so . . . horrible."

"Aye. And when I heard it, both the urgings of the snake and my own conscience drove me from the forests of content to oppose it."

"But how will you? I mean, if the civil war is still raging?"

"That is why I am riding this way. With you."

Here it was. In the zoo the snake had spoken—and rapped—about the disasters in Goloth. About how she was summoned, again, to fix it. She shivered. The only thing she wanted to fix right then was where the hell her dad was and how the hell to get him back to New York. "What do you expect me to do?" she said softly.

Leo took a deep breath. But the question remained unanswered because Huy cycled up beside them. "Hey," he said, needing to steer now as the grasslands had given way to something rockier, "water break?"

Leo frowned. "Ah, my friend needs a drink," she said. "Can we . . ." She gestured ahead.

Leo nodded, called down. "A little farther. There is a pool. We will stop."

The valley had narrowed, the slopes rising higher on each side. They entered a defile, rocky ground rising either side of the track, slowing as Swiftsure negotiated some small boulders. "So?" she said, her previous question still in the air.

"Others, on both sides, have recognized the terrible threat to us all. A secret meeting has been called, three nights from now—the first ever between Weavers and nobles—to discuss a truce and then unity against the common foe."

Elayne thought back to some of the heroic stories she'd read growing up. "And so you thought it might be time for the return of the king?"

"Mayhap."

"But will they listen to you? Obey you?" She craned around to look at him. "I mean, Leo, dude—you oppressed the one and deserted the other."

He looked at her, smiled. "I had forgotten, maid, how direct you are." He pulled the reins back, clicked his tongue. The horse halted. "If they do not want me to lead, I can still offer my sword, my skills in fighting. But kingship? No." He looked away. "Truly, I only seek to fight, as a man of Goloth. Fight against an evil that could destroy our world."

They'd reined in by a bubbling pool. Beside them, Huy laid the bike down and ran over to the water, dipped his cupped hands, drank. Elayne was thirsty too, but didn't dismount just yet. "And me?" she asked.

"Did the amphisbaena not tell you, maid?"

She did not answer, couldn't find the words. "Come," he said, sliding off the horse, reaching a hand to help her down. Keeping it, he led her along a faint path that wound up one steep side of the bowl that sheltered the pool. Huy followed, they climbed for a little while, crested the slope—and emerged onto a kind of rocky platform. The land fell away steeply below them, opening into another valley that swept in a patchwork of forest and meadow across to—

"Whoa!" said Huy. "Quite the view. What are they?"

"The Griffin Mountains," Elayne murmured.

"Aye." Leo was looking, sheltering his eyes like the others against the sinking sun. "Over them lies another land, where man has never gone—the Valley of the Unicorn. So over them lies, perhaps, the fate of Goloth."

Moonspill, she thought again, directing the name over the distant peaks. Got only silence in return. The network was down in Goloth, just as it had been in New York.

Leo must have sensed her discomfort. "Come, maid," he said, offering his hand again. "There is time yet to consider . . . all options. First we must go to the peace council. For if there is no agreement between Weavers and nobles to fight the common foe, then any journey would be in vain." He shook his head. "For there may not be a human or a fabulous beast left in Goloth for the unicorns to save."

14

PEACE TALKS

"Why would we trust you?" The rough, deep voice soared out above the angry shouting. "When you have oppressed us for centuries?"

The shouts crescendoed. For and against. Faction versus faction. It reminded Elayne of live transmissions from Congress during a particularly scrappy debate—if it was held al fresco in a forest clearing and at night, lit only by firebrands placed every twenty paces around the wide circle. If half the congressmen wore masks, as half the participants here did. If the unmasked half wore pieces of armour—though no weapons. Neither side had those—at least showing.

"And why should we trust you?" answered an unmasked man with white hair and beard whom Elayne vaguely remembered from the court, "when you do not even dare to show your faces?"

This was greeted by another huge roar, support on his side, fury on the other. The figure next to her leaned in, lifting his own mask to whisper. "This is going well, don't you think?"

She glanced at Huy. She had only just gotten used to his getup. He'd been most upset the day before that he'd had to remove and hide his velvet frock-coat suit in the village they'd passed through. Leo had demanded they both change if they still insisted on infiltrating the peace council with him—which she did. For one, in every village they'd visited there had been talk of it—so she could only hope that her dad had also heard and that he'd chosen to go where the action was. She still didn't know what Leo thought he could achieve here. But like her, he'd probably find out at the only game in town. Also, she knew if she was going to do this thing—cross the mountains, speak to Moonspill—that the unicorn would need all the information she could bring.

So Huy had reluctantly removed the velvet and donned the uniform of a peasant-weaver: baggy trousers with rope belt, a wool shirt, a smock over it all. What had hurt worst was trading his Ferragamos for clogs. Still, he'd managed to do a lot with little. He'd unwound the belt, then twined it into a decorative pattern—he'd been a wow with a rainbow loom, apparently. The soft, wide-brimmed hat was given an almost military slouch, and the apron was cinched in at the waist. They both wore scarves to conceal their faces, but his, of course, was monogrammed Hermès.

He was undoubtedly the most stylish peasant she'd ever seen. She'd only given up her large backpack, left it with half her stash of things. Strapped to her front was a smaller day pack, with essentials. It gave her a pregnant bulge. She'd also left the bicycle with the pack, both hidden along with Huy's clothes. The apron, shirt and trousers fitted nicely over her sweater and wool pants—for which she was glad. Her down jacket was rolled up on Swiftsure's haunches. The nights turned chilly fast. Mid-autumn, Leo had said.

As she shivered, the gruff-voiced man who'd shouted before replied, "You wonder why we wear masks, high steward? Could it be because we remember all too well the mask of the executioner *you* commanded to take the heads of all who opposed you—you and your king?" Shouts of assent greeted this from his side. "We conceal our faces lest, if by a miracle, the Glanasa are defeated and you again become our oppressors and murder us."

A greater shout came at this, on both sides. There appeared to be just one neutral there, a man unmasked and unarmoured, quite old, with snow white hair, standing between the two jostling groups. He lifted his arms now. "Gentles, gentles," he called, the strength of his voice belying his age. "Gentles! Quiet, pray! Let us be done with insults and suspicions. There is harm on both sides, I warrant." Another murmur swelled at this, and he flapped his arms to calm it. "Let Robert, the high steward, answer."

"High steward no more," said the man Elayne recognized, "for I have no king to steward for. Leo is long missing and most probably dead. So I propose here a council, made up of equal numbers of Weavers and nobles—a council whose first task will be to defeat the Glanasa. Its second, restore Goloth to prosperity."

"With you doing the prospering, no doubt!" the rough voice called back.

Tumult again, the snowy haired man flapping his arms in vain. "My time, I think," said Leo from under his own mask. He had not swapped his leather clothes for a peasant's. Yet he was dressed in neither finery nor armour. "Wish me fortune," he said, and stepped forward. Cupping his hands to his mouth, he let out a perfect imitation of his own hunting dog, who was at least part wolf.

People started, looked about. Only the Weavers nearest him knew he made the sound and most gave back. As the silence spread, he lowered his hands. "Gentles," he called. "Noblemen and noble Weavers. The high steward is right—only if all have a voice in our future will we have a future. And he is also wrong. Because Leo is not dead. Leo is alive." He moved another pace forward and took off his mask. "I am Leo."

She'd expected an explosion of sound; none came. There *was* noise, as everyone on the nobles' side knelt. As some on the other side did too, and took off their caps, the impulse instinctive.

"No!" cried Leo, moving through the ranks of Weavers to join the white-haired man kneeling in the centre. "Up, all of you, up!" He waved everyone to their feet. "Only one man should kneel here," he said, turning to face the masked peasants. "To beg forgiveness for all the wrongs that have been done to you." He paused, looked around the circle before him, before adding, "That man is me."

And then he knelt to further gasps and shiftings from the men he knelt before. "He's good, isn't he?" said Huy, leaning in again. "Will it work?"

"Let's see," Elayne whispered back.

The Weavers were murmuring in wonder, looking at each other. Few had put their hats back on. Indeed, more were taking them off. Smiles were appearing under masks. Though most vanished when that rougher voice came again. "What?" the Weavers' spokesman cried. "You kneel and think that is redress enough for centuries of tyranny . . . *Leo*?" He gave the name a harsh twist. "You think to win us with a show of contrition? It is another role you take on, like in your staged fight in the arena, the hunt of the unicorn."

Gasps came again. However rebellious they were, centuries of conditioning meant that no one spoke to a king like that. And no one ever used his name.

But Leo only smiled. He began to walk toward the masked spokesman, other rebels slowly opening the way before him, speaking softly as he came. "The only thing I seek to win is the war against the Glanasa. The only role I desire is warrior of Goloth." He reached the masked man, halted. "I swear to you, I will never be king again but only and ever a servant to the people." A murmur rose from behind him, from the ranks of armoured lords. Ignoring it, he thrust out his hand.

The man stared at it. Then he reached up and pulled down his mask. Elayne recognized him—the Weaver leader who'd helped her escape from the Castle of Skulls. Slowly he reached out too—and the two men grasped hands around each other's forearms. They stared, as cheers came, from both sides now.

Leo lifted the other's arm he still held, waved for silence, shouted, "Together we can triumph. Especially now. Because we have been given a sign."

"Oh no," Elayne muttered. "Don't—"

"For the one who began the revolution, the one who tamed the unicorn, that one has returned to us in our hour of greatest need." He swept his arm up toward her. "Behold her. Behold . . . the Summoned."

Damn him, she thought. He'd said he'd keep her a secret, only to be revealed at time of greatest need. Yet despite his solo vision quest in the forest, he was back with people now and still, it appeared, a politician. Lying again. "Remove your mask, Alice-Elayne," he called. "Bring joy to the people of Goloth once more!"

"Your royal majesty," said Huy, bowing as he stepped back.

"Shut *up*!" She'd like to run. But really, what choice did she have? Sighing, she peeled off her mask.

Gasps and a moment's silence. Until all there, Weavers and nobles, began to clap and cheer. She looked at Leo who gave her a "told ya so" type nod. She glared at him and shrugged at the cheerers.

Amid all that noise, it took a while for anyone to hear the new voice. Yet eventually a shuddering cry pierced the acclaim.

"The Glanasa!" the man shouted. "We are betrayed! The Glanasa are come!"

It silenced everyone there, Weaver, noble, the man who once was king. Which meant that all heard, clearly, the deep blast of a hunting horn.

It was pandemonium in a heartbeat.

Everyone scattered, mainly through the forest the opposite way the horn had sounded. Elayne clutched Huy when it looked like he would follow. "Leo," she said. "He's coming for us."

And he was, cutting against the flow, dodging around and shoving aside people in his path. He ran up, barely slowed. "Come," he said, running past them and between two trees. It was not the direction most had taken. Indeed, if anything, he led them toward the sounds of ambush. More horns sounded, more shouts came—joined by the clash of weapons.

"But they're this way!" Elayne yelled, she and Huy running nonetheless.

"Aye, some of them," Leo called over his shoulder, "but trust a hunter—the Glanasa want to capture, not kill. They make noise to startle, like a dog flushing a deer and driving it onto the waiting spears. Most of them will be where our men run now, with clubs to hit and ropes to bind. Hurry!"

They ran back the way they'd come. Cresting a small hill, running over it, Elayne saw Leo's horse below, in the dip where they'd left it. It had been the darkest part of the woods, but it was bright with light now—for five men with torches stood around it.

Glanasa.

One man of the five stood slightly apart, an instant vision flash-burned onto her eyes.

He was tall, well over six feet. Wide too, his size enhanced by plates of armour covering his shoulders and chest. His hair was black, accentuating a pale face, and fell in two long, straight shanks down the side of his head from a shaved crown, like a reversed Mohawk. He wore a feathered necklace and some sort of pleated kilt. At each hip she saw— the last thing she saw before losing the battle with slope and gravity, tumbling—two skulls. Both human.

She slid, slowed, grazed herself on dry wood and rough earth, but kept her eyes up—to watch Leo, not slowing at all, unslinging the bow off his back as he ran, stringing an arrow, pausing only to draw, sight, release before charging on. His shot was good; one of the enemy tumbled back, new feathers at his neck—and Elayne noticed what she hadn't before—that the man falling had been standing on something that rose now, shook off a net, tipped back its head and howled.

And with that, and his master's shouts, Wolf leaped on the closest warrior and pulled him to the ground.

Leo kept running, dropping his bow, drawing his sword. She could see he was going to take on the three men still standing. Scary enough— but what was scarier was who was matching him stride for stride.

"Huy!" she screamed. But he paid her no mind, focusing entirely on the warrior before him.

She jumped up. Her hand had settled on a stick about four feet long. It was stout and she picked it up. Then she was running forward too. It was crazy—but what choice did she have?

The man Leo fought had a shield and was using it to fend off the former king's furious attacks. The warrior Huy faced was bringing his huge war club over in great downward swoops, which her friend dodged, weaving and bobbing. The other warrior was on the ground, trying to wrestle off the hound who kept leaping in, savaging, withdrawing.

That left one enemy, the one she'd first noted, turning to her now. She could see instantly that he was more richly dressed than the others, his feathered neckpiece more elaborate, his armour thicker. A leader, then. He was holding Swiftsure's reins in one hand. In his other was a long knife and on his face—painted, the eyes circled in black, emphasizing his dead white skin—was a wide smile.

"Woman," he said, in Glanasan. "I like a woman."

"But do you like this?" she replied. In Glanasan. The shock caused his eyes to shoot wide in astonishment. More importantly it caused the hand holding the knife to move slightly to the side—allowing her to drive the stick hard up under his kilt between his legs where it did not stop—until it did.

His response was understandable in any tongue. "Oof!" he said, folding over, dropping the reins.

Elayne caught them, pulling to steady the horse. When she'd been in Goloth before, she'd been terrified of riding—and they'd forced her onto horses all the time—but she'd taken many lessons since. Let's see if they've paid off, she thought—and threw herself into the saddle.

The horse balked. She controlled it, with thigh, heel and hand. Turning she saw that Huy still dodged before his man, whose sword strikes were slowing. Leo's opponent was using his shield advantage to steadily push the former king back toward the treeline, and all the dangers underfoot there. Only Wolf seemed to have a grip on things. Well, on a neck.

Once, on a nervous mount in Connecticut, she'd made a mistake. Maybe she could make the same one here.

Jerking the reins hard, throwing her weight back, she brought the horse up onto its hind legs—and flailing hooves provided the instant of distraction her friends needed.

As his opponent flinched, Huy dropped low, fast, and hurled a leg parallel to the ground, sweeping the Glanasan's feet from under him. Then Huy leapt high and, with a yell, brought his elbow crashing down into the man's face. Leo, shifting left, let a blow miss his side by a hair.

The heavy sword thumped into the ground and, twisting his wrist, Leo plunged his sword into the gap opened between shield and body.

The man she'd hit with the stick had risen, staggered back to a tree. Now he glanced at his felled men, shot her a look of the purest malevolence and took off into the forest.

Calling off Wolf, who obeyed instantly—though the man he left had ceased moving—Leo was at her side in a moment. She was half off the horse. "Nay," he urged. "Ride, maid!"

"Where?"

"To the Griffin Mountains. Over them to the Valley of the Unicorn. In the valley where we hunted the griffin that time, there is a rough path up."

"But—"

He turned to Huy. "Mount behind her, friend. Be bodyguard still," he said. "And thank you for your courage."

"De nada," Huy replied, vaulting up behind Elayne. "Where will you be?"

Leo looked back into the woods. Distant shouts came, the clash of arms. "Here. I must help to free my people. T'would be a sorry loss to Goloth if we were to lose some of our best fighters this night, Weaver or noble." He took a breath. "After, I will fight where I can. But I do not know how long we can hold them back. That they raid so far inland does not bode well. We will ambush, delay them until—"

"Until?" Elayne asked, though she feared she knew the answer.

"Until you return with the unicorns, maid." He looked into her face, must have seen the fear there. "I know you doubt yourself, Alice-Elayne. But remember: you are the maid, the one foretold. Believe." He reached a gentling hand to Swiftsure, who was twitching at the distant sounds of battle. "And trust me in this: I will look for your father."

"My—" She gasped. "How did you know?"

"I cannot think that anyone else of fifty years would cause you to look so scared whenever you speak of him. Am I right?" On her nod, he continued, "I do not understand the way of it, how and why he came. But I will find him and keep him safe against your return. Perhaps then I will begin to earn your trust."

"Trust?" she echoed. This was Leo, former tyrant, all-round schemer, wasn't it? Yet in the end, what choice did she have?

In that same moment she realized two things: First, that to sit around and mope and hope her father would appear would help no one, least of all him. And second, that what she was being asked to do was what she'd most wanted to do from the moment she returned to Goloth—be reunited with the sole other being in two worlds that she loved completely. Who loved her completely in return.

Her unicorn. Her Moonspill.

Shouts came again, not far off. Glanasan. They looked and saw figures running through the trees, heading to the noise of fighting deeper in the forest. Wolf snarled, and Leo restrained him with a word. He reached up, squeezed her hand, turned. "Wait," she cried. "If we make the mountains, what about Swiftsure?"

He paused. "When you release him, say my name, he will try and find me. With fortune, he will."

"But how will we? If . . . if I succeed, we'll need a rendezvous."

Leo's brow furrowed. "I do not know where the fight will take me."

"And I don't know how long this might take."

"With two on a horse, it is three days to the mountains." Leo squatted, grabbed a stick. There was just enough moonlight for them to see the lines he swiftly scratched in the dirt—rough peaks, a long line ending in a circle. "The city lies two days march south of here, along this river. A rallying point. Do you rally there too," he glanced up, silver on his face, "from the seventh day after the full moon."

She looked up too. The moon was perhaps two days away from its height. That gave her—she gulped—less than ten days. "I'll try," she said.

"Farewell." He took a step away but she caught him a last time.

"Leo? You . . . you take care of yourself. Uh, in the battle?"

"Always." He hesitated a moment, then sheathed his sword, put one foot on the stirrup, raised himself up. "But, Alice-Elayne, a favour?" He leaned closer. "Will you not send me off to that battle with a kiss?"

She snorted. "Don't push it, buddy."

He grinned. "Nay, I will not." Jumping down he looked up at Huy, nodded. "Warrior."

Then he ran, Wolf tight to his heel, slowing only to stoop, snatch up his bow, notch an arrow. They watched until the dark woods swallowed him.

"What?" Huy murmured. "You couldn't have given the cute king dude one kiss for luck?"

Elayne tapped Swiftsure's flank. "Yeah, right!" was all she said as they set out.

They went fast, sounds of battle fading behind them. But they'd only ridden a little ways before Elayne noticed something digging into her back. "What's that?" she asked, squirming.

"Souvenir. Fell off the armour of the guy I knocked down."

They'd just cleared the wood, were riding now across grassland, and the light of a waxing moon reflected silver on what he now reached before her. It was an oval, concave panel, about the size of a plate. As he tipped it, she saw that it had patterns in it, swirling shapes, in what would be a multitude of greens in the sunlight. The closest thing at home would be abalone. Yet this was no sea creature's shell.

"What do you think it is?" he asked.

"Oh, I know what it is," she replied, tapping her heels into Swiftsure's flanks. "It's a dragon scale."

15

THE GRIFFIN

"We're going to climb this?"

"Unless you have a better idea."

It was three days after the Glanasan ambush. They'd followed the sunsets, headed northwest, arrived at the Griffin Mountains that morning. They'd ridden along them for a while, seeking some chink, some crack in the sheer face that might indicate a path up, however steep it might be.

"You sure this is the place?" Huy asked. Again.

"Yes, I'm sure," she snapped, though she wasn't entirely. It certainly looked like the valley where she and Leo had been attacked by a griffin. But she could be forgiven, she thought, for forgetting some of the details of the place—since the griffin had chased them, caught them, damn near killed them both. Leo had saved her life and nearly lost his in the saving.

At least so far she'd seen no sign of the flying monster, nor heard its cry, from anywhere along the stone ramparts that swept each way as far as she could see. She looked up, straining her neck as she tried to gauge just how high they were. Really, really high. It would take two hours to walk up them—if they ever found this mythical path! Only where they'd halted now did it look anything less than vertical, a slight bend to it. She could see some handholds, footholds. She'd spent time on climbing walls with her dad. But he wouldn't be standing at the bottom of this one, paying out the rope.

She turned to Huy. "Hey, don't your people say: 'the longest journey begins with a single step?'"

He raised an eyebrow. "Canadians?"

"No, uh, your family's people. Vietnamese. Buddhists."

He shook his head. "Jeez. You may know every language in the world. But you've got a lot to learn about who speaks them."

"Oh-kay. Still, how's your climbing?"

"Terrible. I'm scared of heights. Any advice?"

"Sure." She considered. "Don't look down."

She went to where Swiftsure was cropping some grass. "Easy there," she said as he shied slightly. He settled, allowing her to strip off the two water skins first, then his bridle, saddle. Free, he shook himself. "Go find Leo. Leo!" she said. "Look after him."

The stallion's ears came forward, as if he were questioning her. Then he jerked his head up and down, snorted, and a moment later, took off across the grasslands to the hills. It was always hard to tell with a non-fabulous beast, for they did not answer in words, but she got the clear sense that Swiftsure had said, "I will."

She lifted her day pack, checked that all the zippers were closed, slipped it on, clicked the waist and chest straps. "Ready?" she said.

Huy licked his lips. "I was born ready."

Huy? A cliché? Elayne thought. Now I'm really going to have to watch him. She looked down. He'd taken off his shoes, stood in his socks, which were patterned with little clock faces. He was dressed again in his velvet frock coat, because he'd insisted they detour back to the village to collect his stuff. "I'm not meeting my first unicorn in an apron and clogs," he'd said. She'd still left her larger backpack hidden there, though she too had changed back into all her clothes.

Still, his suit was looking a tad tatty. And it was hardly climbing gear. "It'll be easy. Just put your fingers and toes where mine go."

"Will do," he said brightly, licking his lips again.

"Let's boogie."

At least her own ancient cliché brought a groan. With a slight smile, she reached her fingers into a crevice at head height.

It wasn't hard going—for a while at least. From below it had looked almost vertical, but in fact once they'd gone diagonally up and over an outcrop, the slope was not ninety degrees at all, more like forty-five. They climbed steadily, not pausing—she didn't want to risk him looking back the way they'd come. She'd done it once, and even though she didn't suffer from vertigo, it had still made her head swim.

They were about halfway up when they hit a problem—an overhang. For a nanosecond she forgot that she was leading someone, took the risk, put her foot in a tiny indent and swung herself up and over. There was more angled slope ahead, an easy haul. She figured they were maybe twenty minutes from the summit.

"Elayne?"

She looked down. The outcrop hid him from her sight. "Huy! Uh, sorry. There's a crack—"

"I c-can't." His voice was all quavery. "I can't move. I can't open my eyes. I . . . I looked down."

Crap! She took a deep breath. She really, really didn't want to do this, but she had no choice. "Don't worry. Stay still. I'm coming for you."

Words came through tight lips. "Staying still."

She was looking down, trying to figure out how the hell she could do that, when the shriek came.

Sudden, high-pitched. "Scree-scree-scree." Eagle, she thought, hoped, prayed. And she was partly right. At least, the cry did come from an eagle's head . . . on the body of a lion.

She looked up . . . and saw the griffin, stooping fast from the sky, its four legs thrust out, six-inch razored talons on each one. She was perched on the outcrop, with nowhere to go—except into it. She flattened herself, pressing herself into rock as if she could dissolve into it. She couldn't, but she must have shrunk just enough. She felt a tug on her back, was lifted, the claws fastening onto her pack. But its plastic must have made it slippery; she fell about a foot, hit the rock face hard, slid, her fingers scrabbling for a hold, any hold. Fingernails ripped, she dug harder and held herself, just, as her legs shot out over the outcrop, into space.

"Elayne!" Huy cried from beneath her.

She tightened her finger grip, tried to find a toehold too. "Don't open your eyes!" she shouted.

"Too late! Holy f—"

His voice was lost to another terrible screech. She glanced back—and wished she hadn't—because the griffin had swung up and out from the wall. Now it dropped, and with three mighty flaps was coming in again, coming fast, parallel to the rock face, wings spread back, talons leading.

"Oh! Oh, oh . . . ohhhhh!"

The cries came from just below her. The last one extending into a wail that diminished fast.

Huy was falling.

"No!" she cried, trying to scrabble around, feeling her own precarious grip loosening. And then her breath was knocked violently from her body as something slammed into her back. She was no longer slipping—she was rising vertically off the outcrop, rising fast—she almost thought of snapping the clasps on the pack, dropping, but that option was gone in a moment as the griffin shot away from the wall—then folded its wings and plummeted toward the valley floor.

"Ahhhhh!" she screamed, then heard it echoed in another scream, Huy's continuous wail from below her, becoming louder quickly as the griffin fell faster than a heavy rock. It looked like all three of them were going to smash into the ground below—until, a moment before that became a certainty, she glimpsed the griffin open its other claws at the same time as it spread its wings—snatching Huy by the back of his jacket when he was maybe ten feet from the ground. Huy reached up, grabbed the huge paw that held him. The lion-bird dropped a moment more, Elayne almost touched earth with her toes, then with a huge flap, the beast lifted upwards and they were rising again.

Instant relief and total horror chased each other through her mind. They were being hoisted straight up, parallel to the rock face. The griffin's huge wings were beating hard, and she got a sense they were a heavy load. She also got a memory. After her first time in Goloth, she'd made a point of reading up on all the fabulous beasts she'd encountered—the myths of her world that were true in this one. The stories. And one told—why did the name Marco Polo pop into her head, why now?—that the griffin would carry its prey above the rocks and drop them close to their nests, dashing them into bite-sized pieces to feed upon at leisure.

As they cleared the ramparts of the wall, Elayne had no doubt that that was exactly what the griffin was about to do.

She didn't usually have to search about in her head for any language, human or beastly. They just came. Now, panic prevented her. Words clashed around. She thought of shouting in Dramach, at least a tongue of Goloth. Then, just as the monster reached its desired height, just as it levelled out and its wings flapped even harder to hold it in a hover, the word came. A word, anyway.

"Unicorns," she screeched, in purest griffin.

The flapping slowed. They dropped, then rose again as the wings again beat hard. But it was not the only sign of the animal's shock. Huy, released, began to plummet to the earth.

"Catch him!" Elayne screamed, in the language now fully recalled. And the beast obeyed, swinging her up, slamming her into its furry belly, folding its wings to stoop—and pluck a yelling Huy about forty feet above the rocks.

They rose again, the griffin working even harder now, judging by its heaved breaths. Yet soon enough they were again poised above the peaks, jagged and rough beneath them.

"What are you?"

The griffin's voice, unlike its hunting cry, was deep-pitched. She'd learned that, like the amphisbaena, the fabulous beasts of Goloth talked without the aid of lips and a normal tongue but with organs of speech somewhere in their throats. All except the unicorn who spoke largely in the hearer's mind.

It was hard to concentrate looking down onto a rock spire she was about to be impaled on. What to say? Swallowing, she settled on her best shot. "I am the maid. Uh, the one foretold." When no reply came she shouted, "I ride unicorns."

It was the wrong thing to say. "Unicorns?" The word came on a higher-pitched shriek, and she felt a slackening of the claw's grip on her back, started swinging her arms to see if she could grab an ankle, like Huy again had, in case the animal released. Then the grip re-established; indeed she was jerked up, turned—to meet a single, black eagle's eye.

"I hate unicorns." That eye narrowed. The griffin shook her. "And how is it you can talk to me? Food does not speak."

"Amphisbaena. Gift of tongues." It was easier to speak in part sentences.

"So." This came on a rumble from somewhere deep, continued. "Curious. Why would you be given such a prize?"

"Oh, you know. To save Goloth. Ha ha."

Another rumble came, though this one sounded . . . Elayne thought it sounded almost like a laugh—one with almost no humour to it. Words followed. "You did not save Goloth. You delayed her doom. Doom to all man, all beasts." They dropped slightly then, the wings needing to beat even harder, the beast's breaths getting louder. "Yet I will not live to see it. For my chick is dying, and I will die the moment after he."

This came on a wash of sorrow. It also came with another slackening of grip. The chat was nearly up. They were doomed unless . . . "My friend there has a medical kit," she blurted. "I mean, he's a healer. He can help your chick."

She felt the grip re-establish. "Only food will help him."

"No! Food will—" she echoed the griffin, "just delay the doom. We can stop it. We can save him."

She had no idea what she was talking about. She just knew that anything was better than being tenderized on rocks to be a griffin's last supper. They hovered, the beast's breaths coming in ever-greater heaves, the black eye upon her. Then, suddenly and wordlessly, it spread its wings to stillness and swooped down to a level patch of mountaintop. Hovering for a moment again, it lowered them to the earth and deposited them as gently as if they were eggs. Then it flapped twice more and settled onto a large, flat-topped rock about twenty yards away.

They both lay there, taking in air in great whoops. Huy particularly seemed unable to breathe. "T-t-t-t-t—" he went.

She crawled over to him. "Asthma?" she asked.

"T-t-t-t-t-terror!" he exclaimed. "D-don't make me t-talk."

"You might have to do more than that," she replied, and turned to face the griffin.

16

THE DOCTOR IS IN

She'd seen one before. Both times the griffin had tried to kill her.

She thought that the one that had attacked her when she first came to Goloth was bigger—more the size of an African elephant. This was about the size of an Indian one. He? She? Though she'd read up on such creatures, she couldn't recall its child-rearing habits—who stayed with the chick? Only its parts: head and wings of an eagle, body of a lion. Ears too, joined by a feathered crest. She recalled there'd been some debate among the ancient experts who'd catalogued them as to whether they had claws or paws. Two of each, she saw now, the front feathered, the rear furred. Each with a wicked set of curved talons. So that's settled, she thought, a giggle rising, swiftly suppressed.

The griffin was looking at them as if they were a meal postponed, not cancelled. She had to delay the feast. Rising onto her knees, she said, "Have you a name?"

"A human name? My kind have had many over the years." The eagle head shot forward, those black eyes fixing on her. "But you only need know one name. That one I took from the Goddess whose chariot I pulled through the sunset of Greece as the heroes fell." It spread its wings wide, rose up onto its rear claws. "I am Nemesis, daughter of vengeance. And you will suffer if you do not do what you said you could. Suffer most terribly."

The words came on a blast of hot breath. "Sure. No problem," replied Elayne, sinking back, then turning to Huy, only now starting to breathe a little easier, coming onto his knees. "OK, you're up."

"I'm up what?"

"I told the griffin that you would heal her chick."

His expression didn't change. "You told her what?"

"That you were a healer."

Now it did. His jaw dropped. "Wha-? I . . . I did one year of pre-med."

"And first aid, right? You have your brother's medical belt. Closest thing round here to a healer."

"First aid?" The idea floored him. "I learned splinting. CPR. The recovery position." He swallowed. "Do you think I should put the griffin chick into the recovery position?"

"Maybe. Let's take a look." Glancing over her shoulder—the beast was still staring at them, her eyes huge, hungry—Elayne leaned forward. "Listen, if I hadn't told her what I did she'd be sorting through our entrails now for the tastiest bits." She raised a hand. "Eugh. Sorry, gross, even for me. But our only hope is . . ." She shrugged. "A quick consultation."

He stared at her for a long, long moment. Then his mouth snapped shut. "Righty ho, then," he said, in a jolly PBS Brit accent. "Let's have a look see, shall we?"

She had to admire his recovery—from death plummeting to Doctor Huy in seconds. Though she still had to steady him, as he wobbled to his feet, and ignore his faint giggling. She looked at the griffin. "Where?" she asked.

The beast inclined its head along the rocky wall on which she perched. To the left, Elayne saw what could be rough steps. Not letting go of Huy, stooping only to pick up her pack, she moved across to them. A little scrambling brought them to the top of a horseshoe-shaped bowl, its ends joining to the rock face beyond. It went back a ways, most of it sheltered by an overhang. Beneath that, in the middle, was a nest of straw. And in the centre of that lay the griffin chick.

She'd expected "a chick" to be small. But she didn't think he was any smaller than his mother, now turning to peer at them as they descended another rocky stair, a rumble of warning in her throat. They crossed, and the chick half-opened one eye. The surface was filmy, gunk-pooled and hardened in one corner. The other looked like it was sealed shut. The chick gave one faint mew of surprise. Then the eye closed again.

"Easy there," Elayne murmured, gently laying a hand on the eagle head. Even through feathers, she could feel the heat within. The chick stirred, and she could sense shock at a human speaking griffin. But he was too weak to even open his eye again.

"Well, Doctor?" she said, assuming a brightness she didn't feel.

With one nervous glance over his shoulder at the mother, Huy turned to the child. "I mean, where do I begin," he said. "I can hardly ask the patient where it hurts."

"I can." She stroked the feathers again. "Where do you hurt, little one?"

It took several seconds during which the only sound that came was the chick's shallow breaths. Then the beak opened a little and the word came clearly. "Everywhere."

"Good start," she breathed, then turned. "How did the sickness start?" she called to the griffin on the wall behind them.

"He . . . flew into the mountain. He was too bold, trying to catch a goat."

"An accident," she said, turning back to Huy. "Things broken maybe?"

"I'm not sure that would account for the smell. Phew!" He took a breath, then reached for the first time to the body, feeling gently up the right wing, manipulating it a little. The beast did not stir. But when he did the same to the left—

The chick twisted, letting out a high-pitched shriek of pain—a shriek immediately echoed in fury by his mother, who hopped down, shot her head forward into the cave, her wicked curved beak halting an inch from Huy's shoulder. "You will not hurt him," she screamed.

Huy had managed to gently lay down the wing he held, before he hunched. But Elayne stepped across, raising her hands. "He is hurt there. We can't look at it without a little pain."

A growl came, more from the lion side than the eagle's. "Be more careful," she rumbled. Then she pulled her head back, about an inch.

Elayne nudged Huy. "Go ahead."

He shuddered. "One of the reasons I gave up on medicine. Patient's families."

He lifted the left-side wing again, to another groan, another growl. Slowly feeling along, moving it a little, he whistled in some breath. "I think—I think this shoulder joint is dislocated. It's . . . it's weird—I mean weird even for Beast World—but where bird wing joins mammal body, it's . . ." He shrugged. "Out."

"I dislocated a shoulder once, skiing. Super painful. Can you put it back?"

"I—I could try. But that doesn't account for the stink." He sniffed, his nose wrinkling. "Smells like rot but the source is farther down."

"To look at that we'll have to move him. A lot, right?"

"Yup."

"OK. Do it." She turned to the mother griffin. "You have to give us some room. This may hurt, a lit—"

She got no farther—because the chick let out a hideous scream, rising from its nest, the one eye that could open shot wide, before falling back. She whipped around to Huy. "What did you do?"

"You said 'do it.'"

"Not till I—"

Another scream, deeper, longer. The mother griffin rose up on her hind legs, her wings spread wide, reaching both sides of the cave. "You hurt him!" she shrieked. "You die!"

She lifted her head as high as it would go. Yet before she could plunge down and end them, another voice came. "No, Tisiphone! No! It helped. It hurt—but it helped."

Tisiphone halted her descent. "It helped, Alecto?"

"The pain is there. Different. Better."

"Bett-er?" Tisiphone—that's what her chick had called her—drew the word out as if sampling it, then lowered her wings slowly, fixing them both with a stare. "Help more."

Huy was licking his lips again as if he wanted to lick them off. "Oh-kay. Can you, uh, can you, um, get him to, you know? Turn." He gestured. "On his, um, right side."

Elayne gave the command. With another groan, the chick—Alecto—shifted, tipping his lion flank toward them.

"Aw!" Both of them moaned, winced, turning their faces away. Partly from the stench, which rose unobstructed now. Mainly from the sight.

"OK," said Huy, after a moment, hand before mouth, "that's horrible."

Elayne also had her hand raised. "Yeah, but what is it?" she said through her fingers.

Gagging, he bent closer to peer. "Um, you know I'm no expert. But I would say, the colours . . . yellow pus? Discoloured skin? Could be gangrene. Or maybe septicemia. Or maybe both." He raised his eyes to her over his hand. "Beyond me, that's for sure. Beyond anyone, I'd guess, even at John Hopkins."

She glanced back up. Tisiphone was peering ever closer. This was not the answer for her. But what could they do? Pretend? Stall awhile?

As she considered, Huy spoke low, from the side of his mouth. "Have a knife in your pack?"

"Yeah. Swiss Army. Why?"

"I don't think Mom will like my diagnosis. And I don't like the idea of that big fall again." He swallowed. "So pass me the knife. I'll hold it to the chick's throat, threaten to cut it, unless she lets us go."

"What? No. I mean how far would we get?"

"True." He looked up. Tisiphone had come so close now that the great lion's chest was about three feet away. "OK. Give me the knife anyway. I'll . . . I'll stab the mother. If I can jab her in the heart . . ." He swallowed. "I think I can remember that much of my anatomy."

"No."

"You got a better plan?" He looked at her hard, eyes bright. "I don't want to die here, Elayne."

"Me neither, but . . ." She looked at the griffin's chest, pressing still closer as the mother stared at her sick son. Huy's plan was desperate— but was it their only chance? "No," she said, exhaling hard. "I didn't come here to kill fabulous beasts. There are few enough of them around as it is. And—" An idea suddenly hit her. "Wait! Septicemia is . . . it's, like, a poisoning of the blood?"

An eyebrow raised. "Not 'like'—it is blood poisoning."

"Thank you, speech Nazi. You, like, sound like my dad. And gangrene?"

"Decomposition."

"Flesh poisoning?"

"Well, kinda—"

She shot her eyes wide. "OMG. I know what to do."

"You know a cure for blood poisoning?"

"No. But I know a man who does. Uh-uh, not a man." She turned, stared up into the great eagle's eye so close to her now. Spoke the words clearly. "We only have one hope." She took a deep breath. "We have to get your son to a unicorn."

She expected a big reaction: a flapping of wings, deafening roars, threats. Instead that same rumble came that she'd heard earlier—though this laugh was even more bitter than before. "Hope? There is none there. There is only death for my child the moment the unicorn sees him."

"Not if I'm with him." She turned to fully face the beast. "Look, did you never hear of me? The maid who rode the unicorn?"

A long pause. Then a reply. "There were rumours borne on winds. What of them?"

"Then perhaps the rumours told of how I didn't just ride one, I . . . I saved the unicorn. I started a revolution, I—" She broke off. In normal times she found the whole legacy, obligation, expectation a burden. But she had to sell this so . . . "I am the one foretold," she continued, her voice stronger. "I am going to fetch the unicorns back to Goloth. And I am going to save the world. Again."

It was as much of a speech as she'd ever made. Huy couldn't understand a word, so he stared at her, astonished, as she grunted, chuntered, and rumbled. Tisiphone understood—and the cynical laugh came once more. "Brave words, maid. But only this is foretold: my son will die— yet not before you and your companion provide him with his last meal." She reared up again, as if poising her beak for a sharp stab down. "For the unicorns will never heed you and heal him."

Elayne threw up a hand. "They will. They owe me. One, especially, owes me." She nodded, thinking of Moonspill, his healing touch. "He will do this if I ask him."

"And how will you find him in time?" Tisiphone's head drooped slightly as she eyed her child, fear in her voice now, not fury.

"Let's cross that bridge when we come to it?"

"There are no bridges there. Man does not live in the Valley of the Unicorn."

"It's an—" She wasn't sure how to explain "expression" in griffin, so she gave up. "First thing we need to do is descend into the valley. Once there I reckon—" She stopped, thought. She'd always been able to "speak" to Moonspill in her head. She'd been too far away for too long. But in his own land? "I'll be able to find him, have no fear."

"I do not fear—except in this." She reached down, past them, to lay her beak softly on her child's neck, ruffling the place where bird down met animal fur. "To lose him. Which I will do, I know I will and soon. So you are right, maid. You are the only . . . hope. And while you are that, you will live. And when you are that no more, you will be what you always were."

Tisiphone had turned as she spoke, shuffled across the cave floor. Once clear of the overhang, she opened her wings and hopped onto the protecting wall. "And, er, what was that?" Elayne asked.

"Food." The word was called back, as she launched herself and flew off the mountain.

For a moment there was silence—until Huy cleared his throat, spoke. "What's happening?"

Suddenly Elayne's legs felt very weak. She lurched across to the bottom rough stone step in the front wall, sat down hard. "I bought us some time."

"Oh good." He joined her, sat heavily too. "Till what?"

"Till we can get the griffin chick to a unicorn."

She decided not to mention the food bit.

17

MORNING FLIGHT

"You awake?"

It had been full night when they'd finally come out of the cave. They'd heard running water nearby. A cascade fed a mountain pool and they'd fetched some in their water bottles, enough to wash the gash in the chick's side. It had cleared the stench, a little. Huy had sprayed on antiseptic from his pack and then used moss from the poolside to patch the wound, since he didn't have a long enough bandage to wrap around the huge body.

When they emerged into darkness, Mama griffin was still gone. But they quickly decided that they weren't going to try and escape. "Climbing's hard enough in daylight," Huy said. "And I've had enough of falling off mountains." So they sat and made a moonlit feast from fresh water and a couple of power bars. Elayne was embarrassed by the sounds her stomach began to make, but as it soon became a chorus of two, they both settled back and ignored them.

"Ever study Latin?" Huy asked out of nowhere.

"Never studied it. Speak it fluently." Elayne smiled. "Why?"

"Their names. Tisiphone and Alecto. Two of the Roman Furies."

"What did they do?"

"Oh, vengeance mainly." Huy leaned back, put his hands behind his head. Elayne had to admire his powers of recovery. The only sign of his recent trauma was a slight tick in the corner of his left eye. "Tisiphone was also known as 'the Avenger of Blood' and Alecto was 'the Implacable.' Though I think Alecto was also a girl, not—" He waved toward the cave where the chick slept. "Still, hardly Dopey and Sneezy, are they? I mean, if unicorns are their mortal enemies, and vice versa, and they attack each other on sight, how will you get them to make peace?"

As they'd tended the chick, she'd told him her plan. Such as it was. It had sounded weak then. Now, on a rumbling stomach? "I have no idea."

"Oh, good."

"I mean . . ." She sucked in air. "I'll just, uh, improvise?"

"Fabulous." He shook his head, then yawned. "Sleep," he declared. She caught his yawn. "You think you can?"

"Watch me." He lay back, pulled his clothes tight around him. Shivered. "Jeez, it's cold," he said.

She was better off in her down jacket. "Body warmth?"

"Huh?"

"I had a teacher, old guy. Had been a soldier. Said he and his buddies used to huddle in foxholes and share body warmth."

"Sounds cozy."

"So, you want to? This ski coat's huge."

He'd turned his back. Now he craned his head around. "Um, sure."

Elayne unzipped the coat, took it off, went and curled in behind him, draping it over them both. "Don't get any ideas now," he murmured.

"I know, I know," she said, "you're gay."

"Canadian," he replied. "We're not forward like you Americans. Never do more than cuddle on a first date, eh."

She laughed, snuggled in tighter. Soon his breath came steadily. She thought it would take a while to fall asleep, as the past few days' events rampaged through her mind. Mostly she found herself thinking about her father. Where was he? Would Leo keep his promise and look for him? "Dad," she whispered softly, half prayer, half message out into the night.

She curled over, cuddling into Huy's back. With her father in her head, she didn't think she'd ever get to sleep.

She was wrong.

It was a heavy sleep, though dream-tossed. All types of beast, normal and fabulous, clashed in her mind. Unicorns, of course. Her father, demanding more Chicken Marengo. A two-headed snake, its image waking her for a microsecond as she wondered where the hell Amphisbaena had got to. Finally, for longer, the griffin.

She went from dream to reality. Opened her eyes—and flinched. For perched on a rock not far away, staring to the northwest, was Tisiphone.

She slipped from the warmth of shared down into a frozen dawn, the rocks nearby glistening with frost. Huy mumbled something and pulled the coat tighter. Though it was growing light, there was no heat in the early sun and she shivered hard as she climbed up to the griffin's perch. The beast did not turn to look at her, acknowledging her presence only with a slight ruffling of her feathered crest.

She looked where the eagle's eyes did. It was different this side of the mountains. Behind, though the foothills were rockier, Goloth was mainly a country of thick forests and vast grasslands. Ahead, it was bleaker, fewer trees and those smaller, she could tell even from that height. There were meadows of green in places but there were far larger swathes that appeared almost purple—gorse, she thought, and heather. Rivers big and small bisected the land, flowing out of the mountains below her—and from the mountains she saw in the distance. Many fed into a huge lake that glimmered halfway between both ranges.

"Do you see them?"

The rumble came low and sudden from the feathered throat. She turned, looked up. The eagle head had not turned. "Who?" Elayne said.

"Unicorns."

The word was weighted with disgust. But she turned, excitedly. Scanned. Saw nothing white against the purples and greens though she stared till her eyes ached. "Where are they?" she asked.

"Everywhere. They come, they go. They hide. Seeking for me as I seek for them."

Again, Elayne felt the fury behind the words. Well, the griffin was named for a Fury after all. "Why . . . why do you hate each other so?"

"Why?" At last the head turned to her, one huge black eye fixing on her. "Because we always have."

"That's not why, that's . . ." She shrugged, thought of all the places back on Earth where people would have answered the same. "Madness."

"Madness?" The head dipped closer on the echo, the eye narrowing. "What know you of it? A girl who has lived a score of years? What know you of the thousands of years of fighting begun in a time lost even to a griffin's memory?"

"But if the cause of it is lost, why not just . . . stop?"

"The cause is never lost. For it is revived each time we meet. When griffin kills unicorn. When unicorn kills griffin. Each death an opportunity—for vengeance."

She spread her wings wide on the word, claws shooting out from all four limbs, eagle and lion. Then she settled a little, her eyes turning back to the search, her voice dropping lower. "You asked why hatred began. It is like asking why light first came to the world. All that matters is that it *is*. That it has always driven us. That when each chose to help man, as he struggled from the swamps, each chose the other's enemies to help." The wings rose again. "In the old kingdom of Egypt, we led the Pharaoh's armies in blood over the king of Ethiopia astride his unicorn. When Alexander rode the horned Bucephalus from Greece, we perched on Darius's chariot and tried to hold him back. And when a unicorn bore Arthur of the Britons into the last battle of Albion, a griffin was there to hurl him from his mount and rend both with her claws." She raised her eyes into the sky, as if seeking something. "When we left behind the world of man and crossed to Goloth, the land of the fabulous beast, when there were no heroes to fight our battles through, at least we still had each other."

Elayne stared up at the great bird head. It had been a couple of years, but she was certain that Moonspill had spoken, not of looking for a fight but of avoiding the griffin whenever possible. Yet if they did run into each other—well, no doubt instinct and millennia of hate would kick in. "And yet," she said, chewing at her lower lip, wondering how she could phrase it without setting the beast off again, "you're willing to try what I've suggested?"

Tisiphone did not reply for so long that Elayne thought her question, and she, had been dismissed. She'd heard Huy stirring, was about to turn and join him, when the rumble finally came. "My hate has lasted two hundred years. The whole of my life. My love has lasted for only five. Five since my chick was born, long after I gave up believing that I would ever have one." A great sigh shook the body, eagle and lion. "So I will try to do the impossible. For Alecto. For love."

"And I will help," Elayne said.

She left Tisiphone to her staring. Huy wasn't where she'd left him but he appeared soon, out of the cave, moving his body like someone who'd spent the night on a rock bed—which he had. "Learn anything?" he asked, tipping his head in the direction of the griffin.

"Only that this isn't going to be easy." She shivered, looked past him. "How's the patient?"

He took the down jacket off his shoulders, put it around hers. "Not good. The stink's back, doubled." He sighed. "I don't think we have a lot of time."

"Then we better get going." Elayne turned, called, "We should leave."

Tisiphone stood straight up on her rear legs, front ones thrust out, talons extended. "Then let us do so. For if you want a unicorn, I have found you one."

Elayne really, really didn't like the way she said it.

"How's this going to work?" Huy jerked his thumb back. "Alecto can hardly move. That dislocated limb may be in, but it's still sore as hell. And the wound—"

He was interrupted—and answered—in the same breath, a griffin's breath. Tisiphone lifted her beak to the sky and let out that eagle-ish, high-pitched caw. It was echoed, if weakly, from the cave. Sounds of scrabbling, mixed with low groans, came. They looked—and the next moment saw first the feathered crest, then the head, then the whole body of the younger beast appear on the top of the wall. He perched there a moment then half flapped, half fell to the ground below it.

His mother was airborne and hovering above her child in a moment. Slowly she lowered, like some feathered helicopter, till all four legs were reaching into and around her son's lion body. "Come! Climb on me," she cried.

"Come on," Elayne said, strapping on her backpack. "Our flight's leaving."

Huy did not move. "You are kidding me," he said. "We're going to fly? On that?"

"On her," Elayne corrected. "Yes. Unless you want to climb down? Not your strength, I recall."

"Jeez! A guy has one small weakness . . ." He buttoned his coat tight around him, walked with her to the wall, climbed it. Together they looked down at the fur and feather back. "Seat belts?" he asked, his voice juddery.

"You cling to the mane. You're stronger than me."

"And you'll be clinging to?"

"You."

"I was afraid you'd say that," Huy moaned, then jumped. He landed, straddled the beast, grabbed tufts of mane and twisted his hands tightly into them.

Elayne hesitated. She looked beyond Tisiphone, over the cliff edge. She was about to fly off a mountain on a griffin. Suddenly the bike lanes of New York seemed a super safe place to be. Sighing, she launched herself.

She thumped onto the back, scrabbled up to Huy. She'd scarcely had time to throw her arms around him when the beast took off. In three heartbeats—and their hearts were pounding—Tisiphone sailed over the edge of the world.

"Oh. Oh. Oh. Oh. Oh!"

Their cries were consumed in accelerating wind. Gusts buffeted them, wrenching Tisiphone this way and that. Elayne caught glimpses of the valley below, flashes of purpling gorse, sunlight on still water. At one point the griffin twisted right and both of them slewed; she felt gravity tug, screamed. Huy was silent, just gripped harder with hands, with thighs. Then Tisiphone righted and Elayne pressed her face into Huy's back and wailed.

They jerked. The great wings were spread above her, buffeting the air, trying to slow their descent. But they'd been falling too swiftly, or the load was too heavy. The wings folded, they dropped again even quicker, all the passengers screaming now, two humans and one chick. Tisiphone was weaving, trying to streamline wings that full out had failed to slow them. They levelled, but only a little. They were still shooting down, an arrow now perhaps, not a stone, but the trees that had seemed tiny were getting bigger and bigger real fast.

And then they were among them. Tisiphone dodged the limbs thrust out, scraping their tips. Then she failed to see one, her wing tip clipped a branch, releasing a pungent burst of pine.

Screaming, the griffin plunged toward the ground.

Unicorn

18

TEMPEST

The unicorn stood beneath a pine tree, close to the great rock wall, scenting the air. Searching it for disturbance, for something different. For anything that might yield even a breath of adventure.

There! A trace of fresh blood. He sniffed deeper. Yes! Beyond the iron tang was the stench of a manticore. Its triple row of jaws were hard to keep clean. Meat from the sheep it slaughtered rotted in gaps between its teeth. A sorry beast, he always felt. The breed missed the flavour of human flesh, it was said, and on occasion one would go mad dreaming of it and have to be . . . dealt with. It was one of the very few chances when his kind got to fight, for they never could with each other. Peace, contemptible peace ruled the Valley of the Unicorn. Yet the manticore, despite its jaws and its ball tail that could shoot poisonous darts, was not a worthy opponent. A few flicks of the horn, a lunge—finished in moments. Or so he'd been told. It had been nine years since it had been necessary to kill one. Half his own life.

He tossed his head, dismissing the scent, sniffing for something other. But what reek could disturb the tranquility of their valley's dawn? *Tranquil.* Another base word. Yet it was what their home was. Plenty of food, grasses and heathers that could easily be dug up even through the snows that were coming soon. Then, in the spring, the Feast of the Pine Tips, the new growth nibbled in delight. How old unicorns like his father loved that! Gathered in the groves to eat and tell their stories of all the heroic deeds they'd done in their youth, the battles they'd fought— against beasts, sometimes on behalf of man. As a colt he'd loved the tales; they'd fuelled his dreams. Now that he was no longer young, though not yet full grown, they disgusted him. He would come no more to listen, running to the mountains instead. It took less than a day to reach his world's limits, in any direction. There, he would wait out the feasting alone.

Alone! He dragged one front hoof across the frosted ground before him, again and again, gouging tracks. His mother had told him that unicorns were meant to be solitary, only coming together for short bursts. In the world of man they'd inhabited for millennia, even in the country called Goloth across the southern mountains, there'd been enough room for that to be true. But the very last of them had crossed over two years before to escape the sorrows of that land, joining the rest of unicorns who had been forced to live in the confines of this valley for decades. In company. Some could not stand it. Every few years one went mad. They did not have to be dealt with like a manticore, though. The mad ones would take themselves off to Chanticleer Rock, where the cockatrice—another exile—dwelt. And when it raised its cockerel's head from its serpent's body and crowed the dawn, the sorrowing unicorn would gallop to the crag's summit—and jump.

He looked down. His gouging had shaped a sort of spire in the earth and ice. Chanticleer Rock. He'd thought of it much lately. Of seeking oblivion there. A chance to be alone . . . forever.

He looked up. Through the pine grove he could see the huge rock face. There was a secret tunnel through it somewhere and he had sought and sought it, to no avail. Some of the older ones knew but they would not tell the younger. They knew what might happen. Yet it was not its lure that had brought him there this day. These southern mountains promised something else, on rare occasions.

The griffin. Sometimes one would descend to snatch up the goats and sheep that abounded in the land and provided food for fabulous beasts—other than the unicorn. It was said griffins only came at night, when their eagle eyes gave them too great an advantage over their old enemy. But one had come a few of the sun's circles before and been chased off. Before this very stand of pines. So he had returned each and every day since hoping to meet it. To challenge it. To fight, perhaps to die—but in the dying to at least become part of the great story of unicorns. To have his story told at feasts. Not to pass his whole life in *peace*. In *tranquility*. In this Valley of the Unicorn.

Suddenly, sounds! Distant cries, terror in them. Then another keen sense took over: scent. More than one, and creatures he'd never scented before. Something else too. Something foul, worse, far worse than rotting flesh in a manticore's jaw. Somewhere close, getting closer, a wound oozed.

Then all senses were lost to one. Sight!

He saw it, the griffin plunging between the trees in the very next grove. Saw the eagle head, the lion body, the claws . . . but clutched in those was another huge something that shaped before his eyes into a second griffin. While on the flying beast's back, there was some kind of growth.

Two! He broke straight into a gallop. Two of the most ancient enemy to kill, or die trying. Would that not be enough for legend?

As he charged across the grassland, Tempest the unicorn parted his lips in an almost human smile.

———

Tisiphone's screech was only the loudest. Everyone was screaming—Elayne, Huy, even Alecto, roused from his torpor by the mad velocity of their descent.

When the griffin's wing hit the pine branch, when glide became a flapping tumble in moments, Elayne knew they were going to crash, crash hard. But the sudden scent of pine turned her; she saw branches each side. "Jump!" she yelled.

His knuckles were white with his grip on the mane. "Are you insane?"

"Now!" she shouted, as the griffin swung into a denser tangle of branches, breaking some, bouncing off others. Her arms were still wrapped around Huy and she used her weight, and her feet in the lion side, to launch herself and him.

"Ahh!" they both cried, then both were being stabbed by pine needles, slapped by smaller branches, clutching at larger ones, even as they fell. Until Elayne caught one, lost it but halted her tumble long enough to grab and hold the next, thicker one. Just below her, Huy did the same. They both flung legs around and clung there, quaking.

A loud bang turned her. A little farther on Tisiphone, freed from their extra weight perhaps, had managed to turn out of the rough main avenue filled with huge trees into a small one. The pine halted her, but halted her in a dead stop—though as Elayne watched she saw the mother manage to lay her injured son gently down the moment before she fell to the ground herself.

After all the noise, the sudden silence was almost shocking. Then some snapped branches that had been hanging dropped, birds started to call, and she was aware of breaths—her own, the two griffins', Huy's. "Are . . . you . . . OK?" she puffed.

"N-no," he replied. "And I promise you this: I am never going to fly again."

Swinging herself up onto the top of the branch, she saw that she was about twelve feet up—too high to risk a drop and perhaps a sprained ankle. "Let's crawl along to the tr—"

She'd got that far when Huy dropped, landing like a cat, legs bent. "Hallelujah," he cried, kneeling to kiss the forest floor. "Earth!"

She'd just reached the trunk, was looking down it for hand and toeholds, when she heard a sound. A new one in the forest that day but not new to her at all. A roar. The roar of an angry unicorn.

Moonspill! She thought the name hard, sending it out. Nothing came in reply—except another roar, louder, closer. But now she heard something else, coming every few seconds and she recognized that too because she'd heard it often enough—the takeoff and landing of four hooves as a unicorn galloped to the attack.

And then she saw him, weaving through trees. Not Moonspill, not as big—but still a stallion and not losing anything in speed by his swerves, building up rather as he made directly for Tisiphone, only now struggling onto her paws. "No!" Elayne cried and scrambled downwards, ignoring most holds, sliding, grazing herself all over.

She didn't care. She had to get to the fabulous beasts before they killed each other.

She ran past Huy, frozen to the spot by the sight of his first unicorn. But her run was more stumble, her legs still weak from fear. She tripped on some fallen stick, landed hard, looked up—to see the great white beast arrive, gouging the earth as he halted his charge suddenly. Then he was up on his rear hooves, front ones flailing out, screaming his challenge. She didn't know if the two creatures could understand each other. Yet even if only she heard the words, there could be little doubt as to meaning.

"I am Tempest," the unicorn cried, "and I am going to kill you both."

The griffin was shaking her head as if trying to clear it. Blood dripped from her left nostril, no doubt from where she'd struck the trees. Still, she took a few paces, placed herself before her chick, then rose up on her rear legs too, spread her wings wide and uttered her own fierce cry. "And you will die as you try!"

Elayne was up on her feet again, moving forward, gaining speed. She didn't know if she would make it in time. But she knew this: a griffin that could not fly had lost its advantage. And the branches on every side prevented Tisiphone from taking off. If Elayne did not do something, a unicorn's horn was about to plunge deep into that lion heart.

Though his legs still beat the air, Tempest hesitated, his head weaving, seeking a spot to thrust past the griffin's extended talons. It bought her the moment she needed. Stooping she snatched up a large pine cone, heavy with frozen dew, and hurled it hard into the unicorn's flank.

He shuddered, his front legs plunged down, and he half turned, one huge eye fixing on Elayne. She had not stopped running, and saw that the griffin was tensing for a leap, to take advantage of the distraction. "No, Tisiphone! Alecto! Alecto will die."

Another hesitation. Elayne covered the last ten yards—and ran between them. "Stop!" she shouted, one hand thrust at each. Then some phrase she'd heard in some old movie leapt into her head and she blurted it. "We come in peace!"

Peace? The word came back, in the way it always used to, from a unicorn's mind. *There can be no peace between us. One must die.*

"No," she said, stepping up to the great white chest, pushing a hand into it, shoving—though she might as well have tried to shove over an oak. "It doesn't have to be that way."

"It does, maid." The voice did not come in her head but deep from within the throat of the griffin. "It was a foolish hope. Stand aside."

"To watch one of you die? And Alecto? No way. We—"

Maid? The word that interrupted her was in her head—though it came as if on a shout. *Why does my enemy call you that?*

She put her hands over her ears as if to protect them. "Because I am. Because—"

No! This roar was in her head *and* in Tempest's throat. *There was only ever one maid. She left, never to return.* The unicorn rose on his hind legs again. Again the front hooves flailed, so close above her head. *Now move away and this will end. Fight me!*

The rumble came from behind her, the challenge answered, as Tisiphone's wings spread again.

"Please don't do this," she cried, hands clutching her head. Hands that were pulled away by another.

"Come on," Huy said, tugging her into the shelter of a tree. "I may not speak the language but I recognize a rumble when I see one. You'll just get caught in the crossfire."

"No, no," she moaned, unable to look. "Please, no!"

And then she felt it—the tremor on the earth as if it quaked. And then she heard them—hoof-falls, many more than one, coming fast. And then she saw them, so many it was like a white mist flooding through the trees.

With a roar like a typhoon, twenty unicorns charged into the forest—and leading the charge was one she knew so well.

Moonspill.

19

REUNION

How often had she dreamed of him, her unicorn? Awake or asleep he was always but a thought away. A fantasy had become real in her life—and now her real life often appeared a fantasy, and a slightly shabby one at that.

For how could anything, anyone, anywhere ever compete with Moonspill? The fabulous beast who'd summoned her through the medieval tapestries, through a portal between worlds that her ancestor the weaver had woven into it. Who she'd ridden—first in terror, eventually in joy—not only through Goloth to the saving of his mate, Heartsease, from the tyrant king, but also through the streets of Manhattan to the saving of her dad's life. That healing, spiralling horn had taken all the cancer from his blood. But even without that gift of life, the love she felt for Moonspill, the love she knew he felt in return? He had been inside her head, caressing her mind with a voice like flowing silk, and there was a space where it had flowed, where he was part of her, that had never been filled since, that could never be filled away from him.

Though it was full now as she took him in again—his huge, muscled body, like molten white marble, far larger than that of any horse. His thick mane and tail and the little beard at his chin. His cloven hooves. It had taken her some time to remember that he was a "monster" in the old sense. Like all fabulous beasts, he was made up of different animal parts. Horse and goat and something entirely unique.

There was something different about him now, though she couldn't tell what straight away—and didn't have the chance for further study. She hoped as soon as she saw him that he would see her too, come to her, rejoice with her. *Moonspill!* She called, but only in her mind, to his, as they had always talked. But she got no reply—for Moonspill's mind was occupied.

"What happens here?" he called, in the voice of his kind. "We heard the wail of the—"

And then he'd rounded Tempest and was able to see who was there—Tisiphone, talons bared, razor beak thrust forward and split in another fierce cry.

Moonspill halted suddenly, then moved sideways in a manner almost horse-like. "What is this?" he cried, as the other unicorns gathered, forming into a shifting, restless semicircle. The eagle head darted this way and that, hissing at them all.

"It is a griffin and her chick. Mine! I found them." Tempest tossed his head up and down. "And I will have the killing of them."

"Did they attack you?"

"They were going to. They flew down into our land." He ceased tossing his head, stared straight into the bigger unicorn's eyes. "So they are mine to fight. To prove myself upon."

Moonspill moved a step nearer. "You have misunderstood our stories, Tempest. We do not fight the griffin to prove ourselves. We fight only if we have no choice."

The younger beast threw his head into the air. "You have fought them. I have heard you boast of it." Tempest looked at the surrounding unicorns—many, Elayne saw, as young as he. "What is it, Moonspill? Haven't you enough legends to your name? Don't want to share glory with anyone else?"

Moonspill took a step in, another, only halting when his horn passed the other's, nearly touching it. His reply came softly. "You would challenge me?"

The younger beast froze. His tail stopped swishing; he ceased tearing at the earth with his hooves. Only his eyes moved again around the circle of unicorns, who simply stared back. "I . . ." he began, in a softer tone, "I only wish—"

"No," interrupted Moonspill, as softly. "I thought not. Now go. There will be no killing here unless I decide there is to be. Go!"

This last was louder. For a moment Tempest stood his ground, staring. Then without another word he took off, straight into a gallop, straight through the other unicorns who parted just enough to let him by.

His hoof-falls faded. Elayne was watching closely, unable to take her eyes off *her* unicorn. So she saw the great shudder that ran the length of his body from shoulder to tail. Saw the head droop now as if the horn was suddenly more weight than he could bear. Saw his great eyelashes fall like a veil over his eyes.

Moonspill, she called again, stepping away from the tree.

The eyelashes shot open, his head jerked. He stared at her. She'd always thought his eyes contained universes. Now, though they were a little misted, they filled with just one thing. *Maid?* he replied, and there was all the wonder of the world in the word.

She ran to him, pressed herself into him. Tears flowed into that warm, white flank. Part of it was the reunion, that touch, that connection. Mostly it was simply relief: for the first time since she'd crossed back into the world of fabulous beasts, she felt completely, utterly safe.

How is this possible? came that voice, caressing her mind. *Why have you returned?*

The amphisbaena came for me. They told me—

A loud hiss broke their minds apart. Both turned.

Tisiphone was on her rear legs again, wings spread, moving this way and that, trying to keep back some younger unicorns who'd pushed closer, horns lowered to nudge at the bundle of matted fur and feathers at her feet—Alecto, his breathing loud now, shallow, erratic.

"Hey!" Elayne yelled. "Back off. The griffin's with me."

They did not retreat. Not surprising perhaps as she realized she'd shouted in English. But then Moonspill stepped forward too. "Move away," he called. He was obeyed, if reluctantly. His voice came again, to her alone. *Why did you bring our oldest enemy to our valley, Alice-Elayne?*

"They don't have to be your—" She cut herself off. This was no time to be trying to heal a ten-thousand-year-old war. Not when she thought that each of Alecto's tortured breaths could be his last. "The young one is sick. Dying. I promised you would help."

You . . . promised?

Of course! She needn't say any of this aloud. *I was coming to seek you. The griffin attacked, could have killed me. Didn't, because I said you'd help her. And also because . . .* She hesitated, listened again. *Because Alecto's just a child. And Tisiphone is just a mother. Please. Please help them.*

Silence. Except in those eyes, those blue-black universes. There, those ten thousand years of enmity shouted. She knew his story, knew he was a warrior, had fought for and against man, fought other beasts, triumphed. It was clear in his eyes, that legacy. Yet, even as she watched, something shifted in them.

I will consider. And on the thought words he turned again toward the griffins.

The other unicorns cleared farther back, allowing him passage—though Tisiphone rose yet higher, her voice a cross between caw and growl. Elayne caught up, laid her hand on Moonspill's shoulder. "He will help," she said to the griffin. In griffin.

One blue-eye fixed on her. *You can speak to her? Ah, of course—the gift of tongues.* Then he turned, spoke himself. "Tisiphone? I know of you. You fought my dam, Salvia, beneath the walls of besieged Orleans."

"And nearly died that day," came the reply. "I am she. So you are Moonspill." The rest came on a hiss. "I would like to fight you and kill you, since I failed to kill your dam."

"Perhaps we will fight, one day. Yet maybe not this day for—" His eyes left the mother, went to the child. "Your child is sick."

Tisiphone, all bristled feather and raised fur, slumped a little. "Aye," was all she said.

"May I?" Moonspill stepped closer, slowly lowered his head, till his horn stretched above the chick. He held it there, closed his eyes, sniffed deep again and again. Then he opened his eyes, peered long before he raised his horn again and looked at Tisiphone. "He is very sick."

"Can you—?" Tisiphone bit back the question, as if she could neither bear to ask a favour—nor hear the answer.

"I—" Moonspill stared long and Elayne watched him closely, breath held. And then she saw him slump a little too—just as he had after Tempest refused his challenge. "I cannot."

"What? No!" Elayne stepped forward, stunned. "But you have to. I promised."

His voice came for her alone again. *The chick is too close to death.*

So was my father!

But I was stronger then. I . . . I do not have that power now.

And then she saw it. Saw the difference she'd noted from the beginning and failed to understand. Clear now in the whiteness of what had been a coffee-coloured mane. In the film of his eyes. In the slump of his shoulders.

In just two years, Moonspill had gotten old.

There was no time to dwell on the shock. Because Tisiphone had risen up once more to her full height, wings spread as far as the trees allowed, beak parted in a cry of fury. "You *will* not, is the truth!" she screamed. "So come then! I cannot take so many. But I will mark many of my enemy with my talons 'ere I die. Some unicorn mothers will weep this day along with me!"

The circle had spread. Now it tightened again, as rumbles came from twenty throats, as twenty horns lowered. Moonspill had backed up, and now used his great body to move Elayne aside. "No!" She pleaded, slapping his flank. "Don't do this."

And then a voice came. A new one, a single word.

"Wait."

It came from behind the circle, which shifted, parted enough to admit the newcomer. Who Elayne recognized immediately. "Heartsease," she cried.

Moonspill's mate moved through the others, came and stood beside him. She was smaller—younger too, Elayne remembered, and whereas his body was still quite muscled, hers was more delicately strong. She touched her horn briefly against his, then looked up at Tisiphone, towering high. "Perhaps no mothers need weep this day, griffin." She tipped her head to Alecto. "May I seek?"

Tisiphone pulsed with anger, with defiance, but then slowly lowered her wings. "Seek," she rumbled.

As her mate had done, so did Heartsease. Bent, closed her eyes, sniffed. But she also passed her horn back and forth across the chick's body, held it long over the wound, from which the stench rose fouler than ever.

Her eyes came open. "I think . . . I think I can do this." She looked at Tisiphone. "But he is so weak, the cure might kill him. Will you believe, one mother to another, that I will try my best?"

This rumble was a while in coming, the answer simple. "Yes."

"There will be pain. He is far gone indeed. But will you trust that the cries he makes are the cries necessary for his healing, if he can be healed?"

Again the delay before the single word. "Yes."

"So." Heartsease looked about her. "Clear back, all. Only the mothers stay."

She was obeyed—except by Moonspill. *My love?* he called, in her head, in Elayne's too. She could feel his concern.

You also, came Heartsease's reply.

He hesitated, then backed away. Elayne followed, laid her hand again on his flank. Now they could only watch.

"Hold him," Heartsease said, and Tisiphone obeyed, unfolding her chick's scrunched body and placing claw to claw, paw to paw.

She began with a low call, almost a song, a run of notes, up and down. Alecto half rose; his eyes shooting wide; a moan of pain escaping his beak. But that was nothing to what came as the unicorn ran her horn back and forth across the lion flank, getting lower, lower as Alecto's screams got louder, louder. His whole body shooting up; his mother thrusting down with full force to hold him. She was moaning too; their three voices like some song of terrible disharmony, until Heartsease at last dipped her horn—and thrust its tip into the oozing wound.

The screeches that came now, from all three but mainly from Alecto, made all the other unicorns back away, snorting, tossing their heads. Moonspill's head lowered and he shook it as if in pain himself.

Elayne *was* in pain, clamping hands over ears in a vain attempt to shut it all out. Tisiphone's cry was an echo of her son's, and though she pushed him down still, her body rose high. For one terrible moment, Elayne thought that the griffin was going to plunge her beak deep into the tormenting unicorn's side. Perhaps Moonspill thought so too, for he took a step closer. But when her chick collapsed with a last great groan, she slumped too; while Heartsease, withdrawing her horn, staggered back and tumbled to the ground, falling hard onto her left flank.

After the terrible noise, a terrible silence. Elayne staggered a pace forward, another, ears unblocked now, desperately listening. But she couldn't hear the griffin chick breathing. Then Tisiphone asked the question, bending as she did, terror in her voice. "Does he live?"

The silence extended from the question—but only for a moment more. Because an answer came. Not in words—in a griffin chick's huge inhalation.

"He lives," said Heartsease, rolling up. "And I think he will."

Everyone else exhaled—every fabulous beast and human. As Moonspill went and helped his mate to rise, Elayne moved over to the griffins. Alecto's eyes were open now and she could see quite clearly what she hadn't before—the light of life, not the flicker of impending death. "Maid," he whispered, and it was a whisper of exhaustion but not of dying. "Thank you. You kept your promise. I will repay that debt one day."

"Oh, it was nothing." She giggled. "But don't thank me, thank—" She turned.

Heartsease was on her feet again, so folded into Moonspill they looked like one twin-headed unicorn, not two. Now she stepped away from him and looked at Tisiphone. Black eyes met blue—then both mothers simply dipped their heads.

After another moment, Tisiphone raised hers, lifting her beak to the sky, letting forth another great cry—this one filled with joy. Then, pressing her limbs around her child, lifting him, she took five paces forward till she was clear of the trees. Then she unfurled her wings and the next moment bore him up, weaving along the avenue of pine, her flight graceful now, easy. Unburdened. She came to a clearing and soared up into the open sky. Her cries gradually faded. Until they were gone.

Another sound came. His voice. "Come, maid."

She'd taken five steps before she remembered. "Huy!" she cried, turning.

"Here." He came to her. His eyes sparkled though his voice was calm. "On balance, and despite stiff competition, the winner of best line was . . ." He struck a pose. "'Hey! The griffin's with me.'"

His imitation of her was near perfect. They both laughed until Moonspill stepped closer with a question that needed neither thought nor speech. "Uh, this is my friend," she said, in English so Huy would understand too, "Huy."

"We what?" came Moonspill's reply in the same tongue.

"Oh, please," Huy groaned. "Not here as well."

Then they both laughed some more, quite a lot more, clinging to each other, while unicorns watched and wondered.

20

TRUTHS AND FISHES

The path up the back of Chanticleer Rock was steep—but nothing to a furious unicorn. As he climbed, Tempest sent out words, in both thought and calling. For this was the domain of the cockatrice, who some called the basilisk. Its special gift was to kill with its stare, striking the beholder dead with a glance. So he summoned them forth from their caves—for he would look in one's eyes. It would save him the long climb to the peak, the shorter fall down.

Yet though he heard stirrings as he passed the entrances, no beast ventured forth to crow with its cockerel beak, to strike from its serpent's tail, to smite him with a glance. Though this was their land, they lived there because the unicorn, shepherd of all fabulous beasts, had given it to them when they all crossed over from Goloth. The valley was too small for each creature to fight as they often had before. All were forced to an uneasy peace. And the unicorn could enforce the peace because it alone of all fabulous beasts had ways to defeat the basilisk stare.

Unless I choose to court it, Tempest thought. "Come forth, cowards," he called. "Fight me!"

He got no reply but a slither, and a hiss.

His hooves ate the slope. Soon, too soon, he was at the crest. Topping it, he swayed—for the drop was sudden, steep, certain. Easeful death lured him.

He stepped. Shale tumbled, and instinct made him retreat. He peered out over the land, its patchwork of forest and plain, the rivers and streams that bisected it. The sun glistened on the great lake that was his kind's main home—and on the mountains that closed off the far horizon, their peaks already bright with the first snows. Winter was coming, an even duller time than autumn.

He stepped through a gap between rocks like a stone doorway and out onto a rough platform. Far, far below and to the distant horizon was the ocean. He lowered his horn to the edge, pried up a slab of granite, sent it tumbling over. He could not see but heard it, smashing, shattering, breaking apart on the jagged crags below.

My fate is as the rock's, Tempest thought. My escape from this coward life. And thinking it, he took a deep breath.

It did not take long to reach the great lake. All the unicorns were excited, tossing their heads as they ran, abuzz with what had occurred, and galloped the entire way. Elayne, atop her Moonspill, rode as she'd done the last time he'd carried her—in total ease, arms flung back, eyes wide to the blue sky and the land that flowed past her. Beside her, Huy, on a unicorn nearly as big as hers, had looked terrified at first. But when she'd called across, needing to shout loudly because of the speed of the wind, that a unicorn would never let him fall, and when his unicorn proved it by swerving left and right only for the fun of jumping huge rocks, she saw him start to relax, his knuckles not so white in the light brown mane. Saw him start to enjoy it.

The unicorns made straight for the water, bending their long necks to drink. *Is the water OK for us too?* she asked.

The reply came on what she'd learned to recognize as one of Moonspill's rare laughs. *Do you not remember that one of our gifts is to make foul water sweet? You think we would ourselves drink anything that was not of the purest?*

"Fair enough," she said aloud, and turned to Huy, adding, "the water's good."

They dismounted, went to a rocky lip, dipped their water bottles. "Columbia U" read the logos on the side. Long way from here, she thought, looking across the wide water to the mountains beyond.

"Water is good," Huy said, capping his bottle as he rose, "but it just reminds me how hungry I am."

Moonspill, she thought. *Have you any food? Uh, human food?*

We eat grasses. Heather. Leaves. Buds.

Yeah. Not so good for us.

He lifted his head, stared ahead. *There are fish in the lake,* he thought to her, then turned as, all along the shore the unicorns lifted their heads as one, turned and cantered away. They headed for nearby woods, and the trees soon swallowed them. When the last had disappeared, Moonspill turned to follow.

"What kind of fish?" she called after. But he was gone, with no reply.

"Fish?" Huy echoed. "Man, I would kill for some sashimi. But how could we—?"

He broke off—Elayne was delving into her backpack. "Ta-dah!" she said, pulling out a telescoped graphite rod, line and hook.

The expression on his face made her burst out laughing. "What?"

"Do you have everything in that bag?"

"Everything that I thought I might need. Been here before right? And nearly starved." She looked at the rod. "Trouble is, I'm not . . . I can't really."

"Stand back." Huy bent and grabbed the equipment from her. "My dad's a fanatic." He quickly snapped it all together, then looked about, his eyes narrowing. "Now, just need to figure out some bait. Not got any worms in there have you? Hey!" he said, suddenly ducking. "See these big flying beetles?"

"See them?" She slapped. "They're trying to eat me."

"Good." He grinned. "You be bait for them, then they'll be bait for us."

She groaned but sat still, holding out bare arms. The creatures that settled looked a little like the deer flies that would persecute her on canoe trips with her dad. Any biting fly loved her—as she now proved again and again to Huy's delight. They slapped, killed, and soon had a little pile. She had to turn away while he mashed, squished, then threaded carapace and wing onto the hook.

"Watch and learn," he said, flicking the rod tip out. The line flew, dropped. It had a small float that he'd adjusted and they watched it bob on the breeze that rippled the surface. Then, after only about a minute it jerked—then disappeared. "Holy!" he cried, "that's a big m—yikes!" He was being pulled about this way, that way, then got his balance, let the line run, reeled it in, let it go again. The fish jumped a few times, flashing silvery scales on a big back. "Got a net?" he cried, as he fought it closer.

"Uh, no!"

"Right. Hold this. Don't let go." She braced herself, he handed her the rod—and then he threw himself into the lake. The water came up to nearly his waist. "Gotcha!" he cried, his hands under the beast's belly. With a mighty heave, he flicked it onto the bank.

It flopped there for a bit, gradually stilling. "Trout," he said. "Or close enough."

"Sashimi?" she asked, pulling out her knife.

He turned bright eyes to her. "Maybe this is the time they're running. And I don't know about you but I am starving."

In the end, six fat trout, each about the length of her forearm, glistened on the grass. Huy gutted one, scaled it, split it along its spine, then cut off pieces of flesh for them to eat. Hunger made them consume one whole side. But when he flipped it to begin on the second, she held up her hand. "I've reached my sashimi limit."

"You full?"

"I could eat more but—how about we cook these?"

"Good idea. And I'm starting to get cold anyway." He shivered. His trousers were soaked from his repeated plungings.

There was plenty of dried heather nearby, and the skeletons of stunted pines. While she got a fire going, he rigged a frame to cook the half-fish. The half filled them, then Huy put bracken on, getting a good smoke going, and raised the other cleaned fish higher above the heat of the fire. "Smoke 'em for later," he said, settling back under the down coat she shared again. Their fronts were toasty but their backs not so much.

"Well, aren't you the mighty woodsman?" she said.

"Every summer with my family, camping in provincial parks. *Every summer!*" He rolled his eyes, threw another stick on, settled again. "And never mind about me. Talk!"

"About what?"

"Your favourite boy band. Duh! About unicorns, of course."

"What do you want to know?"

"Uh." He scratched his chin. "OK, what's with this healing stuff? The griffin and . . . you mentioned your dad?"

She wondered where to start. "OK. So Goloth is the place where all our myths—our human myths—live, yeah?"

"All of them?"

"The ones to do with fabulous beasts anyway. Unicorns, for example. In our world the ancients believed they could heal illness, poisons, that kind of thing. And they could." She shrugged. "Same with the others—griffins, manticores. They all had myths around them and their, um, abilities. They existed in our world for millennia but then basically all but a very few left and came here—which is where they were from in the first place."

"Here?" Huy pointed to the ground. "Goloth?"

She frowned. "You know, I used to think everywhere here was Goloth. But now with the Glanasa, and Leo mentioning other peoples, I think that maybe Goloth is just a country."

"But all this is a parallel world to ours?"

"Um, kinda, I think." She wasn't sure she could handle a discussion on theoretical physics.

Fortunately, Huy was bursting with tangents. "OK, wait. So your dad had cancer and Moonspill cured him."

"Correct."

"So your dad was here too?"

"No. Unicorn made a house call."

His eyes went wide. "Right, I know you told me you were the source of those hoax stories of a unicorn in Manhattan, but I didn't really believe. So they were all true?"

"Uh-huh."

"Amazing! I was always the skeptic, mocking the conspiracy theorists. And now," he grinned widely, raised his arms to the sky, "I'm a believer!"

Elayne smiled. "You certainly seem to be handling it all very well."

"What, you mean apart from screaming like a girl when we fell down that cliff?"

"Higher than any girl I know." She opened her mouth wide. "Ah-ah-hah-ha-ahhhh."

"Shut *up*!" He stuck out his tongue, laughed, then his face changed. "It's not . . . not going to get any easier, is it?" he said softly. "I mean, if it's not crashing on a griffin it will be something else, right?"

"Yes. Yes, I'm afraid it will." She craned back to study him. "Look, Huy, you should go back. This is not your fight. I owe stuff here but you . . ." She slipped out of the jacket so she could take his hand and face him. "If we can just find that damned vanishing snake we can get you home. Safe. Or . . . here's an idea! I could get Moonspill to donate a piece of his horn. You could—"

His grip had been limp in hers—now it tightened, almost to the point of pain. "Uh-uh," he said fiercely. "I'm your bodyguard, remember? Appointed by none other than his majesty. Ex-majesty. Besides . . ." He leaned closer, his stare intense. "I didn't tell you this before but my father—" He broke off, looked away to the mountains. "He tried to settle in Canada. He really tried. But he found it all too, uh, big, I guess." He looked back. "So he waited till I graduated high school and then a week later . . . he just took off."

She squeezed his hand back. "Where did he go?"

Huy shrugged. "We don't know. Probably back to Vietnam. He, uh, he was never much of a talker. Cared but—" He shook his head. "I mean, he was younger than me when they shoved a gun into his hands. He fought and . . . stuff happened though he never said what. So one day I guess he just decided it would be easier on his own."

"I'm so sorry."

"Yup, me too. More for my mom and kid sister, really. Anyway," he gripped her hand again, hard, "I know about missing dads, yeah? And I tell you this: we are going to find yours. Alive and well. Capeesh?"

His stare was a match for his grip. There was no wavering in either and she felt relief cover her like a warm towel. She smiled, so did he. Then he shook her hand once, formally, let go and picked up his fire stick. "En garde," he said, shoving it in. "Didn't we say we were like two of the musketeers? Maybe dishy King Leo is the third, eh?" He poked hard, sending sparks aloft, then added with a grin, "Hasn't got an equally dashing brother stashed somewhere, has he?"

"Not that I know of. But maybe he's . . ." She thought it before she said it, felt some strangeness around the thought, said it anyway, "You know, uh, gay too."

"No, sista," Huy said, settling back, shrugging again into the coat. "Leo has eyes for only one person—and that person is you."

"Get out! He does not!"

"He does too. Trust me."

They fell silent after that, both staring into the flames, despite all the other questions she sensed roiling within him. After a few moments Huy yawned. "I don't know about you but I slept like maybe five minutes last night." An even wider yawn came. "I could so nap. "

"Me too!" She yawned as well. "We could pull up some more of this heather, make a good bed. Build up the fire."

"On it. I'll get the logs, you stuff the mattress."

Huy slipped his trousers back on, dry now, and they busied about. Ten minutes later, they were lying back before a strong blaze. "Ni-night," Huy said, curling onto his side.

Elayne draped her coat over them both, though they almost didn't need it, then lay down too, her back to his. For a while she stared into the moving flames, then up into the bluest of skies. It couldn't have been much past noon. She doubted she'd sleep. She had too much to figure out—especially what to say to Moonspill.

He had to come and help. Not only Goloth. He had to help her find her father. This world was just too big. She and Huy were simply not going to be enough.

In moments, he was softly snoring. She turned and pressed into her friend's back. She was exhausted, but though she tried to sleep, her mind kept flipping between her dad—and what Huy had said about Leo. She didn't want to think about him like that. She'd . . . disliked him for so long. He may have changed after his time in the forest. He certainly seemed to care more. But his total command at the big meeting showed that he wasn't done with leading, not by a long way. Besides, life was too complicated as it was. Complicated—and potentially quite short.

She may not have wanted to think about him. But when her eyes blinked shut at last, she couldn't prevent him entering her dreams. Both as he'd been—the proud, cruel, well-dressed and clean-shaven king—and as he was now, the lean and bearded forest wanderer. He appeared to her in different places, doing different things. She remembered how he'd kissed her in the Castle of Skulls and she hadn't liked it, not at all. But in her dream he kissed her on a street corner in Brooklyn—doubly weird!—and she found she didn't mind it so much.

"Maid," he said. "Come. Awaken and come."

"No, I'm good here," she mumbled.

And then she heard the voice. Not in her dream—but in her head nonetheless.

Maid, awaken.

She sat up. The fire had burned low, twilight had arrived and Moonspill's head was silhouetted against a purpling sky. At his left shoulder, the first star peeped.

His thought was there again. *Come, maid. Ride with me.*

Slipping from under her coat, she tucked it over Huy, who muttered something and snuggled in tighter. Then she stood, Moonspill stooped a little, and she vaulted onto him.

A moment later they were galloping toward the west, to the dimming of the day.

21

PERSUASION

For a while they rode in silent thought, and she let herself enjoy it, this extraordinary rush. Moonspill didn't charge till the passing world blurred as once he would have, didn't take huge rocks in a leap or fly across chasms. But they moved swiftly across the land toward the sunset and the western mountains grew close fast. No matter how often she'd dreamed this, by day and night, no dream came anywhere close to this reality. Two beings, fused as one.

Oh, she thought, *I have missed this.*

As have I.

Soon they were climbing into the foothills. Then, where the slopes sharpened, he slowed, to pick his way through strewn rocks. A rising full moon lit the way in silver. That's . . . moonspill, she thought and spoke.

Where are we going?

I wish to show you something.

The path they climbed was steep and she was forced to grab his mane at last, hold tight. When it got still steeper, the path turned to switchbacks, taking them gradually up the mountain. About halfway to the summit she heard a slithering, then one clear hiss.

She jumped. "What's that?"

Cockatrice.

Yikes! Aren't they the ones who kill with a look?

They will not do so here.

She looked ahead. The path straightened, steepened again, then ended in what looked like sheer rock. But it was an illusion, for when they reached it she saw that there was a gap, between one slab of rock and the next. A sort of doorway.

Moonspill bent. *Go through.*

Elayne dismounted, her legs stiff, then stepped into the wall gap, turned a corner.

"Whoa!"

She had to reach back and hold rock, the drop was just so sheer, falling straight down to a sea sparkling in moonlight. Yet though it was narrow just before her, the ledge widened to her left and she moved down it till she could comfortably let go of the wall and peer.

She'd never seen the sea, or ocean, or whatever this was, in her times in Goloth, though she'd been told of it. The sky above it was cloudless, star-and-moon bright. Though she couldn't see far, there was a sense of immensity, as if the next landfall was a long ways away. Now she was still she could hear it too, the swell, crashing onto rocks far below her. See, farther out, the silvered foam of wave crests surging in. She breathed it, the salt tang, then shivered, wishing she hadn't left her coat with Huy, the cold breeze jabbing through her wool sweater.

It is beautiful.

He'd come as silently as his kind could and stood near her now. *It is,* she replied. *Is that why you brought me here? To show me beauty?*

No. I brought you here to show you safety.

She turned to him. "What do you mean?" she asked aloud.

Now he turned to her. His eyes seemed all black at night, two vast tarns of darkness. During the day it was harder to concentrate on what he said, because she'd get so lost in his gaze. *You stand on the western range. Truly, though, the mountains that surround our valley are one, not several. A great bowl of stone, ramparts that protect us on every side.*

And you are showing me this because . . . ? She paused in her thoughts, then continued, *you could have told me this back at the lake.*

He moved his head up and down, though it wasn't a nod. *Because I wanted you to understand—truly understand—why the unicorns cannot return to the land of men.*

She started. "How did you know that that was what I was here to ask?"

His rare laugh came, the rumble in his throat. *You ask this even as we speak this way.* He craned his neck around. *I am not just in your head, Alice-Elayne. I am also in your heart.*

"Then you should be able to see—" she blurted aloud, then stopped, thought it. *How can you not go back? There is terrible suffering there. There, in a world you love.*

Once loved. Until it became a world where a king wanted to torture me and mine to death.

He's king no more. He's . . . changed. I think. Anyway, he's fighting true evil. She took a deep breath. *An evil that we, you and I, allowed into the world.*

A shiver ran the length of his body. *We did not bring the Glanasa to Goloth.*

So you know of them?

I know of them.

Then you'll know what they do. And if we did not bring them, then by starting that revolution, we took away the power of Goloth to defend itself.

Moonspill looked away, to the water. *You feel responsible?*

Don't you? Anymore? You did once. That's why you stayed there, shepherding the beasts. Because it was you who let the Hunter, Leo's ancestor, into the world, wasn't it?

He tossed his head up and down. She could feel the anger running through him, so joined were they. "Look," she said aloud, reaching a hand to lay on his shoulder, which flinched under her touch. "I know you regret many things. I do too. But maybe . . . maybe this is our chance to put them right. If the unicorns came—"

Why? The single word-thought hung in their minds for a long moment before he continued. *Here, behind our stone ramparts, we are safe.*

For how long? The Glanasa aren't going to stop. When they're done over there, when all are dead or enslaved, they'll come for you here, no matter how big your mountains.

Then we will fight them.

And kill many, no doubt. But all? They'll keep coming and they'll figure out ways to beat you. She thought of the other myths of the unicorn in her world, truths here. *They'll bring mirrors to entrance you. Maidens to tame you. Ropes to bind you. Spears—*

Enough! His thought came hard. *Why are you so certain of this?*

Because . . . because I've seen fanatics back home. Driven by their beliefs in a savage god to murder, slaughter. No matter how many of them you kill they won't stop. News footage horrors from around the world came into her head. She continued. *For the Glanasa have the most savage god of all. They worship the living dragon.*

This word sent more than a shiver down him. Moonspill backed, kicking loose rocks behind him, his tail whipping back and forth. "You know of them too?" she asked.

Yes. He shook, stilled. *They are ancient, far older even than we. They were in your world before us and they left it before we did. By the time the unicorn returned here they had vanished. We thought them extinct.* He turned his face again to the water. *Instead they'd found an island where they could sleep for a thousand years. Until they found a reason to wake up.*

She could sense something in him that she never had before—dread. *Don't you see? All the more reason for the unicorns to go back! Stop the Glanasa before they empty the world of people and the dragon needs more sacrifices. Fight them there before you have to fight them here.*

He turned one eye to her. *You have become fierce, Alice-Elayne.*

Have I? Oh. She looked down, spoke. "I just want to put things right. And there's something else." She took a deep breath. "If you won't come for the people of Goloth, will you come for me?"

What else? I sense a deeper pain in you. Tell me, maid.

My father is here. Somewhere. Lost.

Here? How?

He took the piece of your horn, went through the tapestry. He . . . he thought he was protecting me and now . . . A tear ran down from one eye. *He's in terrible danger. I'm sure of it.* She reached up, laid a hand on the side of his muzzle. *Please help me find him. Please.*

The answer took a while to come—and then was the wrong one. *I cannot.*

"But . . ." Tears flowed fast now. "Why? Why not?"

I am too old. I no longer have the strength.

Too old? Anger came and she wiped the tears away, made her hand into a fist, shook it. *Two years ago you defeated the tyrant, Moonspill! You kicked down the gates of the city! You . . .*

Two years. A breath shuddered through him. *I told you once before that we do not age as other creatures do. For five hundred years I lived strong.*

But when our decline comes, it comes swiftly. My mane is white now. My tail. He shook it. *I have only a few more years.*

"Oh." She laid a hand upon his flank. Her anger vanished and she thought her heart was going to break. Instead, she sucked back the tears. "Then will . . . will you send others? With fifty unicorns I could search wide as well as help the people there. I could—"

No. Alice-Elayne, this is not my decision. We do not have a leader here. All of age have a voice. Today, while you slept, we discussed what I knew you would ask. He turned to her fully now. *We cannot finally decide whether to come or no, whether to risk the very last of us, based only on rumours borne by ravens and gulls. We cannot take your word alone, even if you are the Summoned. So we will send one of our number to see, to hear, to come back and report. Only then will we decide.*

Oh. It wasn't what she'd wanted. The thought of Moonspill helping her had powered her through all that had happened. But a single unicorn? It was a small hope at least. *Who will you send?*

Instead of answering, Moonspill threw back his head and let forth a roar. It wasn't in any words she could understand. But it was a summons nonetheless.

A summons answered immediately. She heard the clatter of shifting shale under hoof. Something was coming fast up the path, heading to the entrance.

And then he was through it, a blur of white, snorting, shaking his head, dipping it up and down so fast that his horn tip struck sparks from the granite. He was moving and it was night but even so she recognized him instantly.

This is the one chosen to accompany you. Moonspill turned. *His name is Tempest.*

"What? No way!"

It is decided.

"But he's psycho! A nut bar!"

These words mean nothing, maid.

"He—" She inhaled deeply, tried to slow her pounding heart. *Look. You saw what he wanted to do to Tisiphone!*

A griffin. Our oldest foe.

But he was—"Auch!" she blurted. "He was totally up for a fight, he—"

"Up for"?

"He—" She stopped, took another huge breath, then another. She needed to be calm. Unicorns were very literal—they didn't do slang or expressions so well. *OK, look. I think he's too young. Too wild. We need a diplomat, not*—She broke off, then thought it again. *We need someone wise. Like you.*

But he is like me. Me as I was at his age, which is less than a score.

Oh great! So you're fobbing me off with a moody teenager?

Moonspill took a step toward her. Behind him Tempest, who had been shaking like a kid who can't control his leg spasms, now ceased his jerks to stare at her.

Moonspill's thoughts came again. *He is young. Wild, yes. We are a wild race too, for all our wisdom. But he only seeks what I sought then— adventure. A chance to prove himself. If he stays here, untested, he will kill another—or he will kill himself.*

"Well, I'm sorry about that," she replied, "but my plan is not to accompany a young unicorn on, what? his 'vision quest'?" She stopped herself, knowing they would have no idea what that was. And then Moonspill spoke again, before she could continue.

But what is your plan, maid?

She considered. It hadn't really gone much past leading the unicorns back to fight the Glanasa and find her dad.

Moonspill could not read her mind when she did not think directly to him—but he must have sensed her doubts. *So. Perhaps you will need his wildness before you find your answer.*

She thought of protesting more, arguing—but then just shook her head. It was no good. Moonspill wasn't a leader as such, a tyrant like Leo had been. This decision had been made by a council of unicorns. It was as good as it was going to get.

She shrugged. *It seems I have no choice.*

Both unicorns jerked their heads up and down as if nodding. Then Moonspill said, *Come then. There is much to do before you leave tomorrow.*

"Tomorrow?" she cried.

With the world as threatened as you say, there is no point in delay.

He moved to the entrance, stopped there, turned to look back at her. *There is something else you should know, maid. About Tempest.*

Ever since her return to Goloth, all she'd wanted was to be with Moonspill, to reunite with him, find her dad from his back, then ride to save the world. Instead he was getting rid of her tomorrow; worse, he'd fobbed her off with a wild kid.

Allergies? Medication? Favourite bedtime story?

Moonspill didn't react, save for a swishing of his tail. *Only this.* The great body shivered. *He is not like me because he is a unicorn. He is like me because he is my son.*

She gasped. Moonspill turned away, went through the rock entrance. But Tempest remained facing her, staring straight into her eyes. His shakes started again even if his thought came clearly, calmly. *Maid, will you mount?*

So that's it, she thought, but not to him. I'm being handed on. Well, good luck with that.

"No thanks," she said, deliberately aloud. "I got a ride."

Their return was even swifter. Moonspill, for all his talk of feeling old, matched his son's every stride despite Elayne on his back. And Tempest pushed hard. When they reached the plain and galloped side by side, she was able to study him. Smaller than Moonspill certainly, but his back was still a good foot higher than her height standing. His mane and tail were the same coffee-brown showing vividly against the pure marbled whiteness of a body heavily yet lithely muscled, and in perfect proportion. Yet it was the horn that took and kept her gaze. The sire's, like the rest of him, showed his years. It had the deep reddish-yellow of old ivory. Tempest's horn was shorter, slimmer, and almost pure white. Four feet of spiralling power ending in a point she could tell was as sharp as any sword's.

Too soon the lake glimmered in the distance. She left her study to focus on the ride, on Moonspill. He'd begun to breathe more erratically, she could feel the shudders running through him, through her. She closed her eyes but failed to blink back the tears when she realized that this could be the last time she rode him.

It was still deep night when they arrived back. This did not stop someone being awake. And very angry.

"Where the hell have you been?" Huy was beside her the moment she lowered herself stiffly to the ground. "How can I handle your security if you just take off without telling me?"

"'Handle my security'?"

"You know what I mean!" He thumped his chest. "Bodyguard, remember? Appointed by his majesty or Lion or whatever the hell he is."

"But I was safe. I was with Moonspill." She gestured to the two unicorns moving away to a grove, where scores of white shapes rose to receive them.

"Just you damn well tell me in future, OK?" Huy growled then turned, looked where she'd pointed. "Isn't that whos'it with him? The unicorn who wanted to fight the griffin?"

"You have a good eye. How do you tell one from another?"

"Hard to forget your first unicorn," he muttered.

"Yeah, well, hear ye, hear ye. His name's Tempest. And he's Moonspill's son."

"No shit?"

"None. And it gets worse." They walked to the lake as they talked, and Elayne knelt on a rock ledge, scooped up a handful of cold water, drank.

"Why's that bad in the first place?"

White shapes were coming from the wood, fifty of them at least. She drank more, splashed her face, stood. "Because the unicorns aren't coming to save Goloth. One unicorn is coming," she said, adding derisively, "to make a report." She pointed at Tempest, in the forefront. "That one."

Huy raised an eyebrow. But he had no time for further questions.

Maid. Moonspill was before her, at the head of a white phalanx. *Is there anything you need that we can give you?*

She turned to Huy. He may not have heard but he sensed the question. "I packed up, just in case we had to make another speedy getaway." He turned. Her pack was on his back. "Smoked fish is wrapped in leaves. I found a bush of . . . well, they're kinda like blackberries. Crammed them into your spare water bottle. Others are full so," he shrugged, "we're ready, I guess. If that's the question."

"It is." She shivered. "Can I have my coat back?"

As he slipped out of her coat, she considered. She could have used a little more sleep—or maybe just a little delay. But the moon was full, and the city was across the mountains and several days beyond them. So she turned back to Moonspill. "We're good to go."

Then mount again, and let us ride.

He stooped for her and she climbed on. She watched as Tempest bent for Huy. Huy had no grudge, got on easily, even excitedly. It was the unicorn who had the problem. It was clear he'd never borne anyone on his back. For a few seconds, he shook, skittered sideways, and Huy lurched. Then Moonspill rumbled, and his son settled. Only his tail still swished, wildly.

Three unicorns rode to the southern mountains, their peaks just beginning to gild with dawn light, for Heartsease cantered alongside, her head close to her son's. Elayne was not part of whatever she was saying, yet their minds were joined the entire way, with Tempest's head jerking up and down often as if agreeing. Advice before the son goes to college? she thought. What does a unicorn's empty nest look like anyway?

She snorted and Huy raised an eyebrow. She had to get a grip. What she was about to do was no tougher than things she'd done before, surely? Bond with a unicorn? Check. Save Goloth? Check. Pass calculus? Check. She snorted again, but this time did not meet Huy's stare because she knew she'd lose it. *Breathe, Elayne,* she thought to herself.

And apparently to Moonspill. *Do you need to rest, maid?*

"No, I'm good." She spoke it, rather than thought it. She was still annoyed with him, didn't want that link again. Not when it would have to end so soon.

Not too soon. They did not ride the same way they'd come from the mountains but turned parallel to them and headed south. She reckoned it must have been a couple of hours, because the sun was full up, though hidden now by clouds that looked like they were snow-heavy, before they cut toward the peaks, the land rising through a stand of oak, giving way to groves of silver birch as they climbed still higher.

They slowed, then stopped. The treeline ended. Across a small stretch of bare ground was the rock face. If it was not quite as sheer as the reverse side they'd climbed—and nearly died on!—it looked sheer enough to her. And obviously to Huy, who gave an audible shudder beside her.

She spoke aloud, so he could hear. "There's not really a path up that, is there?"

No, came the reply. *The path does not go up it. It goes within.*

He bent, so she could slide off. Beside her, Tempest did the same for Huy. Then they followed the unicorns across the scrap of land to one of a few silver birch that had crossed the gap and grew almost flush against the rock face. Almost, but not completely. There was a gap between trunk and stone, and when Moonspill halted and beckoned her on with his horn, she stepped into it and saw.

There was a split in the wall, a jagged crack a few feet wide that ran half her height again. *There is a cave beyond,* Moonspill thought. *At its end a passage curves and rises through the rock, then falls again to the land upon the other side. It comes out in Goloth not far from the spire where we first met.*

Black Tusk? It was a bonus, because it was a part of the country she actually knew. The original tapestry door had been in a tree beneath the spire. Which meant that the new door was in a stream nearby. They'd basically done a big circle and returned to where they'd started.

Hear me, maid. Leave the mountain quickly and with no sign that you passed that way. For if man, of Goloth or Glanasa, were to discover this tunnel . . .

He did not need to complete his thought. If the mountains were breached, the Valley of the Unicorn was, eventually, doomed.

Beside them, Heartsease leaned a last time into Tempest. Something passed—in thought, in the light caress of horn to flank. The younger beast snorted and disappeared into the cave. "He'll be needing to see," said Huy, pulling out a flashlight, following, vanishing.

Moonspill was backing away, his mate at his side. "Hey!" called Elayne, stepping after. "That's it? No advice? No goodbyes?"

Advice? A rumble came in the huge white throat, as if he was considering. *Yes. If you meet a dragon—*

"Whoa! I have no plans to meet a drag—"

If you meet a dragon remember this: like any fabulous beast it has its weakness.

You mean like you and mirrors? Oh-kay. Anything else?

The rumble came again. *Yes. Listen to your heart.*

"Oh. Fantastic." A piece of advice she could have heard on daytime TV!

He'd continued backing away. Now he halted, turned his full gaze upon her. *You are angry, Alice-Elayne.*

"Yes, I'm angry!" She took a step back toward him. "I expected more from you. You said you'd always come if I needed you and now . . . now I do, instead you're sending me off with a teenager. You're—" She felt the prickle in her eyes again. Dammit! When had she become a crier? She sniffed them back, stamped. "You're abandoning me and you just don't care."

Maid. Moonspill came closer, till his chest was an arm's length away. Then he did what he'd done sometimes, rarely, before. He reached her with his mind, touched it as if laying a warm towel upon an ache. *When I said to listen to your heart it is because you will always hear me within it. I have not abandoned you. I never could. Because I am with you always, as long as my years will allow me.*

She could not hold the tears now, let them flow. *But I'm terrified I'll never see you again. Never . . . feel this again.*

A ripple ran down him, from neck to tail. *You may never see me. And you may. Our fates will decide that. But if you do not, yet you will always still feel this. I am forever with you and you with me. For you are my maid. And I am your unicorn.*

It came then, a surge in the warmth he'd laid upon her, like a last, long hug. Then it was gone, he'd turned, moved away, Heartsease at his side, their two whites distinct for a time from each other and from the white of birch bark, before blending into it, vanishing into it.

Elayne watched for a little longer, although there was nothing to see. Then she sniffed, wiped her nose, straightened. "All right, Dad," she said. "I'm coming."

Turning, she stepped once again into the dark.

22

THE DEVASTATED LAND

The light flashed along the ground before her.

"This way," Huy called, flicking it like an usher in a movie house. "Mind the step."

She tripped anyway, on some stone, kept her feet, stumbled over to him. He was at the other side of the cave. Beside him, looming white in the gloom, was Tempest, tail swishing.

Huy played the beam on the wall—on a crack in the wall, not dissimilar to the first one they'd come through. "This is it," he said. He looked up at the unicorn. "Shall I go first?"

There was silence, then the thought word. *Yes.*

"All right then," Huy said, and took a step.

"Wait a minute," said Elayne. "You heard his reply?"

"Such as it was. He said 'yes.'"

"But I heard it too. Usually they speak to one person at a time."

"Well, this guy must be talking on all frequencies. Hey!" He turned. "Maybe we can communicate that way too?" He put a hand to his brow. "What am I thinking?"

"That this sweater really doesn't go with these pants?"

He laughed. "Nice try. Oh well. Could have been handy. Though truly you don't want to know what goes on inside my head. It's murky in there." He turned again. "Ready?"

"Lead on." Elayne dug her cellphone out of her zippered coat pocket. She'd turned it off when they hit Goloth—so there was plenty of battery to power the—"Ta-dah!" she said, using the flashlight app. "I'll bring up the rear."

"Great." Huy stepped into the entrance. "Oh, and it doesn't, by the way."

"What?"

"Your sweater. Go with your pants."

"Move it, man." Huy disappeared and Elayne stepped—then had to stop when Tempest put just his head in, and nothing more. *You next. I'll come behind,* she thought to him.

Yes, he thought again. But he still didn't move.

She sensed something, some disquiet. *What is it?*

Tunnels. I have never . . . He scraped his horn on the rock. *I am used to the sky above me.*

Great, she thought—not to him—a claustrophobic unicorn! But she said, aloud, "If you need to go back. Send another—"

No! The word came hard, angry. Then he lowered his head and entered.

It was tight in there, and got tighter. The roof lowered too, till he had to keep his head down, his horn's tip only just above the ground. She imagined other unicorns, bigger than him, like Moonspill having to really push their way through. It was cold too, as cold as rock. Yet heat came from him, along with the musky aroma of his sweat.

He moved slower than Huy, frustratingly so. Elayne heard her friend's voice get farther away, in his calls back, as they climbed higher and higher. "Watch yourself here! Steps up. Ow, crap! Slippy here, water. Oh, and—"

She didn't hear the last part. It was as if he'd turned a corner. "Huy?" She called, then louder, "Huy?"

Tempest halted, breathing heavily. "Move will you!" she said, but he didn't. The passage had narrowed again, so she couldn't squeeze past him. "Huy!" she screamed.

It took a moment but then his voice came. "Sorry! This is the top. Downhill from here."

"Hey! Come back will you? Unicorn needs your light."

Tempest stamped at that, perhaps hearing some tone in her voice. But Huy returned. "Easy, big guy," he said, and turned and led them up more slowly.

The downhill part was gentler, a little wider. A wind blew up it as well, bringing smells of earth, trees. Tempest started to go quicker. "Not so fast," she called and he snorted but slowed. Then there was light, daylight, and they stumbled out into a sleety rain.

They'd taken no more than two steps when a voice greeted them. A familiar one—in a way. "Did I not tell you to chill? Dogs be here anytime now."

As Tempest backed up, nostrils flared, horn lowered against a threat, Elayne pushed past him. "Baena?" she called, peering through the rain.

"The same, girlfriend. And my homie's here too."

Then she saw them—twin heads rising from a bush. She was delighted—and furious, all at once. "Where the hell have you been?" She stomped over. "You brought us back here and then just took off?"

"Us?"

Amphis's query brought him forward. "'lo!" said Huy. "Came along for the ride. And it's been quite a ride so far."

"Bro! You made it. Give me five."

"Is that even possible?"

"Don't leave me hangin'!" Baena thrust his head forward. Huy shrugged, then patted it.

Amphis spoke again. "Maid, I apologize for absenting ourselves. Baena was not well and needed healing straightaway. And only his mate could do that. We used the stream to take us home."

"His mate? Another—" She indicated the two heads.

"Nay, we mate with ordinary snakes—though, by the heavens above, do not let *my* mate hear that I said 'ordinary'!—and in every seventh egg of every seventh brood an amphisbaena is born. We—" He looked behind her. "But, maid, let us move away and allow all the unicorns egress."

She looked back. Tempest was still standing before the entrance, horn high in the rain, revelling in it, eyes closed. "You're looking at all the unicorns." She shivered. "I'll explain out of the rain. Is there any shelter?"

"The best is the cave you have come from. Enter."

Tempest would not join them. He cantered off, as the others went in, her calls to be wary unacknowledged.

She explained what had happened in the valley beyond, the unicorns' caution. The news silenced even Baena. "But why are you here?" Elayne asked. "How did you know to come?"

"The king-elect, that was," Amphis replied. "We only just missed you at the ambush, found him. He was leading a party of men he'd rescued, fleeing ahead of the pursuing Glanasa. We were able to call in their tongue, lead them into a trap. There was a most bloody battle . . ." He paused, shuddered.

She felt an odd flutter around her heart. "Leo? Is he OK?"

" 'Twas a battle won, maid. Many of the enemy were killed and few of ours. Leo took a slight wound but is well. And while he retreated to the city, he sent us to meet you. For only we alone in all Goloth know this secret passage between the unicorns' land and ours. He asked that we escort you to him. The bringer of hope!"

She looked to the cave entrance. Out there, a single unicorn ran in the rain still coming down in freezing sheets. She shivered. "Not much hope," she said, then shook herself. "Still, we better go. We need to get this news to the city. It's gotta be three days away—"

It was Baena who interrupted her. "Chill, sista. The king has left his crib."

She flushed. "Look! Can you just speak plain English?"

"He finds it hard, maid." Amphis glared at the other end of the body. "Being second born, he is also much given to frivolity. Hush, fool!" As Baena slumped, muttering, his elder by a moment continued. "The city is abandoned. Hunger emptied it, for the Glanasa were raiding closer and closer and too little food was reaching it. It was crowded too, for so many had fled the countryside. And then there were the first victims of plague."

The horrible word hung for a moment before Elayne swallowed and asked, "But where are they going?"

The green eyes widened. "Perhaps here, whence we could lead them through the tunnel?"

Elayne glanced back into the darkness. She thought of the tens of thousands of Goloth going through to a valley only just big enough for the fabulous beasts that already lived there. Bringing disease perhaps. They'd destroy it, and then each other when they starved. "No. We cannot do that. It is what Moonspill most fears. You didn't tell Leo that this was possible, did you?"

"Nay. 'Twas my present thought alone, and foolish." Amphis shook himself. "I believe the plan is for all the people to make for the northern mountains, as far away from the ocean, whence the Glanasa will come, as they are able. They come slowly west up the central valley toward us here, then they will follow the great river north."

Plague! Of all the terrors in the medieval world, was that the worst? And her dad was out there exposed to it? Her heart sped up. "Look, is there any word of my father?"

"I have made enquiries," Amphis replied. "And there was rumour of a man dressed differently, who spoke in a strange manner, begging food in a village not far from the city. About a week past."

"How far? Let's go there now." Elayne had taken a step forward as if to begin running.

But Amphis stopped her with a shake of his head. "He will no longer be there. The people of every village along the route have joined those fleeing the city."

Had he joined the refugees? Had he run into the Glanasa? He should be at home, testing chocolates for his cocoa, not in Goloth begging for food. Dad, she thought, sending it ahead of her like a shout, where the hell are you? But there wasn't much choice. She could only go where he was most likely to be. "OK," she said, rising. "Let's go find Leo. Huy, you ready for—" She jumped. "What the hell are you wearing?"

Huy was covered head to toe in blue plastic. "Poncho," he replied, grinning, running a finger down the inside of the hood. "Hideous, I know. But, sista, when you wear velvet in New York you learn to make fashion sacrifices."

She smiled and scowled at the same time. "Don't call me 'sista.' One's bad enough."

As they left the cave, Baena said, "Show her, bro."

Amphis nodded. "Aye. Follow."

As they slithered downhill along a faint path through the brush, Elayne looked back and up. Towering above was the basalt spire of Black Tusk, shrouded in sleet. Then she lost it to branches as they entered a stretch of forest, crossing that, coming out onto a riverbank. "Hey," called Huy, looking about, "isn't this where we came in?"

It was. The amphisbaena slid to the bank. "Look carefully, maid."

"Eyes wide, homie."

With Baena's end lodged on the bank, Amphis thrust his head out into the stream. "The slit that your ancestor wove into the tapestry was in the trunk of the tree, and was so here too. But that tree rose above the centre of the stream. Moonspill destroyed the tree, which too many humans knew about, so evil would not have access to your world and moved the gate into the middle of the water." He pulled back his head. "You see, below me, a rock on the bed? It has a strange peak, almost like the Tusk above us?"

Elayne peered. She could just make it out, about a foot below the surface. "Uh-huh."

"The door is the whole left side of that. You still have the tip of unicorn's horn?"

"No. My father took it. That's how he's here, remember?"

"I had forgot me." Amphis swung back to the riverbank and rested his head briefly beside his brother's. Then both gave what could pass for a nod. "It is agreed, maid. You shall have . . . this."

And on the word, he did what he'd done back at the Cloisters, spitting up the piece of yellowing horn. It was no less gross here. "Touch it on the rock, as you would the tree trunk, and you will open the door 'tween worlds."

Elayne swallowed. "Uh, Huy? Can you get this?"

"Love to, of course but . . ." His voice came from a little ways away and she looked back to see him in front of a silver birch.

"What are you doing?"

"Marking the spot." He moved aside. He had her Swiss Army knife out and had carved a large heart in the trunk: within it, L and a plus sign. "Nearly done," he said, and added an E.

"You are such a jerk," she said. "And no gentleman," she added, picking up the piece of horn, holding it as far away from her as possible, rinsing it in the stream.

The snake was already sliding away along the bank. "Come," Amphis called, "we must to the rendezvous. Where is the unicorn?"

"Tempest!" Elayne shouted, zipping the horn into a pocket. The beating rain muffled her voice. Nevertheless, they soon heard hoof-falls and a few seconds later the unicorn charged into the clearing.

There are humans near, he thought.

"Scragar's gang?" Huy said.

"Probably." Elayne stepped toward Tempest. "We need to go and go fast. Can you carry both of us?"

She'd never seen a unicorn look contemptuous before—but in his shake somehow this one managed it. *Of course*, came the thought, and he bent.

She leapt atop him—but Huy climbed slowly, struggling up behind her. "What?" he said at her impatient tsk, as she handed him her pack to slip over his back. "It's hard to vault onto a unicorn in a poncho."

"Words you'd never expect to hear together in a sentence," she said, adding with a shout, "Let's ride."

With the amphisbaena forming into a hoop beside them—its speedy form of travel—they set out into the ever-increasing rain.

Tempest was as good as his contemptuous word. He threaded the trees of the woodlands, leaped rocks and streams, while effortlessly keeping them centred and balanced on his back. The amphisbaena spun beside them, equally tireless. It was the humans who had to call for occasional breaks—for peeing, for water, to stretch, to consume smoked trout. At one stop, Amphisbaena slunk off and returned with a suspicious looking bulge at their joined belly. Tempest chewed at grasses and leaves but was always the first to stop feeding, to snort his impatience, to hoof the earth. Then they'd be up and mounted again. She and Huy took it in turns to sleep, swapping places, the sleeper leaning and held against the mane.

The day passed, and half the night. Elayne woke—though she was meant to be the watcher she'd managed to fall asleep too—to groggily shake her head clear and try and make sense of what was before her. *Beneath* me, she thought. The rain had ceased, the sky given over again to moon and stars, but a chill wind was gusting up what she realized was a long slope. Far below, at its base, many lights sparkled.

"'Tis the camp," Amphis said, rising up beside her, confirming her thought. "This is the place where the two valleys and the two great rivers of Goloth meet. Leo suggested it be let known, and the council agreed, that all could rally here, all who would make the journey to the northern mountains. From the spread of firelight, I warrant that few have stayed away."

"So they welcomed him back?" Huy slid off the unicorn, swayed on rubbery legs. "I thought you said he'd been overthrown?"

"The people were so buzzed out they figured his return was fly."

"Huh?"

"What my brother so ineloquently quoth," Amphis sighed, "is that Leo brought some hope of order again in the chaos. He does not rule alone though but as one of a council of Weavers and nobles. They have made an uneasy peace."

Elayne also moved to dismount, but Tempest backed suddenly, forcing her to grip his mane. *Should we not descend immediately, maid? I cannot study the state of this land and its people from this distance.*

It was what she wanted too. Her father could be there. But before she could reply, Amphis—obviously in on the conversation—did. "I think it would be wise if we alone were to descend and fetch Leo here. There have been many rumours of the return of the unicorns, to save the land. If but one were to come . . ." He shook his head, the shake moving down the scales to shake Baena too. "I fear such disappointment may turn men ugly. Remember it was only two years ago that the slaying of a unicorn was seen as a rebirth in this land." They hooped up again; Baena taking his brother by the throat. "We will return soon," Amphis squawked.

They watched the hoop run ever faster down the hill till the dark took it. Elayne dismounted and this time there was no objection. Tempest went to some trees to seek leaves while the humans moved to the hill's reverse slope. They found a sheltered scoop of land there and, beneath an overhang of rock, some old, dry wood. She made a fire; Huy went to a pool nearby and fetched fresh water. Soon they were reasonably warm, drinking, and munching smoked fish and berries.

"What do you think will happen?" asked Huy, pulling a bone from between his teeth.

"I don't honestly know." She sat back, picked up a stick, poked it into the flames. "Tempest is meant to 'report' back. Tell the unicorns if they can come and make a difference."

"If they can come and not all die."

"True." She lifted the stick to study its glowing end. "But you've not seen them fight. Fifty unicorns could drive the Glanasa from the land."

"Unless the Glanasa had a dragon with them. Do they?"

"We haven't heard of any here yet. So far the dragon—or dragons, I am not sure if there are more than one—has been content to stay on its island and have victims brought to it."

"Can't they fly?"

"Maybe. As you can imagine, I've spent a bit of time studying fabulous beasts. Some dragons don't fly, some do."

"Some are Grendel, some are Smaug."

"Exactly." It was good that Huy was also doing a minor in English lit. Made conversation so much swifter. She threw the stick into the pit. "I just wish I trusted Tempest more. He's just so . . . so—"

"Young?" Huy smiled. "About my age. And you trust me, right?"

"Sometimes."

"Well, you definitely trust Moonspill, yeah?" On her nod he continued. "So you don't really believe he'd have deputed someone unless he thought that someone could do the job. Cut the kid a little slack, eh?"

He rose, went beyond the firelight. Elayne huddled deeper into her down coat, stared into the flames. She was annoyed—because Huy was right. Plus, whatever she thought of him, Tempest was the only game in town.

Huy returned at speed. "Someone's coming along the ridge. Listen!"

She heard them. "Hooves!" she said. "Not a unicorn's either."

Hooves—on a horse. The one named Swiftsure. Who belonged to the man riding him. "Maid," cried Leo, out of the saddle before his mount had fully halted. "You have returned. How fare you?"

He ran up close, stopped within a short arm's length. His hands rose toward her, then froze. He looked even more tired than he had when they'd parted. He also looked like the guy from her dream, who'd kissed her on a Brooklyn street corner.

There was a silence—broken by a cough. "Don't mind me," Huy said.

"Quiet you!" Elayne turned back to Leo. "Where's—?"

The question was answered with several sticks snapping as a scaly hoop rolled over them. "Tired!" Baena spoke as he released his brother's neck. He lay down. "While you do the real talk, this brother is sleepin'."

He lay his head down, while Amphis reared up. "'Tis true, maid. We are exhausted. We will contribute what we can but from a coil. We have told Leo what we know." He circled down, his head coming to rest beside his brother's. "Speak," he said, closing his eyes.

Before Elayne could reply, though, there was another arrival. Wolf bounded in and fell at his master's feet. Leo went down to his haunches, threw back his cloak, held his hands out to the fire. She and Huy joined him and for a moment there was silence. Then they all spoke at once.

"Maid—"

"Water?"

"Fish 'n' berries?"

"Aye to both and thank ye," Leo replied. "There is little food to share in a city—a country—on the move." He took the bottles, of water and fruit, opened the leaf that held a fish, ate, his hunger showing in his speed.

"It's bad down there?" Elayne asked.

He paused in his cramming a moment. "Most fled with little but what they could carry, fast consumed. We hunters do what we can. But the land is devastated. Even the animals flee it." He ate again, his eyes on her. "Amphisbaena told me that but one unicorn has come. Where is he?"

"His name's Tempest." Elayne looked around but the fabulous beast was nowhere in sight. "He likes to explore. This is all a big adventure to him."

"That's not quite fair," interjected Huy.

"An adventure?" Leo threw the fish spine into the fire. "I always thought war was an adventure. Until I experienced one." Even in the dark, Elayne could see that deeper darkness in his eyes. "Yes, maid. You can say that it is bad down there." He looked in the berry bottle, took one last fingerful, then sealed it. "You will need this." He handed it back, then he cleared his throat. "Alice-Elayne—" He broke off. Dread added to the dark in his eyes.

"What is it, Leo? Tell me fast."

"Your father. I met your father."

"What?" She jumped up. "Where is he? Down there? Let's go!"

Leo rose too but reached and took one of her arms, restraining her. "I say I met him. It was the eve of the ambush of the Glanasa. He came in with a group of rebels to join us in the fight."

"The fight?" Elayne's eyebrows shot up. "My dad's not a fighter. He's an architect!" she blurted.

"He told me he could use a sword."

"He was a fencer at college!" She gripped Leo back. "You didn't let him fight?"

"I could not stop him." A slight smile came. "I see where you get your determination from, maid. He said he felt he had a responsibility to aid us."

She remembered their conversation now. Her dad saying that it was his duty to help the people of Goloth. Though he didn't even know about the Glanasa then. "But where is he? He's not—"

"Nay. Trust me. His was not among the bodies . . ." He swallowed. "It was a hard fight, at night. There was confusion. The Glanasa who survived fled and we were too tired to give chase. They may have taken him. So he may . . ."

"Be a prisoner in Glana. Where they sacrifice people to the dragon."

She said it coldly. It was the only way she could keep control of a heart threatening to burst out of her chest.

Leo nodded. "I am afraid that may be so."

"Then I must go after him."

She said it in the same steely tone. Huy grabbed her arm, squeezed hard. "Elayne, no. That's impossible," he began.

But Leo interrupted. "My friend, I learned that 'impossible' is not a word the maid heeds." He reached out, took her other hand. "Alice-Elayne," he said, "when the amphisbaena said they would fetch you from your world, when they succeeded and you returned, ah!" His eyes flashed. "It gave me hope. Hope that you could bring the unicorns back to Goloth, ride your Moonspill into battle, destroy our enemies. But now you have brought but one—" His voice cracked; he took a deep breath before he continued. "I am forced to my second plan—which may fit in with yours. It is more desperate, and the chances of success are, I admit, slight."

"What is your plan?"

"To take the fight to the enemy. To journey to Glana and hunt the dragon."

Ignoring the gasps of Huy and the snake heads, both risen, Elayne looked Leo in the eye. "Then we're going to the same place. Two against the dragon."

Three.

It always surprised her how silently a unicorn could approach, without attracting the attention of person or dog. Leo turned slowly, looked up. "So you are the unicorn named Tempest," he said.

The unicorn's words came and it was clear from their attention that all could hear him. *And you are Leo, who once was king. The man who tried to kill my sire and my dam.*

"Your—?" He looked at Elayne, then at the snake. "You did not tell me this."

"We did not know," replied Amphis.

Leo swallowed, then turned again to the unicorn. "Does that make a difference to you? Do you wish to kill me for it?"

This thought came more slowly. *No. For my father once said to me that no one should die for what he cannot help.*

"He said that to me too," said Elayne.

Tempest's eyes flicked to her, then back to Leo. *So now, king, you seek to do the impossible.*

"The impossible? Mayhap." Leo nodded. "Yet I do not go as a king. I never became king. Your father and this maid saw to that. So I go only as a man of Goloth."

Yet if you succeed in this hunt, if you slay this dragon, you will be a hero.

Leo shrugged. "I do not seek that title either."

Yet you will be. The next thought came accompanied by a rumble in the throat. *Unicorns like heroes.* Tempest moved down a few steps into the bowl. *We like to bear heroes to glory.*

Leo's brow furrowed. "Are you . . . are you offering to come with me?" He looked at Elayne. "With us?"

I am. He jerked his head up and down. *I was sent to discover all that was wrong in this world. How can I carry home the news of that without going to its heart? Besides, my mother charged me to mind the maid.*

Elayne looked back and forth between them. She watched Leo smile. And though she was pretty damned sure unicorns couldn't, she'd swear that Tempest did too.

"Wait a second here!" Huy had managed to restrain himself up to that point. Now he was shaking his head hard. "How the hell do you travel to an island that's miles away? Are there even sailors here?"

"There are," said Leo. "Fishermen and some traders on the coast. It is how we got goods to and from the Glanasa—when we were not fighting them." He took a deep breath. "But it is not the traders I shall seek to take me. No one has heard of them since war came and we can only think that they were the first enslaved. But there are others."

He bent, picked up a stick, drew in the mud beside the fire. A rough coastline appeared, mountains above it. "Somewhere along this bay . . ." he jabbed down, "lies a town. No one in Goloth knows exactly where it is because no one who goes there returns. Save one old man who grew homesick and told the tale 'ere he died of wounds he received when he fled." He threw down the stick, looked up at them. "This town is a refuge for all who would live free of any state's laws. Not only Goloth's; some are escaped slaves from Glana. From other lands too. They are sea warriors, though they do not fight for any country, only for treasure. They are—"

"Pirates!" It was Huy who blurted the word. He turned to Elayne. "Pirates! How cool is that!"

"C-cool?" Elayne jerked her arm from his grasp. "You don't think you're coming, do you?"

"Certainly am. Bodyguard, remember?"

"Look, Huy, I've got enough people into enough trouble already. This—"

She was ignored. Leo and Huy were grasping each other again, forearm to forearm. The amphisbaena was laying two heads across them both. The unicorn was lowering his horn atop the pile. And then they were all looking at her. So she sighed and laid her hand upon the others, on flesh, scale, and horn. "So what's this place we're going to called anyway?" she asked.

"Slavetown," Leo replied and frowned. "Though now we must find a place that is on no map."

It was Baena who lifted his head. Scaly lips parted in a grin, forked tongue flicked, eyes narrowed. "Chill, dog," he said. "Me and my brother got this."

4

Here Be Dragons

23

SCARAB

Elayne lay on the hill above Slavetown, staring at the dark shapes of ships on the water and listening to snatches of distinctly slurred song. When she heard rustling behind her, she whipped around. "He's back," Huy said, thrusting his head between the bushes.

She followed him along the path to the little clearing where they'd rested after their two-day hike. She still couldn't quite get used to Huy's new clothes. He'd been forced to lose the impractical velvet frock coat. It hadn't been designed for the rigours he'd put it through and was falling off him. So he'd donned Leo's cast-offs—they were about the same size—and now wore stained leather from ankle to neck—boots, leggings, and a kind of shirt-jacket. The only thing left of the old Huy was the Hermès scarf that he'd rolled and tied around his neck. He still looked totally stylish. Unlike her, she knew, in the farm boy's hand-me-downs Leo had scrounged in the camp—rough wool shirt, a jerkin, some baggy sort-of trousers. She still had her own clothes underneath, and was grateful for the warmth. She'd coiled her thick hair and shoved it all into a wide-brimmed hat. No one knew how women were treated in Slavetown. If pirates shared traits between worlds . . . not well, they all suspected. So she would pose as a boy, and keep quiet.

Not something she was too pleased about. "You took your time," she snapped as Leo entered the clearing.

Leo raised one eyebrow—another talent he shared with Huy—as Wolf bounded up and Tempest came through the bushes. "Because it took time," he said as he knelt by the fire pit. "The snake and I first went to the port. But no vessel was readying for voyage. So we visited the town. There is one main tavern where most people gather. It is a rambling place of many levels. Amphisbaena remains there, hidden and listening. In their talking they hope to hear of a sea captain who might be tempted by this." He pulled a golden coin from a pocket in his shirt. "But in case of difficulties, I will leave the rest of the gold here with you."

"Not with me." Elayne took the coin, flicked it into the air, caught it. "Cuz I'll be with you."

"Alice-Elayne, we discussed this—"

"No. You decided." She lowered her head, fixing him with her gaze. "You should know by now, Leo—I don't really do orders."

He went to speak, then forced the words down. He turned to Huy. "Very well, then you shall guard the camp."

"Nah. I'll be with her."

"But—" Again Leo held back, though his face flushed. He looked up at Tempest. "Will you stay, at least?"

The thought took a little time to come. *I will. Not from fear. Yet the price of passage may be too high if they see who they also have to take.*

Leo bent to rub Wolf's neck. "At least you will hearken and remain. Stay," he said. Then he rose, pulled up the hood on his cloak, and with a curt, "Come," strode off through the trees.

"Tetchy," Elayne said, following. "Still, he was a tyrant. Must be tough when no one obeys you."

"I think he's kinda cute when he pouts," said Huy.

"Oh, be quiet."

They followed Leo down a steep trail that ended on a rough track. Across it, the land dropped steeply to the seashore. They could hear the tide sucking at pebbles. To their left, Slavetown's lights sparkled, with the sound of a shanty coming more clearly, and even more drunkenly. The rain had started again, instantly heavy, and pulling their hats down low, they shrugged into it.

On the edge of the town, facing the water and the main jetty, was a large building, dwarfing those around it. It was the centre of both light and noise. Shouts came, voices raised in argument, song—several different songs, in fact, in several different tongues, none of them blending too harmoniously. A glance through the main door showed a huge black man with an enormous boot at his mouth, drinking from it to encouraging, rising cheers. "This takes me back. Looks like a frat party," Huy said.

"Never took you for a frat boy."

"First year, U of T. Before I transferred to Columbia. Phi Kappa Delta." He shuddered. "It was a ghastly mistake. I—"

"Shh!" hissed Leo.

Another hiss echoed his—and the amphisbaena slid from under the porch. One head rose to Leo's ear; he nodded several times. Then the snake returned to its hiding place, and Leo led them through the swinging door.

All the attention was focused on the man and the boot, the cheers reaching a climax as he tipped it ever higher, beer spilling around his chin. So they were able to enter the hall unnoticed and slip into shadows beneath a gallery that ran around all four sides.

"Very *Pirates of the Caribbean*," Huy whispered.

"Quiet you," she said, but couldn't help her giggle. Because it was, totally.

The people of Goloth, city and town, were mostly fair skinned, tending to the Nordic like Leo with his fair hair and blue eyes. They were usually soberly dressed, in drab greys, browns and blacks. Plus, they were usually sober. In this pub, people were a variety of shades, vividly dressed—and very, very drunk! It was like a Brooklyn bar on a Saturday—if they were holding a pirates and wenches night! The black man now finishing his boot to massive cheers was just one of several, many as dark as him, others lighter skinned. She saw several pale Glanasan, all with their distinctive long, black hair parted each side of a shaved crown. Pale too were the men of Goloth, though these would have been cried out in the streets of their city for their raggedy beards, their big gold earrings, their multi-hued clothes.

The women, though there were fewer of them, were also diverse in skin tone, in dress, in hair and clothes—though most of them definitely favoured the "pirate wench" look: big on makeup and bling, their blouses low cut, cleavage well displayed as they swooped amongst the men, dispensing drink, collecting tankards, fending off some hands with a curse, accepting the gropes of others with a smile. Yet looking closer she saw other women—a few, not many—who were dressed more like the men: not concealing themselves but with breeches, not skirts, and buttoned-up doublets rather than blouses. These women also wore their hair pulled back, gripped daggers at their waists, and had a watchful look in their eyes. Who are you? she wondered.

The sight was one thing—but the sound! It was a true babel of voices, so many tongues mixed in the hubbub that at first it was hard to hear any. She focused on some Golothians nearby, understood their

Dramach, listened to a man from Glana tell a countryman how he wanted the girl with the missing tooth. Then the tavern opened up to her in language. A brown-skinned man was telling another that he was thinking of returning home, if he could get one more big score. A pale man was wooing a wench, saying that if she came to his room that night, he would give her a jewel "surpassing rare."

It was the wonder of the gift of tongues that the amphisbaena had given her—and a gift to be concealed—otherwise she might have warned the wench that the man who offered the jewel immediately told his friend in a different language that it was the best ruby he'd ever faked!

Leo stepped closer, took her arm. "There is the man the amphisbaena singled out," he said, nodding to a table across the room. A Golothian, vast belly poking out of his white shirt, was sitting at a table with two Glanasa. "He looks more prosperous than the others." He pointed to deeper shadows either side in the gloom behind the table. "Bodyguards too. A leader then. A captain we may be able to deal with." He turned to her. "If I ask you—not command you, heavens forfend!—to wait, will you do so? There seems little point in risking all three of us immediately."

She put on her sweetest smile. "Of course, Leo. Don't I always obey?"

He let a little smile come. "No. But use your skill in tongues to learn. We may have to consider other captains."

With that, he was gone. Fending off a wench who called her "hand-some youth" and tried to stroke her arm, Elayne watched Leo reach the table. She couldn't hear, but she could see how it all unfolded—the guards stepping forward as Leo stopped, daggers glinting in the lamp-light. The big man waving them back and gesturing Leo into a chair. The brief conversation that followed. Leo reaching into his cloak and putting something glittery on the table. The pirate picking it up.

The room going mad.

It started with a crash as the big man threw over the table. "Seize him," he bellowed in a voice that cut off all the other sounds, all songs, all conversations instantly. His guards fell on Leo like a storm: the dagger he'd half-drawn wrenched away, both arms pulled behind his back, and his head forced down. Elayne started forward but her arm was seized and she was jerked back. "Wait!" commanded Huy softly. "Too many." He was right and, reluctantly, she settled back.

"There!" shouted the big pirate, pointing, and the guards dragged Leo from the shadows, people scattering before them. "Down!" came the next command and the two guards threw Leo down in the centre of the room, stepped back, cudgels in their hands.

Surprised whispers came, low murmurs. "Quiet!" shouted the pirate, bringing an instant silence. Leo had been right about one thing, at least. The man was a leader here. "Now," he said in a softer tone, stepping forward into the light that pooled in the middle over Leo, "shall I tell you all of a wonder?"

"Tell us, Bullman!" someone cried, and was immediately echoed.

"I will. For see what has come into our home." He pulled a glitter from his pocket and spun it up in the air.

"Noggin!" someone shouted.

"Arse!" came the challenge.

Bullman caught the coin, slapped it onto the back of his hand, made a show of revealing, peering. "Arse!" he cried, to another tavern-wide shout. "And this fool's one for walking into the Dread Serpent with a gold talon what was minted but two year ago. And he's the bigger fool for offering it to me, the Bullman." He waved down the acclaim that came. "For I would sell my own mother for only one of these beauties. And he's offered me twenty more . . ." He paused, looked around the whole room. "To take him to Glana."

Everyone laughed loudly. Bullman let them continue for a while before he raised his hands again. "So I thank him once for the joke. I thank him twice for the gold. And I'll thank him again . . ." He bent, seized Leo by the hair, jerked his head back. "When he tells me where I might find the rest of it."

Leo had reached hands up, seized the man's wrist. But the two guards stepped in; two cudgels fell, on his head and stomach, and Leo collapsed to the floor. Again Elayne lurched forward, again Huy pulled her back, not letting go this time.

Bullman knelt. "What is it?" he said, bending close, his voice false-gentle. "What do you want to tell me, friend?"

Leo raised his head, whispered. The pirate's face cracked into a huge smile. "Friend wants to know if I am the leader here. Alas for him, I am." There was a little muttering at this, and the smile vanished. "I am, ye scum," he hissed. "Scarab's gone. Been squashed by Glanasa, or Tarvians, no doubt. I miss him. I am so very sorry about his untimely demise." The grin that came now was as fake as the sentiment. "But I am the leader now. Anyone got anything to say about that?"

If anyone did, they didn't voice it. Instead, under the hard stares of his two guards, and four more equally large and hard-looking men who came to stand with Bullman in the middle of the room, most people cheered—though not, Elayne noticed as she glanced around for some help, some way out, the three women she'd noticed before in trousers and daggers. "Thought not." Bullman nodded. "And now, friend." He reached again for Leo's hair.

The new voice came quite softly. Yet perhaps it was its depths, its smoothness, its velvet quality that pierced the last of the cheering. "I believe that I do," the voice rolled out. "Have something to say, that is."

The voice came from just behind her. Elayne turned—and when she saw who spoke, she was surprised that she hadn't noticed him before. He stood out, even in this gaudy crowd.

The newcomer was dressed head to toe in what her old Shakespeare teacher would have called "motley"—a riot of textures and colours. This began with the purple cocked hat he was just putting back on, an emerald ostrich feather in its crown; descended through a brocade cerulean doublet, a cascade of golden stars embroidered upon it; spread on through crimson velvet breeches that flared from the hip and tapered to pigeon egg blue stockings that began at the knee; and climaxed in black ankle boots that had both silver spurs on the heels and silver caps on the toes.

It was such a mix it shouldn't have looked good—yet it did. In fact, it looked great. Even the fashion police approved—if Huy's audible gasp was anything to go by. Though perhaps it was the man himself who held it all together. His skin was smooth, the coffee colour of Tempest's mane. His features were even, his nose straight, his lips full. He was poised on his feet, like a fencer, like a dancer, and now moved like one, away from the tangle of a black cloak on the floor that, Elayne realized, must have concealed his finery until a moment before.

He stopped after a few steps, and spoke again. "Not squashed, as you see. Though the Tarvians did try, and the Glanasa tried even harder." He smiled, revealing perfectly even teeth. "Are you going to try now, Bully Bullman?"

The silence that his voice had brought held, so deep that the loudest thing in the room was Bullman's shallow breaths. His eyes, small in such a big face, had enlarged when the newcomer first spoke. Now they narrowed again as he looked away, about him, took in the six men near as big as him that backed him, then settled again on the slim man standing alone before him.

He smiled. "Now, Scarab, me old shipmate, no need for us to quarrel. You know the way of it. You was gone too long. People don't like to be without a steadying hand on the rudder. They don't feel safe. I am that hand now." He raised what Elayne saw was a huge one, fingers like vast sausages. "Because they want me to be." He glanced left and right at the silently watching crowd, up once more at his men behind him, then back to the man before him. "But seeing that my fortunes have changed," he bent and lightly tapped Leo on the shoulder, "I am in a good mood. No need to go through all the usual unpleasantness. So why don't you and yours find another place to drop anchor?" He sucked in his lower lip. "And since I'm feeling generous, I'll give you two bells."

"Me and mine. You remind me." The man called Scarab raised a hand, clicked fingers. There was a rustle in the watchers, and the next moment the three women Elayne had noticed before, the ones dressed to fight not flirt, had stepped up to stand behind him.

Bullman's eyes narrowed again. His voice, when it came, was lower, angrier. "Your three bitches," he hissed. "That still makes three *women*," he gave the word a derisive twist, "and you 'gainst seven of us. More than seven if people want to be favoured by the certain victor."

He'd directed this last with a meaningful glance around the circle of pirates and wenches. Many shifted, uncertain. A few dropped hands onto the hilts of knives. But only one man spoke.

"Seven against *five*," corrected Leo. And as he did he shot his hand into Bullman's groin and twisted as hard as he could.

The man's scream was swallowed by others. A knife and a short club were suddenly in Scarab's hands, drawn crossways like a gunslinger in a western. He was the first to leap, the three women only a step behind, similarly armed, all four yelling. Bullman's six guards shouted and charged, as their leader wrenched himself free of Leo's grip, backhanding him hard across the face. He fell among the stomping, shifting feet.

Elayne yelped, tore herself from Huy's grasp, was across in moments. She didn't know where the strength came from but she had her hands under Leo's shoulders and dragged him to the shelter of a table in three seconds.

She looked back. Bullman was bellowing like the creature he was part named for, dagger and cudgel in his own hands, slashing both at Scarab. He dodged them, while also parrying, ducking and deflecting the attacks of two guards, one on each side, moving so swiftly the colours of his costume almost blended into white. Each of his women followers was dancing near as fast—one of them especially needing to with a brace of men chopping at her. It wasn't an even fight, despite her skills; eventually she missed a block, and a cudgel swept in and took her in the head. She went down, one of the guards turning to double team the next woman—while the other spun, his dagger half a foot from Scarab's side. He pulled it back.

"No," screamed Elayne, rising, grabbing a stool, knowing she could never throw it in time.

But before the man could thrust, there was a shout—and someone else whirled into the middle. "Yah!" cried Huy. The shout caused the guard to hesitate a second . . . a second too long, as Huy swept a kick hard into the man's cheek. He crashed into his comrade. Both fell.

It was a switch of fortune, sudden and clear—which Elayne added to now by hurling the stool. It passed between Scarab and Bullman forcing both men to lean hard back—and the lithe man in motley to then snap forward and pop the tip of his cudgel right between the other's piggie eyes.

He went down. Two of the other guards looked, which they shouldn't have because two more cudgels fell; they collapsed before the two women. Huy, dropping low, swept away the feet of one of the men still before Scarab. While the last enemy, seeing his comrades tumble left and right, yelped, turned and ran.

For a moment there were no sounds but groans. Until the chant began, low at first from a few voices, spreading rapidly and loudly to many. "Sca-rab! Sca-rab! Sca-rab!"

The restored leader was making no attempt to look modest. Beaming, he swept his plumed hat from his head and made an elaborate bow. While holding it low, his head came quite close to Huy, who'd obviously decided to stay put after his last floor-level kick. Elayne was already moving across to help her friend up, but Scarab beat her to it. "The glory is yours to share, my new comrade. What is that kick you did and how did you assay it?" he asked, offering an arm.

"Oh, nothing much," replied Huy, taking the arm, pulling himself up, similarly failing to look less than delighted. "It's called Te Tat. I . . . I can show you some time if you like." His gaze went down. "On one condition."

"Speak it."

"You introduce me to your tailor."

Elayne stepped in. "Really, Huy? Now?"

She pointed. Bullman was crawling back toward the table he came from—and a knife there. Just before his hand closed over it, Scarab crossed and kicked it away. Then he bent, spoke softly—though that steel-in-velvet voice was still loud enough for all to hear. "I'm not feeling generous, my old shipmate. You have till the next bell. Tick tock."

Bullman rose, turned. His left eye was already swollen shut. His right would not be far behind. Still, he managed to squeeze an impressive amount of hate through the diminishing gap. "I will see you again, Scarab. And all your . . ." The head moved, taking them in. "Friends."

One of those stepped forward now. "Mine, I think," Leo said, and reached to pluck the gold talon from the big man's vest.

With a snarl and a last baleful glance, Bullman and his men limped from the tavern.

Scarab turned to where two of the women had helped up the third, the one who'd gone down. "Are you well, Malima?" he asked, in one of the tongues Elayne had heard before, when the man had talked about the fake ruby.

"I am . . . well enough." She looked up, her eyes as dark as his. "Nothing that a little rest and a visit from my master would not cure."

Though those who held her up were fairer—one had red hair, one corn yellow—Malima had near the same skin tone as his, as Elayne saw when he tenderly laid fingers on her cheek. "Then rest aboard and I will visit soon," he said. He turned to the others, and changed to English. "You fought well, my loves. Take her to the ship and I will visit you all there."

"We will." It was the red-haired one who answered. "And it is good to see you returned. Was it a great adventure, master?"

"It was, Caelin. As I will soon relate to you. Though I think . . ." and here he glanced back at Elayne, Huy and Leo, and a grin came, "an even greater one may be about to begin."

It took a little time to tidy up and for most of the tavern's clientele to come over and tell Scarab how they'd rooted for him from the very beginning. Leo's head was woozy for a while but he recovered fast with food and ale, brought by a grovelling landlord. They'd eaten short rations in the two days that it had taken to reach Slavetown and the three of them tucked into stews, breads and, in Elayne's case, one glass of beer too many. So she sat back and let Leo do the talking.

He told the story they'd agreed upon—that they'd been sent from one of the factions of Goloth to offer peace to the Glanasa. Scarab's face never changed in expression, and he never questioned why delegates should be so young—nor asked why Huy didn't look like anyone ever seen in that land before. In fact he cut pretty quickly to his own special interest.

"Gentlemen—and lady," he said, for Elayne had taken off her hat and let her hair fall once the fight was won, "your health." Filling up their tankards again, he continued. "I am a pirate. My mother—may the Gods keep her safe and far, far away from me—told me that from the hour of my birth I was cursed with a grasping heart." He smiled widely, one tooth flashing gold in his mouth. "So tell me about the money. And I will then tell you if it is enough to make me even consider this great risk."

It was—though Leo had to nearly double his original offer to Bullman. Content, Scarab sat back, put his feet up on the table, and picked at his perfect teeth with a small golden spike. "You mentioned animals. How many?"

They had discussed this. No one looked at the other as Elayne answered. "Two. One horse. One dog."

"Hmm." Scarab looked at the ceiling. "A dog is easy. A horse?" He shrugged. "Sometimes they do not like a sea voyage. The waters can be violent. Will he be calm?"

She thought "maybe" but said, "Yes."

"Good." He took his feet off the table, leaned in. "It will take me two days to outfit my ship for the voyage. I will not stop in Glana—they are not fond of me there, especially after my last visit—but once I have dropped you, I will then go on to my own shores with trade goods.

Ah, what a feast will be had at my homecoming. The celebrations of my people! The dancing. The drinking." He looked at Huy. "You should see them."

"I'd like that." Huy looked at Elayne, who frowned at him. "But, of course, the delegation, you know. Have to stick with my friends."

"Of course you do." Scarab studied him a moment longer, then nodded, rose. "I assume you did not offer me *all* your gold?"

"Not all," replied Leo.

"Good. This tavern's beds are the least dirty in the town. I would never sleep in them myself, but then . . ." He flashed a golden smile again. "I don't have to because I sleep aboard the Scarab."

"You named the ship after yourself?" said Huy. "Modest."

The pirate did not take offence. "It is named for my father, and his father before him, and his cousin, and his brothers, the Twins of Terror." He laughed. "It can get quite confusing at home. It is also named for my country, Scarabia." He leaned and tapped the table. "We leave on the night tide, on the second day after this. Be dockside then. But of course if you grow bored and wish to visit me, just ask where the Scarab is berthed." He seemed to direct most of this last at Huy. Then he was gone.

"Will you stop it?" Elayne hissed at Huy.

His eyes went wide, innocent. "Me? What?"

Leo looked between them, oblivious. "Is there something I should know?"

"No," they both said.

"Good." He rose, swayed slightly. "I will go seek one of these almost clean beds. I will take a room and you can both join me later. But will one of you go and tell Tempest what has transpired? And fetch Wolf to me?"

"I'll go," Elayne said.

"We'll both go," added Huy. "And what about Amphisbaena?"

Leo leaned down, lowered his voice. "Let us keep to the plan. The less they know of our company before we leave the better. The snake will see themselves aboard." He reached and touched his head and the gull's-egg-sized lump there. "I think I will sleep well this night."

He went, spoke to the landlord, who nodded vigorously, and pointed up.

"Let's go," said Elayne, stifling a yawn. "Before I fall asleep too."

The night tide two days later was exactly that—at four bells in the morning. Even the tavern before the dock was dark and silent as they left it, the faintest hint of dawn lightening the sky behind it, above the cliffs. They walked down several long jetties to reach the Scarab at her berth. Tempest had met them at the track down from the forest, submitting angrily but silently to the blanket Elayne threw over his horn and head. It looked odd, and she suspected that everyone in Slavetown was either drunk or asleep. Probably both. But it wasn't worth risking the hue and cry if someone saw him.

Scarab awaited them at the top of the gangway. "Why is the horse covered?" he asked straightaway.

"Um, shy?" Elayne began.

But Leo shook his head, stepped closer. "He has to know. We talked of this," he said. Then he reached up and pulled the blanket away.

Grunts of surprise, whistles, curses, all came from his crew—a dozen men, and the three women, now gaping from the gunnels of the high-sided ship. Only Scarab was silent, staring for a long moment before he spoke. "I knew I should have asked for more gold," he sighed. "Horse, hey?" He shook his head. "Get him aboard before someone in the town sees and we have them all down here."

Elayne went to lead Tempest up the gangway but he jerked his head up and down, avoiding her grasp. Two days of rain in the forest had not improved his temper.

Leo moved before him. "Will you follow me, Tempest?"

The unicorn shivered his length, then grunted. *I will*, came the thought.

With Leo leading, Wolf and Tempest both following, Elayne and Huy together in the rear, the quest of the dragon climbed aboard. Once on deck, the unicorn had to be winched in a sling and lowered into a straw-filled hold. There was a cramped cabin at the aft that the three of them would have to squeeze into. It had only one narrow bed—they would sleep in shifts.

"Away ropes!" Scarab called, and men on the dock cast off and scrambled aboard as the vessel started to drift. "Up anchor!"

Elayne had walked the length of the ship. It had taken about forty seconds. When she reached the raised forecastle, where two of the crew hauled on the winch, she leaned over the side and, as the iron anchor cleared the surface, saw who clung to it—and who slipped off the chain and through a porthole with a hiss.

She stared ahead as the ship headed west, away from the sunrise, into the deeper dark, and whispered her thought. "I'm coming, Dad."

24

LAND OF THE DRAGON

On a ship so small, with a crew of sixteen and passengers added, it was hard to find anywhere for a bit of solitude. Elayne craved it, and so spent a lot of time in the one tiny cabin. She was guiltily aware that she was getting more sleep time than the others on the cramped little bunk. They let her though. Huy was always hanging out with Scarab, laughing at something or other. Leo? He seemed to share her hunger for alone time. Perhaps it was the worry over what he'd undertaken, what lay ahead. It was all so bold, to vow to set off on a dragon hunt. But how to succeed in slaying one was something else. No wonder he was so often staring ahead into the endless ocean, seeking land and perhaps his destiny.

A dragon, she thought, sliding off the bunk. There had been so much other stuff to deal with since arriving in Goloth that she hadn't focused much on what lay beyond it. She'd even convinced herself that the contact she'd had with it in the doctor's office—the visitation; she couldn't think of another word for it—was a by-product of the stress she'd been under, the hypnotic state she was in. A dragon hadn't spoken to her across the divide of worlds. It hadn't summoned her. And yet she'd felt, from the moment that she'd stepped aboard the ship, that she was being pulled forward. That something awaited her. Could it be her dad? Did he lie ahead? Was he really a prisoner of the dragon?

Pulling on her trousers, she stumbled a little with the sway of the ship, and kicked the bucket that lay there. It tipped over—fortunately, this time, it was empty. There was another reason they probably let her have the bunk so much. Of the three of them, she was the one who was seasick. It was only this morning that she had truly mastered her stomach.

She stepped out of the little cabin now and, as always, looked ahead. She still couldn't see any land. But there was a scent beyond the salt for the first time in a week. Quite different from the cool, pine-laden breezes off the land they'd left behind. What she got here as she inhaled was warm, rich, yet with a base note to it that was . . . rotten? But that could have been her. She'd taken in some pretty funky smells in her week at sea. She was afraid that she was the source of a few.

The wind had dropped from the near gale that had pushed them so far, so fast. Usually everyone had to shout above the shriek of wind in rigging, the crash of waves against the bow. They were still moving steadily but across calmer waters. And it must have been the relative quiet that meant she heard a sound she hadn't heard aboard before—music. Someone was playing a stringed instrument. She looked all around, couldn't figure out the source. Huy and Scarab were across the short main deck, near the forecastle. They were laughing, as usual, starting to wrestle. They had done little else on the voyage except show each other fighting moves—Scarab's cutlass against Huy's Muay Thai.

Her friend glanced across. "Am I going crazy?" she called. "I'm hearing music."

Huy grinned, and pointed up the main mast. There was a crow's nest at the top of it, the highest point of the ship for the lookout to seek land. She'd not climbed up before—it was hard enough on her stomach standing on the swaying deck, let alone in the rigging. But she felt better now and she was definitely missing her climbing. It had been at least a month since she last had back home. She had decided not to count the Griffin Mountains. She was trying to forget all about them.

She swung easily up the rope netting, the sound of plucked strings getting louder, a mournful tune. Grasping the top of what was essentially a wooden bathtub around the masthead, she raised herself over its sides—

"Leo!"

A harsh discord. "Maid!" He jumped. "You startled me."

She hoisted herself over and in. Leo sat cross-legged on the floor, a small stringed instrument—a type of mandolin, she thought—on his lap. She dropped down opposite him. The mast, rising through the box's floor, was between them. Peering around it, she pointed. "I didn't know you played."

"I barely do. But it was considered one of the knightly virtues that I must learn. I was not diligent, preferred training with the sword. Now . . ." He strummed a chord, a minor, in that same melancholic tone. "I find I like it. One of Scarab's, uh, female friends lent me it. Caelin. The red-haired one."

"The pretty one?" Elayne said, a bright smile on her face. "So are you practising this sad old song to play for her?"

"Nay, the song's not for her. It's—" He broke off, looked away, then down to the strings. "Nor is it old but a tune of my own poor invention. Yet I have discovered that I do not truly have the gift."

"It sounded pretty good to me."

A loud burst of male laughter came from the deck below. Elayne peered over the edge of the nest. Huy must have just thrown Scarab because the pirate was on his back. As she watched, Huy pulled him up and there was a moment when they held each other, smiles on their faces.

"They are good comrades already, are they not?" Leo had risen and was looking down too.

"A little more than comrades perhaps," she said. "Huy's gay."

"Yes, he always seems most happy."

She laughed. It was a joke that hadn't worked back in her world for decades. "No," she said, "I mean he and Scarab are . . . in love."

"Oh. Oh, I see." He sat back down, so she did too. "This is not very common in Goloth."

"You disapprove?"

He was silent a moment, staring back at her. When he spoke, his voice was low. "I do not think I could ever disapprove of anyone finding love in this brief life."

He went to put his mandolin aside. "No, please!" She raised a hand. "Will you play it for me? Your song?"

"I—"

"Please."

"Lady, since you request it—"

He strummed that same chord again, reached up to adjust one of the keys, strummed and nodded. Then he plucked the strings with his right hand, while his left fingers moved over the frets. Closing her eyes to the melancholy air, she opened them again when he began to sing, his voice soft yet true.

"There was a sailor went to sea
Singing ho-heh-ho and the waves sweep by
Who asked his love please wait for me
With a ho-heh-ho and the seagulls cry."

He played another run of chords, then took a deep breath.

"Three years he voyaged to faraway lands
Singing ho-heh-ho, be true and bide
At last was wrecked on desert sands
Singing ho-heh-ho trust be my guide."

Elayne stared at Leo. His face was transformed when he sang. His bright blue eyes, always so direct, so piercing, were misty now, as if he were not looking out of them at all, but in. And then she couldn't see them because he closed his eyes to sing again.

"'Twas three more years 'ere he was saved
Singing ho-heh-ho, 'tis home I'll go.
But there his love was freshly graved.
And he'll sing no more his ho-heh-ho."

The last notes, of string and song, hung in the air for a while. "But, Leo, that's . . . that's beautiful."

He opened his eyes, smiled shyly. "Nay, 'tis but a trifle. I—"

He went to set down the instrument again. But this time it was her hand not her voice that stopped him. "Really," she said, laying her fingers on top of his. "Beautiful."

He looked down at her hand on his, then up into her eyes. "Alice-Elayne," he whispered, leaning toward her, as she leaned toward him.

"Land! Land ho!"

She turned, had to. Both of them peered forward, both indeed saw the thin line of green where there had been nothing but blue.

"Glana," Leo said, and she could hear in his voice the same thing she was feeling inside: an equal mix of excitement and dread.

"Come on you guys," called Huy from below. "Team talk."

Leo gestured. "After you, maid."

So, it was back to "maid." She looked at him a moment, couldn't find anything to say, went.

They clambered down. Leo went to the raised aft deck where Scarab was while Elayne joined Huy at the rail near the prow. The sun was rising though it had not yet breached the horizon; yet it was light enough to make out more clearly the low-lying mass on the still-dark sea.

"Where is he dropping us?"

Huy nodded forward. "Northeast coast of Glana. Scar says—"

"Whoa! 'Scar'?"

"Sure." Huy grinned, picking a thread from the emerald, pearl-buttoned waistcoat Scarab had given him early in the voyage. "Couldn't keep calling him by a beetle's name. Though I did try 'Ringo' for a bit, which he didn't like, so—Scar. Very *Lion King*." He turned back, pointed again. "Anyway, he says that this coast is hard to get to overland so the Glanasan 'authorities' don't venture up much. There are a few small villages, mainly inhabited by runaways. Kind of like Slavetown, but on this side."

"I see. Tell you much else about the place?"

"Oh sure. He knows it quite well. He was a slave here for a while himself." He turned. "He's had an amazing life actually. Warrior, turned slave, turned fugitive, turned pirate. He—"

"Maybe later? How about catching me up? Do we have a plan?"

"We do." It was Leo who spoke, coming up quietly behind them. Leaning on the rail, he gestured ahead. "The island is big—near as big as the whole of Goloth. It is mainly jungle." He sniffed. "That is what you are smelling. But farther south they have cleared vast areas for farmland, built a city. It is where their temples are. Where the sacrifices take place. Where their dragons live."

234

"Dragons plural?" She shuddered. "So there *are* more than one?"

"There are three smaller ones, the dragon's brood. One that rules, mother or father, no one is certain." A light came into his eyes. "It is the one that I must kill."

"But . . . how?" Now they were within sight of land, all Elayne's misgivings returned, doubled.

Leo sensed her disquiet. "It will be difficult—but will it be as difficult as what you achieved before? Saving your unicorn and starting a revolution? I think not." He turned to look at the land again. "Scarab was once a rebel here and led a slave rebellion. It was crushed; he escaped. But fury is a slow fire that burns still. He has been in touch with elements in Glana—"

"How? Skype them from the quarterdeck?"

Leo stared at her. "Once again, maid, I have no idea what you are saying. The contact was made by pigeon."

"Excuse me? Did you say pigeon?"

"Aye. A messenger bird sent out before land could be seen but when it was first scented a day ago. And Scarab received a message back only one bell since." He nodded to the deck where the captain stood. "We are expected. We will be guided by rebels to the city, gathering more as we march. You will ride in on the other bearer of hope—the unicorn, and then, maid, you will start your second revolution." Leo's eyes gleamed. "But I will be guided ahead to sneak at night into their temple. To slay a dragon."

She tried to object. Couldn't. It didn't sound like a plan. It sounded like her nightmares. Her stomach heaved. She was uncertain whether it was a return of seasickness or sheer bloody terror! She turned to the rail, in case, mastered herself—then heard soft footsteps behind her.

"It is time."

Scarab was dressed quite moderately—for him, which meant he was still pretty flamboyant, in pirate chic: mauve, tasseled culottes over bare calves and shoeless feet, a flounced white shirt, an ochre headscarf, one large gold earring. He had a cutlass at one hip, a dagger at the other, palms resting on both. "We land you on a remote beach. The first of your army awaits you there to guide you up a cliff path. Ah, see!" he pointed shoreward.

Such was the speed of their sleek vessel that Glana was much closer already. The light had grown too, and Elayne was able to make out trees, and thick brush climbing steep cliffs. There was a lighter strip at their base, a strand of beach. "I will see you to shore." He looked at each in turn, his eyes resting last and longest on Huy. "T'faith, I wish I was coming with you. What adventures you will have!"

"So come," replied Huy.

"Alas!" He shook his head. "Were I to be caught in Glana, such is my reputation, they wouldn't even wait to bear me to the sacrifice but would immediately separate me into parts. When my parts go so well together!" He spread his arms wide. "Nevertheless, I will sorrow at our leave-taking." He dropped his arms, and his dark eyes narrowed. "I had hoped to deliver you to a proper dock. But my feathered messenger brought warnings of danger. Hence, this." He waved at the rowboat. "As you see, it is small. It will fit all the humans and one dog, but speed is required, and I am loathe to make two journeys. Can the unicorn swim?"

They all looked at each other. "I . . . have no idea," answered Elayne. "I'll ask."

"Nay. I will," Leo said, adding to Scarab, "Will you arrange the winch?"

On his nod, Leo went to the hold, disappearing into it. "What's this?" asked Elayne.

Huy shrugged. "While you were sick, Leo spent quite a lot of time with Tempest. The unicorn wasn't doing well and they . . . talked. I think they've gotten quite close."

"Oh really?" Elayne frowned, pissed. Wasn't she the unicorn tamer?

Huy must have sensed something. "Hey, who're you jealous of? Man or beast?" He put a hand on her arm, adding softly, "Or is it both?"

"Neither. I have my unicorn, right?" She turned again to the shore, much closer again. She of all people knew the power of the connection with a unicorn. And as she thought of them in the hold, their minds linked, she felt a surge of longing for her Moonspill—coupled with a sudden surge of regret for a missed kiss in a crow's nest.

"I'll get our supplies," Huy said.

"OK." She turned at a scraping sound. It was the winch's teeth biting as the sling took the unicorn's weight. In a moment, Leo appeared from below, his attention focused down. In another, she saw the ivory horn. Tempest rose, cleared the hold, was lowered to the deck.

He didn't look well. Stuck in a small space where he could barely turn around and where his horn scraped the roof, unused to the roll of a ship, she'd heard he'd also been seasick. Now she could see it. His normally glossy coat had a slick sheen, his eyes were filmy, his mane, beard and tail hung lank.

Leo rested his hand on the velvet of his muzzle. "Can he swim?" she asked, crossing to them.

The reply came in her head. And in her ear.

I can.

"He can."

"Good." She said it aloud. There wasn't room in there for three of them. She turned away. Dammit, she thought. Huy's right. I'm jealous of both of them.

The cry came from below. She went to the rail. Scarab and Caelin of the red hair were in the rowboat, bracing it against the ship's side—with some difficulty due to the waves. "Come!" the pirate called. "Be swift."

Elayne leaned into Leo. "The snake?" she whispered.

"I heard a clear splash. The amphisbaena can swim this distance, I believe."

Slipping on her backpack, she clambered over the side. Huy and Scarab helped her into the rowboat, then took a squirming Wolf from Leo, who then followed. Once all were settled, Scarab and Caelin began to work the oars, pulling strongly for the shore.

They'd only got about fifty yards when there was a big splash from behind them. All turned, to see a spiralling horn break the surface, followed by a white head. Tempest was kicking hard for the shore.

"Will he be OK?" asked Huy.

"I think so. After a week in that hold, he's probably loving it."

Swimming was perhaps not a unicorn's strong point. He fell behind but appeared to be doing fine. Indeed every so often a larger wave would pick him up and carry the white form several yards on. "A body-surfing unicorn," said Elayne, pointing. "Not something you see every day."

The surf was rougher closer to shore. Scarab skilfully steered them in on it, using a last wave to sweep them onto the beach. Wood ground on sand, and the three passengers and one dog leapt out. Scarab and Caelin dragged the boat beyond the ocean's tug. Then they all looked around.

The beach was long, stretching at least a quarter mile either way, ending in steep promontories. It was also shallow, a narrow strip with maybe fifty yards of golden sand between water and what looked like palm trees. "Nice," said Huy. "Give me a hammock and a Mai Tai, some chill tunes and I could—"

He broke off. All turned to watch Tempest come ashore. The last part was difficult for him; he slipped once, was washed in on a bigger wave, struggled up, stumbled onto dryer sand. There he stood, head down, breathing heavily.

Leo turned to Scarab, who was staring into the treeline. "So where is your guide? I would be swiftly on our way."

"Here," replied Scarab.

There was something in the way he said it, some tone that jarred with her, that made her look at the pirate. And then past him to the treeline where, for the first time, she noticed a large piece of cloth, a blanket perhaps, hanging from the branch of a palm. But she didn't have time to study it—not with the movement below it, the sudden blinding light of the sun dazzling her. Yet since that had only just risen, was behind her out to sea, what was blinding her, moving toward her was not the sun at all but it's—

"Reflection!" she shouted and knew, in that word, another one.

Betrayal.

She turned, shouted. "Moonspill!"

It was the wrong name, of course, born of panic. Still, Tempest looked up at her. "Mirrors!" she managed, just before she was grabbed from behind, further words cut off by the arm around her neck, and the point of a dagger just above it.

"You will all be easy," Scarab said in that velvet voice, with the steel back in it, "or the maid will die."

Fear flushed her, in the pricking at her throat. And there was no time for Huy or Leo to do anything, not with her in danger and a dozen men rushing at them with spears. Through blurred eyes, Elayne could only watch as Tempest turned to look into the five big mirrors being run at him. Watch him caught by his reflection, held by it, entranced by it.

It was a myth in her world, so another truth in this one: the one true weakness of the unicorn, the only way to capture a beast that would otherwise die before it allowed itself to be taken. Hypnotized by his own image, Tempest lost himself to his own vast eyes.

The eyelids drooped, the horn dropped. Another man came past and bound a special harness around the unicorn's head. Elayne knew what that was, how the raised eyepieces would have little mirrors within, and slits for light to enter, constantly showing the beast to himself. Moonspill had been caught once that way too.

At least one of them escaped—Wolf, teeth bared and snarling, was about to hurl himself upon the enemy, heedless of spears. But Leo shouted, "Wolf! Go!" and the hound obeyed him as ever, evading the grasping hands, a thrown net, running up the beach to vanish into the jungle.

It was one joy among so many sorrows. Elayne sank, and Scarab let her, stepping away, sheathing his dagger. Huy was glaring at him. "You traitor," he spat.

Scarab shook his head. "To be a traitor you have to be loyal to something in the first place. Scarab is only loyal to Scarab."

"And only a dick talks about himself in the third person."

"You feel like this now. You will learn to feel differently later." He reached out a hand. "Come."

"What do you mean?"

"You are part of my reward. It is agreed. You do not go to the dragon's feast."

"Oh, no." Huy unbuttoned the embroidered waistcoat, peeled it off, dropped it to the beach, and heeled it into the sand. "I go with my friends."

Scarab frowned. "I could take you by force."

Huy moved into a Muay Thai stance. "You could try."

They stared at each other a long moment. "Well," Scarab said softly. "I am sorry for that. I liked you. I liked all of you. But truly," his eyes hardened as he said, "which part of the word 'pirate' did you not understand?"

Scarab was approached by a Glanasan, gold circlet around his head linking the two hanks of black hair that fell from his bald, pale white scalp. "Your pardon for past crimes," the officer said, handing over a sealed scroll of paper. "And your gold," he added, passing over a cloth bag.

It clinked as Scarab took it. He weighed it briefly in his hand. Then he bent and snatched up the waistcoat. "Take them," he said, and walked toward the rowboat without looking back.

25

Temple of the God

The third day was the worst.

The first two had been in the mountains, so some tracks were steep and often switchbacked, while others went along the edges of the peaks, narrow defiles with long drops to rivers far below. Though their guards were brutal, hitting them on arms and back with short ebony rods when they thought they could go faster, they also took great care. It was clear that they did not want to lose any prisoners, and that the captives needed to arrive in reasonable shape. They were fed often—a foul mix of some kind of grain, studded with stringy, greasy pieces of chewy meat, washed down with green-slimed water. There was no question of refusing the food— sharp jabs in the ribs convinced them otherwise. When they stopped at night, they were allowed to sleep without their arms chained to the yoke—a long bar of wood across their shoulders, which they wore on all but the most dangerous paths—though then a guard walked beside them, club in hand. And there was no talking, pain the consequence when anyone tried.

Leo contrived whenever possible to keep beside Tempest. Elayne knew what he was doing: trying to reach the blinkered unicorn with his mind. But she also remembered that when Moonspill had been captured before, the tiny mirrors in the eyepieces held him in his memories more firmly than any ropes would have done.

Her body might have been suffering, exhausted all the time. But two things were propelling her forward, no matter the steepness of path, the rocks underfoot. The first was a delirious certainty: her father waited at the end of this journey. He was alive. She had a sense of him, perhaps transferred through the earth that now linked them. Somehow she knew he was there. This, at least, gave her some joy.

The second feeling did not. It gave her the reverse.

She felt the lure of the dragon.

It was like the probe she'd received all those weeks ago in Leibowitz's office—except to a factor of ten. No voice came, no words sliced into her. It was worse than that. A will greater than she'd ever known was focused entirely on her, drawing her forward, a cord attached to her chest, dragging her remorselessly on. It wasn't the yoke that made her feel like a prisoner. It was powerlessness in the face of that awesome will.

Everything changed on the third day.

They were woken when there was barely a hint of light in the sky. Forced to wolf down foul food before being yoked then driven onto a path that immediately descended sharply. The mountains had been cool, especially at night. But the lower they got, the warmer they got, until they were soaked with sweat. This attracted bugs, clouds of them, large and small, emerging from the huge-leaved shrubs and vine-wrapped trees of the jungle around them, settling and biting. With their hands bound high on the wooden bar above them they could do nothing to fend them off. They were especially attracted to Huy, whose face was soon red and swollen.

Down they went, down, at an ever-increasing pace. Roots snagged their feet, sent them tumbling. They were dragged up, pushed on again.

On and on, hours blending into each other. Elayne sank into a waking dream, eyes open, legs moving, somewhere else. She began to fantasize—about bug-spray milkshakes rubbed all over her. About slimy iced coffee drunk in a sleek Manhattan café. It distracted her enough to keep putting one foot before the other, to haul herself up when she fell before she was hit.

When she thought she couldn't take another step, after what had to have been three hours, suddenly it was over. The ground levelled, which made her stumble though she kept her feet, staggered on—and emerged from shaded canopy to a blinding sun. Everyone stopped, and they all collapsed onto the ground, squinted into the light. Gasped.

It was unlike anything she'd ever seen since coming through the tapestry.

From the verdant chaos of the jungle to a vast and ordered plain. Everywhere was green, in every shade and tint, so varied and overlapping it made her eyes swim like psychedelia. To her left, a vast area, ten football fields long and wide, was covered with shrubs bearing egg-shaped fruit like avocados. The fields ended in lines of trees, planted in rows, with huge spear-like leaves, their colour matching the bark and of a green that was almost black. To her right, everything flattened to low, narrow-leafed plants, covering an area that matched the fruit shrubs. Iridescent canals of algae-bloomed water threaded these and in them waded men and women in wide brimmed hats. As she stared, she saw some raise their heads and stare back—only for a moment though, before other men, with the distinctive Glanasan hairstyle, stepped forward and whipped them back to work.

"Slaves," she hissed at Huy, before her own guard prodded her up. It was only when she was in line again and moving from the hard-packed earth of the forest trail onto a paved roadway twenty feet broad, cutting like a stone spear through all the green, that she saw what awaited at journey's end.

A giant tower. Trees lining both sides sheltered her from the sun now and she was able to see what had been lost to dazzle. She blinked, disbelieving. Goloth City had some buildings that would have made six storeys back in Manhattan. This was far taller, twenty at least, and was faced with some sort of reflective material that forced her to look away from it every so often or go blind. Then, just when she thought she'd have to simply look down and concentrate on her footing—for the stone paving was irregular and full of unexpected ridges—a cloud hid the sun, the dazzle reduced, and she was able to see what crowned the structure.

A dragon. It was the top, the apex, claws dug into its perch. A beast so huge, its wings were the size of an airliner's, spread wide for flight, as if it was about to swoop down and snatch them up in its vast, fanged jaw. "Oh no," she moaned, the sweat that covered her instantly chilled. She stumbled, nearly fell, a guard catching her, forcing her up, on. She didn't want to look again, at the monster soon to devour her. Had to, did—and saw that the beast was poised in exactly the same way. It hadn't moved.

It was made of stone.

The cloud passed, sun bounced off the temple again, forcing her to lower her eyes. But her main thought, as her party stumbled out of the sheltering trees onto a vast, open plaza before the tower she now saw was a pyramid of steps, was that if this was the sculpture, she did not want to meet the model.

They were driven to its side and there, in its shade, they were allowed to fall over. The yokes were removed, replaced by manacles, and gourds, filled with foul, brackish water the same shade as the canals, were dropped beside them. They were too thirsty to care about the colour. Even Tempest was being watered, his blinding harness, with the mirrors over the eye sockets, lifted just enough for him to drink from a stone trough. They were not alone but part of a mass of prisoners: black-haired Glanasa, others with the brown skin of Scarabia, others still darker who would have been African back home, a few pale and fair from Goloth. What united them all was the glassy stare of the abused prisoner.

She was closest to Leo. Huy, with his eyes shut, was on Leo's other side. The former king-elect looked like she felt. "How are you?" she managed.

"As well as you, I suspect."

She glanced over at the guards. They were digging into other gourds now, pulling out fingerfuls of their cold stew. "At least they're not making us eat anymore of that crap," she said.

"You think that a good thing?" Leo replied. "They have delivered us alive to their god. Their duty of care is done."

"You saw the statue?"

"The dragon? Aye. And those too."

She looked where he pointed—and wished she hadn't. Because about twenty paces away, facing the temple, was a long line of shelves, three high—each shelf crammed with skulls. Mostly human. Some animals. But one especially drew and held her gaze. It had a triple set of jaws.

Among all the victims sacrificed to the dragon had been a manticore.

"Oh God," she said, looking down quickly, mastering her stomach. "We're doomed, aren't we? And it's my fault." Her voice went quavery. "Why did I let us come here? Why couldn't I persuade Moonspill to come to our aid? We wouldn't be here. We wouldn't be—"

Leo's manacles jangled as he laid his hands upon hers. "Alice-Elayne," he said. "It was my foolishness that brought us here. I the one who chose this mad quest. I the one who should have insisted you remain behind. But I couldn't. I . . ." He faltered, looked down, then sharply up again into her eyes. "My courage failed me. I did not want to be alone. I did not want to be . . . without you."

His gaze fell again. She reversed her hands, so she could hold his wrists too, bent till she could find his eyes again with hers. "I would never have let you go alone," she said softly. "We're in this together, all the way. Huy, Tempest. You. Me."

"You—and me?" Leo blue eyes searched hers. "Is there such a thing as you and me?"

She didn't know what to say. Twice before, in her first visit to Goloth when he'd been king-elect, he'd leaned toward her like this. Once, she'd slapped him. Once, she'd let him kiss her, hoping to dupe him. And then, a few days ago he'd sung her a song in a crow's nest. They'd been interrupted then. A final, perhaps lasting interruption was coming now. And she knew suddenly, certainly, that she didn't want to face whatever was coming without giving him something, without taking something in return.

So she kissed him. And he kissed her back.

She felt it tingle on her lips, spread down her body, sensed it vibrate through his. It gave her comfort and the first warmth she'd felt in an age that wasn't made of jungle heat or terror. This was a softer heat within and it lasted a while, as long as a kiss.

And ended. Leo broke off, moved back but only a little, to look at her closely. "I take courage from your lips, Alice-Elayne," he whispered, "and heart too. For I cannot believe that fate would have brought us to this moment, only to pull us apart again. We have breath and so we have hope. We are not done yet."

"We are not done yet," she echoed. "And I've just remembered something else. *Someone* else, who I left off the list." She smiled. "Where's Amphisbaena?"

His smile matched hers. "Indeed. And where is Wolf? Our beasts are out there. We have hope indeed," he repeated and leaned in again.

A voice halted them. "Sorry to interrupt," said Huy, "oh, and may I just say, 'about time'?" He grinned briefly, then pointed with his chin. "But something weird's happening."

"Define weird," she said, turned, saw.

They were about halfway along a rough line of about two hundred prisoners. To their left, toward the end, those who had lain slumped against the wall were now either on their feet or rising to them. No guards urged them, but it was like a ripple passing along. One moment the man or woman was crouched, cowed, the next they were on their feet, some crying out, some just staring wildly above. Then they calmed, looked around as if seeking someone. No one spoke and no guards came near.

The ripple or current—something she felt she could almost see— gained speed along the line then deviated, for it passed to Tempest who stood just in front of the prisoners at the stone water trough. One moment he was in the docility that the head harness forced on him, the next he was up on his hind legs, his forelegs kicking the air as if in a fight, his horn rising and plunging, a great whinny bursting forth.

She heard that. But more, and just for a moment, she heard him in her head, as she hadn't since they'd blinkered him on the beach.

No! You shall not have me! he cried, the thought so loud it hurt. But then a worse one came. *Maid!* he screamed.

She jumped to her feet. *Tempest!* she called. *What is it?*

He was gone in an instant, hooves crashing down, horn drooped, still again—yet the connection between them did not falter. She felt like they were bound by sound waves, linked by electricity. And along it she sensed something coming, bypassing everyone between her and the unicorn, a microsecond's pulse before she was struck, a thought driven into her skull like an invisible spike. A question. A word.

Maid?

When she'd first come to Goloth, panicked and scared, Moonspill had laid his mind against hers, wrapping her brain in warmth, calming, stilling. He'd done it again before they parted at the tunnel. This was exactly the opposite—an icy shaft of pure malevolence thrust into the skull, ripping aside tissue and thought, piercing to her very core. "Ahhh!" she screamed, collapsing. Leo leapt to catch her just before she smashed into the ground. But then he was picked up, hurled aside, his arms flung wide, his legs launching him backwards and away from her. For Elayne the moment of his flinging was a moment of relief, the shaft withdrawn, the pain receded. Until Leo fell and the ice spear drove in again. She was helpless to do anything but curl into a ball and let whatever it was ravage her mind.

She did not know how long it lasted. Suddenly it was gone, withdrawing, though where it had been felt bruised, sliced, battered. Yet even as it left she heard faintly, as if in a distant shout, a command.

Bring her to me.

Eyes glued shut by terror, she felt hands on her, heard Huy cry, "Leave her alone!" heard the blow that silenced him. When her feet lifted from the ground, she forced her lids up, glimpsed water, a river, some boats. Gone as she was run up the steps of the pyramid, her guards' breathing getting heavier as they climbed. They were replaced by two more, a second exchange happening before they reached the top. A flat platform, a low arch, dragged through that into a corridor with torches flaring its long length. Another doorway, more light, much more light— the sun streaming through a vast translucent roof covering a hall filled with stone columns, so vast that the far end was lost to shadows. Into those they ran her, flung her down, removed her manacles. Footsteps receded, sounds faded. Until only her sobs pierced the silence.

Which ended on a voice. *That* voice. Though this time it did not come on a frozen shaft, the words still chilled.

Welcome, Alice-Elayne.

Another sound. Not in her head. From the shadows before her. She forced her eyes open again . . .

And watched a dragon pull itself from the dark.

26

The Dragon of a Thousand Names

At first, the beast was impossible to take in. Partly because terror froze her breath and that made her giddy. Partly because it just kept coming. Thick, powerful forelegs, with claws the length of her arms, scratched the paved floor, pulling it forward. The vast chest and long neck rippled with overlapping aquamarine scales the size of trays. The head was the size of a bull, with crocodile jaws parted to reveal rows of shiny teeth, two fangs like paired ivory daggers thrust down at their centre, a red, forked tongue flicking out between them. Above the twin caverns of its nostrils, the long snout ended in eyes all iridescent green—except in the very centre, where lay slits of red fire.

The head was crested in long emerald feathers. As it ducked into the main hall, the beast rose onto huge hind legs, able to stretch out at last, to thrust those feathers up, reach its long neck toward the roof above, spread twin wings like the sails of a giant windmill, both divided into sections by long bones, which all ended in a curved talon. At their limit the wings near filled the width of the space. The monster flapped them once—and a gale hit Elayne, knocking her straight from kneeling onto her bottom. The dragon kept coming, growing, towering, its head shining, its scaled body glimmering, halting at last to sweep a spear-tipped tail around and wrap it about its huge-clawed back feet.

Elayne shook, the only movement she could make, unable even to turn away. The dragon, having touched the roof with its head, now began to lower that again, slowly winding down, closer to her, ever closer, halting perhaps half a dozen feet away. It's head was so big that the beast couldn't look at her straight on. First the one eye fixed its red-green gaze upon her, then the head turned and the other eye took up the study.

Elayne's breath came in shallow gulps, her mind flushed of anything but pure fear. This close she could smell the beast's breath, a foul mix of half-digested flesh—what kind she didn't want to consider—and something from a dripping, dank cave. This close she could see that the two monstrous incisors had razored edges and were lined in yellow slime. This close . . .

Do I frighten you?

The thought words made her start. But couldn't help her conjure words of her own.

"Would you feel less fear if I talked instead?"

The voice emerged from the throat, as it did with all the fabulous beasts of Goloth, as if the organs of speech—lips, tongue, soft pallet—were buried deep. It was sibilant, a small hiss on the esses. Other than that, it could have been a voice she heard back home, light in tone, in pitch.

Home. The thought word, its normality, calmed her enough to allow a blurted, "Maybe."

"Then I shall speak so. But my appearance?" The head thrust another foot closer and she leaned away. "Yes, that terrifies. I have seen that same fear on ten thousand faces. Would you rather I looked differently?"

"How . . . how do you mean?"

Turn about.

The words were back in her head. A command. She turned, unable to disobey.

Go to the torches.

Behind her, fire burned in the shadows. She rose, staggered, took a breath, another, steadied, walked between two columns. Flames moved on them in iron sconces. And a few feet ahead of her, flames moved again. Reflected.

She heard the scratching of claws on stone. Heard the word in her head. *Closer.*

She obeyed, stepped nearer. Saw herself.

It was a giant round mirror, six feet in diameter. It swung slightly, held by chains that disappeared into the darkness above. She looked again, shocked for a moment by the sight of herself, her thick hair a matted tangle, her face puffed with insect bites, streaked in filth. Mostly she was appalled by the terror in her eyes. She didn't think she'd ever been this frightened. And she'd been frightened by the best.

"Obsidian." The words were aloud again, as the dragon's head lowered, coming in behind her, so slightly out of focus. "A stone, polished for centuries. A seeing stone. I saw you here first, Alice-Elayne. I can show you wonders within it. I can show you . . . anything."

"Like—" She swallowed, forced herself not to squeak. "Like what?"

"Oh, shall we begin with some of my other faces? Since you are so frightened of this one?" Something rumbled in the throat that could have been close to a laugh—if such a sound could come entirely free of humour. "Shall we begin with the face I first saw in it a thousand years ago?"

Elayne saw the dragon in the mirror vanish. Saw another, very different, take its place. This one was as much bird as reptile, each scale of its long, coiled body covered in feathers, dazzling in every shade of yellow and green. Its chest was a vivid crimson; its snake-like head surmounted in a spread crest of blue, orange, and black. As she watched, the face receded till the whole beast was revealed, spreading multicoloured wings, soaring up into the sky, a tail like the longest train on a wedding dress streaming behind in flashing green.

"Quetzalcóatl was the name they gave me."

"Aztecs," Elayne breathed.

"A people I loved, who loved me. A people who knew how to care for their god."

She watched in the mirror as the plumed serpent flew down to perch on a temple, a step pyramid not unlike the one she was now in. Saw a man dragged forward, his limbs spread, saw another man raise a stone knife above him. She jerked her gaze away.

The voice came. "Yes. They are similar, the Glanasa of this land. I have made them similar. But they have not the Aztecs' mind, their imagination, their faith. They do what they do for fear, and for the power the sacrifice brings."

"Nice for you," she murmured, her gaze still down.

"Nice?" The repetition had extra hiss, and steel in it too. "Look again."

"I'm good, really."

Look.

Once again, the thought command was impossible to disobey.

She looked, thankfully to blankness. The Aztecs were gone, as was Quetzalcóatl. For a moment there was nothing in the stone. Until there was.

She took a big breath. Before her now was a beast of many parts. Its head looked almost camel-like; its ears more like a cow's. It had antlers like a stag, a scaly neck, a belly made of clamshell.

"You see me in the phase of the kioh-lung. Before that I was in water. Here I am on earth. I will stay like this for a thousand years until I grow my wings, take to the air, become ying-lung. I am a dragon of the east." She heard the claws scratching, felt the monster move to her other side. "Do you like this look better, Alice-Elayne?"

It was still weird, all those different animals rolled into one. But there was something peaceful, nearly comical about the vision. Though she was a long way from laughing, she said, "Yes."

"Yes," came the echo. "Of course you do. The eastern dragons harm no one. They help. They are benevolent, kind, wise."

Dull.

The word clanged into her head. The image in the obsidian lurched as behind her the dragon swept its huge tail around and sent wind into the torches, making the flames jerk wildly. The kind dragon vanished as all the fires in the stone coalesced into a long, flaming stream. She could see its source—the wide-spread jaws of another dragon.

"I have been them all," the voice came again, crackling with heat. "And if I have not, those of my family have. For if one of us lives a life, all of us live it, so closely are we bound." The breath withdrew, then shot out again. "So closely *were* we bound."

Scrunching her neck down—the flames had come so close she'd felt the hairs on her arm crisp—she still heard the emphasized word. "Were?"

Heat diminished. She risked a glance. The dragon was back as it had been. "What you see is the shape I choose to be. The last shape I was before I was driven from your world."

Look again.

She did, had to. And in the stone, many shapes swirled now, dragons of different sizes yet all with the same look of the one who was controlling the vision, controlling her. But in these visions there were other images too.

There were men. Men in armour. Mounted men with lances. Men on foot with spear and sword.

Men slaying dragons.

Creatures shrieked—and she realized she could hear it now, not just see it, hear the beast's death cries so loud they hurt, see black blood spurt. She forced herself to look down—but not before she saw a maiden wrapping a silk scarf around a sleeping dragon's snout, binding it tight, as a man waited near, concealed by shadows, axe in hand.

She closed her eyes, blocked her ears with her hands. It diminished the wailing—and did nothing to halt the voice in her head.

They found a way to kill us. Too many of us slept, content with what we had. A few woke in time, too late to do anything but die. I was wounded but escaped through the dragon gate of Ishtar, the last gate that was open, destroying it as I passed. I came to this land. I slept. Five hundred years I did not stir. A score of years ago, when I was healed, I awoke—to find a people who, if they were not the Aztec, at least learned to understand my needs. For a dragon who has slept requires a lot of blood—if she is going to grow strong enough to fulfill her destiny.

It took a moment to make any sense. Then, since her hands were useless, she dropped them. But she still kept her eyes shut. "She? You're a—"

Yes. I am a female of my line. I am named many things, in many tongues of man. But you may call me by an ancestor's name: Tiamat. I am also the daughter of Jormungandr. Fafnir was my brother. Yet I am more than inheritor, child, sister.

She didn't want to ask. She had to. "What are you?"

"This." The voice turned gentle. "Open your eyes, maid, and see."

She had no choice. The dragon would just go back into her head and command her. And each time she was invaded like that, it was like the onset of the worst migraine ever. So she opened her eyes, looked in the mirror . . . and saw them.

"Yes," said Tiamat, as three much smaller dragons pushed into her, nuzzled her, "I am a mother. And it is time for my children to inherit the world." Her head bent closer till the face was an arm's reach away. "The world where you grew up. The world where we belong."

"What?" Elayne was so shocked she stared into the huge red slit of one eye for the first time. "Why would you want that?"

"It is their inheritance. But it is more, much more than that. For if the descendants of Quetzacóatl, of Tiamat, of Surrsuh and Jormundgandr are to live on, my three daughters will need to find mates." As she mentioned them, the three younger dragons thrust their heads up to hers. "All over your world, dragons still sleep. It is time for them to awaken."

Up to that moment, Elayne had been too terrified to do more than react, reply. She'd barely put a string of thoughts together not to do with the avoidance of being incinerated. Yet this? This was just too weird, in a world of total weirdness. "But why?"

"I have told you."

"No, but . . ." She raised a hand. "You just said that men could kill you."

"They could."

"Well, they've got way better. At the killing." Flashes came, of machine guns, heavy artillery, attack helicopters—a cruise missile lifting off. "Forgive me but . . . they'd see you coming. You wouldn't stand a chance."

She looked straight in the dragon's eye when she said it. Tiamat stared back—and then the red slit of the iris slowly widened. "They'd see us coming. But what would they see? Because, Alice-Elayne, we have got better too. At the killing." The head thrust closer. "Look in the mirror."

Elayne stepped back, hands raised. "Please, don't—" she began.

Look in the mirror.

She clutched her head in both hands—and looked. Of course she looked. Saw herself, her frightened self. Saw the dragons behind her, the vast reptile head, the three smaller heads beside it. Then flame swirled in the black glass, obscuring all. Shapes moved in mist. Until, as if blown away by dragon's breath, it cleared.

Her head wasn't clear. It couldn't be. Because no dragons stood there now. Instead, in their place, was a woman—an attractive woman in medieval dress, probably in her thirties, with long brown hair. Beside her were three girls, each holding onto her belt. They were identical, triplets with hair as long and as brown as their mother's, the same solemn expressions on their pretty faces. Until, as one, they all smiled at her.

She couldn't help the shriek. Turned immediately because even dragons were better than this. Saw, and fell to the ground, sobbing.

Because dragons didn't stand there now. The mother and her daughters did.

Those dragons you admired for their kindness? They were shapeshifters. They liked to walk with people. It is not something that can be kept up for long. The dragon will come out. Especially when hungry. But for a few hours? A day? Long enough to fool the humans anyway. In my memory, humans are so easily fooled.

Elayne curled into a ball, head under arms. There was a long silence, and then a woman's voice came. Not like the dragon's—softer, warmer, though there was still just a hint of that sibilant ess. "Come, sweet ones," the dragon woman said. "Alice-Elayne needs to rest. She's going to be so good to us. So kind. For she's going to guide us where we wish to go. Come, I have a treat for you. A wonder you have never seen. Shall we go and look at a unicorn?"

"Yes!"

"Yes!"

"Oh yes!"

The children's voices were high and sweet. Footsteps moved away, then stopped. Or maybe they didn't even stop, just transformed without pause into scratching. Elayne stole a look. A dragon and her brood were now moving to the great ramp that led to the outside of the temple. But as she looked, Tiamat halted, glanced back. And the words came into her head again, on pulses of pain.

Your friends will live, maid, as long as you obey me. Well, most of them. One I shall consume in the great ceremony tomorrow as a warning for your continued good behaviour. But which will it be? The boy? The one who thinks he's a hero? The unicorn? It has been centuries since I tasted unicorn flesh. My children never have.

Screeching, the younger dragons hurled themselves into the air. But as Tiamat reached the edge of the ramp, Elayne finally found a little voice. "What is it you think I can do?" she whispered. "I'm no one."

The dragon halted, did not turn, though her thought came carefully, painfully. *No one? The maid who was given the gift of tongues? The girl who towed a unicorn? Who saved and destroyed a world? Oh, Alice-Elayne, you are someone. And you are about to learn that your story is only half told.*

It was too much. Once more the weight of expectation was pressing down on her. She felt as if someone had just dropped a sack of rocks onto her back and she collapsed under it with a sob.

The voice was remorseless, jabbing her again. *There is something more, maid.* The great head turned and fixed her with a single-eye stare.

Another reason you will do all I ask of you. There! There in the room behind the glass.

With that, with a great cry, Tiamat was gone. Her shrieks blended with her daughters', fading, till all Elayne could hear were her tears falling and the crackle of flame.

Behind the glass? She pushed herself up, lurched to the mirror, past it. There was a room in near darkness there. There was also the taint of blood in its stifling air. In its depths she noticed a crack of light. Moved to it, reached, felt an edge of wood. She pulled and it gave a fraction, letting enough light in for her to see that it was a shutter. She found a latch, flicked it, pulled. It opened with a loud creak, light came, she turned, saw. Screamed.

Hanging from the ceiling was a long, narrow metal cage. Wedged into it, upside down, was her father.

27

ℛEUNION

"Dad!"

The first sight of him almost took away her ability to walk. Somehow, she staggered across to the dangling metal cage, slipped when she was directly below it. Glancing down, she saw blood on the floor. Looking up, she saw where it came from.

"Dad!" she called again, reaching. She could just touch the metal bars if she stood on tiptoe.

His eyes fluttered, then opened, though that was hard work as they were gummed with blood. When they did, a little light came into them. "Elayne," he murmured, his voice thick. "What time do you call this?"

"Oh, Dad!" she sobbed. "You're bleeding."

"Yes, couple of places. They play hard, the Glanasa."

"How can I get you down from there?"

He licked his bloody lips. "I'm not sure you can. It took three guys to get me up here."

"There has to be . . ." She looked above. The cage was attached to a bolt on the ceiling. They must have had a ladder or ramp to put it up there. She turned. "I'll be back."

She ran past the mirror, back into the hall. It was a huge, empty space, no tables, no furniture, nothing. Dragons obviously didn't sit— but they had to lie down. She looked into the side hall from which Tiamat had first emerged. It was all spooky shadows. Taking a deep breath, she ran into it anyway.

It took a few moments for her eyes to adjust. But there was some light reaching the gloom—and that light reflected off a thousand glitters. It took her breath. So it's true, she thought. A dragon has a hoard.

She was looking at a giant pile of metals. They ranged from the smallest of silver coins to big pieces of armour—breastplates, helmets, gauntlets, and shields all scattered about. There were different kinds of weaponry, some of which she could name from her visits to the Metropolitan museum—maces, broadswords, falchions, a cleaver-and-spear combo whose name she couldn't recall. Large wooden chests stood out like islands in an iron sea. Their lids were up, contents spilling out— emeralds and rubies in crowns, in necklaces, silver platters studded with diamonds. At a swift glance, Elayne could see some things that looked like they were from Goloth. Most were alien, though, from other lands. There's a lot more to this world, she thought, than I can even guess at.

But she wasn't there to wonder. Her gaze darted about, seeking a ladder, a hoist, a platform—and saw, over at the far wall, what looked like an art installation in twisted metals. Walking closer, she could make out its separate parts: a tall, silver-backed chair, like a small throne; poles and spars, joined by woven rope that could have come from a boat; a great steel yoke, larger but similar to the one they'd forced her to wear as a prisoner. In the middle of it all she saw wheels attached to some kind of wagon or—

"Chariot," she said aloud. She'd seen similar in books on ancient Rome. It had high sides made of wicker slats with thin gold strips twisted through them, forming a U around a platform.

An idea came and she started ducking around, seeking a way to untangle the whole. She walked to the back, inspecting. Then, bending, she put her palms to the chariot's rear end and began to push.

It took a moment. There were many things piled atop it. She needed to bend deeper, use all her strength, heave—and then leap back as the structure lurched forward and bits came a-tumbling down. A spear missed her by inches. But the chariot moved forward half a dozen paces, shedding most of its load. Elayne ran to it, leapt up, threw off spars and struts, left the throne. Then she jumped down, went to the front end, grabbed the main bar that was attached to the front wheel section. Pulled. It came surprisingly easily, the whole section turn-able, the axles greased.

She dragged it out into the main hall and then to the opposite side past the mirror. "I've found something," she said, and pulled the chariot right under the dangling cage. The throne brushed against it, setting her father swinging.

"What the hell are you doing?"

"Trying to get you down."

"The guards might come."

"What will they do? Feed me to a dragon?"

"Elayne—"

"Shh! I need to concentrate."

She centred the chariot under the cage. Climbing up, she tipped the throne-thingy over, then levered it up till it was upside down. It was heavy enough to hold steady. Then reaching up, she swung the cage.

"Whoa!" her father yelped.

Using all her strength, Elayne managed to pin the cage top against the throne's inverted base.

"That's . . . slightly better," he sighed.

"Don't thank me yet," she muttered.

She climbed off the chariot and looked up to where the cage met the ceiling. It was suspended from an iron hook by—she peered closer. Rope. Thick, plaited rope. Someone must have tied it up there.

She turned and dashed out again.

She found a type of broom, very wide at the bristles, solid looking. But minutes of seeking produced no ladder, no crane or platform. Frustrated, she stood, hands on hips, and looked again at the hoard, its jewels, its weapons.

"Weapons." What *was* the name of that cleaver-and-spear combo? "Poleaxe!" she said, as she scrambled up and grabbed it. The top was a long spear point. The rear of the head was a hook. But the front was a huge sweeping axe blade, which she discovered, when she ran her finger along it, yelped and sucked, was sharp as a razor.

With it in one hand, the broom in the other, she ran back to the room.

Her father had slipped into unconsciousness again, his breathing shallow. Just as well, she thought, as she climbed up. The base of the chariot was filled with shallow, raised blocks of wood—for the charioteer to brace his feet against, she supposed. She jammed the broom's butt end against one, then shoved the bristle end hard against the cage. It held there. Taking a wide stance, she leaned back, looked up—and struck with the axe head, aiming for the rope.

She got mainly metal. There was a loud *clang*, and she swayed back and forth on the chariot.

"Now what are you doing?" Her father, awake again.

"This," she replied, and swung again. This time she caught more rope, saw some of the strands sever.

"Elayne, this is not a good idea."

"Best I got," she said, leaned back, and struck.

It was her finest shot. Hit right where she'd hit before, slicing through the last of the rope. She'd figured she would have a moment then. She got slightly less.

"Argh!" shouted her father as the cage parted from the hook and plunged down.

"Oof!" Elayne cried, flinging the weapon aside, reaching up to the cage. It was falling at an angle because its top was on the wedged chair. The broom held it for the moment she needed, before its shaft snapped. Bending her knees she took the weight, the strain, held the cage just long enough to lower its end to the chariot floor. When she was certain it would not fall, she jumped off the platform and sat down, taking huge breaths.

A chuckle came. "I am so glad I renewed your gym pass."

She looked up—and saw close to his feet, and near the top of the cage where bits of rope still clung, a bolt and latch. Forcing herself up, she reached and jerked it open. A section about the length of a man swung open. "Dad. Do you think you can—?"

"Oh yes."

Then, with Elayne steadying the cage, Alan slid from his prison and on down to the floor of the room.

"Oh, Dad!" she cried, and threw herself onto him.

"Easy! Easy! I might break." He wrapped his arms around her. "Oh, my darling, darling girl," he murmured, his face in her hair.

Then all words were lost to tears for a time. Both their tears. She couldn't believe, after all that had happened—to each of them—that she actually had her arms around him again. She kept moving her hands up and down him as if to verify that he was real, not simply another hopeful dream.

After a long while, she pulled back, sat up, stared at his lovely, bruised, cut face. "Oh, Dad," she said, reaching out her fingers, "what have they done to you?"

"Uh—" He pulled himself upright, stretched his arms above his head, rolled his neck. "You know, I'm not too bad. The worst was the hanging upside down thing."

"How long were you like that?"

"Felt like all night but . . ." He shuddered. "Maybe two hours? That dragon came and told me you were on the way and I must be, uh, 'readied' was her word I think." He shivered again. "I decided to resist and so . . ." He gestured to his face.

"Oh," she moaned, "why did you come?"

"Because, Elayne, I could sense what was happening with you. I worried that somehow I'd get careless, you'd get the horn back and then go."

"You couldn't have just hidden it? Put it in a bank vault?"

"No." He put his hand under her chin, lifted her head. "I told you what I felt. That I owed something to this world. Thought I could come and help." He shook his head. "And I did for a while."

"Leo said he met you. That you demanded a sword. What were you thinking?"

"Leo." Alan smiled. "An impressive young man. Is he here too?"

"He is. So's my friend Huy. And we've brought a unicorn. Not Moonspill."

"What?" He shook his head. "Back up. I don't even know *how* you're here. I took the horn, remember."

"OK." She took a deep breath. It didn't take long to catch each other up. They didn't know how much time they'd have. A quick exchange of stories, a swift summation of situation. "What now?" Elayne asked, at last. "Should we sneak out the back?"

"How far would we get?" Alan shook his head. "Besides, what about the others? We can't just leave them. Also, I suspect the dragon has all exits watched. She's not about to let her most precious treasure escape. Not after all the trouble she's gone to." A little smile came. "And I can't believe we're actually discussing this so normally. I mean, a dragon? How cool is that?"

"No, it's not." Elayne came up onto her knees. "Didn't you hear what she said to me?"

"No, I was—"

"She wants to go back to our world. To wake her sleeping kindred. To find mates for her daughters. To kill oh-so-many. And she's going to begin with one of my friends, tomorrow."

"Oh." He came onto his knees himself, then levered himself up off the floor. "You're right. Not cool at all."

He moved then, walking stiffly across the floor to one wall, almost disappearing into the shadows there. "Thought so," he called. "Those guards tormented me with this sound." He re-emerged with a flask, tipped it back, glugged some down, drank, passed it over.

She sipped. "So," she said, "what now?"

"Didn't you have a plan?"

"Sure. Come here, find you, slay the dragon."

"Impressively simple." He smiled. "First two done. How do we accomplish the third?"

"That's just it." She sank again to the floor, her efforts, all she'd been through, making her suddenly very weary. "I mean, you've seen Tiamat. She's huge. She has that army, those daughters. What do we have?"

He knelt, put his arm around her. "Hope. In my little time here I've learned this: a chance will come. Maybe only one, but when it does, let's make sure we take it."

"Dad," she said, and then could say no more as shouts came, distant, growing rapidly nearer. In a moment, a dozen Glanasa burst in, immediately surrounding them. "Bind them!" snapped one in an elaborately feathered headdress. Each raised their hands, and manacles were slipped over them.

"Take them," the leader cried, and they were shoved apart, marched in opposite directions.

"Dad!" she yelled just as she was about to be thrust through an archway.

"Our chance will come!" he called back. "Be ready!"

There came the sound of a blow. Then she was being rushed down a dark corridor, deeper into the pyramid. It led to a door, which opened onto an even darker room. Her manacles were removed and she was flung into it, the door clanging shut behind her, bolts shot.

There was a small window high up, too high to reach. It gave a little light, her eyes taking a while to adjust to the gloom. When they had, she saw a space about ten by ten. It was clean, dry. There was a small bed with a stuffed mattress on it. Five star in these parts, she thought.

There was a table. She crossed to it, found a bowl of grain with meat. It smelled as foul as ever, but she began to eat it anyway. Needed to be strong if she was going to get herself and her friends out of this mess. Take advantage of her dad's one chance.

Friends. Elayne raised her head, looked up to the hole, the square of sunlight. Are you there? Huy? Leo? she thought, sending it out. But there was only one she had a chance of reaching that way. *Tempest?*

Nothing came. And then, like the faintest shout from the far distance, she felt it. A shift, not even a word. Like a cellphone just before it lost the signal. She thought hard, though she had no idea if such a thing could reach him. Kept it simple.

Be ready.

28

SACRIFICE TO A SAVAGE GOD

Be ready.

Did he hear that? Or was it only one more false whisper in a room full of them? Everywhere he looked, *He* looked back—for the place where they'd put him was made entirely of mirrors.

Moonspill had told him of this—of being trapped by one's own reflection. Tempest had listened but mocked the tale, thinking it a weakness, a thing of age alone. He would never be caught so, trapped so.

Until he was. Until he found himself as powerless as his father had been. Until he learned that it had nothing to do with weakness or fear or anything else he despised.

It had only to do with desire.

Moonspill had been right—when he looked, it was not just himself who looked back. For deep within his own eyes Tempest saw them, as clear as he saw the tip of his horn—clearer, for that blurred into nothing when his ancestors strode forth. Then he knew the magic of the mirror, knew why it could trap a unicorn. For how could you ever turn away from the heroes of your blood? Were they not everything you wished to be?

In the mirror, they did not stand motionless as he did. They galloped, leaped, fought. Went into battle ridden by human heroes—for each one found the one who was their destiny.

Bucephalus the Mighty with Alexander of Macedon on his back, shattering the ranks of Persia. Ambrosius carrying the spear-struck Arthur into his last battle. Salvia taking the Maid of Orleans to the saving of all France. His own father, Moonspill, bearing Alice-Elayne to the liberation of Goloth.

Yet even that was not all the wonder of the mirror. For he did not just see them and their mighty deeds. He *was* them.

Again and again he rode with them to glory—to the adventures he'd always dreamed of having for himself.

Until a blink, a flashing past. A moment when he looked into one tiny panel that of all the mirrors was cracked. So small, and yet when he stared into that, his mind cleared, his ancestors vanished, the battle trumpets ceased, he was alone in a hall of mirrors. Where he heard, quite clearly, the maid say, *Be ready.*

He shook, turned away, the thought fading. And an ancestor he had not seen till now came, one he recognized, one he became . . . his own grandsire, Darkheart.

Moonlight silvers a mountain trail. A man in armour on his back, a man named Thorkell Farsight. A quest has brought them here. A treasure beyond price. An enemy beyond terror.

They enter a cave. A dragon rises from her hoard—Tiamat, daughter of Jormungandr. The battle is fierce: his hero fighting with his magic sword Mimung, the unicorn with hoof and horn. And it is horn that pierces first, plunging between leg scales to flesh beneath. Tiamat screams, lifts her head to blast Darkheart with fire—and Thorkell drives his sword, his magic sword, deep into the dragon's chest.

Black blood gushes. She howls, wrenches back, jerking Mimung from the hero's hand, rises screeching into the sky, and vanishes into cloud. A cloud misted by moonlight, frosted in a cracked mirror.

Darkheart went. Only Tempest's own reflection was there again. And in it he heard the echo of the maid's words. Yet now, instead of only listening, Tempest answered.

I will.

She thought she wouldn't sleep but exhaustion took her. When she woke it was bright with the new day, a sunbeam coming through the small hole above. Yet it wasn't light that woke her. It was the drums. It was the trumpet's sudden blast. It was the repeated single word that came in Glanasan, a word she'd have been able to understand anyway, even without the gift of tongues.

"Kill! Kill! Kill! Kill! KILL!"

The last word was screamed, together with the horn blaring one high note. Then nothing but the noise of a murmuring crowd came for a short while—until she heard the soft tippety-tap of wood on skins and, very faintly, distant weeping. There could only be one thing happening beyond her cell. And she could do nothing about it except be ready. So she drank the rest of the cloudy water, ate what remained of the foul food, tied her matted hair back. Her dad had said that a chance would come. And what girl doesn't believe her father?

She sat on the edge of the cot and waited, trying to shut out the screams, the drums. When she heard footsteps approaching the door, she rose to face it.

Though they were a little hard to tell apart with their shanks of black hair descending from their shaven crowns, their uniforms of solid black, she thought that the jailer was the same who'd locked her up.

He was as limited in his conversation. "Out," he said, jerking his head, standing aside.

She walked out of the cell into the middle of four guards who flanked the door. They set off, took corridors, stairs, descending. Finally they made toward the front of the step pyramid. Light grew, as did the sounds of a crowd.

Then she was through an arch and into harsh sunlight. It took her a while to see, after the dark within. But as the guards shoved her forward, she noted that she was on a wide, shallow platform. Craning around she saw the giant stone dragon a short flight of stairs above. While before her on the lip of what was probably a big drop—she could see the jungle below across the fields, the mountains beyond them—was a body-length flat stone that glistened a wet red. Glanasans stood about, their strange hair concealed by great masks with demon faces and brightly coloured bird feathers in a crest. Each man held a weapon. And among them, hands bound, faces lowered, were her friends. Leo, beside Huy, who was next to a hooded Tempest. Lost in his mirrored world, the unicorn's tail was flicking.

She gave a cry, ran across. Not one of them looked well. She turned first to Huy, her friend from Canada who should not be there, laid a hand on his arm. "Are you OK?"

It took a while for a reply to come and, "Look," was all he managed.

His voice was ragged. So she looked where the slight jerk of his head led her. And wished she hadn't. Down.

The entire front of the pyramid was a vast staircase, fifty feet broad, a hundred steps down. At its base a huge crowd stared up. But between her and them, tumbled like broken dolls on the stairs, were a dozen crumpled bodies, the stone around them awash with blood.

"Oh no." She closed her eyes, swayed—and felt hands grip her.

Opened her eyes again and looked at Leo. There was a huge welt across his cheek. His eyes were sunken and bruised. But there was a gleam in them still. He bent closer, laid his roped hands on her free ones, whispered, "We are not dead yet, maid. Be strong."

He broke off. But his grip, even bound, and his words strengthened her.

Movement behind her. She turned—to her father being thrust out by guards. "Dad!" she cried and he, squinting against the sun, saw her. One of the guards shoved him hard in the back and he stumbled across.

"I'm all right," he said, as she hugged him. "They didn't put me back in the cage. They even gave me food." He looked over her shoulder. "Leo. Good to see you, even here." He turned. "And this must be your friend."

"Huy, my father."

"Alan," he said, raising his bound hands, tapping them on Huy's. "I wish we met under better circum—"

Trumpets blasted again, cutting him off. Another great cry came from the crowd below, and then other cries from the sky. Elayne looked up—and watched four dragons descend.

Tiamat landed in front of the stone dragon, on the edge of the upper platform. Her daughters flew a while longer before settling upon the statue itself. So it was five dragon heads—four of scale, one of stone—that peered down.

Words jabbed into her mind like little blades.

Maid, are you ready to do what you must?

No.

You must prepare. Though I have decided something. The thought words paused, came again. *I will not choose one of your companions to die.*

Sudden hope flared in her. She looked up into one of the dragon's huge eyes, into the fire-red slit within the green. *You . . . won't?*

No, maid. There was another pause, like a suspended breath. *You will.*

She felt the attention leave her, saw one of the demon-masked men jerk upright, bow. He came to her and, from a sheathe, drew an obsidian knife. She could see its long edge, honed to incredible sharpness. He held it out to her.

Take it.

The words poked her.

I won't.

If you do not, two will die, not one. Then three.

She was shocked into speech. "I can't. I couldn't—"

Nay, do not fear. I am not asking you to kill. Humans are so weak, it might shatter your mind. And I need that whole for what lies ahead. Something like a chuckle came. *Though I will bind you to me—in blood. You will mark one before you. A simple scratch across a hand. Or a flank, if it is the unicorn you choose to die. After, my slaves will do the rest.*

She stared at the knife. Trying to breathe. Trying to focus. Trying to think. A drum had started again somewhere, a whisper of knuckle bone on skin.

"Elayne!" her father whispered. "What is it?"

She couldn't lift her eyes from the blade in her hand. "The dragon wants me to choose . . . to choose which one of you is to die. Only one, she tells me, and the others will live. Only—"

She broke off. Huy and her father gasped; Leo cursed under his breath. Tempest flicked his tail, still oblivious. She stared at each of them in turn. "How can I choose? All of you are so . . . so precious to me."

We are waiting, Alice-Elayne, my daughters and I. And we are hungry. So decide. Decide . . . or I will decide for you—the two that will feed us.

The voice slinked into her head again, sibilant, sing-songey, teasing.

She sobbed, clutched her stomach as a pain shot through it. Who could she choose?

Then she knew. There could only be one choice here. Stifling another sob, she turned toward the shrouded unicorn. Above her, she felt the shadow of the dragon loom nearer.

Then someone spoke. "Elayne, look at me. Look!" It was hard but she forced her gaze from the horrid blade, all the blacker against Tempest's white flank, up to her father's eyes. "You have to choose me. No, don't speak, just listen." He stepped toward her, laid his bound hands onto her shaking ones. "I was dying, remember? In the hospice, maybe half a day's life left? You came, and you brought Moonspill with you and he . . . he healed me." He smiled. "What a gift! But gifts have to be repaid and I am ready." He looked at the others. "Who else could you choose? Either of these two young men? The one who followed you from our world and has protected you ever since? The other who may be the only leader who can save Goloth from this peril?"

She took a breath, to protest, to shout down his reason, but he beat her to words. "And the unicorn? Child of the unicorn who saved me? That would not be right. That is not the way a gift is returned. But more than that: if the dragons are to be beaten, you will need the unicorns. Tempest is your only hope of them coming."

That shadow swamped them now, Elayne glanced up—to Tiamat, craning over them, eye vast, savouring her pain. "Daughter, don't look at her, look at me. And listen." She obeyed. "I have had two more years with you. I've been able to watch you grow into this wonderful, strong young woman. A father who has a hero for a daughter? What greater legacy could I ask for? What other gift could I ever hope to receive?" He lifted his hands to her. "Elayne. My child. Mourn for me a little. But live and choose your time," he nodded, "to kick this dragon's butt."

She stared into her father's eyes. Saw in them what she sometimes saw in her own reflection, when she wasn't terrified: the strength to do what must be done. But she also knew—if she obeyed him, if she made this choice, she would shatter. If she marked her father and then watched him die, she would be Tiamat's slave forever.

Which could only mean one thing: that this was the chance. The one he'd talked of. The one to do or to die. She could not wait for another.

That different voice came again in a thought like a slap.

Enough, maid. Choose!

She straightened, squeezed her father's hands. "Trust me," she whispered to him and then walked to Leo. He flinched, as she stopped before him. She looked into his eyes, narrowed her own. Huy was next, she locked gazes with him, gave him the slightest of nods. Beside them Tempest's body shivered with whatever vision he was lost in.

She raised the knife and laid the flat of it against his rope-bound wrist. She could sense Tiamat looming closer, feasting on her pain. Huy's eyes widened. Then she spoke to him. In Vietnamese.

"We have to fight now, Huy," she said. Above her she felt the dragon's mind move to her, try to reach her. But she was speaking a language Tiamat could not know and she sunk totally into it, used it as a shield that would only hold for a few short moments. Used those—to slash through Huy's bindings, then reach up to Tempest and sever the strap of the hood before ripping it from his head.

Are you ready?

She shouted the words into him just before the dragon mind reached her, wordless, a thrust into her mind that bent her in agony, knocked her to her knees. But as she fell she saw the unicorn's eyes clear—to focus first on her, then on the demon faces around her.

Ready!

Tempest roared, rising on his rear hooves, flailing his front ones, crashing them into the men with the demon masks, striking down those who were too slow to get away, or foolish enough to reach for him. The platform was pandemonium in a flash and she felt the dragon's mind thrust into her one more painful time, before it pulled away to focus on the mayhem.

Huy snatched up the knife, turned and, in one stroke, severed Leo's bonds.

It was not a moment too soon. Three of the guards not scattered by Tempest's hooves were running at them. Leo bent, picked up a fallen spear, snapped the shaft into the first guard's head, drove the butt of it into the second's belly. The third raised a war hammer high—and Huy drop-kicked him in the face.

Every guard was down and for a moment there was almost silence. It had all happened so fast. Now noise returned as the crowd below gave one great roar and fifty armed men started up the stairs. They had a long way to come—but they would be there soon enough. While above them, her wings spread wide, her long, scaly neck thrust close, her great jaws open, was Tiamat. She let out a roar and it reached them on hot breath.

Leo reversed the spear and hurled it. It bounced off the dragon's armour. "How do we get past her?" he yelled.

It was another voice that replied. In their minds.

This way.

The mirrors in the headdress had been tiny. He had not been able to see every ancestors' adventures. But one had come, again and again—Darkheart, his grandsire, powering up a mountain, a hero named Thorkell Farsight on his back. Together they had fought a dragon—the same dragon above him now.

Tempest charged. His speed extraordinary, he was at the top of the steps in moments. Tiamat jabbed her head down at him, jaws spread wide. But he had seen it so often, had experienced what Darkheart had done again and again in the mirrors of his prison. So he dodged the thrust fangs, dipped under one flapped wing . . . and plunged his horn straight into the dragon's leg, exactly where his grandfather had struck, in the gap between scales that had never completely overlapped again.

Black blood jetted out. The scream caused the guards running up the stairs to falter. Only Tiamat's daughters did not quail. They'd risen from their perch, and now they swooped toward the unicorn.

But the maid and the others were running past him. "Come," she called. Tempest swung his horn hard, striking one dragon, driving back the others, and followed.

Just inside the archway they halted, and Huy slashed her father's bonds. Tempest joined them in a clatter of hooves, slipping, nearly falling, as he hit the polished floors inside. Close behind him was a pursuing dragon-daughter. But Alan grabbed a spear that was just inside the door and he hurled it, clipping the monster's left wing.

She vanished with a screech. But her sisters' cries were building, and the shouts of men were getting closer, coming up the temple stairs. "Where now, maid?" Leo shouted.

"The temple backs onto a river. There are boats."

Huy stepped closer. "That the best you got?"

"I'm sorry. Shall we hail a cab?"

She led and they ran, fast. It was the same columned hall where she'd been before and she took them to the right. As they came into the treasure hall, the others slowed. "Yeah, I know, gold and silver and jewels. Just keep moving!"

All but one obeyed her. "Maid," said Leo, stopping. "Look!"

He was staring at a sword. It was at the top of a heap of dazzling gemstones. But the giant emerald that formed its pommel gleamed brighter than any others.

All halted then, despite the cries of men drawing nearer. The guards had to be close to reaching the entrance. But over them, words came into her head yet not addressed to her.

It is Mimung. The sword of Thorkell Farsight. The weapon that nearly slew this dragon once before.

"Then I shall take it," said Leo, "and try to finish the good work."

"Leo, there isn't time!"

"Elayne," said her dad, "for this I think there must be time."

Shouts came echoing into the halls. The guards reached the platform at the same time that Leo reached the sword. Seizing it, he slid fast down the pile of coins and jewels, hit the ground.

He grinned. "For you, Alice-Elayne."

She thought he was being all knightly, offering her his sword. But what he held toward her was black . . . and plastic. "My backpack," she gasped. "How—?"

"With the sword. Her most special treasures."

They smiled at each other. "No time for that," yelled Alan. "This way."

They ran out into sunlight and a view. The river was wide, with at least three vessels tied up at a dock, next to a narrow bridge. It was a lot of steep stairs down, but with the shouts filling the halls behind them they had no choice but to take them at extreme speed and pray they did not trip. If they didn't break their necks, they would deal with whatever awaited them at the bottom.

They survived—and there were a lot of people gawping at them. Mainly chained prisoners, newly disgorged from the boats, squatting on the dock. But there were also at least twenty Glanasan guards, recovering fast from their astonishment. And they all had weapons in their hands.

Cries from above. Elayne turned—a horde of soldiers was running down the stairs. "Jungle!" she yelped, and ran to the foot of a tall-arched bridge that spanned the river.

"If we all go they'll catch us, " said Leo, stopping. "But you must get away. Take word back to Goloth." He turned to Huy. "Mount the unicorn, bodyguard. You too, honoured father. Get her away."

"We can go together!" Alan said.

"Nay, sir, we cannot. We are too tired, too weak, and they will catch us all. But I can hold them here for a while." He raised Mimung into the air. "For do I not have a hero's sword?"

"But—"

A howl turned her, turned them all—to the sight of a grey shape bursting from the jungle, running across the bridge, moving so fast it took time to realize that it was . . .

"Wolf!" yelled Leo, bending briefly to rub the great grey ears, then straightening to lift the sword high once more. "Now I know I can hold them. We can!"

"No, we must—" Elayne glanced back. Perhaps the sight of the wolf dog had slowed them. But the guards were massing—and many more were running down the pyramid.

"Alice-Elayne, the maid who always argues." Leo smiled briefly. "For once, do not. You and the unicorn are Goloth's only hope." He turned to Huy and Alan. "Go! Take her!"

Men closing in from the dock. Men running down from above. "No!" she shouted again as Huy grabbed her around the waist and lifted her toward Tempest. She twisted back, looked at the fast-descending Glanasa . . . and so saw what happened.

It was five men at the back who fell first. They brought down more near them, who brought down even more. In a moment, the whole troop was tumbling, all the guards who'd been running now crashing onto their bellies. While rolling fast through the last of them, stretched to its full length, was the amphisbaena.

It slowed to a stop near their feet. Two heads rose. One spoke.

"Ah, glory! The quest is reunited."

"Guards," yelled her dad, turning with the sword he'd snatched up from the hoard. The reinforcements may have been tripped but the dock guards, at least twenty of them, had regained their courage and were marching toward them now.

"The bridge," called Leo again. "Go!"

It was then that the voice shouted from behind them. It sounded familiar. "Archers!" They all winced, turned, expecting to hear the thrum of arrows aimed at them, and saw, on the prow of the vessel—

"Scarab?" Huy called.

The pirate did not pause to acknowledge him. "Shoot!" he shouted, and from the vessel nearest them downstream of the bridge, rose three more figures. Each was a woman, each had a bow, each released and shot, notched, released and shot again, and again, as did their leader. In moments, a dozen arrows ripped into the guards. Those not hit turned and fled.

Scarab ran to the head of the gangplank. He was wearing his multi-coloured doublet, his yellow breeches, his red head scarf, his black cloak flapping behind him like a spread sail. Had a bow in one hand, a cutlass in the other, and a smile on his face. "Now, don't just stand there, friends," he shouted. "All aboard!"

They were all aboard fast, the pirate's other commands obeyed as rapidly. Oars hit the water, the main sail was unfurled, the ropes that held them to the dock were cast off. With Tempest the last on, the gangplank was pulled up. Yet even as the ship began to gain speed in the river's swift current, screeches came.

"Dragons!" Scarab yelled. "Shoot!"

The daughters of Tiamat swooped low. But the women of Scarab shot and shot again, driving them away, up, to hover out of range. "Fortune for us that their bitch of a mother isn't with them," Scarab called as he ran aft and took the wheel.

"Tempest stabbed her," said Leo.

"But . . . but why are you here?" Huy climbed the steps to the wheel deck. "You had the gold for our betrayal. You had your pardon."

The contempt was clear in his voice. And it briefly drove the grin from Scarab's face. "But I did not have you, my friend," he replied softly. He looked about. "Nor these others, whom I had also grown to like. Though I do not know you, sir." He bowed his head to Alan, who bowed back. But before introductions could be made he continued. "I came scouting—and then I met a wonder—a two-headed snake, who told me a story." He grinned. "Besides, have you not learned by now how changeable I am?" The smile widened. "Indeed I am forced to ask again: which part of the word 'pirate' do you not understand?"

Everyone laughed then. But Elayne stopped first, as she lurched to the side, and felt it in her head as much as she heard it. The wind was strong, that and the current already speeding them quite far from the temple. So Tiamat could no longer hurt her, perhaps. But the dragon's words, though like a whisper, whipped her anyway.

You will not escape me, maid. No matter how far you go, how fast you run. I will come for you, you and all you love. And I will destroy Goloth.

Last
Stand of
Goloth

29

FINAL HOUR

Two weeks later . . .

Elayne sat on a rock on the crest of a hill, peering east. She knew the grassland fell steeply away from her perch and ended in a forest that swept in its turn to the sea, and the beach they'd landed on one week before. She just couldn't see farther than the next rock, less than twenty paces away. The rain prevented her, though this was like no rain she'd ever known; it fell horizontally as much as vertically, soaking, not stinging her face. If she licked, she got a salty tang like tears. It was as if she were in a steam room, if steam could chill. Her down jacket, which she'd recovered along with all the rest of her stuff, might have been good against the snows of Colorado. But it was pierced pretty easily by the fall mists of Goloth. She was cold and wet all over.

She shivered yet again but still did not move. Because a rider had come into camp an hour before to warn that the Glanasa had landed at last. Huy, Scarab, his women followers and fifty pirates recruited from Slavetown had harried the invaders on the water, harried them as they tried to land, and would keep harrying them in the rainforests of the coast. But the message was clear: they could not delay so big a host for long. Be ready.

The messenger brought other news too: Huy had been hurt. He was on his way back.

And so she waited, guilt overwhelming her way more than chill. How hurt was he? Huy should be safe back in New York, his most difficult daily choice being whether to wear velvet or tweed. He should not be risking his life hourly for a land that was not his. She had no choice. She was responsible for so much of what had happened. "Overthrow the tyrant" had such a cool ring to it and she'd helped do it. But what had come in tyranny's place? Enslavement, slaughter—and perhaps now the total destruction of Goloth. She should change her name to Pandora. She'd opened the box for a microsecond—and shut it way too slowly to trap the consequences.

She shivered again, nothing to do with the cold.

Something black ruptured the grey ahead—a man on a horse. She jumped up, ready to run if it was an enemy.

The shape came closer and resolved into . . . "Huy!" she shouted, running forward. The horse shied, but Huy brought him swiftly under control. Another skill he'd acquired.

"Elayne!"

He dismounted, limped toward her, hugged her one-armed, the other keeping the reins. He was not dressed in velvet or tweed but in a pirate's cast-offs—a much-patched green doublet, a scuffed leather coat, boots with holes for toes, a mangy cloak over it all. Strangely, he still managed to look cool. Maybe it was the bow and quiver across his back, the short sword at his side.

"You're wounded!"

"This?" He reached to a blood-streaked bandage about his thigh. "Flesh wound." He grinned. "Really, it's, like, yea deep." He squeezed his thumb and forefinger tight. "But Scarab is such a wimp—and for a pirate he's very wussy about blood. 'Ooh, Huy, you bleed apace. You must be tended to.'" The impersonation was dead-on and Elayne smiled. But then Huy's face darkened. "Actually, I think he just wanted me away. It's getting pretty rough back there, in the trees. But he also wanted you and Leo to know what you're up against."

"The messenger said—"

"The messenger was just a general warning. I bring the details."

"How long?"

"Scarab's going for one last ambush. That'll buy you maybe . . ." He sucked air between his teeth. "One hour?"

"Really?" They moved toward the rock she'd sat on. Whatever he claimed, he was limping quite badly. "You ride," she said. "I'll walk."

"OK."

They'd reached the rock. As he mounted, she dug into her backpack, pulled something out. "Here, I saved the last one for you." And she shoved an energy bar into his hand.

He stared at it. He took a while to speak. "Guava and Pomegranate," he read. "That is just so . . . random."

He laughed, ripped the foil off, devoured it in four mouthfuls. "Oh-my-God," he said through a crammed mouth, "that's delicious. Especially after a week of smoked squirrel."

"Seriously?" They moved off again. The mist had begun to ease a little, and they could again see into the valley. There was movement in its base, men. Horses. "Was it, uh, bad out there?"

"Bad? You could say that." He reached up, picked something from his teeth, ate it. "But good too. You know my dad was a soldier. Didn't talk about it much. But he did tell me once that, however scared you were, there was also a . . . a buzz to it. Doing what's right. Fighting for what you believe in."

"And you believe in Goloth?"

"I believe in my friends. And I've seen the alternative up close."

"Huy," she said, "you've become a warrior."

"Yeah." He grinned. "Pretty good for a gay boy from Ottawa, eh?" He nodded. "We slowed the Glanasa a lot. But there are so many of them. And they'll be coming fast."

"Is . . . ?" she began, hesitated, continued. "Is Tiamat with them?"

He shook his head. "Didn't see her. Or her daughters. But we retreated after the first wave of ships finished landing and there were many more following. I guess they'll be along soon, now that her army's landed." He reined in the horse and they stopped. "But what Scarab wants to know—what we all want to know—is if all the fighting so far's been worth it. Did we buy you enough time?" He leaned down, his eyes burning. "Elayne, have the unicorns come?"

She held his gaze for a moment, then dropped hers. "Not yet," she replied.

In his sharp indrawn breath were all her terrors too. She looked up again as Huy and his mount lurched forward. "Tempest went, straightaway. He didn't say much—*think* much!—before he left. Just, 'I will tell them all.' But what they'll decide?" She shrugged. "I thought of following, trying to persuade Moonspill myself. But Leo needed me here."

"Uh-huh. How, uh, how're you two doing?"

"Look, it was just a kiss, OK? Spur of a dangerous moment." His skeptical look made her blush so she hurried on. "Besides, there's not been any time for anything other than, you know, rallying the kingdom. Except, of course, that Goloth's not a kingdom. He can't just command. He has to persuade, cajole. Still, everyone's so terrified they're listening to him. Agreed to make the stand here in this valley. He's got five hundred nobles in armour, about a thousand Weavers—"

The horse halted again. "What? That's not nearly enough. Elayne, there's five thousand Glanasan warriors coming at least."

"Yeah. We sort of guessed that—though we haven't told anyone. Which is why Leo needed me here. He's a great fighter one-on-one, knows all about raids and ambushes. But he's never fought in a battle so . . ." She gave a little bow as she walked. "Meet General Alice-Elayne, tactical adviser to the former king of Goloth."

"Wait! So suddenly you're a military adviser as well as a unicorn tamer?"

"Uh-huh. The joys of being an only child raised by a single-parent, history-obsessed dad. We spent every summer holiday in Europe traipsing through battlefields and too many winter nights playing war games. On boards, later on computers. Thousands have died at my . . . thumbs." She waggled them. "Dad was happy with a daughter—but he really wanted a son too. So I was both. I can talk you through most battles from Thermopylae to Agincourt. We stopped once gunpowder came along. Dad thought it unsporting."

"Yeah, well, I'd take an AK-47 now, just to even the odds." Huy laughed. "So where is your dad? Is he a general too?"

"Nah. He gave me the adviser position and joined the snakes."

"How's that again?"

"The amphisbaena's been recruiting too. They have unorthodox methods. Dad now considers himself more a guerrilla fighter. Plus he likes rap." She shuddered. "It is truly one of the more embarrassing things in life to have a father who's into the music I am supposed to be into."

Huy smiled. "So what have you got planned?"

"I'll show you in a while. Let's find Leo first. He'll need your report." The wide valley funneled down and they were soon among people engaged in various tasks. Large pits were being dug. Long stakes were being sharpened. As each worker raised eyes from their task and saw her, each bowed low. A woman came and kissed her hand. Elayne bent and whispered something in her ear, and she returned to her work, a smile on her face.

They moved on. "You're popular."

"Leo . . ." She hesitated, then went on. "He told me I had to get over the 'I'm only a girl' routine. That what these people needed was hope, a belief in something greater."

"And they believe in the maid and the unicorn?" Huy nodded. "I can see that."

The land began to rise again quite steeply if not for long, the hill running perpendicular to the valley, like a stop at its end. Tents were on top of the hill, pennants fluttering from their main poles. "He's in that big one, with the lion on the flag."

As they drew nearer, as more people crowded by, staring up at Huy with a mixture of hope and dread, he leaned down to ask softly. "So— do you think he will come? Moonspill and the rest?"

"I still hope. He's cutting it pretty fine if—" She broke off, shook her head. "I don't know. Would you? Come to the rescue of a land where your last experience was torture and death in an arena?" She shivered. "It'd be kinda like a bull in Spain coming to save the matador."

They reached the tent's flaps. Huy dismounted and someone took his horse. They entered the tent.

Of the many men leaning over the large table at the tent's centre— some in full armour, others in the gown and doublet of the rebel Weavers—Leo saw her first. His eyes gleamed with pleasure. "Alice-Elayne!" he said. Then her friend stepped around her, and the former king's eyes narrowed again. Like his people, he knew what news a messenger might bring. "Master Huy! You have returned." His gaze lowered.

"And you are hurt. A chair," he called. One was brought immediately and Huy sank into it. "Ho, one of you," he called, "fetch a physician."

"It's fine, really. Just rest it a little." Huy raised a hand, halting the man about to leave. "And we haven't the time."

Every man in the room took and held a breath. "How long do we have?" asked Leo softly.

"Scarab figures . . . less than an hour." Over the massive exhalation, Huy continued, "The Glanasa seem very keen to get on with it after their long voyage. Scarab says he will slip to their rear, harry them still, keep some always facing back. But most will march straight here. They do not know you are waiting for them, of course, but it is the direct route from the sea so—"

"How many?" Leo's voice was low. "How many will we face?"

Huy looked around the anxious faces. "Do you trust everyone here? Sorry to ask but . . ."

"Everyone here, Weaver and noble, is sworn to stand, no matter the odds . . . and to secrecy. All know it is our only chance. So tell us."

"OK." Huy sat up straight. "Scarab thinks around five thousand."

"Gods!" It was one word but it came from a dozen mouths.

Only Leo did not utter it. Instead he looked around sharply. "It was more than we expected. But our plan still stands for even this much." He turned to the table, to a great hand-drawn map spread there. "Maid, do you wish to show our friend what we have planned, in case he must return and inform Scarab?"

"I'd rather show him." Elayne nodded to the tent walls, to what lay outside. "And I'd like to check that everything is in place."

"Good." Leo reached for the sword on the table. Mimung was sheathed now, but the emerald in its pommel glowed in the lamplight. "And I will carry this to show our men the power we have too." As he was buckling on the scabbard, he looked again at Huy. "Does the dragon lead her horde?"

"We have not seen the dragon, nor her brood. But I left when only the first boats had come ashore so . . ." He shrugged.

"Then perhaps she is not there. Perhaps she waits for her forces to conquer so she only has to arrive and feast on the dead. Tiamat is used to slaves bringing her helpless victims. But we will show her that we are nonesuch." He looked at each man in the room. "To your positions. I will walk the field one last time."

All went, leaving the three of them there. Leo sagged, leaning back onto the table. "I tell you both now—it is hard to convince others that I have no fear when I feel so much inside."

"If you had no fear, you'd be mad—and then dead." Huy nodded beyond the canvas walls. "I learned that out there from Scarab. And neither madmen, nor dead men, win battles."

"You are right there, friend." Leo stood straight. "Are you well enough to walk?"

Huy stood too. "I'll be fine—with maybe a stick?"

There was a rack of slim throwing spears outside. Huy grabbed one to pivot on and the three set out to their left. "May as well start from the one end," Elayne said. "Do you want—?"

She'd turned to Leo. He shook his head. "Nay, maid. 'Tis mostly your plan. You tell it."

They started at the left end of the hill. The slope fell steeply there to a fast-flowing river that curled around the hill to their rear. Stones were piled up—to be hurled at anyone foolish enough to run up. "So unless they want to climb those," Elayne gestured to the mountains on both sides of the valley, "they won't outflank us here. They'll be funneled into the valley before us, where we've dug the pits you saw. It will bunch them, help us concentrate our fire. Our armoured nobles will be in the middle here with a lot of Weavers with slings and bows." She smiled briefly. "It's basically Agincourt with a bit of Battle of Hastings thrown in."

"I remember that one. Read about it in social studies." Huy frowned. "But we're the defenders here. Didn't the defenders lose?"

Elayne shrugged. "Yeah, but from all accounts it was really close."

They were walking back the way they'd come. The frown didn't leave. "Something else I remember about Hastings. The invaders landed in England, then burned their boats."

"So? It was just a tactic to inspire them. It says there's no going back."

"That's what I mean." Huy swallowed. "The Glanasa burned their boats."

Leo started. "Truly? Then they come to triumph or die?"

"Guess so."

Leo grunted. They'd reached the other end of the hill. This side did not descend to a chasm but to a small forest that ran right up to the mountain slopes beyond. "Maid, I must leave you. There are things I must attend to. When the trumpet sounds, do you both rally to the centre."

As Leo strode off, Huy looked down to the trees below. "Now I may not be Napoleon. But even I can see this . . ." He waved. "This *flank*, yeah?—could be turned."

"You're right," she started down the slope, "which is why we keep our secret weapon here."

"Intriguing. What is it?"

The slope was short. In a few moments they were under the first of the branches. "It's—" she began.

The first snake dropped from the tree onto Huy's shoulder. He screamed, would have brushed it off if it wasn't a constrictor that instantly curled around his neck. In a moment, a second was gripping his left leg, a third his right. He tottered, fell, and from right before him a cobra rose up hissing, its neck flaring wide, while to each side there came the distinct rattle of very different beasts.

"Off! Off!" yelled Elayne. "Friend! Friend!"

A familiar voice said, "Loose, varlets!" the words followed by a hiss. At that, all the snakes released Huy, who collapsed onto the ground. The snakes vanished—into the undergrowth or up into the canopy. All save one. The two-headed one.

"Dog!" said Baena. "Welcome to Snakesville."

"Shit!" said Huy, staring up resentfully. "Thanks for that, Elayne."

"Sorry." She reached a hand, pulled him up. "I didn't know they'd do that."

"They are keen for the fight, maid. I warned them to await our command." Amphis turned to peer at Huy. "They did not bite, did they?"

"I-I-I . . . don't think so." Huy felt himself up and down, then gave a nervous laugh. "How . . . how many have you got here?"

"Several hundred."

"Secret weapon, see," Elayne said. "They couldn't fight out there; they'd be chopped to pieces. In here—"

"In here, we got game." Baena's scaly lips spread in a smile. "And that's not all we got. Tell him, brother."

Amphis reached forward. "Twin chimeras have answered the call. And three manticores."

"You've not met one of those, have you? Want to?" asked Elayne.

"I'm good." Huy stepped away from the cobra coiling near his leg. "Um, shouldn't we be getting back?"

"Yep." She turned to Amphisbaena. "An hour. Maybe less."

"We are ready, maid."

"Straight. We got this."

"Where's my father?"

"He is around, training other men with swords."

She'd have liked to hunt him down, even though they'd said, "See you later," about forty times. But she had to get back. She looked at the two swaying heads. They were her friends and, like her, they were going into a tough battle for the first time. "You, uh . . . you take care of each other."

"No choice, sista."

They began to walk away. Amphis's voice stopped them. "Alice-Elayne," he spoke softly, came closer. "If all else fails, if Goloth does not hold and we are able, we will come for you. We put you in this danger, you and Huy. In the end, this is not your fight."

"Oh, but it is," said her father, stepping out from behind a tree.

"Dad!" She peered. "Um, what are you wearing?"

"This?" Alan flicked at the leaves that covered him, head to toe. "A little something I wove from reeds, threaded through with all this foliage. Voila!" He gave a flourish. "Instant camouflage." He came to her, then took her hand. "Elayne, I'm going to fight here. The snakes needed some men to do the, uh, things they can't. There's about twenty of us, so—" He swallowed. "So I need to know that you'll take all reasonable precautions."

"Trust me, Dad. Every reasonable precaution a girl can take in a medieval battle, I will take."

He nodded, then hugged her. His face close to her ear, he whispered, "You took the chance, Elayne. And that bought Goloth another. We're going to win this."

"We are." She hugged him back fiercely. Suddenly the only place she wanted to be was in those arms. Yet she knew she couldn't be, not yet. They'd come this far. And they both needed to fight. "Reasonable precautions to you too?"

He smiled. "I'm fly, sista."

"Dad!" she groaned, breaking away. "I love you."

"And I you. Be safe."

Turning, he blended swiftly into the trees.

She and Huy had not gotten twenty yards up the slope when they heard it: the loud, long, deep cry of a trumpet. It faded, came again. "That's the signal," Elayne said, breaking into a run.

They reached the ridge, ran along it, dodging through all the men and women stepping forward to stare down the valley to the forest ahead. They made for the lion pennant, now planted right in the centre of the hilltop.

Leo was under it, surrounded by twenty of his nobles, all on horseback. "Maid," he said, as they ran up.

"Are they close?" she panted.

"They are here," he replied. "According to the last person to come from the forest."

He pointed down. Twenty feet below them, Scarab's woman, Caelin, was sitting drinking from a water skin. Huy immediately joined her and they had a whispered conversation.

No one else was making a sound. All were listening, their ears as strained as their eyes. And then another sense took Elayne. She sniffed. "I smell smoke," she said.

"You do." Leo continued looking ahead. "I burned the bridge behind us."

"You did what?" Elayne gasped, swung around to stand before him. "But that means we can't retreat."

"Like those who come." His gaze came onto her now—and there was cold steel in his eyes. "Triumph or death."

She wanted to say something, anything, but couldn't think what. And then she wouldn't have been heard anyway.

"They come," was the cry that burst from everyone's lips. She looked to the forest, expecting to see the first Glanasan warrior.

Right in the middle of the green semicircle something stirred. But no human enemy stepped out there.

An elephant did.

30

THE LAST STAND OF GOLOTH

"War elephant."

A groan from a thousand throats ran down the line. "Calm! Calm!" cried Leo, left and right, Swiftsure less than calm beneath him, his head jerking up and down.

Elayne turned to look up at Huy, mounted again. "You didn't say!"

His face was white. "I didn't know! They must have landed them later, after we retreated from the beach. Caelin?"

The red-haired woman leaned forward and spat. "We did not see them either. But we withdrew before the last boats came that must have brought them. An elephant moves fast."

Leo looked down at Elayne, standing near his stirrup. "Maid, have you any knowledge from your history of this? How do we kill it?"

"Well—"

"Not it. Them."

Huy's harsh whisper turned them. All looked again to the forest. Where one had stood, six stood now.

The groans from before became shouts. "Devise a plan," Leo snapped at her, then turned and spurred his horse down the rear of the line, shouting, encouraging, forcing men back into the ranks with his horse. The other mounted nobles all turned to Elayne.

She had no clue. She couldn't let them know that. *Improvise, Elayne,* she thought and said, boldly enough, "Hannibal. Fought the Romans with elephants. So they, uh, uh, they formed squads. That's right. Covering archers. Swordsmen going in. Cut the hamstrings. Here!" She ran a hand across the back of her leg.

She knew Huy was staring at her, open-mouthed. She just looked ahead, at the man who had been Leo's high steward and was now his second-in-command. "Good, maid," he said and turning to others around him, started a low, harsh whispering.

"Hannibal?" said Huy quietly.

Elayne let go of the breath she didn't realize she was holding. "It's all I got."

More trumpets sounded from the other end of the valley, many more. She looked to see the elephants move forward, the spaces behind them filled in by soldiers. Dozens emerged, then hundreds, finally thousands of Glanasa, their black armour gleaming in the pale sunlight that had broken through the shredded clouds. It had stopped raining at last. She didn't know if that was a good thing. Her tactical analysis was all used up on elephants.

These came in a rush now, driven on by men sitting astride their necks who beat them with small sticks about the ears. On their backs were wicker baskets, their walls a man's height, protecting the half dozen archers within. Behind them ran the Glanasan army, trumpets blaring, yelling their war cries. These came in a mob, as unused to fixed battle as their opponents. It was, for the moment, the Golothians only advantage.

"Steady! Hold! Hold!" Leo cried, riding the lines.

"That's it," Elayne urged softly. "Straight on. Straight on!"

The elephants' charge had taken them at least one hundred paces in front of the soldiers. Their line was uneven, the slightly smaller ones on each flank racing even farther ahead. And Elayne could see just before them what they'd hoped running men would not notice—the slightly darker green of pine boughs, the brown of freshly dug earth. "A little more," she whispered. "A few steps more."

Snap! They could hear it, distinct, even above the shouting, as the first elephant stepped onto the pit and the branches gave. They could not hear the give from the other pit. The loud screams that both elephants made as they fell drowned all other sound, halting, if just for a moment, the roar of the Glanasa. The silence was filled by the huge cheer that erupted from the men and women of Goloth. But it was cut off fast, as the other four elephants surged on, their riders slowing them with blows and shouts, steering them away from what now looked more obvious to Elayne, the four other pits.

But the pits did another job too: forced the charging army to slow, to funnel through the four gaps. She'd hoped it would be men jammed together, a huge target for Golothian bows. But it was the elephants who came through; those had to be the targets now.

"Loose!" cried Leo, leading by example, still mounted but turned side on, his great war bow in his hands, the first shaft dispatched. Elayne tried to follow its flight, lost it in the cloud of arrows that followed a second behind. Hundreds of arrows poured down onto the four elephants, and even if they were armoured, with thick wicker on their sides, wound rope on their legs and dragon scales protecting eyes and ears, some barbs must have reached them, judging by their shrieks. Reached them, slowed them, but did not stop them. Each shook themselves as if from biting insects and came on.

They were perhaps one hundred paces away now, and the arrows were falling less thickly. They were gaining speed and behind them the soldiers were thrusting through the gaps between pits. Then something flashed in Elayne's eyes, coming from her left, from the steep fall to the river. It burst over the lip of the bank—yellows, blues, reds, startlingly different from the blacks and dark greens of the enemy.

It was Huy who put a name to her confusion. "Scarab!"

She saw him then. Saw the pirate leader and his crew charge straight for the elephant on the riverside. They came so fast not the beast itself, nor its rider, nor the men on its back saw them coming. Some pirates halted close and shot arrow after arrow while, covered by that barbed rain, Scarab, followed by two women, ran on, ducking under the beast's belly, disappearing . . . and then reappearing the next moment the other side . . . just before the elephant reared up on its hind legs and, shrieking, tumbled over.

Scarab was the last to emerge. He was almost clear of the fall. But just as he took a step toward the hill, the elephant's trunk crashed down and smashed him over.

"No!"

Huy had already urged his horse to the very crest of the hill. Now he was over it, charging down, Elayne's shout to him unheard. She took a step . . . but could only watch as her friend galloped down. The Glanasan foot soldiers were following behind the elephants fast. But Huy, sweeping past the two women who'd turned, bows in hand, to cover their fallen leader, was there, off his horse and back on it in three heartbeats, his friend flung before him. "Yah!" he cried, kicking in his heels, and his mount took off, with the first Glanasa just ten paces away.

"Shoot!" cried the high steward from beside her, leading by example. Arrows flew over the fugitive's heads, halting the first men of Glana. Huy galloped up, the ranks parted to admit him, then closed behind him. In a moment he was off his horse and lowering the pirate gently to the ground.

"Scarab!" he called. "Scarab! Are you alive?"

The pirate's eyes fluttered, then opened. "A piece of me." He tried to sit up, yelped in pain, clutching his ribs.

"Easy," Huy said. "Lie still." Scarab's three women rushed forward. "Back off!" Huy hissed, a fierce gleam in his eye. "I got this."

Scarab clutched him hard, smiled, then frowned. "The elephants?"

Elayne jerked her gaze back. Three elephants were down. But there were still three coming—the two bigger, slower ones in the centre, only just now clearing the central pits; the other faster one on the right flank, already at the base of the hill, thirty paces from the line. The line was wavering, men falling back.

Then she saw him—Leo. He'd dismounted, was running downhill with twenty armoured men. Two got ahead of him. Two died: one impaled on a tusk, one knocked aside by a sweep of the trunk. But Leo dodged under the beast's swinging head, arrows shot from above glancing off his shoulder plates, his helmet. He clutched Mimung and, dropping to his knees, he put the blade flat on his left shoulder then swung it, a great scything blow that slammed into the elephant's leg. It had ropes bound there to protect its tendons from common weapons. But Mimung was not common and it sliced through the rope and into flesh. Leo held it there but a moment before he stepped and ripped it hard through.

The beast came onto its rear legs, its front flailing. It gave Leo the room he needed to place both hands on the grip and drive the sword straight up into the belly.

With a scream, the beast fell away backwards. Leo turned, and sprinted back up the hill, the survivors of his party around him.

Elayne ran along the hilltop. As he stumbled through the ranks, she caught him. "You did it!" she cried.

"Aye, the poor animal's dead." He knelt, taking huge breaths. "And now I must kill the others."

They both turned. The two biggest elephants were still alive, clear of the pits in the centre, and starting up the hill. A mass of soldiers, yelling war cries, was behind them. The men and women of Goloth were wavering, some slipping away to the back of the hill. More arrows were flying up now than down. Leo lifted his great shield, held it over them both, as arrow after arrow thunked into it. Then he forced himself up, as if he was about to charge into a rainstorm.

"You can't!" yelled Elayne. "You'll die! We'll have to wait for them. Try—"

A cry cut her off, filled with wonder, horror. Fewer arrows fell, and she peeked under the edge of the arrow-studded shield. Saw. Gasped.

They came, silently and fast on folded wings, swooping down through the last shreds of low-lying mist. It was only about twenty feet above the elephants that they spread their wings wide, slowing them just enough. Swinging their rear legs forward, the griffins Tisiphone and Alecto sank their talons deep into the last two elephants' necks.

There was a moment, a frozen moment, that Elayne knew she would remember for the rest of her life. She thought all sound had somehow gone, that time itself had halted. It was a moment to capture with a camera, if such an object could exist in Goloth. The griffins appeared perched on the elephants, both sets of animals unmoving, with every human on the field doing nothing but stare. A moment lasting less than a breath before time resumed—in wings folding then flung wide, griffins straining up, lifting the elephants from the ground. In screams of man and beast.

They didn't take them high. It was too huge a load to carry. Tisiphone and Alecto flapped hard, rising perhaps thirty feet before they released their claws.

Elayne turned away, couldn't watch, wished she couldn't hear as the elephants screamed in terror as they fell. The men beneath them screamed too, but she found she cared less, much less, about them. They had chosen war. The elephants had no choice.

A voice boomed out, rising above any other. The deep voice of the griffin. "Is my debt repaid, Alice-Elayne?" Tisiphone cried.

It was weird being called like that amongst this whole crowd. But she knew she couldn't be shy. "No! They still outnumber us. Fight with us. Save Goloth."

"We will."

It was Tisiphone who answered. But it was Alecto who let out a great shriek of joy, spread his wings wide again, swooping low over the Glanasan ranks who cowered under his flight. And together with those screams she heard others. A large group of the enemy had swung wide and entered the forest on the right, seeking to outflank their foes. They must have met Amphisbaena, her father, and various chimeras, manticores, and snakes.

"Oh my God," whispered Elayne. "We can do this." She turned to Leo, eyes wide. "We can do it."

The joy lasted for only a moment, the short one before the dragons came.

The three daughters of Tiamat swept in over the forest, their cries higher-pitched even than the griffins', who swerved in the air and only just eluded the claws extended to snatch them. Five fabulous beasts now rose in a twirling, twisted circle. Jaws jabbed, claws and talons ripped. They spiralled high fast as they at last reached the clouds, burst through them, were gone, leaving only their screeches of fury to echo over the field.

Leaving one dragon behind.

She glided in as her children had, her great wings spread wide, her huge tail swaying back and forth as if that was what powered her—a perfect combination of bird and reptile. As she swooped low over her army, the soldiers gave a huge cheer, formed again into their rough order, came on, all shouting. "Dragon! Dragon! Dragon!" Yet Elayne barely heard them, as if they called from a great distance, their cries cut off by the single word that moved in and occupied her mind.

Maid.

She bent over, hands smothering her head, uselessly. Tiamat's voice had poked her before and it had hurt. Now it was as if the dragon thrust one of her talons deep into the soft flesh of Elayne's brain.

She cried out, fell to her knees. Hands reached for her, whose she had no idea. Only the voice mattered.

Alice-Elayne. Did you truly believe I would not come for you? Did you think that these puny efforts would protect you from me?

She could do nothing but moan.

You surprised me when you escaped—me, who has not been surprised in five hundred years. The stories of you were true. Ah, what a pair we shall make when you take me to your home!

Home. It was an absurd word there, on that battlefield, with a dragon occupying her mind. But it was like a drop of water in a forest fire, the briefest flash of respite. It let her think a word, just one.

Never.

The feeling changed. The talon was withdrawn, but it was like a great iron weight pressed her down, in her head, in her body. She collapsed from knees to ground. At the same time, she felt Tiamat's attention go elsewhere, outwards. *Kill them,* the dragon thought. *Kill them all. My daughters and I are hungry.*

Somewhere in the distance Elayne heard a great cheer and a voice she thought she knew cry, "Loose!" From that world away came the whistle of arrows in air, the sound of steel on steel, the fall of war hammers, the cries of the men and women of Goloth killing, dying. She tried to slip free from what held her. Beyond, her friends were fighting. Her friends . . .

Maid.

Another voice inside her. So different from the dragon's. Velvet to steel. Warmth to chill. She knew it, for she had loved it better than any other in either world, except perhaps her father's.

Maid, Moonspill said again and added, *I am here.*

Velvet slipped under the iron that pressed her, its softness forcing the hardness up, off. She was able to move, her eyes at least, open them—to the wonder of his, those blue universes gazing down at her now. "Moonspill!" she cried, sitting up.

Mount, maid. The fight is in the balance.

She rose. Everything came into her senses now—the surge of battle before her, nobles in armour, Weavers in cloaks and skirts, the metal plates and plumed headdresses of the Glanasa. The sound was extraordinary, the blows, the fury, the agony. As she ran to Moonspill, hurled herself onto his great white back, she felt it, like the slam of a great bird into a window, the dragon's mind driving against the unicorn's, striving to reach her. But Moonspill did not give her up, and then she was aware of Tiamat only when she saw her rise up shrieking above her army's ranks.

"You came!" she cried. "Just you?"

Nay, maid. Look.

She did—and saw fifty unicorns run up the back of the hill, shaking the river water from their flanks. The next moment Heartsease was beside them.

"Tempest?"

It was Heartsease who answered. *There.*

Elayne turned again, to the front. And there the young unicorn was indeed, already deep in the black ranks. But he was not alone—for on his back, sword raised high, was Leo. Behind him came about twenty mounted nobles and they were driving an armoured wedge deep into the Glanasan ranks.

Moonspill rose up onto his rear legs, let out a great roar. *Now!*

And with that the rest of the unicorns followed the king of Goloth into the heart of the fight.

Then she was only aware of what was close to her—flailing hooves, shattered armour, horns thrusting, men falling. She did not fight, did not have a weapon, wouldn't know how to use one if she did. But she knew this: she was the Summoned, the Prophesied, the maid who rode the unicorn. And she could feel, as if she could touch it, the men and women of Goloth take heart when they saw her, and the men of Glana quail.

"Goloth! Goloth!"

She heard Leo's cry, from not far away. Spotted him, sword waving on Tempest's back. Then saw what he could not—Tiamat, with wings folded, falling from the sky upon him, reaching with her claws. "Leo!" she screamed.

To no avail. Tiamat seized Tempest by the neck, stretched out her wings, rose, lifting mount and man. But Leo, hanging on with one hand to the unicorn's mane, his legs dangling beneath him, still had his sword in the other hand and he swept it around now. The blade smashed into the dragon's foot a hand's breadth above where the claws dug into the unicorn. The dragon screeched, released, blood spurting. Tempest fell, stumbled but stayed on his hooves, and Leo got his balance again.

Tiamat had lurched sideways. She tried to right herself, spreading her wings for the thrust that would carry her up, away. But the tip of her left wing smashed into some of her own soldiers, she skittered to the side, and her right wing crashed into the ground.

"Now!"

Now.

The word. His thought. Her shout. Instantly acted upon. Moonspill gave a great leap toward the fallen dragon and, as Tiamat came up onto her rear legs and spread her wings again for flight, the unicorn drove his horn straight into that huge scaled chest. It did not pierce, but the force of the charge was enough. The dragon was knocked back. Yet even as she fell, she shot her long neck forward and fastened her jaws, driving those terrible fangs deep into Moonspill's neck.

Elayne was two feet away from the great green eye. Tiamat regarded her now with a look that was malevolent, triumphant. Moonspill shook and twisted, helpless in the fanged grip. And in that terrible moment, Elayne realized she was wrong. She did have a weapon. So she reached to her belt, pulled the can from its holder, flicked off the safety guard— and shot bear spray straight into the fiery centre of the dragon's eye.

Tiamat shrieked between her teeth, louder than she had before. Twisted her head hard, released her fangs, the force of it throwing them to the side. Moonspill crashed over and Elayne didn't have time to get her leg out. As they hit the ground, she heard the snap, a moment before the terrible pain came.

She screamed, tried to pry herself out from under Moonspill, screamed again at the movement. But another cry drew her. She looked up to see, through misting eyes, Tempest with blood pouring down his flanks and Leo still on his back, charging straight at the thrashing dragon. Tempest plunged his horn into the same spot he'd plunged it back in Glana—straight into Tiamat's leg.

The dragon shrieked, then swept her barbed tail around, knocking Tempest's hooves out from under him. The unicorn fell but as he did Leo leapt from his back and threw himself right under Tiamat's upreared head—just under the eye that was swelling, closing and could not see. Instinct told her of danger, she snapped her head around, saw him—and Elayne saw fires leap in her throat. Tiamat had not used that terrible power yet, perhaps for fear of killing the maid she needed. Now they grew—and Elayne could only cry out, "Leo!"

But the microsecond's delay of the blinding had given Leo time . . . to squat, grasp the sword two-handed, throw himself up—and drive Mimung straight into the chest at the only other point where a wound had never fully healed, where scales had never quite meshed.

The blade did not stop. It sank deep, so deep that the shaft, guard, and grip all vanished into the monster's body, forcing Leo to let it go. It was as if a great basin had burst, for black blood gushed out, hot and smoking, completely drenching Leo and Tempest, who had rolled back onto his hooves. Leo cried out, staggered aside—and not a second too soon, for Tiamat tumbled down, to fall between man and unicorn.

There was a moment when Elayne, through the mist still in her eyes, looked into the dragon's open one. A word came, the same word.

Maid?

But it was only a question now. It had no power to hurt her. And it was her final thought, as the scaled eyelids rolled down.

Tiamat, last of the great dragon queens, was dead.

31

ᴀFTERMATH

The Glanasan army fled.

Elayne didn't care. She was aware of the great moan they gave as one. Aware of the cries of triumph from the Golothians, turning rapidly to shrieks of vengeance. Both armies poured off the hill, the chaser and the chased. Sounds of fighting, of killing, faded down the valley.

She was only truly aware of two things—one, the terrible pain in her left leg. The second—

"Moonspill!" she cried, reaching her hand up to his neck, his poor savaged neck. White agony blinded her and falling back, she cried, "Someone help! Help here!" even as she started to faint.

She was dimly aware of hands under her shoulders, of being pulled. The pain of it snapped her back to consciousness. She looked up. It was her father dragging her clear. "I've got you," he said. "I've got you." Gently, he laid her down, moving around to peer at her leg—and wince. "Elayne, that doesn't look good."

She didn't care. Even the joy that he was alive was overwhelmed by what was before her. "Never mind me. Moonspill! Moonspill." Drawing blood from her lips with a bite, she forced herself to sit up.

Three unicorns were before her. Heartsease and Tempest were standing, bent over the one on the ground. They were running their horns up
and down over the great, white body. From their throats came a low
rumble like a song.

"Take me over there."

"You shouldn't move. You've—"

"Take me or I'll drag myself!"

Huy had joined her father. Together they bent, lifted her between
them. The pain nearly sent her back into oblivion but she held on,
until they'd laid her down and she could reach out and touch the
fallen unicorn.

Moonspill's eyes were closed. But they opened at her touch, the
thick eyelashes unfurling like a veil over those huge blue orbs. His voice
came into her head.

Alice-Elayne. You are hurt.

She could hear it, even though she couldn't "hear" it—the weakness
in his voice. *So are you. But we'll both be fine. Right?*

You will be.

So will you. Because . . . She looked up, at Heartsease and Tempest,
moving their horns over him, crooning deep in their throats. *Your mate.
Your son. They are healing you.*

Nay. Moonspill gave a quiver. *Horns take away poisons. They cannot
heal wounds. The dragon has hurt me too deeply.*

If she'd been standing, Elayne would have stamped her foot. *Then
what the hell are they doing?*

A rumble came, that rare unicorn laugh at her anger. Then words.
They are easing me away.

"Away?" She said it aloud. Thought had become too intimate, too
painful. "Away where?"

Why, my dear, to my next adventure.

"No!" She moved then, crying out as she did, needing to get her arms around his neck, that great white neck, so reddened with blood now. "You're not going anywhere without me."

I am. I cannot carry you in that world. For your time in this one, and in the one beyond the tapestry, is only just beginning.

"I won't let you go." She hugged him even tighter.

You have always been a wonder. But even you cannot conquer this.

She was sobbing full tilt now—until his mind reached to her, as it sometimes did, laying its velvet upon her, warming her, calming her. His words came again.

Alice-Elayne. Maid. You must see this as I do. You knew from the beginning that all I ever yearned for, from the time when I first heard the stories of heroes, was to be part of such a story myself. I made so many mistakes because of that desire. And even though you and I achieved so much before, there was still that yearning in me, the doubt that I had truly done enough to live forever in memory beside my forebears. I thought my chance had gone. But now . . . The lashes fell, then opened even wider, his gaze going up into the clouds, beyond them. *Now I can see them all waiting for me. I see Bucephalus, who bore Alexander to glory. See Ambrosius, mount for Arthur of the Britons. See my mother Salvia, with Joan of Arc on her back. See Darkheart*—the lashes began to flutter again—*my father, the greatest hero I ever knew, waiting for me. There's a place right beside him, amidst them all, there in Elysium. For did I not help to slay the dragon?*

"What will I do without you?" she sobbed.

This thought took longer to come, as if from a greater distance. She heard it faintly, but clearly. *You will search in your heart. And you will always find me in it.*

He was breathing more shallowly now. His eyes closed again. A different voice was in her ear. Her father was reaching hands under her again. "Come on," he said.

"No! Let go of me. I must—"

"Elayne," he said gently, "you have to leave him to them."

He was right. She sank into his hands, letting him pull her a few feet away. Far enough so that Moonspill had just his dam and his son and their horns moving over him, their song lulling him. Close enough to see his flanks give one last, great heave.

Alan crouched behind her, holding her upright so she could see. As her unicorn breathed his last, she buried her face in her father's arms.

It was night by the time Leo found them.

They hadn't moved far, what with Elayne's leg and Scarab's busted ribs. Huy had bound both of them as well as he could, with bandages torn from cloaks. The former king-elect walked stiffly into the firelight and fell to the ground next to her. "How fare you, Alice-Elayne?" he asked.

She'd found it hard to talk for a while now. Huy replied for her. "Not well," he said, handing over a water skin, which Leo quaffed greedily. "Her leg's badly busted in three places. Are you OK? You look like one of the walking dead."

Leo might not have got the reference but it applied anyway. He looked down at his armour, which was thickened with congealed blood, dabbed a finger into the ooze. "Near all this came from the dragon," he answered. "It has soaked me through to the skin and I have had no chance to clean it off."

"'Near all'?" echoed Elayne, sitting up slightly. "Are you wounded?"

"Nothing too much. Other blood may belong to . . . other people." His eyes darkened. "We chased our enemy back to the shore. My people had the blood lust upon them, though once my battle fury passed, I soon discovered I'd had my fill. Indeed, methinks I have had enough for my lifetime."

"Are there any of Glanasa left?" Alan asked, leaning in, offering a hunk of bread.

"Aye, a number." Leo took it, ate as greedily as he'd drunk. "And not all their boats were burned, or more came late. They did not need many to take home those who remained." He peered into the fire. "We need not fear them again. For who will inspire them to vengeance now that their god is slain?"

"What happened to the daughters?" Huy asked.

"They vanished when their mother died."

It silenced them, the memories of Tiamat that came. Until Elayne spoke. "Not only the dragon. Moonspill—"

She found she couldn't say it. Leo reached out, took her hand, squeezed it gently. "I know, maid. I saw his great body. I grieve for you. We will bury him, or burn his body, with great honours as befits such a hero."

No.

The thought words, which all heard, were as startling as a shout. Those who could, stood, as Tempest walked into firelight that glistened on his dragon blood–soaked flanks. More of his words came. *My dam and I will return with my father to the other side of the mountains. There we will mourn him as our rites demand.*

Elayne shook her head. Between the pain and the painkillers Huy had given her for it from his kit, she was more than a little fuzzy. But she remembered the narrowness of the tunnel, and Tempest's terror within it, clearly. "But how can you do that?"

The griffins. Tisiphone and Alecto will bear his body home.

Elayne's eyes went wide. *I thought you were the oldest of enemies?*

Even ancient foes can make peace eventually.

"They can." Leo stepped forward, raised his hand to Tempest's muzzle, and the beast did not shy away. Indeed, he dipped his head to the touch. "You and I proved that, did we not?" He smiled, teeth bright within the blood on his face. "Together we slew the dragon."

The reply came, along with a tossing of the head to each of them. *Together we all did.*

"Aye." Leo nodded, ran his hand down Tempest's neck, the claw wounds there. "So do you have to cross the mountains at all? Goloth is your land too, and it has changed completely. Why not return to it? Why shouldn't the unicorns come back and share this land? Why shouldn't all the fabulous beasts? Together we won it. Why not help us make Goloth the paradise it could be?"

No thought words came for the longest time, until . . . *It is something I have thought too. Goloth—and the world beyond it, of which I am only beginning to learn. A world perhaps of adventures enough even for me.* His gaze took in Scarab before he continued. *But this must be considered by more than myself. Discussed by all unicorns. For now, we will return to the valley across the mountains, winter there. And I will bring you an answer in the spring.*

"Good," Leo replied. He stood straight, then pressed his head into Tempest's flank, and thought, *And if all is settled, perhaps you and I can do something together.*

Tempest's ears flicked, as his thought came back, *Do what?*

You talked of this world. I share your curiosity. Leo stepped back, so he could look the unicorn in the eye. *I have been thinking of all the peoples we saw in Glana. Many more than I ever knew about. There's a big world to explore. There are adventures to be had. You, me and Mimung. If you would care to explore this world together?* He smiled. *That is, if you consider me worthy of such a quest.*

Tempest looked around at all of them, one by one, staring longest at Elayne before turning back. *My father found his hero in the maid. Now I have found mine, dragon slayer. So I shall look for you in the spring. Within one week of the equinox.*

Leo laid his hand again on Tempest's neck. Looked again into his eyes. *Consider it a rendezvous.*

Throwing his head up and down, Tempest turned and vanished into the dark.

A great cry came, from a griffin's throat. All looked, to see something huge and white being borne up, vanishing rapidly into the dark. Then for a while all they heard were hoofbeats until even their echoes were gone.

Leo turned to Elayne. "Now, maid, to your hurt. There are those among our people skilled in the setting of bones. I will—"

It was her father who spoke before she could. "Huy tells me her leg is not just broken. It has a compound fracture. The bone has penetrated the skin and she could get blood poisoning or worse. She could certainly lose the leg. Face it, there's not a doctor in this place who could deal with it." He put his hands on his hips and looked Leo square in the eye. "So I'm taking her back to New York."

There was silence for a moment. Elayne wanted to speak, maybe to argue, but couldn't. She knew they were right, her father and her friend. And she also knew she needed—wanted!—to go home.

A new voice broke the silence. Or rather, voices.

"And we will see you through the portal."

It was Amphis who spoke, and Baena who added, "Come on, dogs—let's jet."

———

In the end, all the dogs jetted. Even the real one, Wolf.

Alan, under Huy's promptings, was determined not to delay. "Don't like the look of it," he'd said, pointing at her leg, whenever anyone suggested resting for a few days.

So next morning, having scraped a meal of dried bread and even drier meat, and having washed the worst of the blood and battle filth off themselves, they set out. Only Leo, who was filthiest, had actually bathed, though dragon blood had stained his normally pale skin a reddish-black. He also had clothes at the camp nearby, though he chose the more recent leather he'd worn as forest hunter rather than the fancier garments he'd worn as king-elect.

"I do not want to be different from my people now," he said, as he walked alongside the cart where they'd placed Elayne. Swiftsure, his horse, was tethered to the rear, and Leo never left her, more often than not contriving to have his hand in hers.

"Commendable," she said. "Going for the democratic style. Though you might want to watch the way you say 'my people.' Still sounds a little patronizing. If you want to lead, you'll have to smooth your image."

"Ha!" His eyebrows rose. "You see, maid, how I need you? Not only as a battle adviser but as someone who can 'smooth me.' Is that right?" He smiled. "I have so much to learn. To begin, what is this . . . democratic thing?"

"Democracy? It's—" She shrugged. "I can give you a primer. But you really need to take a class. It's—" She broke off, wincing, as the cart bumped over a rock.

Instantly Leo bellowed, "You two! You hurt the maid! Pay more attention to our road and less to each other!"

Huy and Scarab, who'd been walking arm in arm and leading the cart horse between them, broke apart. "Sorry," they chorused, though their immediate giggles made them seem not very.

"Dolts," Leo said, stepping back to his place beside her.

"Oh, give 'em a break. They're in love. You know what it's like."

"I do," he said, "now." And he took her hand again.

Oh, she thought, letting her hand lie, not squeezing, not pulling it away either. She wondered if her father was watching—though he was spending most of his time rapping with the snake. She thought of how she looked—her clothes a mess, her hair a ruin, her face drawn with sleeplessness and pain. And yet, Leo didn't seem to mind. In fact—"Leo," she began a sentence she did not know how the hell she would finish.

And then she didn't need to. Amphisbaena rolled up, hooped. Amphis unclasped Baena's neck and spoke. "We are close. And we have found the rest of your clothes."

The snake had detoured via the village where they'd stashed some of their things. It dropped Elayne's larger backpack on the ground before them. Huy let out a whoop. Both he and Elayne had forgotten them in all the subsequent upheaval.

Elayne swallowed. "So we're nearly there?"

"Aye, maid. Turn and see."

She swivelled with some difficulty. Black Tusk was perhaps half a mile ahead over the rolling land. The door was in the stream beneath it. Her eyes brightened at the thought of home, of help—then darkened again as she saw the expression on Leo's face. She looked over and saw the same mixed emotions on the faces of the young men standing at the horse's head. She was pretty sure they mirrored her own.

It was as if Amphis spoke to their thoughts. "Maid, my brother and I have been thinking about time in our two worlds. The hour we went before. The hour Moonspill told us you arrived. We think it would be better to wait till nearer evening. That way it will be the middle of the night in your world and you may be able to arrive with less . . . fuss."

"You down with that?" contributed Baena.

"For sure," Huy said, taking Scarab's hand again. "Hanging's good, don't you think, Elayne?"

She wasn't sure it was. She hated goodbyes anyway and the longer they were, the worse they got. But the snake was right—the later they got through the tapestries at the Cloisters, the better it probably was. She grunted and laid back.

They came soon enough to the stream and their stash. Her decision to leave some of their food in her pack turned out to be a popular one as the energy bars and chocolate were shared out, making a great change from squirrel jerky and stale bread. Huy put on his velvet frock-coat suit again and strutted up and down, making them laugh—well, making Scarab, her dad, and the snake laugh anyway. Leo stared at her a long moment then excused himself, walking off into forest with Wolf, bow in hand—"to hunt fresh meat for our journey back," he called over his shoulder when she asked. He didn't return, even as the shadow of Black Tusk grew longer on the ground before them. Huy and Scarab went off later too, hand in hand. Only her father hung out, and he soon fell asleep.

The pain was getting worse again, the last of Huy's pills consumed some hours before. Somehow she fell into a fitful sleep, tormented by dreams. She woke to darkness and a flapping noise, listened as whatever it was—some birds?—flew off into the woods. Then the snake was beside her. "'Tis time, maid," Amphis said.

"What?" She sat up too quickly, winced. "Ow! But where are the others?"

"Huy will join us at the stream. He is saying farewell to the pirate. Will you bear her, Alan?"

"Gladly." Her father bent, lifted her, and carried her closer to the stream.

It was dark, the moonlight fitful through fleeting clouds. She saw vague shapes before her. Huy, Scarab. "Where's Leo?" she said.

"Listen, Elayne. No easy way to say this." Huy came forward as he spoke, and there was something about him that seemed strange, though she couldn't see him properly in the half-light. "I'm not coming back."

"What?" she gasped. "You can't mean that. You can't stay here. It's too dangerous."

"It is." Scarab stepped forward. "Yet from what he tells me of your world, that is dangerous too. And as long as he has someone to protect him . . ."

He put his arm around Huy's shoulder. Her friend nodded. She could now see his bright smile in the dark. "But . . . but . . . your family. School? You—"

"Family will be fine. I'm not saying its forever, just—" He shrugged. "And as for school . . ." He grinned. "Think of this as a sandwich year away. Research."

"But . . . but . . . my dad can't manage on his own!"

"I will help him."

It was Leo who spoke as he stepped into such light as there was. Her eyes had accustomed enough to it for her to be able to see what had confused her about Huy before—he and Leo had swapped clothes. "May I?" he said to Alan, and her father nodded, released her.

Leo carried her into the shadows of the birch tree, out of sight. It was the one Huy had jokingly carved her and Leo's initials into within a heart. She'd mocked it then. Now . . .

She wasn't sure what she felt. It was as confusing as it always was around Leo. He was coming back with her? For her? She felt her heart beat faster. Joy and panic merged. "Wait! You can't. You promised to rendezvous with Tempest in the spring."

"And I will." He leaned closer, spoke softly. "But that is six passings of the moon away." She went to interrupt, but . . . "So I will come and I will take class? I am certain I can learn all there is to learn of this 'duma-ocrocy' in that time."

"Not really. And anyway . . . seriously?" she replied. "Huy's staying so he can play hooky and you're coming so you can go to school?"

"Nay, maid," Leo replied. "You know the reason I am coming. It is because I cannot—will not—let you go."

"But—"

He stopped her words then by the simple method of pulling her close and kissing her softly. In the kiss, all her questions, all her fears, even her pain, melted. So she kissed him back, not softly at all.

A voice called. "'Tis time!"

They took the few steps to the stream's banks. Leo laid her down at his feet and returned to Scarab, who was keeping his hand on Wolf. Leo knelt, and whispered in the dog's huge velvety ear. Huy came and sat beside her. "Promise you'll eat some pho soup for me."

"You sure about this?" She glanced at Scarab. "Giving it all up, for . . . love? I mean, you're a cute couple and all but—"

Huy grinned. "Think of the beautiful babies we could make together."

"Uh, yeah. You . . . know that's not possible, right?"

Huy fixed her with the sort of look that would have benefitted from his pince-nez. "Elayne," he said, "in a world where a two-headed snake raps, griffins fly, and dragons fight unicorns . . ." His grin returned. "Anything is possible!"

He leaned in, pecked her on the cheek, rose, and went.

"Fare thee well, maid," Amphis called.

"Yo, Alan," Baena added, "don't you come back without some sick beats, bro. Deal?"

"Deal, dog," replied her father, stepping into the water, pulling the key to the door between worlds from within his sweater.

Leo bent, lifted her and followed, keeping her above the water.

Alan held the key up. "So how do we do this?"

"We hold onto each other. Leo's got me, so if I . . ."

She reached and grabbed her father's shoulder. Leo looked down at her. "Ready, my lady?"

"Ready, my lord." She smiled up at him. "For anything."

Alan plunged the horn down—and vanished. She and Leo were sucked after and immediately the chill swept through her. Then it was gone and they were falling, together, not separately, her hand in her father's coat, Leo's grip on her never slackening. She felt a slight tug on one leg, a little like when Huy hitched a ride to get to Goloth. But it was her broken one, and full of odd sensations.

There was air and darkness, then there was cloth and light. Suddenly and again, she was in the room with the unicorn tapestries in the Cloisters Museum, in New York City. Her father was standing in the middle of the room. While kneeling on the floor, still holding her tight, was Leo of Goloth.

He frowned. "What's that?" Leo said, shaking his head as if dodging something. "Why are there birds inside a building?"

She sensed flight, rather than saw it—something moving away. But travel between worlds could be disorientating, she knew. It was nothing important, she was sure. "We better go," she said.

He stood, lifting her effortlessly. "Whither, maid?"

"That way. Fast, before the guards come." She smiled. "Or, in the immortal words of a snake I know: 'Let's jet.'"

Author's Note

It is such a thrill to be writing the Author's Note for this book. Mainly because it means I am near the end of a process that was just a dream, an idle fancy, for so many years.

I often feel that the beginnings and endings of stories are arbitrary. Unless it starts with the birth and finishes with the main character's death, I always close the book and wonder, "OK, that adventure's over. But what happened next?" Especially if you have a problem with "Happily Ever After." (I do!) So if you love the characters, as I tend to love mine, you want to answer that question. You want to hear from them again. Even when I dive into a new novel, make new "friends" who I grow just as passionate about, I cannot forget my old friends nor ever stop wondering what they are up to.

This was definitely the case with Alice-Elayne. I wrote three adult novels after the publication of *The Hunt of the Unicorn*. Became immersed in new adventures, with all kinds of wonderful, vibrant, scary people. But unlike with some of my books, where I know the story ends with the publication, I never felt that way about her. To begin with, she was sixteen when the novel ended. She'd had all these extraordinary adventures that concluded with her freeing the unicorn she loved and starting a revolution. Which made me think: how does she go back to math class after that? How important is an update on Instagram going to seem to her? How did she cope back in her old, so-called "real" life?

Not well, I decided. Not well at all.

When I get an idea for a book, I visualize it as a file folder that I create on the hard drive of my brain. It may only have one document in it for a long while, one sentence—"What ever happened to Alice-Elayne?"—but even as I am engaged on other projects, something—an image, a piece of action, a line of dialogue—will start in my subconscious, make itself known, then be "filed" away for later. By the time I get around to considering actually starting to truly think about the novel, there's quite a bit of stuff accumulated. Mainly questions I am by now itching to answer.

The main problem I have as a writer is not writing. It is "not writing." If I finish a stage of a project—send a draft to my editor for appraisal, say—I will often take some time off. Even though I know it is much harder to get going again later. Even though I know that I am happiest when I am at my desk every day, making stuff up.

I was working on *Fire*, the second book in my Restoration London series. I sent it off. But instead of stopping I just dived into what you hold now. Opened that folder in my head and scanned its contents. Asked the questions. Began to write.

I was blessed in this way especially: I already had interest in the idea from Doubleday in Toronto. Most especially from the editor I'd wanted to work with for several years, Amy Black. She had actually contracted me to write a YA novel which, for reasons too long to go into here, I'd decided to drop. So I owed her a book. She never put the slightest bit of pressure on me to give her one. Yet every time I was in her office in Toronto I'd find myself talking about Alice-Elayne and "what happened next." Finally, when the folder was open and I'd developed the idea a little, Amy said, "Go ahead."

She didn't know when I'd begin. She certainly didn't know I'd written the first draft when, four months later, we met for dinner before the event where I was about to win the Arthur Ellis Best Crime Novel Award for *Plague*. But she was pretty happy when I pulled out the manuscript and handed it over—as usual, tied up with string. (I always try to hand deliver it thus bound and I am still not sure why!)

Even though *The Hunt of the Unicorn* had done moderately well, five years had passed. No one was holding their breath for a sequel. So with Amy's smart, gentle but firm guidance, I discovered what Alice-Elayne and everyone else had been up to, but did it so no prior knowledge of the characters was required. Made it stand alone. The first book became nothing more than the character's back story, which any novel would contain anyway. The good thing for me was that I didn't have to make any of that up. I also needed to come up with innovative ways to convey the information—which led to what my twelve-year-old son felt was a totally embarrassing exploration of rap. (Something I was able to transfer into the novel with the daughter similarly appalled by her father's "youth" musical tastes!)

I have to say, I loved being back in this kind of story, revisiting Goloth, the land of the fabulous beast. But as the characters had all aged a couple of years, I wanted the themes to reflect that. Love gets more of a play in this novel. All kinds. And I introduced the first major gay character I'd ever written. Not for tokenism. Just because he is. As our still relatively new Prime Minister of Canada replied when asked why he had chosen an equal split of men and women in his cabinet, "Because it's 2015." I feel the same way about Huy Phan—who is also a Thai boxing master and a computer genius.

So here it is. What you are holding is that cram-full folder opened and thoroughly explored.

There are so many people to thank, as ever. Books do not happen by themselves, far from it. My Doubleday team is tremendous—from the boss man, CEO Brad Martin, and my publisher Kristin Cochrane, both always so behind me; to Max Arambulo, my tireless publicist. As well as all the people who design, copy edit, print and deliver my books, not to mention the wonderful booksellers who hand sell them. (And I will mention one—the terrific and funny Adina Hildebrandt of Salt Spring Books who takes "supporting the local author" to extraordinary lengths.) My hair cutter in Vancouver, Tracey Tran of Icy Hair Design, deserves special thanks for giving me the Vietnamese translation of my weird snake aphorism. My family, of course: my son Reith for letting me read him the first draft in bed—and forgiving me for my deeply embarassing attempts at rap. My wife Aletha, who also read early and encouraged mightily, especially suggesting I brought out the humour even more. Even Dickon my cat, always on my desk when I write, even now as I write this.

Finally, again, ultimately, Amy Black.

Oh and by the way? A new folder has been created. It has only one file in it, with just one sentence written down so far. "Shapeshifting serial killer dragons terrorize New York—and only one girl can stop them."

See you in two years.

C.C. Humphreys
Salt Spring Island, BC
September 2016